BOXED IN

BOXED IN

PENNY GRUBB

Cover design by Gabi

ISBN (eBook): 978-1-914060-10-6
ISBN (paperback): 978-1-914060-09-0

To the memory of Shaun Russell Grubb
1967–2018

CHAPTER 1

The camera lens high on its pole looks down into the heart of the yard. It was designed to swing back and forth, covering the wide entranceway and across to the box-shaped offices, but water got in last winter and now it rests its beady eye straight down, the edges of its vision stretching to surrealist curves.

Red Boy hasn't got round to getting it fixed.

He's there now, with two others; striding out from the elongated distortion at the edge of the lens. A fourth man, small and wiry, sits in a cab above them from where he operates the crane that keeps the flow of giant containers smooth.

Someone's messed up. The man in the cab leans out to watch. Above him, the camera looks down on them all.

Red Boy grumbles his way between two of the giant boxes. The metal surfaces distort his voice, bury it.

Small-and-wiry leans forward as though to eavesdrop but he's too far away. He reaches for the door catch.

The camera's view is unobstructed as long as the giant containers are stacked no more than two high. But there's a lone tower of three. It creates a blind spot.

'There's been a bloody dog in,' Red Boy grumbles, kicking out at an irrelevant pile of debris the wind has heaped in a corner.

1

'Cats. It'll be cats.' Small-and-wiry is down there with them now, huddling into his coat against the creeping cold. He fights them on every level, even cats versus dogs, even at a time like this when he's noticing that stack of three as though he's not seen it before, as though it wasn't his crane that constructed it.

They watch as Red Boy's gaze runs across the metal panels automatically seeking serial numbers. It's the container at the bottom of the stack that looks out of place. It's solid but weathered, its paint many years old but all-encompassing.

'Fuck's sake,' Red Boy mutters, reaching for one of the metal shafts that litter the site.

Small-and-wiry feels the tension twist his gut. *I did it off the docket,* he'll say, because Red Boy can't sack a man for doing his job, and he must have done it off the docket, though truth be known, he doesn't remember this one.

Red Boy clangs a metal spear against its wall, then screeches it across, metal on metal, setting his teeth on edge.

'Fuck're you doing?' One of the others too is cringing.

'Serial number's painted over.' Red Boy's voice is steady, in control. He can open any container in this yard but only when he finds its ID.

He leans in, putting his weight behind the metal shaft, and chips at the surface. The paint's old. Years old. It doesn't take long.

They watch Red Boy as he checks his list. Nothing but his fingers move as he scrolls through the information. After a moment, he looks up, his stare landing on his crane driver. 'Get the bolt croppers. It's not one of ours.'

'You can't do that!' It's almost a whisper. Small-and-wiry

looks at the speaker. Their eyes meet. The look says, why aren't you telling him, too?

He swallows, mouth dry. It's all moving too fast to get his thoughts in line.

'Bolt croppers!' snaps Red Boy.

'Check the docket first, yeah?' He hears the words from his own mouth. 'Could be anything in there.'

They want to move back, but Red Boy's the boss, and that compelling stare nails them to the ground. They won't step nearer but they daren't retreat. So they just stand and gape until Red Boy's voice, incredulous, yells, 'Fucking bolt croppers!'

They all jump, but it's small-and-wiry who spins round to race for the office. Can he take the time to flick through files, grab the docket, see if it sheds any light? But how can it, if the crate's not meant to be here?

His hand reaches for the tool shelf, hesitates between the big bolt croppers, the ones that could take off a man's head, and the tiny ones that might at least delay Red Boy's suicidal move. But he daren't go back with something that'll barely cut toenails; he needs this job.

Enough to die for it?

Walking across the yard is like wading through treacle. And now he has to move even closer to that alien crate.

Red Boy glares, tapping his foot with impatience.

'Boss,' one of the others is pleading. 'It might be anything.'

'We'll soon find out,' Red Boy growls, as he braces the teeth of the croppers against the lock.

The other three exchange glances. They've read the briefings, seen the films, heard the warnings ...

Small-and-wiry can't believe he's let it come this far. It might be booby trapped. 'Boss,' he screams, 'could be explosives in there.'

His words barely precede the crack of the lock as it flies open.

CHAPTER 2

Police Constable Jennifer Flanagan let the distinctive blue light up ahead guide her through the maze of roads to the right entrance gate with its "Redman's Yard" sign. An ambulance was pulling out. It was a relief to see its light flashing because that meant there was a life to be saved. As she opened her window and flagged it down, a hard wave of cold air blew in, fresh off the estuary; a background hum of voices carried on the breeze indicating people at the far end of the yard, words indistinguishable but the tone sounded angry.

'Do you know who, what …?' She asked the question staccato, nodding towards the back of the vehicle.

The driver shook his head. 'Had another call. Nothing to be done back there. Long past our help. Left them with the responder to wait for you.'

She nodded, *Good*, to the news of a responder waiting behind. 'What did you see when you got here?'

The man shrugged. 'Vagrants sneak in for the heat of the generators. By the looks of it, some poor sod timed it wrong and starved in there.'

She nodded. The emergency call had said *vagrant*. 'Man … woman …? Did you check the body?'

'Only to be sure it wasn't a tailor's dummy. A man. I went in with my colleague back there. He can tell you the rest …'

So there was a 'rest' to be told.

She gave him a quick nod of thanks and waved him off.

A lone vagrant found dead in a corner. Not the first of the winter and wouldn't be the last. If the body matched a missing person report, there would be difficult calls to nearest and dearest, but often there was no one.

She drove across the tarmac of the yard, noting the glint of a lens on a high pole. A small wiry man looking both hangdog and defiant was the butt of a low-voiced tirade from his younger well-built colleague who she guessed was the Mr Redman who'd made the call. Two others looked on nervously. The paramedic sat in the responder car, window part open.

Voices shut off as she drove up. The paramedic climbed out of his car.

She walked unsmiling towards the now silent group. Chances were she would be okaying the removal of the body and letting them go on their way, but she wouldn't take the easy option just because it was cold and late. The dead man deserved the full protection of the law whoever he was.

Her gaze ran across the high fences and stout locks, the all-seeing camera. The paramedic had said vagrants got in, but he'd clearly not stopped to consider how.

'Where?'

Following the line of Redman's pointing finger showed a container, at the bottom of a stack of three, with its door gaping on to a dark interior, the lock hanging jagged and twisted.

'It looks different,' she observed.

'Shouldn't be in a three,' he said. 'I'd have to check the

paperwork. They're stacked by an algorithm that maximises efficiency.'

'Computer says where to put 'em,' clarified small-and-wiry.

A glare from the boss to his diminutive employee. 'Reg operates the crane,' he told her. 'Reckons he doesn't remember this one.'

'Can't be expected to remember them all.'

Without being able to put her finger on why, she wasn't happy with this set up and she'd yet to see the body.

She insisted they all walk across to the front of the container, but took only the paramedic inside. They picked their way round fallen boxes and pieces of furniture skewed at odd angles, to where the body lay. The comment about tailors' dummies made sense as she looked down on the shrivelled form lying in the pool of light from her torch.

'Who's been in here?' she asked the paramedic.

'They all have, I'm afraid. If this is a crime scene, it's been well trampled through before I got here. Is it …? A crime scene?'

'I couldn't say either way as yet. Could you hazard a guess about cause of death?'

'No, sorry. He's been battered about but, state he's in, I can't say how or when.'

She flashed her torch round the interior, imagined the man weakened or perhaps already dead when the container arrived, the crane lifting it, swinging it into position. It was clear even to a cursory glance that not all the contents were adequately tied down.

Turning back to the paramedic, she asked, 'What do you need to tell me?' He shot a quick glance behind her to the open door. 'They can't hear you, not with the wind whistling through. What's bothering you?'

'I challenged the little guy. They'd disturbed the body. He said his boss wanted to know who it was. They went through his pockets. He swears they didn't take anything. It's all on that box there.' He pointed and she aimed the torch beam. 'There's a wallet looks like it has money in it, but he told me there was no ID.'

'Do they know who it is?'

'He said not.'

'You think they do?' She watched him but he only shrugged a don't-know.

Jennifer Flanagan looked at the small pile of the dead man's possessions. Beside the wallet was a handful of used tissues and a ball of green wrapper in a twist of silver paper, the remains of a packet of mints. Last meal? Was that all he'd had? How long had he been in here? She aimed the light again around the metal interior; tea chests, stacks of furniture, some lashed to the walls with thick ties, others toppled and broken with the ties hanging free.

She pulled out a pair of latex gloves and slipped them on, picking up the wallet in one hand, using her thumb to flick it open. No ID, or at any rate no obvious ID there now.

She was going to call it in as suspicious, but she'd be doing it in the face of what little evidence there was. It was certain to land her on the wrong side of the new DI who had been parachuted in and was building a reputation for either being invisible or for butting in where he shouldn't.

Her latexed finger ran across a wad of notes, counting them. All twenties, quite a sum. She pulled out a plastic evidence bag and swept in the small heap of belongings, dropping the wallet on top.

Something glinted from the floor. She bent down and picked up a broken plastic disc, sweeping the floor for any sign of its missing half. Could have fallen out of the wallet, or it might have been lying on the floor all along. The play of light on the uneven surface showed up the remains of a metallic coating and ridges where the surface had been embossed. She could make out the letters H-A-V-E running into the jagged break, along with part of a logo. Shipping containers ... docks ... A memory half-glimpsed from when she'd worked in Hull years ago ... some kind of shipping outfit the other side of the Humber estuary ... Haven-something Docks. It would come to her in a moment. She slipped the disc into its own evidence bag. It was time to herd everyone back into the warmth of the office and then radio in.

She stayed outside to make the call to her sergeant and said all she wanted to say, spelling out every last shred of unease, and telling him about the broken tag. 'There's an outfit called Havenmere Docks the other side of the Humber, it could have come from there.'

The call left her both annoyed and dissatisfied. It wasn't often she regretted her decision not to chase promotion and a high-flying career; she enjoyed the sharp end of the action away from the responsibility, but occasions like this brought home the frustrations of being experienced beyond her rank. She'd pleaded for some backup so she could at least get some proper initial statements, but had found herself competing with a nasty RTA up on the A63 that was threatening traffic chaos. What evidence she'd picked up would churn through the system, and there would be a post-mortem, but no forensic results for weeks. She was going to have to leave this site unsecured.

As she strode back towards the office, Redman came out to face her.

'It's getting late, Constable. We've a shipment coming first thing. Can we not have that unfortunate victim taken away and get on with things?'

'We'll get things moving just as soon as we can, Mr Redman. I'll just take some contact details from you and your colleagues.'

'Well, all right. Then let's get on with it.' He held out his hand to usher her back inside.

'It's a converted container,' she said, looking at the office. 'I hadn't realised. 'What is it that makes it look different?'

He turned a blank stare on the giant box with its neat corporate layout. 'Well, what else am I going to use? I'm not going to pay to have buildings erected when we convert used shipping containers for a living.' He gave a sharp bark of a laugh. 'It's the paint you're seeing. Basic weather-proofing, hard-wearing, extra coats. Don't want to be repainting every five minutes. Colour's different too so we don't have some dozy git in the crane trying to lift us off the ground when they don't read the docket right.'

'I think what I meant was … it's different in the same sort of way that that other one's different. The one where you found the body.'

He glanced across the yard towards the looming silhouette of the stack of three. 'Yeah, I see what you mean.' He sounded surprised. 'Hard-wearing paint, layers of it. But it's a rogue. It's not ours and it's not our paint. Anyway, time is money, so could we get on?'

Before she could reply, her phone buzzed an incoming call. A glance at the screen made her pull in a breath. DI Davis. What in hell did he want that he was ringing her in person? 'Just let me take this and I'll come in and get everything sorted.'

He gave her a hard stare and retreated inside to the warmth.

She hadn't made too much fuss about her unease ... not enough for anyone to have reported back to him, surely. And even if they had, it wasn't his business to be on to her like this. More likely he was after a grunt to run some damn fool errand for him.

'PC Flanagan,' she answered tersely.

'Ah ... Flanagan.' The slight pause told her he'd tried and failed to remember her first name. 'This body. The people who found it disturbed the scene, is that right?'

'As far as I can make out they called for an ambulance, then they went through the pockets, trying to find out who he was. One of them told the paramedic. I've not spoken to any of the witnesses properly. I'm on my own. Don't really want to conduct a group interview.'

'Do we know who it is?'

'I don't. If they do, no one's saying.'

'No ID then?'

'No obvious ID. I haven't been able to conduct a proper search. If he'd been in that container as long as it looks like, he might have stashed things.'

'OK, get him sent to the morgue, but get photos before he's moved. When we've got some data we'll have a look at missing persons, and see what the PM turns up.'

So he'd rung to confirm that she could get the body

moved. It made no sense, just added to the image of him as a meddler.

'Yes, I was about to get that sorted.' She hardened her tone to air her annoyance at being told how to do a job that she already had in hand. 'They're impatient to get their yard back and get sorted for the morning.'

'Did you say you're on your own? Where are the witnesses now?'

She heaved a sigh. Since he'd taken the trouble to call, he might at least pay attention to what she was saying.

'The witnesses are in the office. I can see them from here. The paramedic's in there with them. They've not had any chance to confer since I got here. Before that, who's to say? And yes, I'm on my own.'

She braced herself for a put-down, but his reply wasn't what she expected. 'Keep them there. Speak to the paramedic to organise taking the body but I want you to oversee it. Make sure they don't take away any evidence we can use. And no one else to go near that container. I'll get a couple of PCSOs on their way. Sorry, that's all I'm going to be able to muster.'

'Uh … right. Yes, guv.'

'And if you have any trouble with any of them, Flanagan …'

'I won't,' she interrupted. Something that he needed to learn if he was going to keep on with his meddling was that no one pushed her around.

'OK. So where did the container come from, the one they found the body in?'

'I don't know. No one knows. It's not on their paperwork.'

'When you called it in, I'm told you said that either the

12

victim or the container could have come from Havenmere Docks. Why did you say that?'

'From …? Oh yes, I found what might have been an ID tag … part of an ID tag with a bit of a logo. The letters H.A.V.E. are clear, but that's all. It …' The office door opened. Redman stood there, foot tapping impatiently as he tried to stare her down. She narrowed her eyes, faced him square on and spoke into the phone. 'It could be anything. Just a moment, guv, I …' But Redman had reconsidered and disappeared inside. The Flanagan flint-eyed stare had done its work. 'I only said "might", Guv. That broken tag thing could have come from anywhere.'

'I want proper ID,' Davis said. 'Photograph the witnesses in case anyone's after pulling a fast one. And soon as you can separate them, start taking first accounts. And Flanagan, the words "Havenmere Docks" do not pass your lips again, not to anyone, not until you're back here reporting personally to me.'

CHAPTER 3

The incident stayed in her mind over the following days. She'd reported back to Davis the same night, finding him disappointingly unforthcoming, reiterating that she wasn't to 'gossip' about it, which had annoyed her, but also kept her from asking around because she'd only transferred back into Hull a couple of months ago and hadn't yet built up the sorts of relationships where she could be comfortable tapping people for information. After a week with no further news, she'd shelved it as a case that had gone nowhere.

It was a fortnight later she was told she'd be staying late. She'd heard about a big event at the Bonus Arena, that there might be trouble. Officially exasperated at the short notice, she was secretly pleased. It would be an opportunity to pitch in with new colleagues, to become one of the gang and not the newbie. She'd always liked the adrenaline of a busy city at night as long as it didn't get insane.

She made herself sound regretful when she phoned home. 'Hi Caitlin. I've just been told I have to work late, sorry. Big event on in town.'

'Yes, it's been all over the local radio. Don't stress. See it as a bonding opportunity. And be safe.'

'I'll be fine.' She smiled as she ended the call. Caitlin knew her better than she knew herself.

She set off down the corridor, stopping when a familiar voice called her name. 'Jen, is that you? What are you up to?'

'Doing my duty as a law-enforcement officer,' she said, as Detective Constable Tommy Marchant approached. 'Searching out a good cup of tea before it all kicks off.'

Tommy laughed. He'd been an island of stability in all the changes she'd found when they'd moved back to Hull. She'd begun her training here, had quite a traumatic time as a probationer, almost bailed out, but then stayed around a few years before moving south. When they'd returned just a couple of months ago, she'd felt unsettled without knowing why.

Caitlin had got to the nub of it. 'You were expecting everything to have stayed the same, weren't you?'

It was true, but the city had moved on while she'd been away. The stations she'd worked in were gone. A whole new HQ had been built and she couldn't picture what had been on the site before the huge fortress had been erected. Running into Tommy Marchant had been a relief. She'd never known him well, but they'd worked a few jobs together, and now here he was, the same Tommy, the same rank, the same air of being at ease with the job. All that distinguished him from memory was an ugly raised scar that snaked up behind his left ear and vanished into his hairline. It wasn't especially noticeable except that when lost in thought he rubbed at it, running his fingers absently up its length. When she'd first known him, he'd irritated her with his lack of ambition, she now understood him perfectly. She too had chosen family life and outside interests over the stresses of climbing the promotion ladder.

'Go get your tea, Jen, while you've got the chance. You're wanted upstairs.'

She pulled a face. 'Davis, I suppose.'

The meddlesome DI had been gone for over a week, and she'd seen nothing of him since he'd grilled her on that body found in the shipping container. A sudden spark of interest. Had some forensic result popped up showing something untoward? She'd known from the start something wasn't right.

'Not Davis,' Tommy said. 'His sidekick, Sergeant Shiny Boots.' She laughed. The epithet suited the upright and starched Detective Sergeant Ayaan Ahmed who arrived in Davis's wake. 'Saints preserve us from shiny new sergeants, especially the prissy ones,' Marchant went on. 'Come on, let's get that tea. He can wait.'

'He'll be Inspector before long,' she said as she matched step with him. 'You should watch your P's and Q's.'

'Another one wet behind the ears, fast-tracked up the ladder.'

'He's not. He came up the hard way.' She wasn't sure why she was defending Ahmed, and noticed that Tommy's fingers had moved to the side of his head to trace the line of the scar.

'How come you know so much?' he said.

'I asked him.'

He glanced at her. 'It's some kind of regional syndicate stuff, isn't it? They're not just here to cover.'

'Course it is. Have you seen much "cover" going on?'

'What are they after, then? Best guess.'

Unexpectedly the answer, *Something at Havenmere Docks*, popped into her head, but she just shrugged.

Fortified by her tea, she headed towards the office where Ahmed was camping out while he was here.

'Hi Jennifer,' Ahmed smiled but though he used her first name, his greeting felt formal. 'Remember that body found at Redman's Yard? We've had an ID. It's a William Marshall, 58 years old, reported missing by his wife six weeks ago. Next of kin have been informed, confirmed the ID ...'

'When?' she asked. 'When did you ID him?' She felt the frost in her tone. Behind the words she was saying why didn't I know, why didn't anyone tell me? I was there that night.

'Uh ... about a week ago.'

He had the grace to look shamefaced. Anyway, he didn't meet her eye. Or maybe his attention was elsewhere. She would tell Caitlin that he'd looked shamefaced.

'Not a vagrant then?'

'Semi,' he told her. 'Prone to going AWOL on benders. String of minor offences. She didn't report him missing until he'd been gone the best part of a week and by then he'd have been dead. We kept back some of the stuff we found in the container but we've done all we can with it, there's nothing of interest. I'd like you to take it back to his wife when you're done here today?'

She glanced at the clock. 'I'll not get back for the briefing.'

'What briefing?'

'Tonight, big event at the arena. I've been told I'll be working late.'

'No, that was me. I asked for you for this. She's outside Hull, near Brough. Finish up here, then take Mrs Marshall her husband's stuff and go home. I'm sorry,' he added. 'We've no one else, and with you being there that night ...'

17

She felt a shaft of disappointment that she would miss the camaraderie of a busy night, but at least she wasn't being asked to break the bad news.

'Is it just the stuff from his pockets or did you find more?'

He reached down the side of his desk and pulled out a carrier bag. She heard the clink of bottles. 'He took a couple of bottles of whisky in with him. We found them stashed in one of the cupboards. He'd made a start on one of them.'

'And they're definitely his, not part of whatever was stored in there?'

'His fingerprints were on them … he'd taken the bottles with him. His wife mentioned it when she reported him missing. She thought he'd be gone his usual two or three days. And anyway, there was no evidence of anything like that in the original shipment.'

'You know what it was, then? Where did it come from?'

'We've traced the container from the serial number. It was carrying a shipment of furniture from ex-pats coming home from the Middle East twenty odd years ago.'

'Twenty years?'

'Yup, it left its destination all fine and dandy but never made it to this country until it turned up in Bristol earlier this year.'

'How does a container that size go missing?'

'Convoluted story,' he said, as she took the carrier bag from him and peered inside. 'The ship lost some cargo in a storm. When this one didn't show up, it was presumed to have gone overboard. The insurance company did its own investigation and decided it almost certainly hadn't. Paperwork backed them up. It looked like it'd been unloaded.' He spread his hands in a who-knows gesture.

'They'd had to make an unscheduled stop to get the cargo re-balanced. It could have been unloaded and left behind … accident or deliberate fraud … No one really knew until it turned up.'

'In a dockyard?' she asked and saw his eyes snap up to meet hers, with the sharp look she was beginning to associate with every mention of Havenmere Docks. 'In Bristol,' she clarified, wondering if the container had bounced off Havenmere Docks before coming across the Humber to Redman's Yard.

'No, not a dockyard,' he said. 'An outfit not unlike Redman's Yard. It was probably meant to be stored there temporarily, but they boxed it in.'

'Deliberately hid it?' She supposed the one place you might hide a shipping container would be a place like Redman's Yard.

'Who knows? It's a couple of decades ago. In all the chaos of dealing with an unscheduled shipload of containers, they had to find temporary storage. This one got painted in during routine maintenance on an office block, the sort of job that's only done once in a blue moon. It took years before anyone had the nous to realise they were painting more roofs than they had rooms inside. It might have been deliberate to start with but over time it was gradually boxed in and forgotten.'

'Presumably it belonged to an insurance company by then.'

He nodded. 'They sold it to a firm near Middlesbrough. It should have arrived around the time William Marshall went missing, but it did another disappearing act until it turned up at Redman's Yard with Marshall inside it.'

'So had he been to Bristol? Is that where he got in it?'

Ahmed shrugged. 'That's where the old contents were re-tied down, so he'd have had the opportunity. Once it was on its way, it shouldn't have been re-opened.'

'But can't you tell? Forensics on the lock … CCTV from Bristol. There's CCTV at Redman's. Have we seized it?'

'You know the score, Jennifer. Whose budget's going to take the hit? It's going to be classed misadventure. We've nothing to justify chasing it.'

'How did he die?'

He scrunched his face in a way that said this wasn't easy. 'He must have been in there almost the whole time he was missing. Looks like he'd been dead about that long too. We can't get chapter and verse after all this time, but there was a head wound that finished him off. Hopefully he was already unconscious, sleeping off the drink.'

'I didn't see a head wound,' she murmured, knowing she hadn't really looked, that it wouldn't necessarily have shown. 'But how?' she interrupted before he could speak. 'How did he get in? It was locked. From the outside. What was he hit with?'

'I'm not saying we have all the answers, but there's nothing pointing to anyone else's involvement. A lot of the ties inside that container had rotted; some had been redone, but they didn't tie everything down as securely as they should have. That container's been on at least one lorry, probably more, before Redman's crane swung it about. He could have died anywhere along the journey. Let's hope it was quick and he knew nothing about it.'

'Hang on, Sarge, you said he was hit over the head. That's potential manslaughter if it's not murder. He could have got in a fight, and someone lashed out. We've all seen it. You said he'd been drinking. Someone picks up the nearest weapon and it's goodnight Vienna.'

He shook his head. 'The "weapon" in this case was an oak sideboard. The damage fits the moulding on the edge. There were fragments of wood in the wound. As soon as that container went at all off level, it was putting strain on the ties that were half rotted anyway. Something that big suddenly breaks free and he's in the wrong place, he's no chance, conscious or not.'

She supposed he had a point. 'There's something missing.' She reached into the bag to move the bottles aside. 'That tag thing, Havenmere Docks.'

'You told DI Davis you'd found it on the floor of the container, not in his pocket.'

'I did, but it could have fallen out of his wallet. I wasn't the one who emptied his pockets if you remember.'

'I do.' His unsmiling stare met hers briefly, as though he was reprimanding her for that.

In a deliberate attempt to needle him, she asked, 'Do you want me to ask Mrs Marshall about it?'

It worked. 'No! Don't say anything about–'

'The words "Havenmere Docks" won't pass my lips,' she parroted.

CHAPTER 4

'Havenmere-sodding-Docks.' Miriam Marshall muttered the words under her breath as she trudged up a road that was proving longer than she'd anticipated. She pulled out her phone, clicked in a number and put the handset to her ear.

Foregoing any greeting, she said, 'Have you found out yet?'

'Not yet,' the voice said, a mix of amused indignation and apology. 'Give us a chance.'

She ended the call and looked at the surrounding buildings with distaste. She wouldn't normally venture anywhere near an area like this; and would have brought the car if she'd known how far it was from the city centre.

She slowed, not wanting to arrive hot and bothered. It would make her late for her appointment but that wasn't going to worry her, and if they tried to make anything of it … well, just let them try. They knew to expect trouble from her. She'd made that very clear when she rang.

Over and above arriving composed, she didn't want to cry. Not that she'd considered the possibility when she'd set out. Will had died almost two months ago but she'd only known about it for eleven days. It hadn't been a shock. Not as such. She'd been expecting it for ten years, ever since Havenmere Docks.

Here at last.

She looked up at the façade. Their offices were on the first floor and those upstairs windows hadn't seen a wet cloth in decades. A sign hung there, not quite level, its font too fancy, its apostrophe incorrectly placed. She'd found them in a magazine after Will had been gone for a week, longer than the usual bender, and no word. The advertisement had been neat, understated, professional; nothing like this ramshackle set up.

The police weren't looking for him, not with his record. In the circumstances, a private investigator had seemed the right way to go. And now? She wasn't the sort to shit on her own doorstep but she wanted vengeance for Will; she owed him that. It was when she'd gone through Will's stuff that the game had changed. She'd found a whole stack of paperwork, a sharp reminder of something she'd forgotten. Could she use this tinpot agency to work it out for her, in exchange for the crappy job that they didn't manage to do? There was a number on the card given to her by PC Jennifer Flanagan who'd returned Will's stuff, but that would be making it a bit too official. The part of her that thirsted for revenge wanted the world to know, but she didn't want the fallout hitting too close to home. She had a lot to lose.

She'd set out today to complain and demand her money back. If she was honest, she was spoiling for a fight and anyone would do, but perhaps she would hold back, see what the Thompsons and their agency had to offer.

* * *

23

Jennifer Flanagan spun round at the sound of a familiar voice. 'DI Davis,' she called loudly seeing that he had stepped into the lift and it would swallow him before she could get there.

He didn't look up from punching a number into his phone, but he put his foot between the closing doors, so they clunked and slid open again as she caught up.

She joined him in the metal box. 'Sergeant Ahmed sent me to take Mrs Marshall her husband's things.'

'And?' Behind his question she could hear the muffled sound of a ring-tone from the phone at his ear.

'He told me to report back verbally if there was anything to report.'

'And did you?'

'He's not been in.'

'He'll be in tomorrow.' He dismissed her with a wave of his hand as the lift jolted to a halt and turned his attention to his call.

As the doors began to open, she said, 'That ID tag, Havenmere Docks. It *was* William Marshall's.' She shimmied out and set off towards the staircase.

'Flanagan!'

When she turned, his phone was nowhere to be seen. 'I'll catch up with Sergeant Ahmed tomorrow,' she said.

'No, no. Come with me. I've … er … a few minutes … er … What's your name again?'

'PC Flanagan,' she said, deadpan.

'First name.'

'Jennifer.'

'Ah yes, Jennifer … Jennifer,' he repeated as though impressing the name on his memory. 'Well, Jennifer, I'd like

24

to hear about your chat with Mrs Marshall. Come through to the office.'

Where we won't be disturbed, she added to herself, saying, 'Sure,' as she fell into step beside him.

Ahmed hadn't been as clear-cut in his instructions to report back as she'd implied. He'd said, 'Don't bother emailing me, I'm too swamped, it'll get lost. Just let me know sometime how it went.' He wasn't expecting her to have anything of interest to report, but at the same time he was discouraging her from putting anything on the record. Why would he do that?

She ran her gaze around Davis's office, trying to pick up clues about their real work. She'd not confided her latest suspicions to Tommy Marchant because he was too much of a gossip but maybe Davis and Ahmed were nothing to do with any regional crime project, just deliberately giving off that vibe to hide something closer to home. Like an anti-corruption squad.

* * *

Miriam Marshall climbed the stairs towards her appointment and found herself met on the upper landing by a blond-haired man, mid 30s she judged, with a nice smile and an outstretched hand.

'Is it Mrs Marshall? I'm Mike Connaughty. I hope you found us OK.'

She cooperated in the proffered handshake, but wasn't about to be mollified by a nice smile. 'You're very out of the way up here. I was expecting something a bit more upmarket.'

'We're hoping to relocate,' he said. 'Timing's down to the owners of course.'

'Who I'm expecting to meet today.' She kept her tone clipped. *I want to speak with whoever's in charge*, is what she'd said, and had no intention of settling for less.

'The owners have no role in the day to day business. They leave it all to their executive officers.'

She allowed herself the ghost of a scornful raised eyebrow at the grandiose *executive officers*, and said, 'A Ms Raymond I was told.' She ignored the hand that was now trying to usher her off the landing and into an office.

'Annie and I run the agency together,' he said. 'She won't be long. Would you rather wait? It's the funeral on Monday, isn't it? I … we wondered if it would be OK if we send a representative. We didn't know him of course, but to pay our respects.'

She tipped her head, finding herself touched that he'd thought of it. 'If you like.' Her tone was ungracious. 'It's at Chants. Ten-thirty.'

He smiled his nice smile again. 'Can I get you a coffee?'

She thought about the policewoman's reaction yesterday. It had been fleeting but PC Flanagan had been surprised to hear that Will used to work at Havenmere Docks. And surely that was something she should already have known. She might try a similar throwaway comment on Connaughty and see how he reacted.

All that money in the returned wallet, it was as though Will had made sure she would be OK while things were sorted. Had he wanted to give her options? There might not be enough for that. Again the unexpected tear pricked the back of her eye. She turned and headed for the room he'd been trying to get her into. 'OK, let's make a start. I don't have all day. And yes, I could do with a cup of tea. Dash of milk, no sugar.'

It was a relief to sit down. The tea came in a generous mug, steaming hot and just the way she liked it. 'That young girl, Lois, you sent me, she was hopeless, found nothing. I paid good money and it was the police who found him.'

'It must have been awful,' he said. 'I gather he was trapped inside somewhere. Do you know … uh … how long?'

'A shipping container. Nearly the whole time, they think. Took a while for them to find out who he was. You see what I mean? I pay good money and even now you don't know the basics.'

She took refuge in her tea. It was less Mike Connaughty she was annoyed with, than the police for labelling Will a vagrant. PC Flanagan said that the vagrant tag had kept the press away, which might be true but was hardly tactful. At least that slip of a girl Connaughty and co had sent managed to stumble out an expression of regret, though that had been all about fear of losing her job.

'I got nothing for my money,' she went on. 'That girl was supposed to chase up his colleagues, friends, find out if anyone had seen him. She said she'd find who he'd been with, where he'd gone. Well, she didn't.'

'Uh … certainly, it was early days and her lines of enquiry–'

'Lines!' she interrupted. 'Her *one* line was to chase up his boozing mates from the pub. Fat lot of good that did. I'd done that myself. Nothing to do with them. And he didn't just die, whatever anyone says, he was killed and I know who by.'

27

She lifted the cup to her lips and stared towards the window that looked out on to an enclosed yard, showing the blank walls of other ramshackle outfits like this one. Hadn't meant for that to come out. She knew how it sounded; irrational and hysterical, even to her.

'What do you think happened to him, Mrs Marshall?' It was a woman's voice from behind her. She spun round to see a stocky blonde, about the same age as Connaughty. The woman stepped forward and proffered her hand. 'I'm Annie Raymond. Sorry I'm late. I hope Mike's been looking after you.' Annie Raymond pulled round a chair. 'I've looked into the file,' she said. 'We sent you someone inexperienced and she wasn't up to the job. I'm sorry. There'll be a full refund of course.'

The reaction from Mike Connaughty was fleeting, as easy to miss as had been PC Flanagan's surprise last night. The Raymond woman hadn't checked this with him. It made her feel slightly better.

She nodded an unsmiling acknowledgment of the offer. No need for effusive thanks; it was no more than her due. She weighed what to say next, feeling her hysterical outburst about killers had narrowed her options.

'No one seems to have done their homework on my husband,' she said eventually. 'He was found in a shipping container. He worked on the docks for years, him and his father before him, until he was sacked. Havenmere Docks. He's behind it. Small mean-minded git. I knew the moment I heard. And that policewoman didn't have a clue. Tried to hide it, but nearly dropped through the floor when I told her where he used to work.'

Annie Raymond said, 'Tell me more.'

28

CHAPTER 5

Annie returned from seeing Mrs Marshall off the premises. She avoided Mike's eye. 'Coffee?' she asked hopefully, reaching for Mrs Marshall's empty mug.

'Annie! We can't take this on. If there's been foul play, it's a police matter.'

'William Marshall wasn't murdered,' she said. 'You know it. I know it. And his wife knows it. She's just kicking off about an old feud because she's angry. He went on a bender and got locked in a shipping container. Him working at Havenmere Docks explains why he got in it … familiar territory.'

'Did you get the impression she was on the verge of telling us something?'

'Yes, for sure. To do with why he was sacked, is my guess. I'm wondering if he stole something. Maybe it wasn't the drink, maybe he was a thief.'

'He must have been found at Havenmere Docks,' Mike said, thumbing through the thin file. 'Lois hasn't recorded any detail and I didn't want to press Mrs Marshall to go through it; I could see she was fighting not to get upset.'

'She's nursing a grievance about his sacking, but that was ten years ago.' Annie slid past Lois's shoddy note-keeping before Mike could have a pop at Barbara for inadequate supervision. 'Who knows how many hangovers he's slept off like that? It's no wonder he was kicked out whatever else he did. You can't have people around those places drunk.'

'So why tell her we'd take it on?'

'We fucked up, Mike. We shouldn't have sent Lois; she's not been with us five minutes and frankly she's not very good. Give it a day or so and I'll tell Miriam Marshall it's a dead end for us. If she wants to go further, she'll have to make it official. She'll be happy. She gets some extra work and her money back.'

'Are you sure there's nothing more to it? She looked quite cagey.'

'All I can think of is …' She paused to reached for the Marshall file and flicked through Lois's scant notes. 'Apparently, he went back to Havenmere Docks after the sacking and his boss got shirty about it. *Kept a key,* it says here.' She turned to the computer and pulled up a search screen, typing in *Havenmere Docks.* 'He might have been working cash in hand somewhere. Miriam Marshall would keep quiet if he was, because she could lose out to HMRC or whatever.'

'How does that have a bearing?'

'I'm thinking dodgy site, some kind of accident, covered up to avoid a health and safety inspection, but Havenmere Docks doesn't look like that sort of outfit, even supposing they'd reemploy a drunk. Looks like he sneaked in under the radar and got himself boxed in. If there'd been the whisper of that sort of accident, the official investigation would have joined those dots.'

'And it'd still be across the line for us. And anyway, we

didn't fuck up. Barb did. She hired Lois, and her put on that job. She should have kept an eye on her.'

Annie spread her hands. 'Buck stops with us, Mike. We shouldn't let Barb run with stuff like that; it's not where she's strong. It should have been one of us, but we were busy.'

'This just illustrates my point, Annie. How many times have I said …' She braced herself for a lecture. If she'd done this. … done that … how they wouldn't be saddled with Barb … how he would have done it differently … She set her face to 'listening' and let his words flow by.

When he'd come back into her life bursting with all the managerial skills she lacked, and raring to go at a new challenge, she'd welcomed him with open arms. His arrival had smoothed what would otherwise have been an impossible transition as she took over the agency where she'd once been the solitary worker to the Thompson sisters' queen-bee duet.

Then he'd seen the deal she'd signed with the two investors who had swooped in at the eleventh hour, saving the Thompsons and their agency from financial ruin. 'We had no choice, Mike. We were out of options.'

He'd wanted more. 'Who are they? Why did they want you in charge? What do you know about them?'

'Not much,' she'd admitted. It was an understatement.

Her London boss, Pieternel, had run a mile from them which should have rung alarm bells, but their offer had been too tempting. 'It's Ms Dyson and Mr fforbes to us,' she'd told Mike. In truth she doubted those were their names. 'They wanted someone who knew what they were doing. I was here. Right place, right time.'

31

She'd had to rein him in from asking questions.

'Mike! Stop asking about them. Stop mentioning them by name. They're "the owners". Leave it at that.'

'You're paranoid,' he'd mocked her. 'What do you think they'll do?'

'Frankly I don't want to think about it. They're not involving us in anything dodgy. Leave it at that!'

'You mean they're laundering money through the agency?'

'Well no, they're not.' Annie had made the same assumption initially and wanted to glide past the fact she'd been desperate enough to overlook it.

Kicking back, he'd taken to calling them Penn and Teller which infuriated her.

Not that it was Dyson and fforbes who'd tied her into retaining both Thompson sisters, and to keeping their sign hanging illiterately from the upstairs sill; that had been some quick thinking on the sisters' part. Since then an air of lethargy had grown over the agency, almost as though their fate was in someone else's hands so there was no real point any more.

Something about the Marshall case harked back to the more vibrant less secure days. There *was* an element of mystery; why had he gone back to the place he'd worked, what had he been planning to do? The police wouldn't have closed the case if they'd had any doubts so she had no qualms about making a few extra enquiries. In fact, she intended being more proactive than she would admit to Mike. Financial security tied her to a desk far more than she'd anticipated. It would be good to get out in the field if only for a few hours. No one need know.

'Jeez!' Mike rolled his eyes.

Annie realised she'd let her 'listening' face slip, and snapped it back into place.

He shot her a hard look and repeated her earlier question. 'Coffee?'

They walked along the landing to the small kitchen. 'It's not forever,' Annie said as she swilled Mrs Marshall's mug under the tap. 'We can't sack them, but we could buy them off … or something.'

'Drop a hint that the owners are looking to cash in their investment,' Mike said. 'That'll scare them into jumping ship while there's still money in the coffers.'

A door banged downstairs. A heavy tread creaked the rickety staircase. '… and didn't I tell you …?' A querulous voice floated up.

Mike's face hardened. 'If they fell and broke their necks, I suppose they'd sue.'

Annie spooned coffee into a cafetière and thought through her plans for first thing tomorrow, plans she would not share with Mike until after the event.

* * *

Jennifer Flanagan eyed the chip in her cup and spun it to lift the undamaged side of the rim to her mouth. Marchant, opposite her, held his mug in both hands ingesting hot tea via a noisy suction operation that involved no obvious contact between lips and crockery. How he avoided a permanently stained shirt front she had no idea.

He'd known she'd been in to see Davis before she'd mentioned it. He seemed to know everything.

'What've you found out, Jen? What're they doing? It's like having Special Branch in, the way they're all behind closed doors all the time.'

'You think they'd confide in me? It was just loose ends about that body in the container yard.'

He glanced around as though checking for hidden watchers. 'It's being run from York, whatever it is. Just watch your step, that's all. People talk. The new girl closeted up with the parachute squad. Didn't you see anything?'

She shook her head. 'Desks clean, no papers out. Best guess? I'd say drugs. They seem to have a focus on … uh … on shipping … on the port.' She pulled herself up, had almost said Havenmere Docks.

'You said you'd something to tell me. Come on, Jen, spill it.'

His manner was comfortable. She could imagine him instilling confidence in a certain type of interviewee. There was something about him that made you want to help him out. Not that she would fall for it, but he was right, she had something to pass on.

'Davis took a call while I was in with him. From York, I assume. He cut it short, said he was with someone, but whoever was at the other end asked after you.'

'Me?' Marchant looked blank.

'Davis said, "Tommy Marchant? Yeah, he's fine," then when he'd done he said to me, "Tell Tommy the guv was asking after him." So, what's that about?'

'Oh right,' said Marchant. 'Webber. Detective Super.' His hand went to the side of his head, his index finger tracing the scar.

'So why would he ask after you?' She watched him

34

closely. He didn't look so comfortable now. Was it an oblique warning, and if so, to whom? She'd looked up both Havenmere Docks and Redman's Yard and found nothing much. Havenmere, south of the Humber, was a slick outfit dealing in international freight. Redman's Yard recycled used shipping containers, but the boxes she'd seen in their yard were dwarfs compared to the giant containers in the photos on Havenmere Docks' website. If the two sites were linked, it was nothing obvious. And Davis and Ahmed might be here to look into something closer to home. What if Tommy was involved? Maybe he was the one she needed to steer clear of.

'You could say we shared a fire one time, me and Webber,' Tommy said at length.

'A fire?'

'Nasty case. Complicated. I'd as soon not talk about it. But why did Davis call you in?'

'I'd taken the guy's personal possessions back to the widow. He wanted to know if she'd said anything. But when you say shared a fire …'

He put down his tea, and placed his hand on her arm. 'Jen, which part of "I don't want to talk about it" are you having trouble with?'

CHAPTER 6

Annie pulled up outside a huge gate just before 7.30 the next morning. Mike had left early to meet an old friend in Wakefield, someone from his former life in merchant banking. He'd talked about business synergies and had invited her along. Luckily she'd already turned him down which allowed her a window to drive across the Humber Bridge, scout around Havenmere Docks and be back long before he missed her. It would be a good ten minutes before the sun's rays cut across the estuary, but the lights inside the high metal fencing lit the scene comprehensively enough to make day and night an irrelevance.

The road was marked out with lines and symbols she couldn't decipher, although the double yellow lines she stopped on were not open to misinterpretation. Leaving the engine running, she climbed out of the car and went to peer through the metal slats. Busy had been her first impression, but for all the lights and clanging of machinery, it was a ghost town; empty of any human presence.

High above her head a lens looked down. In keeping with the mechanised landscape inside the boundary, the gate made no concessions to human limitations. No bell, no sign, no intercom.

'Morning, Miss.'

She spun round. A liveried car had pulled up behind hers. She looked into an unsmiling face that held a hint of satisfaction; a predator who had cornered his prey.

'Uh … good morning.'

'You can't park here. What's your business?'

'I've come to see Mr Small,' she said, jerking her thumb to indicate the operation behind the fence. It was the only name her rushed search had unearthed. She'd been cutting corners for speed, assumed she'd be able to wing it.

'Is he expecting you?' He hadn't necessarily swallowed the lie, but he wasn't yet disbelieving her.

'I'd like to think so,' she said with a smile, adding silently, *but I can't because I've not been in touch.*

'If he's not answering the gate, you'll have to move on. You can't park here or you'll be towed.'

'Yes, sure. Uh … I couldn't figure out where the intercom is.'

He pointed over her head. 'If he knows you're coming, the ANPR'll let you in.' His tone was neutral, though he'd not lost the mean glint in his eye.

She looked up at the high lens. As an expected visitor she must sit her vehicle in front of the gate and hope for the robotic eye to recognise her.

'Oh, right. Thanks. I didn't realise.' She scuttled for her car and slipped it into gear. This had gone from casual to complicated in the blink of an eye. He had tipped towards disbelief and was going to watch her try to gain entry. And when the gates didn't open to admit her …?

She'd been caught uncomfortably close to the autocracy of the border where Customs and Excise held sway. A sinking feeling in the pit of her stomach told her that far from being back home before Mike showed up, she would be ringing him to come and bail her out.

Hoping to keep the movement below his line of sight, she slipped her phone from her pocket and reached across to push it into the glove box. It wouldn't survive a search of the car but things surely wouldn't get that far. Her clone phone, the one she would rather lose should she end up in custody, was already in her inside pocket; routine insurance that she'd practised for years.

She made a meal of manoeuvring the car to get it in line with the gates in the hopes that the man in uniform would get bored or be called away. It might have been better just to drive off.

He was already speaking into a handset as he watched her. She kicked herself for naïve stupidity. How long would it have taken to make a phone call? This was not the sort of place that could be cold-called.

Her car was nosing towards the gate now. For want of anything better to do, she opened the window and leant out, craning her neck towards the watching camera as though to plead for entry, maybe hoping that officialdom would label her a fool who should be allowed to retreat.

The liveried guard put down his radio; his door began to open. He wasn't going to let her leave quietly.

A heavy clanking sound followed by a screech made him pause.

She fought to hide her amazement as the giant gates clanked sideways. The moment the gap was wide enough, she eased her car inside.

With a slam of its door, the official vehicle drove off, rather too fast, and she was left alone, inching her car forward across an asphalt expanse, trying to work out where it would be safe to park.

An echoing crash made her jump. Her foot slipped off the clutch and the car jolted to a stalled halt. Up ahead a giant frame had clamped shut on a huge container and was lifting it from the ground. She peered up, looking for a cab … an operator … anyone …

From behind, a metallic scream signalled cogs reversing their motion. Before it had fully opened, the tall gate began to slide shut.

Suddenly she regretted the mean-faced uniform in his liveried vehicle. Trapped inside a fully-mechanised yard chock-full of unpredictable machinery with swinging cranes and metal arms, any one of which could knock her off her feet, she felt the need for a witness. Had William Marshall been trapped? He would have known his way about this place. Maybe he'd dived into an open container to avoid a swinging robotic arm only to have it lock him in to starve.

CHAPTER 7

Annie restarted the car, but couldn't see where to go. There were no markings, just a wide expanse that looked as though it was waiting for heavy loads to be dumped on to it. Why had the gates opened for her? There seemed to be no one here, yet the automatic number plate recognition system couldn't have let her in because no one knew she was coming. Was it the man in the car? He'd made a call and then the gates had opened. Had she allowed him to trap her in here?

She started to swing the car in a wide arc that would head it back towards the gate, whilst keeping distance between her and the more active of the swinging arms. If the system had let her in, maybe it would also let her out.

'Hey, you in the car!'

She stopped.

Hurrying across the empty expanse was a tall man dressed in pullover and jeans. He was waving one hand frantically, signalling her to move off to the side, out of the way. Half his attention was up high, fixed on the blind spot she couldn't see through the car's roof. His gaze tracked something; his expression a mix of annoyance and concern as his gestures grew more urgent.

A shadow grew out of nowhere. Some part of the

clanking chaos was right above her and descending fast. Her foot flattened the accelerator and she swung the wheel to follow the man's pointing hand. The car slewed across the asphalt, accelerating away from the growing shadow, and into the shade of the building, seeing at last a semblance of road markings aimed at conventional vehicles. Round the back she found a neat row of parking spaces, only one of which was occupied, and pulled into one labelled Visitor. She climbed out of the car and took a moment for a few deep breaths.

Before she could head back to see what had happened, the man was striding round the corner, radiating indignation.

He glowered as he marched up close. 'I overrode the ANPR to let you in because I can't stand the officious toe-rag who wanted to arrest you, but I can call him back any time.' He stood in front of her, arms folded, foot tapping.

She thought better of offering a handshake. 'Are you … uh … Mr Small?'

'I'm asking the questions. Who are you and what do you want?'

'My name's Annie Raymond. I'm here about Mr Marshall, Mr William Marshall.'

At once, his expression softened, his gaze dropped and he shook his head sadly. 'Poor old Jobsie,' he murmured. 'I heard about it. Listen, the funeral. It's tomorrow, isn't it? Do you know where … what time?'

'Uh … Chants Ave, ten-thirty. Um … can you tell me anything about how it happened? I mean what he was doing and that?'

He shook his head again. 'I've not seen Jobsie in the best part of a year.'

She had to ask. 'You *are* Mr Small, aren't you?'

'Rob Small.' He stepped forward, holding out his hand to give her a firm handshake. 'How did you know Jobsie?'

'I'm afraid I didn't. I only knew him as William Marshall. We … uh … Forgive me but are you thinking of going to the funeral? Only I thought that you and Mr Marshall were daggers drawn. Didn't he work for you once?'

For the first time a smile crossed his face. 'You've been talking to Miriam. And no, me and him weren't at daggers drawn, as you put it. Last time I saw Jobsie, we went out for a beer.'

'But …' Annie's words were drowned in a high-pitched squeal of metal on metal.

Small glanced up. From here, only the tops of the cranes dancing over the yard were visible. 'Could you use a coffee?' he shouted over the clanking. 'I've just put a brew on and it's quieter in the office.'

The easy nickname, Jobsie, suggested Rob Small had known Marshall well. This was a real opportunity to get all the background that should have been unearthed in the first place. On the flip side, she had no easy exit from this complex. She'd broken a cardinal rule in coming here and telling no one of her plans. The office might well be quieter, but it would be even more isolated.

'Thanks,' she shouted back. 'I'd love a coffee.'

Rob Small led her to a wide metal staircase that clung to the exterior wall. To the crashing and clanging of machinery, they zigzagged up three flights and in through a reinforced door. As she stepped out of the whistling wind and continuous noise, Annie felt her eyes widen. A lobby led to a space-age control centre, all gleaming metallic surfaces, consoles and screens. Overlying it was the welcome smell of quality coffee.

A panoramic view across the yard showed the sun's rays spearing in from the east, low and harsh, glinting off the giant rigs. The larger screens showed the same landscape from subtly different angles. Side by side with the windows, the impression was surreal. Sunlight versus a softer version filtered through a network of cameras.

She'd had a close shave with the 'officious toe-rag' outside, and was breaking rules to be here alone. It was high time she got out from behind a desk and refreshed herself on the realities of the job. She'd got sloppy.

'You should keep your plates cleaner,' said Rob Small as he reached towards a shiny expanse of stainless steel she'd taken to be part of the all-encompassing console but saw now was a built-in drinks machine.

She stared, immediately coveting it for her own domain. He handed her a cup and as she tasted the quality of the brew, the futuristic machine jumped to number two on the list for moving day; one: smash the old sign, two: buy one of these.

Rob Small said, 'With you in a mo,' and turned towards the main console where he typed briefly at one of the keyboards.

He's bored, she thought. He might have a state-of-the-art operation but he's on his own too much. Robots aren't built to be good company, not workhorses like these. He would be happy to talk, and looking around at all this advanced technology, she was only too keen to listen.

'What d'you mean,' she asked. 'Keep my plates cleaner?'

'When I say I overrode the ANPR, I can't actually do that. I had to input your reg.' He pointed at one of the screens then moved a joystick. It zoomed in on her car outside the building. The plates were muddy and indistinct. 'Lucky I guessed right or I'd have left you to your fate. So what was it you wanted to know about Jobsie?'

'Oh my God!' Annie stared at another of the screens. 'I stopped just there.' A huge metal box sat on the spot where she'd stalled the car. 'How close was I to …?'

'You'd have been fine.' He laughed at her discomfort. 'Look, I'll show you.'

She moved closer to the multiple displays as he pointed out the schematics that represented the crane that had been set to crush her. At first, she thought she wasn't interpreting the symbols correctly, but … 'Uh, do you have underground storage?'

'Well spotted.' He looked delighted, giving her a nod as though encouraging a favourite pupil.

'So if I'd stayed in the car …' She tried to follow the logic of the chart the crane had been following. 'The ground would have opened up, I'd have fallen in and it'd have dropped that huge box thing on my head?'

'No, no.' He looked disappointed. 'There's no underground storage. I set the parameters so the crane sees the ground three metres lower than it actually is. Then I tell it to set the box there sharpish.'

Annie shot him a look, unimpressed with his light tone. 'So it would've have smashed the box down on top of me three metres faster than it should have done, though I suppose I'd be just as flat either way.'

'You'd have been quite safe. Leastways …' He laughed again. 'I hope you would. I can show you how it works if you're not in a rush to get away.'

Annie considered. There was plenty of time before Mike would be back, and anyway why was she worrying about explaining anything to Mike? She was in charge. He wouldn't question why she wasn't there when he got back because if she'd gone anywhere dodgy she would have let him know. He wouldn't worry until late tonight or maybe tomorrow morning when she started missing appointments. Hell, she thought, she'd worked enough dangerous cases to know when things were sticky. This guy was fine.

'Yeah, it's Sunday. I've nothing else on. I'd love to hear more. I mean I'd like to find out about William Marshall, but I'd be fascinated to know more about this place.' It was no lie. As she cradled her cup, her gaze was riveted to the metallic ballet being played out by the huge machines.

Another jarring metallic shriek resounded through the site.

'It's normally far quieter than this,' he said. 'They go about their business good as gold, none of these jarring stops and emergency breaks.'

Every few moments he leant in to study one of the readouts, or to run his finger along the line of a graph that drew itself across one of the screens.

'Why isn't it normal today?' she said.

'I'm running everything through its paces. We've an HSE check next week.'

'Health and Safety?'

'Yup. They test everything to its limit, beyond its normal limits. Margins for safety. Your car, say. Not that I expected you to come in and park in the firing line like that. I assumed you'd come round to the car park.'

She shrugged. If there had been signs pointing the way, she'd not seen them.

He went on, 'The crane was all set to stand a box on a floor it thought was three metres lower than the ground. I'd told it to move fast – faster than we'd usually run. But no matter what the software says, its sensors are going to see the ground where it really is. They'd have seen your car too. It'd have stopped within maybe ten millimetres of your roof. The car would have been fine, but you'd probably have had a heart attack when you realised what was coming down on top of you. That's why I came out. Didn't want the hassle of calling out the medics.'

He gave her an amused glance.

'Well thanks. How many trespassers have you frightened to death over the years?'

She watched him closely, thinking of Marshall. 'None,' he said. 'We don't get trespassers. They can't get in.'

Marshall did, she thought, but said, 'Nothing's a hundred percent secure … can't be.'

'Good as, these days. If anything breaks its way in here, it'll be brute force, a tank through the fence, and even then every alarm in the place'll be shrieking fit to wake the dead.'

'What's that one doing?' She pointed to a red crane lifting one of the giant boxes.

'Same sort of thing, false levels. The system's telling it to put it down on top of a phantom stack of three. It'll get the nod that it's fixed in place. That should trigger it to let go.'

'It lets go?' she asked, feeling the tension build as the crate rose, as though watching someone blow up a balloon to the point of bursting.

He laughed. 'No way! They never let go, ever, not until

the thing is unequivocally placed and stable. Just like it'd have detected your car and held the box above-' He stopped abruptly. Annie saw his eyes narrow in thought.

'What?'

'There's always something,' he said. 'Possibilities are infinite, that's the thing. When you've been doing this for years you fall into thinking you've thought of everything. I'm wondering now what it would have done about your car. I know it would've worked round mine or the HSE inspector's or anyone else routinely programmed in, but I put your number in on the fly. What would that have done to its priorities? My car, it'd have put the box down beside it. Yours, it might have called in one of the trucks and shoved it out of the way. Might not have done it much good if it'd pushed it sideways … uh … good thing I came out.'

Annie allowed one of her eyebrows to rise. His *Good thing I came out* was an afterthought for her benefit. She was sure he'd much rather have known. Well, he could test that out on his next unexpected visitor.

'That's why it's making all the noise,' he went on. 'Full speed, false levels … It's the emergency brakes and clamps scraping, that's what the noise is about. When it's all running on its own, it's quiet as a graveyard.'

He had an unfortunate turn of phrase. 'Is it because of William Marshall?' she asked. 'That you're having the inspection, I mean.'

He looked blank. 'No, it's routine. Why would it be about Jobsie?'

'Well … he died here … in one of your containers.'

He stared at her for several seconds before he spoke. 'Who in hell told you that?'

47

'Mrs Marshall said …' Annie paused. Miriam Marshall hadn't said where he'd died, just where he used to work. 'Uh … she said he used to work here. I … I just assumed.'

He looked shaken. 'You'll get yourself into trouble, assuming stuff, throwing round accusations. Jobsie's not been near hand nor by Havenmere in a twelve month. He was found in some recycling yard the other side of the river, that's what I heard.'

'I'm sorry,' she said. How many more apologies was she going to have to issue before they'd put this case to bed? 'I misunderstood.'

… worked on the docks for years, him and his father before him … he's behind it, small mean-minded git … Miriam hadn't been talking about her father-in-law, though that was how Annie had interpreted it. She'd meant: *He's behind it – Small.*

This man she was effectively locked in with was the one Miriam had accused of killing her husband.

CHAPTER 8

It was warm for a November morning, the sun bright as Mike drove them in through the tall metal gates and into the landscaped grounds of the crematorium.

'Good timing,' Annie said, pulling on her gloves. 'I want to check out who's turned up before it kicks off.'

She'd downplayed her trip to Havenmere Docks, not letting on how worried … how threatened she'd felt. Because for much of the time she'd been in Rob Small's company she'd felt relaxed and safe. She wouldn't have wanted to have been in that yard without him, with the giant robotic cranes screeching and clanking all around her.

'It was a spur of the moment thing,' was what she'd said to Mike. 'I wanted to check out Miriam Marshall's story. Everything Lois put in that file, it's all come from her. She didn't check anything.'

He'd laughed and said, 'The times your boss in London was on at you for doing unpaid work! I'm getting where she was coming from.'

She'd laughed too. Not just that he was right, but that it no longer galled her to have people refer to Pieternel as her boss. *We're equal partners*, she'd always been quick to point out, but they hadn't been. Despite her own heavy

49

investment in the firm – with money that had never been hers – Pieternel had always held the reins. But now Pieternel had vanished into a new and doubtless successful life, and Annie was back with the old firm, the Thompsons.

And also back with Mike.

They'd said what they'd taken to be their final goodbyes years ago when he'd left her to pursue a dream she couldn't share; a dream of a comfortable home, two-point-four children and a conventional life. It hadn't worked out. The woman he'd married was a real person, not a personification of his long-held happy-ever-after aspirations. His ex-wife and their two-point-four, in reality two, children remained an important part of his life, but his marriage had become just an interlude in their own long-standing relationship.

She linked arms with him as they walked from the car park down to the chapel where William Marshall was to be laid to rest.

As they approached, Annie appraised the crowd already gathered. Mainly men she thought, but when she did a quick count, the gender divide was equal, the male contingent somehow dominating the throng. These would be his ex-workmates, his drinking buddies. There would be people here who'd worked with him at Havenmere Docks. Her sharp gaze ran across them. If Rob Small was in amongst them, she would pick her targets by who he was talking to, but he wasn't there. All-in-all she was relieved he'd decided to stay away.

She wanted stories to compare to what Small had told her, not that she had any reason to doubt his account. Small's father, who had founded Havenmere Docks, had given Marshall's father his first job. The two sons had gone to school together and eventually it was Small Junior employing Marshall Junior, or Jobsie as everyone seemed to call him. Marshall, by the sound of things had been quite a thorn in Small's side; he'd been a shop steward conscientiously putting the rights of the workers he represented ahead of his friendship with the Smalls. His account to Annie had been punctuated by rueful laughter and rolling of eyes. 'Jobsie,' he had told her, 'could be a royal pain.'

Had the resentment run deeper than Small admitted? Assuming the bare facts of Marshall's employment were accurate, Small had been more than fair with his old school-friend, keeping him on longer than any of the workmates who were automated out of their jobs as the robots took over.

'He hated the whole idea of automation,' Small had told her. 'He should have been the first to go, not the last, but you know … old family ties. He was drinking back then. Anyone else, I'd have fired him, saved the redundancy payment, but he had to go. He saw that in the end. He could have walked into another job at one of the smaller yards. I'd have given him a reference. He worked here and there, on and off, but mainly the drink took him.'

'How did his wife take it?'

'She understood. She knew he'd been lucky to be kept on as long as he was.'

'But I thought she …'

'Ach, she blew hot and cold. Loyalty, you know. She wasn't going to bad-mouth him but he was a demon when he'd been at the whisky.'

Since it hadn't been Havenmere Docks where he'd died, she'd tried him for details of where it had happened.

'Some yard near Hull is all I heard. What did she say that made you think he'd died here?'

It was at that point he'd slapped his hand to his mouth. She remembered a dawning horror in his eyes and a creeping fear in her own gut. Without knowing why, she hadn't wanted to see him looking scared.

'For God's sake it wasn't one of our crates, was it?' He'd spun round to stare at his console as though it had an answer. 'No, it can't have been. They'd have been round asking questions. Do you have the ID?' He'd reached again for the console. 'The ID of the crate?'

She'd had to tell him no, she knew nothing but the few bits they'd had from Marshall's wife.

There was a movement amongst the crowd jostling outside the chapel doors. People were drawing back. The hearse and family were winding their way through the grounds.

'I want to be sure she knows I'm here,' Annie murmured to Mike. 'Keep an eye out for reactions.'

She snaked through to the front of the crowd. Her plan was to chat with one or two of the mourners after the service, before everyone made their way to the wake.

She'd asked Rob Small, 'Do you think he had a job there, the yard where he died?'

He'd said, 'Dunno. Could have. I've not been asked for a reference for Jobsie in a good few years.'

He'd been open with her, perfectly friendly and had topped up her coffee cup several times. Then when she'd said she needed to go, adding the lie that someone was expecting her, he'd walked outside with her as though to keep the mechanical giants at bay while she left through the huge sliding gates. Despite everything, she'd found herself heaving a sigh of relief once the gates were behind her.

The hearse was open; men in long black coats were milling about behind it. A uniformed chauffeur opened the door of the first limousine. Miriam Marshall emerged, expression flat, emotionless. A tall man climbed out and offered her his arm. Annie stared.

As the couple walked past the congregated mourners to take their place behind Marshall's coffin, Miriam looked resolutely ahead, sparing no glances for anyone, but the man at her side inclined his head briefly to acknowledge one or two in the crowd.

He nodded to Annie, holding eye contact for a moment before moving on. She barely managed a wan smile in return, and followed their progress until they were swallowed up into the crowd processing inside.

'Are you OK?' said Mike's voice from behind her. She felt his hand squeeze her arm and realised a shiver had gone through her as she stared at the tableau playing out in front of them.

As they attached themselves to the back of the crowd, she murmured, 'The man with Miriam; that was Rob Small from Havenmere Docks.'

CHAPTER 9

Annie and Mike followed at an awkward stop-start pace as the crowd tried to avoid disrespectful jostling through the bottleneck of the entrance. Up ahead, Rob Small, painted by Miriam Marshall as the villain, was now chief mourner alongside her at her husband's funeral.

Annie thought about Marshall losing his job, turning to drink, giving his wife hell in the absence of anyone else to lash out at; Rob Small extending the hand of friendship for old time's sake, rebuffed by his old school-friend, but maybe Miriam had needed a confidant. Had they had an affair?

She imagined Miriam watching her husband descend into a whisky-soaked malaise; Rob Small, family friend, on hand to lend a sympathetic ear. It wasn't hard to see how things might have developed, and no wonder Miriam felt conflicted. Yesterday Rob Small hadn't known the date of his old friend's funeral; today he was back at the heart of the family.

Annie and Mike were among the last to cram themselves in and stood at the back. A song that had topped the charts a few years ago played through the speakers allowing everyone to shuffle into place. As the music faded, a man in a suit read a short account from a written sheet, giving

William Marshall's full name, date of birth, date of death, and noting that he'd died as a result of a tragic accident. William Marshall, he told everyone, would now be remembered by his friends and family.

The name William Marshall was not heard again as a stream of people, all male, stepped up behind the lectern to say their piece about 'Jobsie'.

The order was haphazard, remembrances bouncing randomly around the chronology of Marshall's life.

A rotund man read from a sheaf of papers that charted an emotional account of his friendship. 'If it weren't for Jobsie fighting my corner, I'd have been out of work with young bairns to feed.' – Marshall, the shop steward, thought Annie, pushing herself up on tiptoe to watch Rob Small. His profile showed the hint of a quiet smile, every inch the old friend appreciating the tributes.

The man loosened his collar as he read from the page in front of him. 'We've all heard Jobsie saying it, "The fat cat bosses mustn't be allowed to trample on the workers who make their money for them".' The quote, probably meant to be declaimed passionately, became a mumble as the man shot an apprehensive glance at Rob Small.

Annie leant towards Mike and whispered, 'It has to be years since he worked at Havenmere Docks, but he's still wary about Small.'

Mike whispered back, 'If he's in the same field, his current boss could be a friend of Small's.'

As the rotund man scuttled thankfully away from the limelight, he was replaced by someone much older who launched at once into an account of Jobsie's prowess at the darts board. Whisky wasn't mentioned but the story felt steeped in it. Annie looked at Miriam. Her face remained blank, expressionless.

Then it was back to old work colleagues and more talk of Jobsie's dedication to his role as shop steward, these later speakers unaffected by Rob Small's presence. Annie watched him and thought that his quiet smile became markedly fixed at points.

Miriam's face remained unchanged until a trio of young children were led to the front, then she allowed herself an encouraging smile at them. They recited a long poem they'd written in memory of their 'Uncle Jobsie', sacrificing scansion and meaning in the absolute pursuit of rhyming couplets throughout. A ripple of applause was led by Miriam whose face reverted to a blank as they returned to their seats. It would have been a good place to end the tributes but there were more to come.

Annie took note of ex-work-colleagues versus more recent darts compatriots. One who particularly interested her was a bull-headed man with a pugnacious stare who opened, 'I'm Richard Redman. It was my son as found poor Jobsie. Now he didn't never know him, more's the pity. And it's many a year since I saw hide nor hair of Jobsie but he were a good mate to all who knew him. Came to work for me after he'd been kicked out of Havenmere where he'd worked his fingers to the bone. Broke his heart that did … No offence …' The man tipped his head towards Rob Small before going on.

It wasn't the first mention of Marshall's sorrow at losing his position at the dockyard, though it was the least disguised attack on Rob Small.

Annie had heard enough. The secret Miriam Marshall

had been harbouring was her relationship with Rob Small. Maybe back in the agency's office she'd vowed to forget about him, even going as far as to drip poison in Annie and Mike's ears, with some notion of revenge for a long-ago slight. But Rob Small was now at her side offering support.

It left the mystery unsolved of how and where Marshall had climbed into that shipping container. As to why, the simple answer was that he'd wanted somewhere to sleep off the whisky, and these giant boxes were places he knew. The investigator within her wanted to unravel every thread, but she wasn't going to work on it unpaid just because the agency was financially stable. Mike was right. He'd been right all along. She and the Thompsons had grabbed at a financial lifeline that had left them under the yoke of dodgy twosome, Dyson and fforbes who now owned them body and soul. They needed to get out before they became pawns in someone else's bigger game.

The service was ending. It was too late to make a discreet exit the way they'd come in. Those doors were barred and everyone was bottlenecking out of a side door. She watched Mike go ahead, using the cover of a knot of people, to bypass Miriam and Small, while she waited in line to murmur condolences; since she'd shown her face, it would have been churlish not to. As she shuffled closer she saw Rob Small step away from Miriam's side and lean in to talk to Richard Redman.

Maybe she wouldn't have to talk to him at all, or maybe she would end up talking to them both.

CHAPTER 10

Jennifer Flanagan cradled her vending machine tea as she took a breather in a quiet corner. She'd dodged out of Tommy Marchant's way, wanting to avoid the cosy chats that were becoming too regular.

She'd been talking to Caitlin about him last night while they prepped vegetables and readied the flat for an evening with Caitlin's friends from work. 'Just how I remember him from years ago,' she'd said. 'Always on hand if someone boiled a kettle, but invisible when there was work to be done.'

'All workplaces have a Marchant,' had been the response, though Jennifer knew it wasn't true of the small team Caitlin led. 'Look how he's been pumping you for information about that case in the container yard.'

'Not a case any more. Misadventure. No evidence of foul play. Even our covert team from York seem to have lost interest. It was Havenmere Docks that made Davis and Ahmed jump, not William Marshall, who – his wife told me – kept his ID after he was kicked out.'

She hadn't confided any of it to Tommy but confessed to Caitlin she wouldn't be surprised if he got to know anyway.

Caitlin had said, 'People don't always keep things behind closed doors. Look at the things you've picked up.'

The words were suddenly prescient as footsteps approached and she heard a voice say, '… one of those things, you know … consorting with people they shouldn't …'

It was Ayaan Ahmed's voice. The bend in the corridor hid him from sight. She held still.

'Not much option at times,' Davis's voice replied.

The words, 'consorting with people they shouldn't,' chimed uncomfortably. Could they be talking about her? She'd been off on Monday and had called in on William Marshall's funeral. After all, she'd been first on the scene at Redman's Yard. It hardly counted as consorting. No one else from the investigation had bothered, not that there was an investigation any more. She'd kept a low profile, far lower than intended once a certain face had popped up.

Now Ahmed was spelling out something that she couldn't follow. Figures and percentages were mentioned. She imagined him flicking through documents on a tablet or phone. From what little she could glean this fitted the drugs theory of their presence here, but said nothing about whether their guns were trained inwards or at an external target.

She cringed inwardly. They'd come close to the corner and then stopped, presumably to look at these figures. It put them uncomfortably close to her without knowing she was there. She didn't want to try to retreat silently because they might catch her, but it was too late just to march round the corner as though she hadn't known anyone was there.

The funeral had provided an unwelcome blast from her past. Jennifer silently counted back the years as Ahmed said something about York and Davis responded. They were heading out, not together, that must be why they'd stopped to chat in this supposedly quiet corner.

Go to your office and shut the bloody door, she wanted to shout to Davis. Forget so-called discreet chats in corridors to save time, you've no idea who's listening.

It was thirteen years since she'd been a probationer in this city. That was when she'd first encountered a private investigator with whom she'd later fallen into a casual friendship. The woman had left Hull five years later and they hadn't kept in touch. Back then, they'd both been rookies in their own professions and found themselves entangled in the trauma of a missing child case. It wasn't a memory she took out and aired very often, its overtones still hung unresolved. She thought of it as the case that had almost ended her own career before it began. Maybe she was kidding herself. Wasn't the truth that it had done just that? Where had all her drive gone, all her determination to make Inspector before she was thirty? Where was it, if not dead in the ashes of that case? These were questions she'd routinely dodged during those early years. They rarely surfaced these days, but out of nowhere the past had come back to slap her in the face.

'It's bitty,' Ahmed was saying in response to a question from Davis, 'but we have the paperwork, such as it is. Marshall's not involved, nor was that container.'

'We pretty much have to eliminate Havenmere Docks, too, now.'

Jennifer Flanagan felt her eyes widen. If she'd been out in plain sight, she'd have said, 'Are you sure that's wise?' despite her fragmentary knowledge.

Private Investigator Annie Raymond had been at

William Marshall's funeral, looking much as Jennifer remembered her from all those years ago. She'd watched her nod recognition to Miriam Marshall; seen more, too, after the service as she stood in the shadows by the door. Things she ought to tell Davis or Ahmed but, as more than one of her colleagues had said, they only ever turned up when you didn't want to see them. Ahmed had already made clear he wasn't keen on an email trail.

As soon as Jennifer had seen Annie Raymond walking down towards the mourners, eyes darting everywhere, she'd ducked behind the cover of the crowd. No question that Annie was still in the same profession, as her later brief enquiries had confirmed, but how did she fit in with the Marshalls and Havenmere Docks?

With a murmured, 'Prioritise getting someone on to that,' Davis cut the discussion and two pairs of footsteps receded. She let out a long sigh of relief that neither of them had come her way.

She drained her cup and turned to head back, only to run into Tommy Marchant coming the other way.

'Wossup, Jen? You OK?' He looked down at her leg. 'What d'you do that on?'

'What?' She followed the line of his gaze and saw a brand new rip in her trouser leg, just below the knee. 'Shit, when did that happen? I'll have to sew it. Who'll have a needle and thread round here?'

'Shiny Boots'll have the full kit for sure,' he said, and laughed. 'But he's just gone off out again. Davis is around too. Have you seen them?'

'No.' She shook her head. It was the exact truth. She'd seen neither of them.

On balance she was glad Davis was here and Ahmed was gone. Davis might try to dismiss her unheard, but Ahmed was more likely to subject her to an uncomfortable interrogation. She mustn't let on that she knew Havenmere Docks had been discounted from their investigation; but then she'd never officially been told it was in the mix in the first place.

Leaving Tommy, she hurried off, rehearsing what she would say to Davis. Did she start on Miriam Marshall employing a private investigator or that Marshall was linked to Havenmere Docks by more than an old entry on his CV, and that the man who completed the circuit was the father of the guy who'd found his body?

A diversion to effect a running repair with sellotape took only a few minutes and she was at the half open door of the upstairs office, knocking on the panel before realising who was inside.

'Hi Jennifer,' said Ayaan Ahmed, slipping a sheaf of papers inside a folder. 'What can I do for you?'

Sodding slapdash Tommy, she thought. His network might be impressively wide but she'd forgotten how unreliable he was on fine detail. It hadn't been Ahmed on his way out, it had been Davis.

Too late to back off now.

'Did you know that Miriam Marshall had employed a gumshoe?' she blurted out, and immediately felt foolish. It was neither what she'd intended to say nor how she'd intended to say it.

He stared at her. 'Who? Why? How d'you know?'

He looked as wrong-footed as she felt. It calmed her, and she answered him coolly. 'I don't know why, but I know who. I recognised her. It's a woman called Annie Raymond.'

A fleeting blink of surprise. So he knew who Annie was. She wondered how. He was from York; Annie was well settled in London, last she'd heard, except she'd plainly moved on … or moved back.

There'd been a time she would have felt compelled to fill the silence, to frame some kind of apology or justification for an imagined misdemeanour. Not now. Think what you like of me, she said silently, I've gone past that. For all your stripes, you'll be another decade before you know as much about the job as I do.

'Recognised her where?' he finally managed to get out.

'On Monday at William Marshall's funeral.' And before he could react or not to that, she hurried on, 'Robert Small was there, MD from Havenmere Docks, sharing a limo with the grieving widow. After the service he approached Annie Raymond, clearly knew her, and introduced her to Richard Redman. He's—'

'I know who Richard Redman is,' Ahmed interrupted, finding his voice.

For a moment, he held her gaze; she couldn't read his expression. Then he said, 'And I know a good deal more about you than I did last time we spoke. We looked up your record.'

Her heart plummeted. She had to look away before she gave in to the urge to throw herself at his feet and plead, *Please … that's all in the past … let me leave it behind … I'm getting my life on track now …*

'Can I just—?'

'No.'

CHAPTER 11

The walls of the cramped space pressed in on Annie, but she wasn't about to give up and move her desk back to the larger room. She'd insisted on clearing out this former storeroom/dumping ground to make a private office for herself. New boss, new start. It had never been satisfactory, because it was the only private space they had. She was forced to vacate it anytime anyone else needed quiet time with a client.

If the owners would just let them re-locate, she would be right on top of her game again – new premises, genuine new start, and never mind whether or not the Thompsons came too. Her fingers itched to pick up the phone, to try to get across the malaise that was smothering the agency, but she knew she couldn't. Direct contact was for emergencies only – a line she crossed at her peril.

She was waiting for Lois, who had come to them just a few weeks ago having heard they were looking to employ a junior. Someone to help with the admin had been the plan, but Lois, though nice enough, had proved slapdash, unable to do anything without errors or omission. Giving Lois a task more complex than brewing coffee simply meant having to do it twice. She'd morphed into Barbara's personal assistant, but they couldn't keep paying her to pick up Barbara's shopping, and had agreed to let her go at the end of the probationary period Mike had insisted on.

Annie had never fired anyone before. Back in London, Pieternel had done all that – callously, brutally, no hint of empathy. Mike insisted that wasn't the way, and had taken her through the process, step by step, but she was dreading it. They should never have taken Lois on; it felt part of the lethargy that was overtaking them all.

Footsteps from outside and a knock at the door.

'Come in, Lois, have a seat … You're coming to the end of your probationary period. We won't be keeping you on.'

And there, it was said. Simple statement of fact. None of the softening phrases she'd practised … *I'm sorry to have to tell you … I'm afraid that … you did well in some respects but …*

Make it sound like you're doing it reluctantly, Mike had told her. 'Hurts you more than it hurts her kind of thing. It's bullshit but people react better. She'll feel you're on her side and she won't kick off … well, not to your face. But see her early before there are any clients in. If she's going to kick off, you don't want an audience.'

What did Mike know? Her way was more honest. Lois, as he'd predicted, was now sounding off. Annie watched dispassionately as the young woman fired a volley of low-voiced epithets, impugning her ability, integrity and paternity. Annie was thankful for the low voice, but otherwise felt no more than the detached interest of an outside observer. Sitting behind this desk had fundamentally changed her.

A single barb made it through her shell.

Lois, fighting back tears she was clearly determined not

to shed in Annie's presence, jumped to her feet. 'They're right,' she screeched. 'You're a heartless cow. You think you know everything, but you don't. Mrs Marshall's husband found something out before he died. She was g … uh … she showed me. It wouldn't surprise me if you're in this cover up as much as they were.'

With that she spun round and stormed out. Annie's office door crashed into its frame, the main door banged. Footsteps clattered down the stairs and even from the back office, with two recently and determinedly closed doors in between, Annie heard the street door rebound on its hinges as their former employee left the building.

She replayed Lois's outburst. If Lois had had solid evidence, she'd have produced it. That tripping on words had been heading for, 'She *was going to* show me.' Whatever Miriam had said to her, it had not developed into anything.

Lois was now a footnote in the agency's history. It was time to make some real decisions about the future.

* * *

'Jen Flanagan's not gone out, has she?' Tommy Marchant asked at the desk and received a negative shake of the head. Puzzled he went back inside. A recent initiative had provided resources to target embryo drugs rings, schools stuff, nip them in the bud. He'd been assigned parents to call on, to have difficult discussions with. He wasn't convinced. Pissing into the wind, he was sure, but orders must be followed. He wanted to take Jen with him. She was good at that sort of thing.

He went to the central atrium, glancing upwards at the

closed door of the office Davis and co had commandeered. She'd joked about going up there to borrow a needle and thread, but even if she'd been serious, it couldn't have taken this long. He'd have to take someone else, but Jen was the sort who made people want to show their best side. If she was with him he wouldn't have the hassle of people going off on one.

A voice from behind rapped out, 'You still here, Tommy? Who's going with you?'

'Everyone's tied up, Sarge.'

'I'll come with you, Tommy. I could do with a breath of fresh air.'

'Right you are, Sarge.' Not Jen but a fair substitute, someone to carry the can if anything went pear-shaped. They would have to talk football and he'd sooner talk fishing but he'd have had no audience for either with Jen.

It was as they turned to head off that a movement caught his eye from the floor above. A door opened, Jen emerged followed by Shiny Boots. He couldn't see her expression from here but something in her body language made him stop. She waited while Shiny Boots locked the door behind them, then they strode off down the corridor together, Jen slightly in front, her head inclined away from her companion. He didn't like the look of it.

'Come on, Tommy! You dropped off to sleep there?'

'Sorry, Sarge. On my way.'

Jennifer was was lost to sight though he heard the whine of the lift as they went past.

Their trip across town was uneventful. In what was more a monologue than a conversation, the local football team's current owners were forensically shredded. As they reached the doorstep of the target residence, Tommy beat a brisk tattoo on the door, then murmured, 'Of course, they've put in a lot of money. You have to give them that.'

Then the door opened and it was down to business.

On the way back, the monologue changed shape, vitriol turned on to the team's manager. 'That performance was down to bad management decisions, Tommy, however you look at it, and you can say what you like about those holding the purse strings, but they've done a lot for the team … for the area … put in a lot of money.'

Tommy nodded sagely as he pulled on to the main road towards the station. He privately bet himself he could generate another about-face before they were indoors again, and began to craft a comment about money and undue influence.

His thoughts were snatched away as a car whipped by in the opposite direction. His stare bounced from rear view to side mirror but he couldn't see it clearly before it was swallowed by the traffic.

It took frustrating minutes to park and get inside but as soon as he could, he hurried round to the desk.

'Did I just see Jen Flanagan on her way out?'

'PC Flanagan's gone off sick.' The words were accompanied by an unsmiling stare. 'Why? If you need her for something you'll have to see–?'

'No, no. I was just following up on something we were talking about. It's not important. She seemed fine when I spoke to her earlier.'

He recalled the body language. Her marching along with Shiny Boots on that top corridor. No, not marching along … *being* marched along. He didn't like it one little bit.

* * *

Jennifer was surprised to see Caitlin's car parked outside their flat as she arrived home. Caitlin shouldn't be back for hours yet. Sudden worry blossomed inside her. Had something happened? Not today! Not today of all days.

Taking the stairs in twos, she fumbled the key into the lock and rushed inside.

At once there was a crash from the living room as the door burst open and Caitlin flew to meet her. 'Jen! Oh my God, Jen! What happened? Where were you?'

Jennifer clasped Caitlin in her arms, felt her shaking as she buried her head in the familiar soft hair. 'What's happened?' She returned the question, her mind spinning. 'Why are you home so early?'

Caitlin pulled back to glare into her face. 'Why are *you* so late!'

'I'm not,' she said bewildered. 'I'm bang on time for once. I'm on earlies. What are *you* doing here?'

'Jen, you left work over an hour ago!'

'Oh, how … uh … how did you know?'

'I know what happened, Jen. I know everything.'

CHAPTER 12

A gust of wind pushes in from the estuary, slamming the long side of a giant metal container. It can't dislodge it from the steel arms that hold it, making no difference to the predetermined move from point A to point B – at any rate, no difference discernible to the naked eye. It's the software that interrogates the sensors and reports a delay. The gusting wind will add a tiny fraction of a second to the overall operation.

Up in the control room, Rob Small turns from the screen to watch out of the window as he murmurs, 'Why didn't you lower it?'

There's no one to respond but his fingers tap the keyboard as he tells it to simulate the move closer to the ground.

'There's no safety issue; there's no one down there.' He rehearses justification to the HSE inspector who is not here to watch these manoeuvres, but who would object for sure if he were.

'Well, thank you, boys,' says Rob Small to the console. 'That's interesting.' There have been more tiny fractions of seconds added … considerably more. Turns out that far from being sheltered at the lower elevation, the stacked crates have made a wind tunnel. It's a complex calculation.

There's the energy it takes to lift and then lower the thing versus the energy it takes to move it against the wind. Taken all together, the system chose the most efficient route.

He smiles. These fractions of seconds add up over the months.

The surveillance camera from the road shows the route from which the private investigator arrived a week ago. He remembers her wide-eyed admiration for the whole set up, likes it that she appreciated what he's done here.

A car pulls up. His expression hardens. It's an expected visitor, but he makes no move to welcome him.

Richard Redman knows his way.

A few minutes later, a large bull-headed man pushes through the door to the control room, breathless from climbing the stairs.

Rob Small, his pose overly nonchalant, turns his head as though mildly surprised.

'Rich.'

'Rob.'

No smiles, no handshake. The newcomer is not invited to sit but lowers himself into a chair anyway.

'What was all that at the funeral?' Rob Small's voice holds a seam of resentment. 'I've never done Jobsie no harm, stuck my neck out for him a time or two with my old man. You know that better than anyone.'

'He took it hard being sacked.'

'He wasn't sacked. He was redundant. He got his payout. I didn't have to go that far. I could have sacked him a dozen times in that last year. You saw yourself how he was losing the plot.'

'Painful episode all round.' The visitor's tone has undergone a subtle change, swerving away from the potential confrontation. 'We all need to move on, not spin it out. Miriam deserves better. She's had a right old time with Jobsie these last few years. She deserves some happiness.'

'With you, d'you mean?'

Rob Small's tone is cutting. Richard Redman works hard to take it as light banter and manages a cracked laugh. 'Better me than you, eh?'

'She's safe from me. I'm closing my account with Jobsie. I'll make sure she's sound now he's gone. Loose cannon from start to finish. What a finish. Poor old Jobs. Dead in a crate. No surprise I suppose, he'd been heading that way a long time, but a crate of all things. You want to make a go of it with Miriam, I'll not stand in your way. Just do right by her, that's all.'

Richard Redman pushes himself up out of the chair and walks across to the big window. The condescension chafes, the assumption that it is in Small's gift to ease his path to Miriam. 'Not much going on,' he says as he looks out. 'Business bad?' It's as close as he dares go to a put down.

Their eyes meet.

'What d'you want, Rich?'

'That crate Jobsie died in, where did it come from?'

Small shrugs. 'How should I know? Look, they came asking about it. Jobsie had his Havenmere tag on him. I checked it out. The nearest it's ever been is your lad's yard with Jobsie's body in it.'

'It came from Bristol.' Redman's stare is accusatory.

'If you know the answer, what're you asking me for?'

'I want to know how it landed up in my lad's yard. Jobsie of all people. I want to know if Havenmere had a role in it.' As he speaks, Richard Redman glances pointedly at the small screen beside his chair.

This is perilously close to an accusation. Eyes are narrowed, hard stares exchanged. Outside, a sheet of rain rushes over, sweeping across the windows; the wind whistles between the containers. There's a low hum as though from a giant concertina. Metal clanks on metal as clamps fight the weather to swing giant boxes across the yard.

Rob Small pushes against the console, sending his wheeled chair skating smoothly towards where Richard Redman is sitting. It stops uncomfortably close. One more hard stare and Rob Small's fingers play across the keyboard. 'You got the number?' he says.

Redman nods, pulling a scrap of paper from his pocket.

'Then look for yourself.'

Redman turns to the screen and reaches out to work the mouse, then types in the ID code.

No match.

He is mildly surprised that Small has given him access so readily, but these are the local records, the ones that Small could have doctored. What he wants is access to the external data, the data that Small can't manipulate, but this requires access neither he nor his son has. A set-up like Havenmere Docks has the capability, and he's way more competent with these online systems than Small will give him credit for. Now that Small has opened up the gateway, all he needs is a few moments on his own.

He sighs, sits back, raises his hand as though in

surrender and gives Small a not-unfriendly smile. 'I had to be sure, Rob. You understand that, don't you? I can tell Miriam I'm sure now. No hard feelings?'

Rob Small gives him a speculative look. 'Is that what Miriam wanted to know, is that why she talked to me? I thought it was a bit soon for all to be forgiven.'

Redman glances at him as though embarrassed.

'OK,' Small pushes his chair back. 'How's about a drink?'

He's reaching for the coffee machine, when Redman laughs. 'For old time's sake, Rob, I hope you're gonna offer me something stronger than coffee.'

Rob Small pauses and then chuckles. 'Why not? But I don't keep liquor in the office. Those days have gone. I've some beers in the back of the car.' With that he gets to his feet and heads for the door.

Richard Redman dives at the console, grunting in frustration as he navigates the unfamiliar interface. But he knows what he's looking for. He finds it then curses as a login screen pops up in front of him. A quick glance at the monitor shows an empty car park. Small is still on his way down.

He clicks into the space labelled *username*.

A set of options appear. He picks the top one, *HavenmereDocksRSmall,* then clicks the mouse into the password box. Smooth as anything another list appears and all he needs do is click on the one that says: *Use password for HavenmereDocksRSmall*, and he's in the system just as Rob Small appears on the monitor and edges towards his car, keeping to the shelter of the wall, avoiding the rain.

Glancing at the paper, he types in the ID number, and with impressive speed, the container's history is laid out in front of him. He stares at the twenty-year trail. It gives him far more than the bare bones the police gave Red Boy.

Notes and codes. He knows how to interpret it. The story is transparent to him:

… presumed lost at sea … but obviously not.

… unexpectedly unloaded … and then lost for a very long time …

… rediscovered …

It doesn't tell why it was lost for so long, but it tells him where, and he chuckles because he's been in the business a long time and his network stretches a long way. He knows someone who'll be able to fill in the gaps. He pulls himself up and shoots a glance at the monitor. Small is reaching to close the boot of his car. Looks like a bottle of whisky in his hand, not beers.

… 21st September it leaves Bristol for Middlesbrough by road …

… non-scheduled unloading in Birmingham … technical problem with the lorry … no record of a pick up …

… then it's in Red Boy's yard. 1st November is when he spots it. How long was it there? There's no docket, no nothing, it's a crate without an arrival date, without a record of which lorry it came on, without anything …

He feels the heat of anger. That crane driver should have had the paperwork straight before he stacked it, must have let it in blind. It could have been anything. And even if he could forgive that lapse, alarm bells should have been clanging when he got dockets telling him to stack two more on top of it. They never stacked three high.

Small has gone from the monitor, must be on his way back up the stairs.

Richard Redman's gaze rakes the data one last time. These aren't Havenmere Docks' records he's looking at, these are central, these are accurate. He closes down, logs out, and is sitting back watching out of the window when Small returns, bottle in hand.

Outside the rain eases as the wind tears in off the estuary. One of Havenmere's cranes lifts a box up high into the teeth of the gale. Richard Redman accepts a glass and clinks it with Rob Small's. He has to believe it now. Rob Small has been playing straight. As he sniffs the aroma of good malt he nods his head towards the scene beyond the windows. 'Those robots of yours are not as clever as you think. If you had a man in that crane, he'd have had the sense to keep that crate low, out of the wind.'

CHAPTER 13

'Monday morning,' called Annie, poking her head round the shower curtain. 'Let's make it a new start.'

The case they'd taken on for Miriam Marshall had brought home to her the stagnation they'd fallen into. It was just over a week since her visit to Havenmere Docks and four days since her untidy sacking of Lois; both incidents now felt uncomfortably amateurish. The truth was that a backer with ulterior motives had given them a financial cushion, the need to hustle for business was gone, and they'd fallen into coasting.

All but Mike.

She stepped out of the shower and reached for a towel, watching him through the open doorway to the bedroom where he shuffled through his many ties. He'd been out there pushing for new business that might pick them up and give them real independence. How could she criticise Pat or Barbara when she'd been as bad? It was time to get behind Mike, to find a way out of their dependence on Dyson and fforbes.

He'd made new contacts and one of them had bitten. Face to face meetings were being proposed.

She drove them in, but diverted to the multi-storey, glancing at him as she made the turn. He gave her the ghost of a wink, so she knew he approved. Parking here gave them a brisk walk to the office so they had to be sharp with their timekeeping, and started the day energised. In the old days, Annie had walked everywhere; she'd had to, on the wage the Thompsons paid. It was only now she realised how valuable fresh air and thinking time were.

They strode through the not-yet-busy early morning streets in companionable silence until Mike tutted and said, 'We've no milk.'

He veered off towards the minimart as she continued on her way. Opening the office while he diverted to the shop had been a practised routine.

She carried on past the all-hours café, glancing through the steamed-up glass.

With a jolt of surprise, she found herself staring at Lois who sat in a window seat cradling a mug.

Lois seemed to give her a long look before turning away. Annie pulled in a breath and hurried on. She recalled the woman's not-so-veiled threat. It couldn't have substance; she'd not had access to any files that might have given her leverage.

It was still early but the road became busier with knots of people chatting, smoking, vaping, catching up on gossip before the working day got underway. She didn't know any of them. There'd been a time she would slip downstairs to join the crew in the accountants firm for a coffee before the Thompson sisters rolled in around ten, but it was a different set up down there now, a consultancy with a reception barrier preventing casual interactions.

At the other side of the road, half a dozen women stood chatting in a cloud of vapour, one at the back half obscured, bending to check her handbag. Annie kept her eye on them. People were supposed to sense when they were being watched, but the chat went on unabated.

She turned to the door and let herself in.

Upstairs, she moved from desk to desk, turning on the machines, checking voicemail, glancing at diaries, then at the board that listed key priorities. All OK; everything covered. She walked the length of the upstairs landing to the tiny kitchen to fill the kettle.

The downstairs door clicked open, and Mike's step sounded on the stairs. Annie moved closer to the window that overlooked the street, suddenly convinced that Lois was on her way to ambush them. The group over the road was breaking up; the handbag rummager broke free and headed across the road. No sign of Lois.

When Mike joined her, she was pouring hot water on to a heap of coffee in the cafetière.

She wanted to say: I should have taken your advice and been gentler with Lois, but greeted him with, 'All set?'

'There's good regular contract work here if we play our cards right.' She heard a tinge of pride in his voice as he spoke about the new clients he was reeling in. He was affirming himself in the business.

She was pleased she hadn't blurted out anything about Lois who might have a hundred reasons for being in that café at this hour, including that she had a friend in the area. It was how she'd heard about their job in the first place.

They took their drinks through into the office and sat in Pat and Barbara's chairs. Neither of the Thompsons would show their faces for a couple of hours.

The downstairs door clicked again as they settled down.

'They're starting earlier downstairs. Have you noticed?' Mike said.

Annie wasn't listening. Lois's hundred reasons had shrunk to one. Footsteps ran lightly up the stairs.

'Mike, I should have told–'

But there wasn't time. The door swung open and a tall woman stood framed in the doorway.

'Annie,' she said with a smile. 'You've not changed a bit. I really–' She stopped abruptly as she stepped inside and saw Mike. Her smile gave way to a flash of surprise and irritation. 'Uh … sorry, I … ah, I should have realised … Early morning used to be the time to catch you on your own.'

Annie had been so certain it would be Lois coming through that door, she couldn't get her brain back on track, and was painfully aware she was staring with her mouth half open as an inner voice clamoured, *I know that voice … I know that face … the clothes are wrong.*

Mike went as though to rise, his expression begging her for a lead.

The movement was enough to kick-start her. 'Oh my God!' She felt a grin break across her face. 'Jennifer. You've not changed either. It must be … six … seven years?'

'Eight,' supplied Jennifer Flanagan, returning her smile.

'Sorry … Come in, sit down.' Annie leapt to her feet. 'Mike, this is Jennifer. I met her when I first came to work for Pat. PC Jennifer Flanagan … well …' She laughed. 'Probably Chief Inspector these days. Jennifer, this is Mike Connaughty. He and I run the agency together now.'

'Not so exalted,' Jennifer said, taking Mike's hand. 'Still just a humble PC.'

As Mike reorganised furniture to pull forward a comfortable chair, Annie looked afresh at her old friend. She had changed in one respect. Her taste in clothes had improved immeasurably. She was the handbag rummager, the one hiding at the back of that gossiping group.

Early morning used to be the time to catch you on your own.

Jennifer must have seen Mike enter the building and assumed him to be the first of the downstairs office arriving.

'I'll get Jennifer a coffee,' Annie said to Mike, 'then take her into my office so we don't disturb you.'

As she carried the drinks through to her inadequate inner sanctum, and pulled out a chair for Jennifer, she said, 'So how are you doing? You … look well.' She hoped her slight hesitation wasn't evident. Jennifer did look well, but something wasn't right. Why the slightly furtive approach, she wanted to ask, but instead said, 'Still a PC? How come? You had such ambitions.'

'Oh … life takes some funny turns. I was happy in the job as it was. You of all people know how it can swallow you up. Your father …'

Annie nodded. She'd seen her father's whole universe become defined by *the job*. 'My father had his reasons,' she said. 'What were yours?'

'Family. I met someone. Family life was more important. How about you? Last I heard you were a high-flyer in London.'

Annie pulled a face. 'This opportunity came up. Mike and I got back together. That's the short version. What about you?'

Jennifer told how she'd met Caitlin, how their plans had blossomed, their recent move back to Hull; how surprised she'd been to find not only that the Thompsons were still in business, but that Annie was now in charge.

'Tell me about your big plans.'

'We're going to start a family.'

The announcement was made with some pride, and Annie had to give herself a mental kick to react appropriately. She smiled and nodded as Jennifer talked but her focus was on the indistinct rumble that was Mike's voice on the phone in the main office. He would be making calls she should be making, keeping things shipshape while she drank coffee with an old friend, just as though she had all the time in the world. This wasn't the new start she'd envisaged, but she wasn't going to cut things short, not until she knew why Jennifer had been so keen to see her on her own.

She was relieved when she heard him moving about, clearly preparing to leave for his meeting.

'So you're going to take maternity leave,' she said, 'but Caitlin will give up her job?'

'It makes sense. I can get the well-paid maternity leave, but Caitlin's better placed to take a career break.' Jennifer gave a rueful laugh as she picked up her coffee and stared into it for a moment before taking a sip. 'But you know, best laid plans …'

A theory began to shape itself in Annie's head. Somewhere in the mix was a biological father, maybe someone they knew, maybe not. They needed enquiries making and it was outside the scope of what PC Jennifer Flanagan could do in her official role.

Annie's instinct was to refuse. They had to stay the right side of the owners, and they wouldn't do that by taking on a case like this. On the other hand, the owners need never know. Good relations with the local police were always a plus, and if it put a local officer in the position of feeling under an obligation to them, that was an added bonus.

However, Jennifer had come to her as an old friend, and Annie wouldn't betray her trust if she didn't have to.

'We've worked it through,' Jennifer was saying. 'As long as I stay at work, Caitlin can step out for five years. I might not be a high-flyer on paper, but I've a lot of experience. And I've built up a contacts book to die for. I'm good at what I do.'

She looked Annie in the eye.

Annie struggled to work out what Jennifer was getting at. 'What do you want?' she blurted out, then made an effort to soften her tone. 'I mean … what is it, exactly, that you want from me?'

'A job, Annie. I want you to give me a job.'

CHAPTER 14

It was mid-afternoon before Mike came back. He was in their midst before Annie had any chance to tell him to keep quiet about their early morning visitor.

He beamed at them all as Pat said, 'Well, how was the big meeting?' and Barbara, 'So were they worth the thick end of a day?'

His grin signalled that they'd been very much worth it. He was bursting to tell all and had forgotten about Jennifer.

Annie had spent the day mulling over Jennifer's unexpected request. She'd asked a lot of questions. Jennifer too was at the edge of a new start, with a past that could scupper her plans, but it wasn't straightforward, and she'd given no definitive answer.

'I'll have to think it over, talk it through with Mike.'

Pat's voice bombarding Mike with questions dragged her back to the present. 'Who have they been using up to now? Do we know them? Can we get an inside track? Have they had issues?'

These were the right things to ask. They would have been her questions if she'd been listening.

'No issues,' he said, 'but they could use someone who can be a bit more proactive in their target spaces.'

'Target spaces!' The contemptuous curl of Barbara's lip

signalled no truck with management-speak. Then she added, 'They've been paying up on time, have they? We don't need bad payers on the books. Costs an arm and a leg to chase them.'

'I did the due diligence before I approached them in the first place.' There was an edge to Mike's voice. Barbara had been the one to sign up Miriam Marshall.

'Due diligence, pah!' Barbara rumbled.

Mike slipped out of his jacket and sat on the edge of Pat's desk. 'Anyway,' he said. 'With the areas they're expanding into, they're going to need …'

As his account unfolded, a new angle on Jennifer's proposal occurred to Annie. Mike might have this big new client on the hook, but they weren't landed yet. An impressive debut that outdid the competition in slick efficiency would do it, and who better to help than someone with the sort of contacts they could only dream of?

As Mike leant in to show Barbara a document on his phone, Pat pushed her chair back to come close to Annie, murmuring, 'No questions from you?'

'No need. You're doing it all.' It was true. For once both sisters were stepping up to the mark.

Pat shot her a glance. 'The boy's done good. Give him credit.' And she turned back to Mike.

Annie was taken aback. Surely Mike didn't think she resented his success. She caught his eye and flashed him an encouraging smile.

Thankfully, the clock now ticked towards Pat and Barbara's cut off point. No longer being in charge, they took a prompt end point as one of their perks. 'How do they justify their flexible mornings?' Mike had asked soon after he'd arrived. 'We don't talk about it,' she'd told him, 'and if we've a big job on, they'll do the hours.'

Barbara stood up and headed for the coat-rack, tapping Mike's arm as she brushed past. 'Good work.'

He gave Barbara a nod. It held more warmth than the brief glance he shot Annie. As soon as the Thompsons were on their way, she would explain.

'Anyone up for a beer?' he said, as the sisters made for the door.

Barbara's keenness to get home to family evaporated. Annie slumped. Too late to signal that she needed a private word. Pat and Barbara were bustling back in.

The four of them walked together, Barbara quizzing Mike, until they reached the pub where they did a verbal dance around who would buy what for whom, that ended with Mike carrying his own and the sisters' drinks while Annie reached for her beer, on edge to divert anything that could lead to Jennifer.

With her attention on the trio settling themselves at a corner table, she was unprepared for a drunken voice to erupt in her ear.

'You smug cow!'

She backed off instinctively from a face pushed uncomfortably close to hers. Lois.

'You evil bitch! You've really lost the plot!'

Lois screamed imprecations. The pub quietened as everyone turned to watch.

Annie braced herself, in case Lois tried to take a swing at her. She was too drunk and staggered, half catching her balance on the back of a chair that clattered to the floor. The pub's lone barmaid jumped out from behind the bar.

86

Annie had Lois's arm up her back and was hustling her to the door. The words, 'Marshall … papers … shipping …' rang through a chaotic jumble of slurred threats.

Between them, she and the barmaid got Lois outside where the fresh air brought her partly to her senses. 'I'll show you!' She tacked an unsteady path away from them, stopping to look back from the middle of the road. 'You're so wrong,' she shouted. 'I'll show you! I'm really gonna show you.'

'Don't bring trouble in here,' the barmaid told Annie brusquely as they returned to a sea of faces watching expectantly, but losing interest now the drama was over.

Shaken, Annie headed for the corner table. Looking to Mike for a sympathetic glance, she was aghast to be met by an exasperated glare.

'I forgot to ask you,' said Barbara with a laugh. 'How did it go with young Lois?'

Annie could have slapped her. I was clearing up your mess, she wanted to say.

'I take it you ignored all the advice I gave you,' Mike snapped. 'Why do you bother asking when we both know you'll go your own way regardless?'

'No, it wasn't like that.' Annie found herself on the defensive.

Mike shot her one hard stare and turned to Pat. 'All OK with the court papers for next week?'

'Yeah, yeah. Me and Babs went through them this afternoon. All shipshape.'

Annie felt awful. She'd somehow wrecked his big moment and everyone thought she resented his success. Then he was looking at her again, clearly making the effort to move past the awkwardness.

'So, Annie, what did she want this morning, that pol–?'

She kicked his ankle, harder than she'd intended. 'No, nothing. Just a social call. Uh … Pat … let's get Miriam Marshall's file out tomorrow. Just check through Lois's notes again. Dot the I's, cross the T's. It'll be bluff but no harm in checking.'

Pat gave her a knowing smile. She'd seen the kick.

As Pat and Barbara exchanged small talk, Annie and Mike sat in uneasy silence. Eventually, the sisters drained their glasses and pulled themselves to their feet.

'Tomorrow then,' from Pat.

'Nice work today,' from Barbara to Mike, who accepted the compliment graciously.

Annie watched his gaze track their route to the door.

He picked at his teeth and spoke without looking at her. 'What the hell's going on?'

'Not here. I'll tell you when we get home. Mike, I'm sorry … I …'

'Not here.' He bounced her words back at her and they sat in silence.

She had to convince him she was fully on board. The more she thought about her own news, the better it seemed in the light of what he'd done, but he was going to need room to see it.

As they left the pub and set off towards the multi-storey, Mike said, 'Has something bad happened? Is that what's up with you?'

'No, not at all,' she said surprised. 'It's good. I just wanted to tell you first. Pat and Barb don't know yet. I've got good news too.'

'Good enough to eclipse my little coup? Were you

sparing my feelings by not shouting it from the rooftops?'

'No, nothing like that. What you've done is the best thing that's happened to this agency since ... since ... probably forever.'

'Might even give us a chance to stand on our own two feet.'

'We might be able to relocate under our own steam, without needing a big handout.'

'We'd still need permission. It's written into the agreement you and the dynamic duo signed.'

'Yes, but we've been asking them to bankroll us. If things go well, we won't have to.'

For the first time since the sisters had left them he turned to look at her. 'It'd be an interesting question to ask.'

She half nodded but said nothing. He was right. It would be a challenge to their largely invisible owners and backers. Would they be pleased to see the Thompsons' Agency going up in the world under its own steam, would they be indifferent, or would they show their hand as to exactly why they'd backed this hole-in-the-corner operation?

'This good news of yours. I assume it's to do with your police officer friend, Jennifer Flanagan.'

'It's cold and it's starting to rain. Let's at least get to the car.' Annie wrinkled her nose as they arrived at the concrete stairway. Autumn damp did nothing to enhance the background odour of stale cigarette smoke and urine.

'I'll take that as a yes.'

Annie's gaze raked the surrounding cars. These places were too easy for hidden watchers, for threats. 'It's complicated ... or rather it's more complicated than it seems at first,' she said. 'I've had all day to think it through. Can we leave it till we're home, then I'll tell you everything.'

'Yeah, OK, but make sure it *is* everything.' His tone had softened. He rarely stayed mad about anything for long.

CHAPTER 15

As they arrived at the flat, Annie felt hungry and irritable from the early beers with the Thompsons and the confrontation with Lois.

'We should have stopped for fish and chips.'

They both paused and looked back. The drumming of rain on the porch roof redoubled in ferocity.

'We've got pasta,' Mike said. 'There'll be something in the fridge to go with it.'

She began the story while he poked about in the vegetable rack for onions and she put water on to boil and opened their last tin of tomatoes.

'Jennifer's leaving,' she told him. 'She's going to resign before Christmas. She and her partner are starting a family.' She told him what little she knew about Caitlin and their plans. 'She was going to wait and take maternity leave, then go back to the job, but she's had enough of the hours, the risks, new crime initiatives every five minutes, everything on a shoestring. But she doesn't want to leave it behind her entirely. She has a lot of experience.'

'But no ambition?' he asked, taking a knife to a fat onion. 'If she's that good why hasn't she climbed the ladder?'

'As far as I can gather, she met Caitlin and decided that family life was more important. She said it's frustrating at times, taking orders from people who haven't half her experience, but she's enjoyed the job until recently.'

'Why? What's happened recently?'

'Uh … I'll get to that. We've some spring onions. Can we bulk it out with those?'

'Yeah, why not? So what did she want from you?'

'She wants a job. She wants to work for us.'

He half nodded as he ran oil round the frying pan, heating it before tipping in the onion. 'I suppose it's not an unusual career path, and she'll have the relevant skills, won't she?'

Annie nodded. 'And some useful contacts?' she murmured, making a question of it.

'And some useful con–' He stopped in the act of removing the lid from a jar of dried herbs and spun round to face her.

She smiled. He'd got there right away. Of course he had. His head was already full of his earlier meeting and its potential ramifications.

'Useful contacts,' he repeated. 'But will she be allowed to access them? To use them after she's left? Aren't there rules and such?'

The kettle rumbled to the boil and clicked itself off. Annie lifted it to pour the hot water into a pan on the stove. From the window, they had a narrow view of the estuary. Even through the rapidly steaming glass she could see raindrops bouncing on the rippling surface. 'It'll be a factor, but she can't just stop knowing people,' she said, focussing on the dried pasta she was tipping into the pan. 'And people know her … like her … they won't cut her out. She'll be the most use to us when it's all fresh.'

'Yes but ... Shit! That could have been perfect.'

'It will be perfect, Mike. Couldn't have been better timed.'

'No,' he said, giving the frying pan an irritable shake before upending the tin of tomatoes. The mixture hissed and spat. 'We need her now, not Christmas. She can't work for us, Annie, not while she's a serving police officer.'

'Well ...' She used the excuse of lifting plates from a cupboard to keep her back to him. 'Maybe there's a way.'

'How? I can't see it. It'd be great to have someone like her on board, someone with a work ethic for starters, but ...'

'Mike, don't jump to conclusions. Listen to the full story first.'

His eyes narrowed slightly, but he nodded. She wasn't telling him things in the order she'd planned, but she'd piqued his interest.

Jennifer had laid out the bare bones and left her to chew on them, so Annie did the same with Mike, giving him the rest of the story in a rush, ending with, 'She's facing a disciplinary and she's suspended, but as long as we're careful, she could come on board right away.'

Annoyingly the timer started to bleep the moment she stopped talking.

She watched Mike place the colander in the sink and dump the pasta to drain. Then he pulled in a breath and began to ladle food on to their plates.

'Lois is right, Annie,' he said, as he brought the plates to the table and sat down. 'You've lost the plot. This changes everything. We can't consider taking her on at all. Not now, not Christmas. Not until we know exactly how this pans out. And no way on earth can we try to pull a fast one and get her on board early.'

'But Mike, if–'

'If nothing, Annie! She's on a disciplinary suspension. She might not even be allowed to resign.'

'Oh, she was pretty sure–'

'Well, she would say that, wouldn't she? She's desperate for a plan B. Really desperate from the sounds of it. What exactly has she done?'

'Nothing, it's all a misunderstanding …'

He gave her his old-fashioned look. 'If that's the case, why all the talk of resigning?'

'I told you, Mike. She's been thinking along these lines for ages. This is just the catalyst. And because she's on suspension, she–'

'Stop racing ahead of yourself. One question: did she tell you exactly what it is she's done … supposed to have done?'

She met his eye, thought about staring him out, but then sighed and scooped up a forkful of pasta. 'No, she didn't, but like she said, it's–'

'Spare me whatever excuse you fell for. She's an old friend. It's clouded your judgement.'

The comment rankled. 'I'd like to know what makes you the expert,' she muttered.

'Distance, partly, but I know how these things work. If it was trivial, she'd have told you everything. It's clearly not. She's shit scared of being kicked out with nothing. She's trying to secure something while she can. Why would she offer to work for you now on the QT? Why not just test the waters and offer to start once she's off the force?'

'Well, I suppose …'

94

'I'll tell you why. She knows how valuable she could be to us, and she wants to get on the books right now, get some money banked. She's not confident she'll be in a position to work for us after the dust settles. I'll bet you she's facing potential criminal charges. She thinks she might be going down for a stretch.' He took a mouthful of pasta and sauce, watching her as he chewed. When she said nothing, he asked, 'Can you honestly say you think I'm wrong?'

She smiled at him as she shook her head. Of course he wasn't wrong.

He shot her an exasperated glance. 'So if you'd figured all that, why didn't you quiz her more?'

'No point when it was clear she wouldn't tell me. But if we don't know, then what's wrong with her helping us out?'

'It wouldn't be legal for starters. Suspension or not, she's a serving officer.'

'We don't know that. Is it illegal for us?'

He went to speak, then stopped, looking uncertain.

She pressed her advantage. 'Just think what someone with her network could do for us, Mike, even if it was only for a few weeks.'

'It's … it's not right.'

'C'mon, Mike, on whose scale? Who would we be hurting?'

'Ourselves if we're found out!'

She thought back over some of the milestones in her own chequered career. Mike knew about most of them. She thought back to her earliest real case, the one where she'd first met Jennifer. 'She knows right from wrong, Mike. She knows what risks she's taking.'

'I don't care what she's risking. It's us I'm bothered about.'

'Exactly! Our risk is negligible. And just think what we have to gain.' It was time to stop talking and let the ideas brew. She tapped her plate. 'This is nice for something just thrown together.'

'I'm a man of many talents.' He paused a moment. 'I know it's a mad idea and I'll wake up tomorrow wondering how I ever gave it head room. Just warning you, it's going to be a no, but let's sleep on it.'

'Good idea.' She nodded towards the monitor on the wall. 'Shall we finish watching that film?'

'You mean watch a bit more before we doze off again? Are we getting middle aged, Annie?'

'Hey, you speak for yourself. I'm in my prime.' A yawn overtook her as she spoke, making him laugh. She laughed too. He was relaxed. He thought he'd made the decision to refuse Jennifer and that Annie had accepted it, but he was wrong. She knew that by the time he woke tomorrow morning, he would have changed his mind.

CHAPTER 16

Annie woke to darkness and the even breathing of Mike beside her, sound asleep. She twisted to lift her phone from the bedside table. It was just after five am.

She slid carefully out of bed and padded through to the living room, where the window showed pinpricks of light in a soupy blackness. The sun would burn off the early morning mist, though this looked thick enough to hang around all day. On a clear morning, the lights from the industries on the far bank were visible; today, she couldn't tell if she was looking at the windows of other early risers or boats on the estuary. The air was still. Machinery at Havenmere Docks would be swinging large containers to and fro as they stacked and packed for maximum efficiency. Rob Small had assured her it was a largely silent workplace, but she found that hard to believe.

She pulled her running shoes from the rack, tossing them on to the settee with her tracksuit, then headed to the bathroom for a shower.

When she emerged towelling her hair, she heard cupboard doors clicking open and closed from the kitchen. Mike's face in profile looked pensive as he reached to return the big pan to its rack.

'Coffee, Annie?' he called through.

'Not for me. I'll get something on the way in. I'm going to walk.'

Mike glanced through but didn't otherwise react. There was a time he'd have badgered to know why. 'It's a long way. You can go out for a run when it's warmer … when it's lighter … what if you need the car?'

He came through with his own coffee as she had one foot up on a chair tying her laces. The water in the estuary was now a black sheen through the mist. In the half light it could be just a narrow muddy stream, not a wide and dangerous shipping lane.

She named the coffee shop where she'd seen Lois. 'That's where I'll stop for a drink,' she told him. 'Meet me there?'

It was unlikely Lois would be conscious after yesterday's bender but if she was going to be a regular fixture, then Annie was going to face her down.

'OK, I'll be there in an hour and a half.'

Sometimes she strode the city's streets to think through a tangled case; sometimes she just needed to move fast, not knowing what she was running from or towards. No such uncertainty this morning. Mike had veered towards her point of view. She could see the conflict in his face as they both avoided mentioning Jennifer. Her problem was that she'd veered too. Maybe he'd been right. They'd talked about legal risks, but what if Dyson and fforbes found out? They would not approve of Jennifer. As things stood, the dodgy twosome could pull the plug at a moment's notice. Had she been swayed by an old friendship? Would she have entertained the idea from anyone else?

She set off at a run into the damp autumn air.

* * *

By the time Mike joined her in a corner seat by the café window, the streets were beginning to fill, the fog had lifted and the day promised to be bright. She cradled an almost empty glass of orange squash as she sat back, muscles recovering from what had been a faster run than originally planned. The last half mile had taken it out of her – getting soft, she supposed. She preferred *soft* to Mike's *middle-aged*. The café was packed, though few people stayed longer than the time it took to queue and collect. No sign of Lois.

Mike smiled down at her, made as though to sit, then changed his mind as he watched her drain her glass. 'Coffee in the office?'

She nodded. 'And let's talk things through properly.'

'Yup. Sooner the better.'

'You've not come round to it, have you?'

He wobbled his hand in a yes-no gesture. 'More than I expected to, if I'm honest. Your friend could be a real asset, and one we could really use just now. But all I'm saying is that I can see the advantages. That doesn't make it a good idea.'

As they walked up towards the office, she slipped her hand under his arm. 'I've had time for it all to sink in, too. I'm not as sure as I was.'

'We've a couple of hours before the Thompsons show. Things are pretty much sorted for later unless Barb's set more hares running that we don't know about.' As he spoke, the sky darkened as though to match his tone. 'There's one aspect we've not touched on. If they find out, how are Penn and Teller going to take it?'

'Mike!' She slapped out at him as she looked round. 'I've told you not to call them that!'

He gave her a mock bow. 'I mean of course, the esteemed Ms Dyson and the equally esteemed Mr fforbes, two small effs.'

'Just call them the owners,' she snapped.

'How old d'you think they are?' he asked.

'Hard to tell. Well over forty, for sure.'

'And under eighty, yeah?'

She'd been going to say forty to sixty but hesitated. 'Well … not eighty.'

'And those aren't their names and it's all done through a holding company, and no one knows jack shit about either of them.' He stopped and she had to stop too because she was still holding his arm. They were outside their building now. The sign swayed drunkenly above them. 'They hold the purse strings, but we could manage without them. I genuinely don't know why you're so in awe of them.'

'If I'm right, I hope we never find out,' she grumbled, pulling her arm free and reaching for the door. It was unlocked. The downstairs consultants had beaten them to it. 'Because I sure as hell don't want to know. It's one where I'm going to trust my instinct.'

He said nothing but she was pleased to see he looked troubled as they stepped out of the cold.

'They're earlier than–' Annie stopped abruptly at the sight of the shuttered reception counter. The downstairs office was empty.

Noises from above had them both stare towards the stairs and then at each other.

Voices … indistinct … a sudden laugh …

Mike's mouth had dropped open. 'Is that Pat?'

Annie had to clear her throat before she could speak. Surprise had taken her voice. 'Yes,' she said, 'but … but it's Barb too.'

'But what the hell! They never … Why today?'

'Let's go up and see.'

Annie pushed her way in front of him and was first into the upstairs office. A drone of tuneless humming signified Barbara in the small kitchen at the far end of the landing. It was Pat sitting at the desk, beaming at her.

'You've always underestimated me,' Pat greeted her, radiating satisfaction, her index finger pointing at Annie's face said. 'Babs too.'

'Maybe once,' said Annie, taken aback, 'but not now.' It was true. She'd learnt to respect Pat's talents. 'What d'you mean?'

'I guessed. Him speaking out of turn.' Her thumb jerked towards Mike. 'I made a few enquiries.' Thumb now indicating the kitchen along the landing. It took a moment for Annie to realise that the sounds from the kitchen had morphed into footsteps coming their way, and not just one set. 'We think it's a great idea, but we need to keep things under wraps for the time being, especially from …' – Pat tapped the side of her nose – '… you know who.'

'Penn and Teller,' murmured Mike.

'Morning all.' Barbara entered with a brimming cafetière.

Behind her, bearing a tray holding five mugs, came Jennifer.

CHAPTER 17

Annie shared a brief glance with Mike as she accepted a mug of coffee. She felt outmanoeuvred, and struggled to hide her amazement. She couldn't believe Pat had worked it out from a standing start. She must have had had a tip off.

'We're not without a few sharp operators round here, are we?' It was a quiet comment from Barbara, meant only for Annie and Mike. Annie saw all Pat's triumph reflected on Barbara's face. 'Maybe we should put Pat back in charge.'

'Pat was always a sharp operator,' Annie muttered back.

'We both are. We were getting out of tight corners before you were knee high to a grasshopper.'

At your weight, thought Annie uncharitably, you'd never get into one these days. Mike leant in to ask Barbara, 'So how did you work it out?'

She smiled. 'Nothing to it. Piece of cake.'

'Cake?' Pat paused her discussion with Jennifer.

Mike rolled his eyes and said, 'How come you're both in so early?'

The sisters met his question with blank looks, just as though they were always in at this time.

'I know how busy you are,' Jennifer said. 'So don't worry about me. Pat's given me some stuff to do. Though I'm afraid

I'll have to duck out around lunchtime. I'll get back if I can but I'll be at least a couple of hours. I wasn't expecting to start so quickly and I've a few commitments I can't get out of.'

'Uh … yes … that's fine,' said Annie. Jennifer had warned her that the disciplinary action would unfold into interviews and meetings that she would not be able to avoid. Did the Thompsons know the real story?

As the sisters settled to their tasks and Jennifer crammed her chair next to Pat, Annie headed for the sanctum of her office.

Mike followed her and closed the door. 'How did they find out?'

'She didn't just work it out, that's for sure. Pat has a contact in the local force. Remember, we had a tip off a few months ago … that tax thing … that was from Pat. Maybe someone's mentioned Jennifer coming back, knowing that we knew her back in the day … maybe mentioned that she's in trouble …' The amorphous train of thought tailed off.

'Do you think Jennifer's confided in someone that she's approached us?'

'God, I hope not. If she's blabbed to a colleague, word'll get out.'

'I wonder if Pat knows what Jennifer did wrong.'

'Hard to tell but we need to make sure they know enough to keep their mouths shut.' Last night, she'd have pulled him up, not *did* wrong, *alleged* to have done wrong. She'd moved further towards his way of thinking than she'd realised.

'I suppose it'll do no harm having her help with a bit of paperwork.'

His doubtful tone matched her own reservations. 'Just nip

out there, will you, and see if you can see what Pat's given her.'

As he opened the door, Annie could see Jennifer at one of the filing cabinets. She watched as Mike leant in close to Pat.

After a moment, he was back. 'It's OK. She's set her on tidying up some admin loose ends on a dead case, says she was waiting to talk to you before letting her near anything current. Interesting, isn't it? We seem to have welcomed her in, but none of us trusts her.'

'Wise precaution,' said Annie. 'She's a serving police officer.' They had two live cases delicately balanced at the point of out-of-court settlements. 'If the wrong person got wind of some of the stuff in those files …'

'You think she'd dob us in to help her own position? She'd just get in worse trouble, wouldn't she?'

'We can't know for certain that she wouldn't. I thought we'd have space to work through all this. I wasn't expecting to be bounced into taking her on so soon. Oh, and it won't be a problem to let her loose on your new clients if you reel them in.' The thought surprised her. It brought home what a different world he was leading them towards.

He gave her a satisfied smile. 'Exactly. Completely different ball park.'

Annie looked out at the shard of grey sky visible above the confines of the small yard. 'Pat and Barb have pushed us in feet first. We could throw her out but I don't want to burn bridges to that extent. Let's give it a day or so.'

* * *

'Lunchtime.' Pat pulled herself to her feet and headed for the small kitchen.

Jennifer had already gone, having come apologetically to Annie soon after ten o'clock to say she'd had a call.

'My meeting's been brought forward.' She'd put brief emphasis on *meeting*. 'No idea why. I'm going to have to go. It shouldn't be more than a couple of hours.'

Barbara had been quick to take advantage, hauling herself to her feet. 'I need to pop home,' she'd said. 'I was going to go later but now's as good a time as any.' She turned to Jennifer. 'I can drop you in town if that'll help.'

Annie's eyes narrowed. With the early start, Barbara had already worked a far longer morning shift than she'd done in years.

It was a quiet morning after they'd both left. She, Mike and Pat concentrated on their own paperwork. For their current clutch of live cases, success depended less on any quest for truth, than on pristine documentation with every 'T' crossed and 'I' dotted.

When Pat announced it was lunchtime and went to the kitchen, Annie murmured to Mike, 'We'll get it out of her over lunch, while no one else is here.'

'OK, but don't get into a fight over it. Jennifer's here. That's what we have to deal with.'

'She's cock-a-hoop at getting one over on us. She'll love telling all. But we really have to work out if this is a good idea. If Jennifer comes out intact at the end of this whatever-it-is, we want her on our side.'

He nodded. 'And if it goes badly for her, we don't want her knowing stuff that could damage us.'

It was an uncomfortable idea. Did they have information Jennifer could use to get her out of this hole?

Jennifer wouldn't do that.

She didn't voice the thought because it had been eight years. The Jennifer she'd known would have been on her way up the promotion ladder by now. 'C'mon, we're going to have lunch with Pat and get some answers.'

They joined Pat at the tiny kitchen counter looking out over the road, Mike positioning himself so his back was to the skew-whiff corner of the sign.

'I want to talk about Jennifer,' Annie said without preamble, as she reached a tin down from the cupboard.

'Should we wait for Babs?' Pat rummaged through a Tupperware lunch box, as though interested to see what was inside, though as she lived alone, she must have been the one to pack it.

'No, you can catch her up.' Annie cracked the ring-pull on a tin of tuna. 'I want to get some things straight before Jennifer comes back. How did you figure it out?'

Without taking her attention from the food in front of her, Pat gave a smile. 'Surprised you, didn't I? But I've a confession to make, Kid. I heard the other day that your old mate, PC Flanagan, was back in town. Meant to tell you but clean forgot. It didn't even click when I heard we'd had an early visitor.' She glanced up at Annie. 'Yes, I keep up with the local grapevine. I like to know what goes on when I'm not here. I assumed some random cold caller, then I saw you shut him up in the pub. Bet you've quite a bruise on your shin.' Mike narrowed his eyes but said nothing. 'I put the pieces together and decided to test it by giving Flanagan a ring. I might have led her to believe you'd told us about her – which you had, you just hadn't meant to – and she told me how she's leaving, wants work with us.'

'And you told her to come in and start work without even talking it over with me and Mike?'

'Sure. Where's the down side? She's just the sort we want. Where else are we going to pull in someone of her calibre? They mostly run a mile when they see this place. Who would you rather have, her or Lois?'

'How did you ring her?' snapped Mike. 'How could you get her number?'

Pat tapped the side of her nose. 'I've been round the block a time or two, Kid. Same place I picked up that she was back.'

'I'm gobsmacked,' Annie said, letting her amazement show.

'You want the truth,' Pat went on through a mouthful of flaky pastry. 'I was pretty sure you'd turn her down. He's good.' She indicated Mike with a jerk of her thumb. 'But he's too cautious by half. I thought yeah, why not? I'll take the decision for them. I'll tell her to start first thing.'

Stuffing the last of the pasty into her mouth, Pat retrieved a thick sandwich from the bottom of the box, and took an enormous bite. Fragments rained down into the now largely empty box. Annie took another forkful of tuna. Mike asked, 'What case did you have her working on?'

Annie smiled. Pat was back on board. Maybe she'd never been gone. The three of them could thrash out this whole thing between them.

'Don't worry,' Pat said. 'I wasn't putting her near anything that's heading for the courthouse. I've had her on that job you gave me yesterday, tying loose ends, that stuff Lois was sounding off about.'

'No, you said–' Annie stopped. Pat had said admin loose

ends on a dead case. And that's what it was. But a knot in her gut told her she'd rather Jennifer had been digging anywhere but into the Marshall case.

CHAPTER 18

They had been back at their desks a scant twenty minutes when Barbara clumped up the stairs.

'I'm ready for a coffee,' she said. 'Come on, our kid, give me a hand. We'll do a pot.'

The sisters headed for the kitchen.

'I didn't think we'd see Barb again today,' Annie said to Mike.

'Me neither, I thought we'd see Jennifer back first. How long's she been gone?'

Annie glanced at the time. 'Close on four hours. Say it was Clough Road she went, what's that? Half an hour? She must have been there three hours.'

'We need to keep track of these absences. It'll give us a clue how serious it is.'

'Three hours sounds serious enough.'

'Yeah, but you don't know what these bureaucrats can be like. They could have had her sitting waiting for hours. Let's see how she looks when she gets back. Speaking of which, did you see how Barb looked just now? Cat with the cream. What are they up to?'

She took note as the sisters returned with coffee for four. Mike was right. They both looked suspiciously pleased with themselves. 'I don't want this paperwork under Jennifer's nose,' she announced. 'So let's get through it before she gets back.'

They returned to their desks, and Annie to her sanctum, but she kept the door open. She thought about calling Pat in to ask what was going on, but she could see her scowling over a spread of papers, her glance bouncing from desktop to screen; it wouldn't do to break her concentration. It had been a tricky case and the outcome now rode on them getting the fine detail just so.

By the time Jennifer's step sounded on the stairs, it was after four o'clock, and Annie thought she'd worked it out. Pat and Barbara had found out that Jennifer was in trouble, and assumed Annie and Mike didn't know. She would bide her time and see if they came forward with the information. For the good of the agency, it came under the heading of things she needed to know. Odd though that it had been Barb coming back with secrets to share, not Pat.

An eddy of hard autumn air swirled in as Jennifer, breathless, came through the office door. 'Sorry I'm so late,' she said as she slipped off her jacket and stepped to the threshold of Annie's door. 'May I …?'

Annie was aware of three pairs of eyes watching curiously as Jennifer stepped in and closed the door.

'I'm sorry, Annie. I have no control over how long they keep me. This is going to be happening for a few weeks at least.'

Annie waved this aside. 'Don't worry. You warned me. How are you? Was it tough?'

Jennifer nodded. 'They're scrupulously even-handed, and they don't show it outwardly, but they think they've got the whole story straight in their heads. They want a confession from me; so much quicker than waiting for the evidence mill to grind through.'

'But once it does, you'll be cleared, yes?'

'Oh yes, no question, but it takes so long that people's ideas get fixed in their heads. I could never go back after this, even if I wanted to.'

'Pat and Barb,' said Annie. 'How much do they know? I mean do they think you've left already; do they know anything about the disciplinary stuff?'

Sixteen tiny panes of glass rattled in the small window as a breeze scooped through the back yard. Jennifer glanced up as she answered, 'Not from me. I wasn't sure what you'd told them so I've been careful not to speak out of turn.'

'They've heard nothing from me, but they might have guessed that things are not entirely above board. I don't think it's a problem. They'll keep shtum where they need to. There's something else; your fee. Given the circumstances, I'm not clear how or what we can legitimately pay you.'

The worry played at the back of her mind. *Eight years … I've not seen her for eight years …what do I really know about her?* If Mike was right, then she was desperate to build some kind of nest egg before the disciplinary process played out and the axe landed.

'Yes …' Jennifer half met her eye and half didn't. 'We wondered if that would make things difficult.'

'Having you on the books is not as straightforward as I'd want it to be.' There was an understatement. Amongst a tangle of issues, sat the owners who had access to every financial transaction from Pat and Barb's biscuits upwards, not that Annie would enumerate these concerns to Jennifer.

'Caitlin works for a high-end design consultancy,' Jennifer said. 'I know you want to move. She could do some concept work for you.'

Keeping her expression neutral, Annie asked, 'Do you mean you do the work and we pay Caitlin?' The answer was going to be an unequivocal no, but she wanted to see if Jennifer was genuinely suggesting it.

Jennifer shrugged. 'Well …'

'We'd have HMRC down on us like a ton of bricks.' Annie allowed a seam of steel into her tone.

'No, I didn't mean it like that.' Jennifer backed down at once.

Annie let that pass, though it was hard to see how else she'd meant it.

Jennifer talked unconvincingly about the agency employing Caitlin for real, when their move was underway, but then went on, 'Can we come to an agreement, between friends, nothing in writing, that however this all unravels, we'll agree on how you pay me for the work I've done once the dust's settled?'

It was a good outcome. Mike would approve. Jennifer would be in the position of unpaid intern which might raise insurance issues, except that they wouldn't send her on any jobs that needed specialist cover. Once she'd bedded in and got up to speed with Mike's new clients, they would have her working flat out helping to reel them in, and could only pray that the disciplinary process wouldn't interfere unduly. If and when she came on board properly, she could have her 'back' pay in the form of some manner of bonus – all above board.

Jennifer returned to the main office to take her orders

from Pat. Annie kept her door ajar and wasn't surprised to hear Barbara chip in after a few minutes.

'So, Jennifer … uh … you got your business sorted OK, did you?'

'Yes, thanks,' Jennifer responded breezily. 'How about you? Did you get your shopping done?'

Touché, thought Annie. Barbara's many absences from her desk were *never* labelled shopping.

As they wrapped up for the day, Annie heard Jennifer say to Pat, 'You've nothing to worry about in here. Your operative, Lois, doesn't have anything she could use against you.'

Annie stepped closer to join the conversation. 'That's what we thought, though I suppose Mrs Marshall might have said something to her that didn't get into the file.'

'Maybe,' said Jennifer. 'But it wouldn't matter. William Marshall was obsessed with an ex-employer who'd made him redundant. He was a drunk and he got all wound up in conspiracy theories. Miriam Marshall had no truck with any of it. She knew he was lucky to have kept his job as long as he had. She just wanted to find him, but after he died she might have bought into his conspiracy theories a bit. Did you know he'd stolen some stuff from from his workplace? What if Mrs Marshall told Lois about it? Not that it was anything significant but is Lois the type to think she could make trouble out of something like that?'

Annie recalled the way Miriam Marshall had been on the verge of saying something to her and Mike. They'd guessed at theft, but Jennifer was extrapolating far beyond the file's scant contents. 'How do you know all this? It's not in the file.'

'I was the one called out when they found Marshall's body. I wasn't involved in the investigation but I met Miriam Marshall. I took her husband's stuff back to her. I looked him up to see if he had form.'

'This previous employer,' said Annie. 'You mean Havenmere Docks, don't you? What did he steal?'

'A stack of technical papers. He broke in using his employee pass. We talked to the person in charge … not me of course, but whoever was dealing with it back then. Routine operational records for some safety testing. Nothing incriminating. The place is squeaky clean according to the Health and Safety Exec.'

'If Miriam Marshall wanted to cause trouble, do you think she'd try to play Lois?' Annie asked the room at large. 'I'm hoping Lois has cooled off and decided to put this behind her, but there's a chance of her approaching Mrs Marshall. I don't want them getting together to make things difficult for us.'

Barbara laughed. 'After what Miriam Marshall had to say about the investigation, I doubt she'd give any of us the time of day, and certainly not Lois. If you've done, Jennifer, there's someone you need to meet before you go.'

'Who?' said Annie.

'The kids who work behind the desk downstairs. We want them to know which are the legit faces up here,' said Barbara. 'Come on, Jennifer, look sharp. I want to introduce you before they all pack up and go home.' With that, she flapped and chivvied Jennifer out of the office and down the stairs.

'Not that they'd lift a finger if they saw a gang of masked thugs heading up.' In theory, it was a good idea, but Annie was annoyed at the way Barb had interrupted their conversation.

Pat aimed a glare at Mike. 'Was a time we looked out for each other in this building, back in the day.'

'Don't blame me,' said Mike.

'Anyway, listen, Babs has got her out of the way so I can tell you.' Pat moved towards the door to peer down the stairs, before easing the door shut. 'This morning when Babs went out, she didn't go shopping.'

'I really don't care whether she was shopping or not,' Annie snapped.

Pat rolled her eyes. 'You might be prepared to trust someone who parachutes in like this, but we're not. This isn't about where Babs went. This is about where Jennifer went.'

CHAPTER 19

'What do you mean?' Annie glanced warily at Pat.

She glanced at Mike. He must be as amazed as she was to learn that Barbara had successfully managed to tail Jennifer. If Jennifer was going to come and work for them properly, she was going to have to get her act together. *You're not strutting about in a uniform now,* Annie imagined herself saying.

'Said she had a prior commitment, didn't she?' Pat said. 'Then changed the time. Typical tactic to put people off the scent, claiming some third party has changed the time.'

'Or maybe someone actually did change the time,' Mike murmured.

Pat barely spared him a glance. 'Me and Babs had it all arranged. Babs would offer her a lift.

'Where did she take her?'

'Bus station.'

'OK … And?'

'Where was she before she came back to Hull?' Mike asked suddenly.

'Uh … Bedfordshire, I think,' said Annie.

'Yeah, that's what my contact said,' Pat put in. 'But she's been quite the peripatetic copper since we used to know her. I did some digging. She's had a crop of secondments, quite prestigious, liaison with various HQs and that. The wonder is she's not chased promotion over the years.'

'She certainly had ambition when I first knew her,' admitted Annie, 'but she was little more than a raw recruit then.'

'How come you're happy with her swanning off in the middle of a working day?'

'We took her on really quickly. She still has loose ends to tie.'

'So she goes back to her old station, does she? Where's that, Clough Road?'

Annie replayed her conversations with Jennifer. It had never been specified. 'I think so,' she said. 'Why? Isn't that where she went?'

'No, it isn't. Babs took her to the bus station, parked in Tescos, said she was going to shop. They walked up to the concourse together, Babs made like she was going in the supermarket and Jennifer went on towards the bus station. She was in a hurry, Babs said it wasn't easy to keep pace, but she didn't get on a bus.'

'Taxi?'

'No, she got on a train. The 11:10 to York.'

A pause …

'Then what?'

'That's it. Babs couldn't get on the train with her. She had her shopp– uh … she had things to do. But what's she playing at, d'you reckon?'

Mike had pulled his keyboard towards him and was typing furiously.

'York?' murmured Annie. 'Why would she be going to York?'

'Good question, but we keep an eye on her from now, yeah?'

When they got downstairs, Jennifer was gone. Barbara was in her car outside waiting for Pat. Annie gave them an absent wave then fell into step with Mike as he strode down the road towards the multi-storey. She pulled her jacket tight around her as the wind strengthened. She'd chosen the wrong time of year to reinstate their brisk walk at both ends of the day.

Mike was uncharacteristically silent. Annie looked at him curiously. 'What are you thinking?'

'Jennifer's only been back in Hull five minutes,' he said. 'She's not had time to get her feet under the table, let alone do something bad enough to be kicked out? And just because she caught the York train, that doesn't mean she went to York.'

'She could have hopped off at Brough and caught a train south.'

'Not to Bedford, she couldn't. She wouldn't have had time.'

'She was gone six hours.'

'I looked up the trains, the connections. She couldn't have done it in the time.'

Ah, that's what he'd been doing. 'Where then? York? But why York?' Annie flinched as it began to rain in earnest. Clutching her hood tight around her head she set off at a run to cover the last fifty metres to the car park entrance. Once they were under the dank concrete cocoon, she turned to Mike. 'So it's happening in York, not Hull. That wouldn't be unusual, would it?'

Annie climbed into the car and put the keys in the

ignition, but delayed turning on the engine. Vehicles were queuing to get out. Better to sit here for ten minutes than in a fog of smoke on a ramp.

Mike shrugged. 'If they're taking it off her local patch, I think that makes it more serious. And I'm not sure she went to York.'

'Where else? I suppose she could have got off at any of the stops along the way, but …?'

'No, it's just that the police are all regimented about this stuff, meeting times and such, and unless it's some kind of internal tribunal that's going to go on all day, it's not usually going to take hours. I mean who has the time? If she went to York it was too long for any kind of preliminary thing, but not long enough for a tribunal and anyway, she said that wouldn't happen for weeks yet. I know it's speculation, but if she went to York, I'd have expected her back by three.'

'Where then?'

'What if she changed trains in York?'

'To where?' From York, Jennifer could have caught a train to almost anywhere.

'Northallerton,' Mike said, a tinge of triumph in his tone. 'North Yorks HQ. That crop of secondments, liaisons with various HQs. What's the betting one of her recent stints was up that way? She had time to get to Northallerton and back. It wouldn't have been a long meeting but do you remember how puffed she was when she got back in the office?'

'She was puffed from running up the stairs.' As she said the words, Annie realised how absurd they were. Fit copper, Jennifer Flanagan, out of breath from climbing a single flight of stairs. She'd been at full speed, on edge at her long absence. And she'd diverted everyone with fulsome apologies before diving headlong back into her work.

'I don't like not knowing stuff,' she said. 'I mean it's not her fault that we got bounced into taking her on so quickly, but I feel like we're being played and I don't like it. She doesn't want us to know what she's done. She's turning us the wrong way so we don't ask questions of anyone who might have the answers. And if she's that desperate we don't get to know, then I think we need to find out.'

CHAPTER 20

There was rain in the air, the outside temperature showing close to freezing as Annie slowed the car to count up the numbers on the houses to her left. Most were shrouded in darkness. It was just a hunch, but she was sure her target would be an early riser, and smiled as she saw lights behind the drawn curtains. Parked cars lined the street. She had to drive round a curve in the road before she found a gap.

She'd left Mike asleep; had thought about waking him but it would have been hard to explain quite what she thought she'd found. Jennifer's odd trip. They'd followed the logic to rule out Bedfordshire and settle for either York or Northallerton, but maybe those timetables had diverted them from something closer to home. What if Jennifer's meeting hadn't been rescheduled? What if she'd wanted the extra time for something else altogether?

She recalled the surprise revelation yesterday that Jennifer had not only been the police officer on the scene when William Marshall's body was found, she had met Miriam Marshall. Something that Jennifer hadn't mentioned when she'd first been given the file.

Miriam had mentioned a policewoman who *didn't have a clue* that her husband had worked at Havenmere Docks. That must have been Jennifer. Annie thought back to her own visit to the dockyard, her chat with Rob Small, and the following day, a brief and rather spiky exchange with Richard Redman after the funeral.

Maybe William Marshall was already a person of interest to the police. Hadn't Jennifer said that he'd stolen something from his ex-employer? Was this case sitting at the periphery of something much bigger? Jennifer had given the impression that she'd finished reading through the paperwork after she got back, but that was absurd. She could have had the wafer-thin file by heart during her short morning stint. Had she read something in there that had extended her 'couple of hours' absence to six?

Annie imagined Jennifer rushing off early to see if she could grab some unexpected evidence on her way to the meeting; something that might earn her brownie points, perhaps soften the blow of whatever was likely to land. They'd talked about her changing trains in Brough, but what if Brough had been her destination. She wouldn't even have needed the address from Lois's file. She already knew her way to the Marshalls' house.

Annie walked back down the road, hugging the high garden walls that afforded some shelter from the weather.

When the Marshalls' house came into sight, she saw more than one silhouette moving behind the curtains. Miriam wasn't alone. That was annoying. She didn't think they had children, but maybe there were relatives staying.

She paused in the shelter of a hedge. Dawn was barely breaking through a clouded sky, but the illumination from a streetlight pooled outside the Marshalls' gate. Undecided she stood in the shadows, feeling the cold seep through the denim of her jeans.

Then the front door swung open, spilling light down the short pathway to the garden gate. Annie gaped at the unmistakable figure of Rob Small in the doorway with Miriam behind him. She crouched low to peer through the inadequate cover, unable to distinguish words from a low-voiced exchange.

There was nothing in his body language or Miriam's to suggest anything other than a brief visit; nothing to hint at the relationship she was sure they'd had at some point. In fact, Rob Small's hair and coat were damp as though he'd arrived only minutes ago.

With a quick look at the pair on the doorstep, she dropped to one knee, feeling the hard cold of the pavement penetrate to her skin. Down on a level with the car bonnets, she stared along the line. Most of them sparkled with a thin veil of frost, but one was shiny clean and shimmered. As she heard footsteps and the slam of a door, she pushed backwards into the spiky hedge and held still.

Rob Small emerged through the gate without a backward glance, his key fob held out. The car that had shimmered a still-warm engine acknowledged him with the flash of its lights as it unlocked its doors. So he too had been an early visitor.

And Jennifer, she would lay odds, had skipped the train at Brough and spent time with Miriam Marshall before going on to her meeting.

As Rob Small's car disappeared, Annie pulled herself free of the bush, brushed the twigs off her sleeves and headed for Miriam's door.

CHAPTER 21

A door banged from downstairs. Footsteps sounded. Annie shot out of her small office to meet Mike at the top of the stairs.

'Quick, in here.'

'What's up? What're you in so early for? Why didn't you wake me?'

'Never mind that and be quick before anyone else arrives,' she flapped. 'I've got to show you while we're alone.'

He laughed at her. 'Annie, it's not eight o'clock yet. We've a good three hours before the dozy duo show up.'

She tutted her exasperation. 'No, they'll be early. Jennifer, remember? They're going to be in on the dot the next few days just to show how conscientious they are.'

'Jennifer's not coming in. Pat rang me an hour ago; said Jennifer had been in touch because she hadn't been able to raise you. Some last-minute problem and she won't be in today.'

'Oh right.' Annie's hand went automatically to her pocket, but her phone was on her desk. 'My phone's ... I probably didn't turn it on again. Things got a bit ... it slipped my mind.'

Mike stared at her. 'You turned your phone off? Where've you been? Why didn't you tell me?'

She tried not to radiate guilt. 'Look, it was just an impulse. Nothing dangerous. I went to see Miriam Marshall. Remember how Jennifer read Lois's file in the morning, then after she came back, she had all that info at her fingertips. I think she might have wanted the extra time to go to the Marshalls.'

'And did she?'

'I don't know.' Annie opened her arms in a gesture of surrender. 'It didn't go the way I expected, but Jennifer doesn't need to know anything about it. I don't want to keep stuff from Pat, but ...' She glanced at the clock. 'Yeah, they'll be ages. Let's make coffee. Then see if you can make any sense of this stuff. I'm going cross-eyed with it.'

As they returned from the kitchen, Annie saw Mike's gaze light on the rarely used 'Do not disturb' sign she'd hung on the door to her office. Its use was contentious. It smacked of hierarchies and boundaries, a reminder that the factotum was now in charge of her erstwhile bosses.

She watched as he took in the wide ribbons of paper in the small office; tacked to the walls, draped over the desk, strung from the filing cabinets.

'What the hell is it?'

'This isn't the half of it. It's old-fashioned computer printouts. It's what Miriam Marshall gave me.'

He reached out to rub the paper between thumb and fingers as he looked closely. 'This hasn't come off an old printer. It's custom paper, good quality print. What did she say it is?'

'She didn't.' Annie told him how she'd watched until Rob Small's car was out of sight, then gone to ring the doorbell. The door had been snatched open, Miriam snapping,

'What is it now–?' before doing a double-take, and staring towards the road with a look of alarm.

'She thought I was Rob Small,' she said.

'Had he been there overnight?'

'No, and I don't think there's anything between them. Not now anyway. He'd called round early just like I had.'

'Did you ask her why?'

'I didn't get the chance to ask her anything.'

Miriam had grabbed Annie's arm, pulled her inside and slammed the door. 'Stay there,' she'd barked before striding down the hallway and vanishing into the darkness under the stairs. She'd reappeared clutching a fat supermarket carrier bag, stuffed so full of paper it had started to split. Annie had sagged with the weight of it as Miriam pushed it unceremoniously into her arms.

'Miriam, is this–?'

Miriam had shushed her with an upraised hand, and kept her voice low as she'd re-opened the front door, peered cautiously out into the street and then all but bundled Annie back out into the cold.

'I don't want to see that again. Now go!'

'But, I–'

'Go now! Hurry up before anyone sees you.'

'Miriam, wai–'

But she'd been talking to a closed door.

'The bag was heavy,' she told Mike. 'There were a dozen splits in it and the wind was getting up. I just hauled it back to the car.'

Mike sipped his coffee, peering from one page to another. 'She didn't tell you anything about it?'

'Not a thing, but it must be the stuff William Marshall

stole from Havenmere Docks when he broke in using his old employee pass. Jennifer said he'd lifted a stack of technical papers. I wonder if this is what Rob Small was there to reclaim.'

'Then why didn't she hand them over? Why wait and give them to you?'

'Good question.'

'What are you going to do?'

'Work out what they are?'

'Annie, this isn't a paying case any more.'

'I know, but it will be. She's going to come back and ask us to decipher it. She wants to know. I saw it in her eyes. When she comes back, we'll be a step ahead.' She looked at the snakes of linked pages that she'd pinned to the walls.

'I think that's the start,' she told Mike.

'Start of what?'

'I don't know yet.'

He looked at the heap of paper still to be unravelled. 'There could be hundreds of somethings in that lot.' Then he leant in to study one of the shorter pieces; his finger moving along the disjointed lines. 'It's some kind of system spec, but without documentation to know what it's for, it'll take an age to piece together. That looks like the dateline ID.' He pointed at the header on one of the sheets. 'See, it's the same on that one … and that.'

'Does that tell us what it is?'

He shook his head. 'Not unless you can find the system that runs it.'

'I'm wondering what I can get out of Jennifer,' said Annie. 'Discreetly of course. Clearly it was never recovered after the theft or it wouldn't be with Miriam; it'd have gone back to Rob Small, but presumably Rob Small specified what was taken when he reported it.'

'Speaking of Jennifer, Annie, I've been wondering about getting her on board for next week.'

She spun to face him. His efforts with the new clients had been bearing fruit and she'd had her head buried in this stuff. 'Wow! They've been back to you already?'

'No, no, but I intend to be proactive, and Jennifer could be my ace card if I can rehearse her, but is it too early to draw her into something like this?'

Annie considered. 'If we're going to use her, let's use her properly. It's not the sort of thing where she could do us any damage. Yeah, good idea.'

As he headed for his own desk to start work, Annie told herself she would spare an hour to get a handle on one short sequence, while it was fresh in her mind.

But when Mike called, 'Pat and Barb are here,' she was appalled to see that two and a half hours had gone by.

She leapt up, ripping the sheets from the walls, struggling to recreate the neat concertina of pages, stuffing it all into a box. Dumping Miriam's carrier bag, still over half full, on top, she pushed it under the desk.

CHAPTER 22

The stairs' creaking treads announced the sisters' approach, as she returned slightly breathless to the main office.

Before she could say anything to Mike, her mobile rang, showing Jennifer's number. 'Hi Jen. Everything OK?'

'I'm so sorry, Annie. I'll get my act together by next week, honest.'

'Sure, don't worry.' She could feel Jennifer's frustration at being largely absent as she started this new role, but no one had expected her to be on board the day after she'd asked for a job. There were bound to be teething problems.

'I can get in for a couple of hours later this afternoon if you want.'

Pat and Barbara bustled in, setting their coats just-so on the hooks by the door, Barbara pushing her shopping trolley into a corner, Pat making minuscule rearrangements to the things on her desk before they both lumbered out towards the kitchen. An arrival routine; setting out their stalls for the day.

'Four-ish?' she said into the phone. 'Yes, that would be good. There's a case I'd like you to work on with Mike. New clients. While you're on, you know that case you looked at for Pat? You said William Marshall had taken something from his ex-employer, that his wife might have shown Lois. What was it? There's nothing in Lois's notes.'

'She's not making more trouble, is she?'

'No, I just want to make sure there's a coherent note in the file in case this pops up again in a year's time after we've all forgotten what it was about. What did he take?'

'Technical papers. Detailed specs for safety testing, I think. The guy he stole from didn't want it back, said it was no more than waste paper.'

'I wonder why he kept printed copies at all,' said Annie, thinking of the weight of the carrier bag.

'Oh, I think it was Marshall who did the printing. He got into the control room and printed stuff at random. I don't know the detail. It happened before I was here. I saw the file in relation to Marshall's death.'

'So nothing sensitive or secret?'

'Nothing like that.' Jennifer laughed.

'I'll make a note on the file. Thanks. See you later.'

As she ended the call, she murmured to Mike, 'Don't mention that Jennifer's coming in. If we're going to have her here, it's not just to take Pat and Barb's work off them, so I want her properly started on your stuff. I'll send them off after three to hand-deliver those tribunal papers in town. They won't bother coming back.'

Mike reached out with his toe to poke the tartan shopping trolley parked under the coat hooks. 'That'll be stuffed full by this afternoon. They'll barely have done a four-hour day with shopping, coffee breaks, lunch etc. How those two kept this business solvent longer than five minutes beats me.'

A part of her wanted to say, They'll step up when they need to, but she wasn't sure she believed it any more.

She pulled headphones on to check the morning's voicemail. After a handful of routine messages, a voice said, 'Let Ms Raymond know I need a word with her.' She recognised Rob Small. 'She has something of mine. I'll call later.' Without any pre-planning, she'd given the impression she was a casual acquaintance of Miriam's; the phrase *private investigator* hadn't cropped up, but if he hadn't known her profession then, he certainly did now.

Mike's attention was on his screen.

She didn't want to have the conversation again about why she'd visited Havenmere Docks without telling him. Instead, she strode across to the filing cabinet, and plucked out Miriam's file, flicking through for the number which she thumbed into her phone before slipping into her office and pulling the door shut behind her.

'Mrs Marshall. It's Annie Raymond. Have you told Rob Small you gave me those papers?'

'No!' The denial was robust and immediate followed by a shocked, 'And if you tell him. I'll deny it.'

'I've not spoken to him, but he seems to know.'

'How? What do you mean?'

She repeated Rob Small's message word for word.

'Oh that's nothing.' Miriam's tone relaxed. 'That'll be Rich Redman. He asked about Will's things. I told him I'd hired your firm to find him, that young girl you sent, barely out of school. He wanted to know if she'd had access to Will's stuff. I didn't say she had … but I didn't say she hadn't. He might have got the idea she'd taken something away behind my back.'

Annie allowed an incredulous, 'Pah!' at the idea of anyone being surreptitious with that bulging carrier bag. 'If Rob Small asks me, why wouldn't I tell him?'

'No, you mustn't! Please. Tell him you got them from Lois.'

'Why would I drop her in it?'

'Tell him … anything … just don't say it was me. What about client confidentiality?'

'You're not a client, Mrs Marshall. You want me to lie for you. It's a big ask.'

'Have you looked at it? Do you know what it is?'

'You only gave it me this morning. There's a hell of a lot to check to say no one's paying me to do it. What do you think it is?'

'I want you to find out.'

'Since you ask, I think I have a bit of a handle on what it might be.'

'And have you found a link to Will?'

'Way too early for that and, like I say, it would be a lot of work to take it further.'

A pause, then, 'If I employed you again, you'd look at it properly? And you'd be tied by client confidentiality. You wouldn't say anything to anyone about where you got it?'

'If you were a client again, then yes, I guess that would be about right.'

'I'm not sure … I … uh …'

'Just get back to me when you're ready, Mrs Marshall.'

Annie felt good. She'd reeled Miriam Marshall back on to the books in record time. She wouldn't say anything to Pat or Barb yet. If Rob Small spoke to them, they would truthfully say they didn't know what he was talking about. She could take the initiative and contact him, but he'd said he would get back to her.

His call came mid afternoon, just as the sisters were leaving.

'See you in twenty minutes ... half an hour,' Pat said.

'Unless the traffic's really bad in town,' from Barbara.

Annie met a sideways glance from Mike. Barbara was manoeuvring the now bulging shopping trolley; its weight thumped from stair to stair.

Annie looked at the caller-id, swallowing involuntarily as she picked up the phone. 'Thompsons' Agency.'

'Is that Ms Raymond?' asked Rob Small's voice.

For a second, she toyed with the idea of pretending to be someone else. Her skin felt clammy, there was something nasty underlying this and she had no clue what it was or who was involved. 'Ah, is that Rob Small?' she said brightly, aware of a sharp look from Mike. 'You left a message. How can I help you?'

'That day you called into the dockyard, you never told me you were a private investigator working for Miriam Marshall.'

'I try not to broadcast who I'm working for,' said Annie, carefully missing his point.

'I meant you didn't say you were a private investigator.'

'I'm sure I did when I introduced myself.' Annie allowed a sliver of indignation into her tone. 'Though now I think about it you'd just tried to drop a giant box on my head, so I might not have been as clear as I should have. But who did you take me for then?'

Mike's full attention was now on her call.

'An interfering friend of Miriam's if you want the truth. But the fact is that you've been working for Miriam and she's given you some stuff that by rights belongs to me and I want it back.'

'Just slow down, Mr Small. For starters, it wasn't me who

was working for Mrs Marshall. One of my colleagues assigned the case to a junior operative. It was a standard missing person scenario. Mrs Marshall was worried about her husband being out in the cold weather. He was found before our enquiries had got off the ground. Mrs Marshall didn't give us anything. She met our junior colleague a couple of times and that was all.'

'I understand she complained about a shoddy job.'

Annie felt her eyes narrow but wasn't surprised that Miriam should have passed this on. 'That's between us and Mrs Marshall,' she said primly.

'Well your junior, the one who did the shoddy job, has lifted some paperwork from Miriam and I want it back.'

'Why would Mrs Marshall have your paperwork? You told me her husband hadn't been anywhere near your place for years. There's nothing of yours in our file.'

'You need to talk to your young colleague, Ms Raymond, and you'll find I'm right.'

'The fact is, Mr Small, she no longer works for us. I'll look in the file again of course. What exactly am I looking for?' Annie felt her index and middle fingers slide to cross each other. Would he let slip some clue that might help her decipher those streams of paper?

There was a pause. Her crossed fingers tightened. She had a feeling she'd convinced him.

'Jobsie broke in two years ago, used his old employee pass.' She listened to Rob Small confirm what Jennifer had already told them, though he was less forthcoming on the detail. He went no further than 'technical papers', but confirmed that it had been William Marshall who had printed them.

'I'm trying to envisage a printer and I can't,' Annie murmured into a pause.

'Built in. Rarely use it. Don't need to. That toerag Jobsie almost cleaned me out of paper. It's custom, it's not cheap. He wasted more in that couple of hours than I use in a year.'

'Wow,' said Annie. 'How much did he take with him?'

'The whole bloody lot.'

Then Mike was signalling to her, pointing towards the door. Sounds from downstairs. Jennifer saying hello to the downstairs crew. She was early.

According to Jennifer, Small hadn't wanted the papers back, but he certainly wanted them now.

She tried to imagine a sequence where William Marshall stole paperwork from Havenmere Docks, the police recovered it, Rob Small said he didn't want it back and then … what? Surely it would have been kept as evidence or destroyed, not given back to the thief.

'But Mr Small,' she said. 'The police would have kept it as evidence. You need to go and ask for it back, and I wouldn't hang about; it might get destroyed now he's dead.'

The door swung open and Jennifer walked in opening her mouth to speak but closing it again seeing Annie on the phone.

Against Small's voice in her ear, Annie acknowledged Jennifer as she replayed the things she had said: *technical papers, specs for safety testing, didn't want it back, Marshall who did the printing, I don't really know the detail.*

'I didn't report it,' said Small. 'The police weren't involved.'

CHAPTER 23

Annie gave neutral responses as Rob Small vented about 'Jobsie'. She took care not to mention any names, saying, 'OK, I'll get back to you,' before she hung up. His comment, *I didn't report it*, had been a testy aside to his vitriol about his old friend, Jobsie, but when Jennifer had said, *I saw the file in relation to Marshall's death*, they'd been talking specifically about the burglary. There could be any number of explanations. It didn't necessarily mean one of them was lying. She and Mike would knock some sense out of it later.

She wanted to talk to him anyway, but Jennifer's early arrival had put paid to that, so she gave him a zipped-mouth mime as Jennifer turned to hang up her coat, murmuring, 'Catch up later.'

The office felt oppressively dark despite the overhead light. Annie reached forward to click on Pat and Barbara's desk lamps, creating pools of brightness that thickened the shadows in the corners of the room.

'We need a better bulb in this office.' She turned to Jennifer. 'Mike's been talking to some new clients. We're planning a meeting next week and I'd like you to go along with him. He can spend the rest of the afternoon getting you up to speed and you can start digging into the detail tomorrow. You'll need to be absolutely on point for this but I think it'll be right up your street.'

Jennifer looked surprised. Annie saw her glance at Mike almost as though expecting him to contradict her. 'Uh … yes, of course, but what about the Marshall case? I thought you said you were having bother with Lois.'

'No, that's all sorted. File closed.' *And definitely closed to you,* she added silently.

Mike looked up. 'Speaking of Lois, I was in the kitchen this morning, just before Pat and Barb came in. I'm certain I saw her across the street. Barb said she thought she'd seen her too the other day.'

'We don't own the road,' Annie snapped. 'Let's not get paranoid. Doesn't she have a friend who works across the way; it's how she heard about us in the first place. If she was going to cause trouble, she'd have done it by now.'

'There's no point you trawling through paperwork for next week until you have a grasp of the background,' Mike said to Jennifer. 'Shall we nip down the road and have a chat over a coffee? I could do with the fresh air. We can check for dangerous ex-employees while we're there. How about you, Annie?'

She rolled her eyes but smiled. 'Good idea, but I've stuff to do here and I've had enough coffee to last me a month. You go with Jen and get her up to speed. I'll see you later.'

She retreated to the sanctuary of her office, hanging the 'Do not disturb' sign just in case. There were other things she should be doing, but a clear hour to have another look at Rob Small's paperwork was too tempting an opportunity to let slip. No hanging reams of papers this time. She wanted a proper grasp on one small element and the rest would fall into line.

The box with its bulging carrier-bag on top was an irritating obstruction under the desk, an obvious obstacle to anyone who sat there, as they all did when they needed private space with a client. She pictured Barb hauling out the box with a huff of exasperation, the cascades of paper unravelling. She would probably dump the lot into the recycling container then lecture them on office tidiness and fire hazards.

It occurred to her that the recycling container was just the place to keep it out of the way until they decided what to do with it. Simply letting it go with the next recycling collection was an option.

She removed the ribbon of paper that she wanted to look at and manoeuvred the rest to sit in the container beneath the few sheets of waste paper already there.

CHAPTER 24

When they'd finally found time to relax that evening, she told Mike where she'd put the paperwork, adding that Miriam Marshall might come back on board as a client. 'She wants to know what it means. I'm not going to spend any more time on it, but I went over one bit while you were out with Jennifer.'

'And did you figure it out?'

'It was a really long-winded spec for moving something from right to left at a particular angle.'

'Moving what, a shipping crate?'

She shrugged. 'Could be. Or could be the detailed spec for one tiny cog in the mechanism. It was only the move, not even the angle. The bit that determined the angle is probably in the box taking up at least as much paper again.'

She reached for her inside jacket pocket, retrieving the wad of paper, folded tightly to fit, and smoothed it out on the coffee table.

Mike gave her a look. 'Are you going to bring it home strip by strip or shall we just give in and get the whole lot tomorrow?'

Annie laughed. He was already getting to his knees to help straighten the pages and was peering at her annotations. 'No, it's staying right where it is until we decide what to do with it. I can think of three options.' She counted them off on her fingers. 'Give it back to Rob Small. Destroy it. Give it to someone else.'

Mike pointed to the annotations she'd made. 'You've cut out your first option if you don't want him to know you've crawled all over it.'

'We can just bin anything that gets written on.'

'Even if Miriam Marshall comes back on board as a client, we'd need specialist help, and she wouldn't have that sort of money, would she?'

'Rob Small would know, but we can hardly ask him. Maybe Richard Redman, but he'd just go blabbing to Small.'

'Would he?' said Mike. 'They didn't look like best mates at the funeral.'

'I thought the same about Miriam and Small.' She remembered her surprise when Small arrived as mourner-in-chief at Miriam's side.

'I'll get us a beer.' Mike got to his feet, adding, 'William Marshall, if we're listing people who'd know but who we can't get the information from.'

Annie narrowed her eyes as she watched him go. 'No, not William Marshall,' she said as he returned. 'Marshall didn't know enough. Small and Redman might. Technical papers, safety testing, stolen by a guy who bore a grudge. What if this shows something safety-related going wrong?'

'If he had time to print that lot, why not grab the electronic record?'

'I'm not sure he could have. It's not a standard set-up. You couldn't just plug in a memory stick and grab the data. I had a good look while I was there.'

'Annie?' Mike's tone was suddenly full of suspicion. 'You

140

said you went there just to talk to Small. Why would you check it out like you planned to rob him?'

'Habit, I suppose. Sorry.' They'd agreed everything must be strictly above board from now on. With a pair of dodgy financial backers who could upend them at any point, it was vital they could show that their own dealings had been blameless and beyond reproach. 'Remember, we only had Lois's notes,' Annie went on. She wiped the bottom of her beer bottle on her sleeve before setting it down on top of the relentless technical listing. 'I thought William Marshall had died there. Rob Small's surveillance cameras could have cleared everything up. Maybe grabbing the printouts was the best that William Marshall could get.'

'But why so much?'

'I'm not sure it is. Believe me, that stuff delves into excruciating detail. It could be the technical outline of a few minutes' worth played in real time.'

Mike leant forward again to run his finger down the listing. 'Maybe we could share it between us, work out the bits then plug them together?'

She shook her head. 'It's taken me the best part of four hours solid to get as far as I have. I can't even put it in order where the paper's come apart. Something moved from right to left at an angle. I don't know what, I don't know how far, I don't even know the angle. Supposing we put the whole jigsaw together, all we'd have is more of the same. Things moved this way or that at this or that angle. Probably one of these moves should never have happened.' She pointed at the papers draped over the coffee table. 'Maybe that's the smoking gun right there. Without context, we could spend forever on it and never see the

141

wood for the trees. Hell, we wouldn't even see trees, we're several metres under the forest floor.'

Mike nodded his agreement. 'That dateline ID might be useful but only if we found a system that understood it. So back to your options. We return it to Small so he can bury it. Or we let it go for recycling – at least that way some good comes of it. Or we give it to someone else. You mean the police, don't you? If they can't decipher it, they'll give it back to Small. And with no other evidence I can't see them putting in the resource. It's a two-year-old robbery that was closed even before the perpetrator died.'

'Ah …'

He looked at her sharply. 'What?'

'I haven't told you this bit.' She told him what Rob Small had said.

'Didn't take it to the police? But he must have.'

'Why would he lie? And if he's telling the truth, what case notes did Jennifer see? One of them has it wrong. I don't want to think it's Jennifer, but I can't see what Small gains by lying.'

He was silent for a moment, staring into the middle distance, then said, 'Talk me through that control room again.'

Annie took him back through her visit to Havenmere Docks, from entering the space-age control room to Small escorting her back down the external staircase.

Mike sat back, hands closed around his beer bottle, fingers tapping absently on the glass.

When she'd finished, he sat up and said, 'What about this? He knows someone's broken in, his various security alarms tell him, but they weren't as good as they are now and by the time the police get there, Marshall's gone with his stash. Small works out what's gone, but he says it's irrelevant technical stuff and worthless. When the police catch up with Marshall, Marshall claims he threw it in the river or whatever, but they don't chase it up because no one wants it, so why would they? Then later Small realises that Marshall has actually captured something significant, maybe illegal, so he doesn't go back to the police, he tries to find out if Marshall really destroyed it or not.'

'Maybe Marshall told him he still had it,' Annie broke in. 'Tried a bit of blackmail?'

'There you are then,' Mike finished with an air of triumph. 'Small doesn't want the police involved because what Marshall has shows a health and safety breach. So when you said to go back to the police, of course he claimed they'd never been involved.'

As he spoke, Annie's gaze drifted to the window. 'Yeah,' she said, looking out at the night sky. 'That would work.' She thought back to Small saying, *I didn't report it. The police weren't involved.* A throwaway remark in the middle of him bitching about Jobsie. 'I didn't have Rob Small down as that good an actor,' she murmured.

'He's had months to embed his own version in his head. He probably believes it by now.'

Mike was right. Tone of voice, body language, general demeanour – they'd all been shown to be horribly unreliable markers of whether or not someone was telling the truth.

'I really want to know what Jennifer's disciplinary is all about.'

'Then ask her,' said Mike.

'She'd have told us before now if she was going to.'

'Don't go looking for conspiracies. Maybe she's said nothing more because you've not asked.'

'It's weird, though. Why would we take someone on without finding out something like that?'

'We didn't. If the Thompsons hadn't bounced us, we'd have made enquiries.' He paused. 'How would you go about that? You can't just ask for details of internal disciplinaries, not from anywhere, let alone a police force.'

'We could ask around.'

'Ask who?' challenged Mike. 'You've told me time and again that your contacts from the old days have all moved on.'

'True,' she conceded. 'And anyway, Jennifer was the one I'd have gone to for something like this.'

'So ask her,' Mike said again. 'She must be expecting you to.'

'Pat has contacts. She's got quite sharp in the years I was away.'

'You mean she's learnt that good networking saves her a lot of hassle.'

She shot him a glare. He was relentless with his digs at the Thompsons and where she could rarely disagree when it came to Barbara, Pat was different. She and Pat had been through a lot together. 'I think Pat might have the contacts for this one.'

'Ah but you'd have to let on to her about Jennifer, and you promised not to.'

'What's a promise worth if she's not being straight with us?' Mike looked taken aback so she backtracked. 'No, of course I'm not going to tell Pat, but I think she has a contact who already knows. She didn't work it all out about Jennifer on her own. She smelt a rat and got on to someone. And even if that someone didn't tell her the whole story, they probably know.'

'But you can't contact them direct. Those sorts of contacts, you've always said they're unofficial and we keep them to ourselves.'

'Yes, of course. It's the safest way to do it.' She didn't think Mike had any contacts, not the unofficial sort to be kept below the radar. It wasn't the way he'd been used to doing business. 'I'll think about it,' she told him. 'There might be a number on her clone-phone. I'll see if I can grab a look while she's having lunch.'

'Uh … maybe she just worked it out.'

She caught his hesitation and looked at him sharply, but he was fiddling with the TV remote. 'That's hardly likely. Mike …?' What was the matter with him? He was radiating guilt. 'Was it you who told Pat?'

'No!' He stared indignantly. 'Of course not.'

'Then what–? Oh no, not again! Where's your phone?'

'Here.' He reached over and pulled it out of his jacket, making a poor attempt at nonchalance.

'Your clone-phone,' she growled. 'You know what I mean. Have you forgotten it?'

'Sorry, I left it in the office. It's the first time in ages. It just seems so–'

She grabbed the handset from him and scrabbled to turn it off. 'For god's sake, Mike! It was on, wasn't it? How many times! If the phones aren't close enough to show up as a single signal on a tracker, then one of them must be off. It's basic stuff. You've got to be on the ball with this kind of thing.'

145

'It might have been basics when you were working with Pieternel, but she was the person they invented paranoid for. We're not in that kind of world any more. We're moving on.'

'And until we've actually moved, this is basic stuff and we keep it up. Who knows what we could get dragged into?'

Too late, the conversational traps opened up ahead of her.

'Yes, exactly! And isn't it about time we put together a proper strategy for getting out from under Penn and Teller's yoke. They're not laundering money through us, not doing anything except throwing us enough scraps that we stay afloat. We're sleepers, Annie. We all know it. They've no other reason for investing in us. We're a bit of incidental insurance for them, but if they ever decide to put in a claim, we're going to be stuffed every which way.'

He was right, of course he was right, but what was the point in talking about it? Until they were in a position to get out from under the yoke, it was all pie in the sky.

She sighed, tossed his now-dead phone back to him, and said, 'See that it stays off till it's in the same building as its twin. D'you fancy another beer?'

146

CHAPTER 25

Tommy Marchant was annoyed. He'd no sooner arrived at work, than he'd found himself collared by the night Inspector who, from her expression, had not had a peaceful shift. Her face tight with anger, a phone handset clamped to her ear, she'd stopped him with a peremptory raised hand and an order to 'Wait.'

He hung in limbo for a moment, then began to shoulder his way out of his coat, only to be halted by her knuckles rapping the desk. 'You're going out again,' she snapped, signalling firmly for him to stay put. He stayed put.

'I don't give a damn about that,' she barked into the phone. 'I want to know why our computers went down ... well, they went down here ... *This* is priority! Don't give me that claptrap about– What? I'm well aware of that, and ...'

Tommy glanced round. None of the vital tech would have gone down. They had UPS systems and all manner of gizmos. He'd bet she'd screwed something up and was looking for a scapegoat.

He'd arrived today all set to chase up Jen Flanagan. It had been clear something wasn't right from the moment he'd seen her being marched along that corridor by Shiny Boots. Whatever it was hadn't blown over, and he was going to get to the bottom of it. When all was said and done, he was a detective of several decades' experience, and anyway he liked to think that someone would take a bit of trouble if he just stepped off the face of the earth the way she'd done. He'd gone as far as to talk it over with Dugs the previous evening.

'You want to ask that new sergeant from York,' had been her suggestion, quickly followed by, 'Don't you go meddling into anything that'll put you on duty over the weekend. We've got our Jess coming over.'

In a sense, her instinct was right. Shiny Boots would know the answers, but he'd get nothing from that source. He'd tried the desk sergeant earlier in the week, recalling their brief exchange the day he'd hurried through to find out where Jen had got to. *PC Flanagan's gone off sick*, was what he'd been told; the words accompanied by an unsmiling stare; the expression of someone who knew the real story behind the flimsy excuse. But it turned out to have been just the expression of someone irritated at the loss of an officer when it was busy and they were already stretched.

He'd trying ringing her … mobile and home number … she wasn't picking up and neither was the lass she was shacked up with, not since his original call when she'd known no more than he had. Jen herself hadn't responded to messages other than a brief text saying she was fine and she'd catch up with him when she was back, not that he believed a word of that.

And here he was now all set for a concerted effort to find out what was going on, but he'd failed to spot Inspector Impatient on the warpath and had been nabbed. Rookie's error.

She banged down the phone and turned to him. 'Missing woman,' she rapped out, pushing a piece of paper towards him. 'Adult, 20s. Her father rang in. Expecting her last night. They left the door on the latch when they went to bed. Not unusual for her to be late. No sign of her this morning and the door still unlocked i.e. she'd not been and gone. Log it in and get round to the parents' house pronto. Give them a ring first just in case she's turned up.'

He looked at the time written at the top of the page. 'Why's it not been logged?'

'System went down. Yeah, I know, backups should kick straight in, well it turns out they don't, not everywhere.' She pointed to the paper in his hand. 'Probably nothing but I'm not happy about it.'

It wasn't until she'd gone that he was able to explore the background buzz of conversation, the air of tension as the shifts swapped.

'What's going on?'

'It's not bloody stopped … well, not till this last hour or so.'

Other voices pitched in to describe an unexpectedly busy night. 'Shit kicking off all through … worse than …'

'Summat behind it?' he asked.

'Nah … random … nothing to put your finger on.'

He nodded. It happened sometimes, but it had put people on edge. If Thursday was bad, what were they in for tonight and Saturday?

He blew out a sigh and sat down, smoothing out the paper he'd been given. He could see why she'd given him a verbal summary. Her notoriously small store of patience had barely held out through the scribbled account.

He scanned the phone number; was that a 4 or a 9, and did it end on 6 or zero? He could do with a name, but the best he could decipher was Suffering, Stifling, Stuffing or at a pinch Starling. Since he had a legible address, he went to the electoral register which gave him Suffling, but only the parents were registered. He looked up their phone number and peered again at the scrawl that was the daughter's name. An initial E followed by an undulating line that might be Elizabeth, though it wasn't really long enough, so maybe Eliza, though that felt wrong for a 22 year old.

He could talk about 'your daughter' and she might have turned up by now.

The phone was snatched up at once. 'Ellie? Ellie, is that you?'

A man's voice; its underlying desperation sending a tingle down Tommy Marchant's spine. He thought of his own daughter, Jess. The stats say it'll be fine, he wanted to reassure the man, but he understood why the night Inspector hadn't been happy.

He told them he was on his way.

Ellie? That wasn't a diminutive he'd ever heard for either Elizabeth or Eliza.

* * *

Annie watched Jennifer settle herself at Pat's desk and start to thumb through the data Mike had given her.

'I'll make the coffee,' she said as she headed for the door.

'Not for me, thanks,' from Jennifer.

Annie glanced at her. She couldn't see her face, just the

top of her head. *What are you keeping from us?* She had to push aside a spark of resentment. Even Lois had joined the morning coffee ritual. But she shouldn't complain if Jennifer wanted to get on with things. She'd already said she would have to leave early. She was conscientiously trying to get in a reasonable number of hours.

More than could be said for some people.

Mike, coming into the small kitchen behind her plucked the thought from her head. 'So much for the dynamic duo mending their ways while Jennifer's here. I bet you they don't show before eleven.'

'Give them a break, Mike, it's barely gone eight. They'll be here for nine.'

'I see downstairs were up and running before us again today.'

'Happens sometimes. Probably got a rush job on.' If he was making a clumsy comparison between the downstairs consultancy and the sisters' time-keeping, she wasn't going to bite.

Nine o'clock came and went.

For form's sake, Annie retrieved the Marshall file and read it with care, delving into every detail, almost as though Rob Small was at her shoulder. She'd told him there was nothing untoward in it, and there wasn't. The paperwork he was desperate to reclaim was sitting at the bottom of the recycling container. By any reasonable definition she'd lied to him, and Rob Small made her uneasy. All her instincts screamed that he was not a safe person to cross, but she'd burnt that bridge when she took the stuffed carrier bag off Miriam. Or maybe she was projecting the man on to his giant robots. She wouldn't want to be the wrong side of those.

He'd been annoyed with her when she'd arrived unannounced and got in the way of his cranes, but been happy to show off his tech and chat about 'poor Jobsie'. His recent hostility stemmed from someone, presumably Miriam, telling him that Lois had the stolen paperwork. She was on flimsy ground; the case file was woefully inadequate, no background, no attempt to substantiate anyone's story. Miriam herself might have led her husband to his death.

The door clicked open. 'Refill?' Mike stepped in and reached for her mug anticipating her affirmative.

She smiled and stood up, stretching the tension out of her shoulders as she walked through to the main office.

'How are you doing, Jen?'

'Yeah, good. Fascinating stuff. I'll be honest, I didn't know you operated at this level. I'm impressed.'

Annie gave Mike a wink, acknowledging his success, and finding herself disproportionately pleased that Jennifer had recognised how far they'd brought the agency.

Mike nodded towards the clock and gave her a 'told you so' look. Ten past eleven. No sign of the Thompsons.

It might be Mike's nagging, but their lax time-keeping was beginning to annoy her. She'd been so certain they would up their game for Jennifer, or anyway that the act would last longer than a couple of days.

The phone rang. It was a client's solicitor asking for Barbara, wanting to clarify loose ends. Annie wasn't familiar with the specifics, so had to get files up on screen and bring herself up to speed on the fly as they talked their way through the detail. It took concentration and the thick end of an hour before she emerged from the call with the beginnings of a headache.

Barbara's phone went to voicemail. Annie cursed, but under her breath, this wasn't a feud to play out in front of Jennifer. As lunchtime came and went, her anger receded. Missing lunch went beyond bad-timekeeping.

Jennifer left at two o'clock, with a promise to be in on Monday morning.

Less than half an hour later, Annie's mobile rang. When she saw Pat's number on the screen, her anger boiled up again. 'What the hell do you–?'

Noise exploded in her ear; shouting and clanking against a background hiss and roar. The mental image was of towering cranes, robotic killing machines swinging giant boxes.

'Babs!' Pat's voice was yelling over the din. 'Is Babs there?'

'No,' Annie shouted back. 'Where are you?'

'Has she been in? Have you seen her?'

'No,' Annie shouted again. 'Where are you?'

'Are you sure? Any call, email, message? Was she in early?'

Early? Barbara? 'No. No message. No nothing.'

'... not there ...' Pat was still shouting, but not into the phone.

'Pat, where are you?' Annie yelled. 'What's going on?'

'It's ... There's– Look, I'll get back to you.'

Suddenly the cacophony was gone. Her head rang with it, but the uproar was no longer there. Pat had cut the call.

CHAPTER 26

Annie gaped at the silent handset. Was Pat in trouble? Had she really sounded scared?

Mike stared at her. 'What's going on? Was that Pat?'

'Who did you think I was talking to?' snapped Annie. She'd shouted Pat's name loud enough to feel the abrasion in her throat. 'She said–'

'I could hear what she said. Where was she? Christmas party?' His voice was hard.

'I think she's in some kind of trouble. She–'

'Bollocks! She's putting it on. She knows they've crossed a line. Just look at the time.'

Annie became aware of the gloom in the office, as though the sun had barely made the effort to rise at all.

'I don't think she was putting it on,' she said. 'That racket … She was outdoors.'

Mike reached for his keyboard, then swung the monitor to face her. 'There's your answer.'

The office diary, single day view, stared back. Pat had a client coming in at three o'clock. She peered closer to read the name. 'I guess I can deal with that.'

'She's playing you, Annie. They both are. You shouldn't have to keep carrying them. They've got to go.'

It seemed pointless to repeat her mantra. *They'll step up*

if they need to … they do more than you think … I owe Pat a lot … Was that the nub of it? Her years-old supposed debt to Pat, for giving her her first job, for letting her run with things when she could have held her back, for saving her life one time in a dark empty car park behind a deserted racecourse? 'Let's at least wait till we find out what's going on,' she said quietly.

'Ring her back.'

Annie put her handset to speaker and returned Pat's call.

The auto-message cut in immediately: *The person you are calling knows you are waiting.* Two beeps. *The person you are calling knows you are waiting.*

They watched the handset in silence, listening to the double beep, the message, the double beep, waiting for Pat to connect the call. But she didn't.

Annie looked at Mike. He'd worked in a cut-throat industry where people didn't get second chances. 'The thing is,' she said. 'Pat doesn't try to hide that she's lazy. If she stayed home to watch a film, she'd say. She wouldn't make up an elaborate cover story. Something's happened and I want to hear what it's about. Now I'm going to get some fresh air.'

He followed her out of the office and they walked side by side down to the coffee bar.

She rang again when they arrived, got a ring tone but was cut off, red-buttoned.

Ignoring Mike's heavenwards glance, she texted, *Do you need help?*

The reply came almost at once: *Yes but not a. Will call.*

Mike leant over to read the screen. 'What the fuck does that mean?'

Annie looked at the disjointed set of words. Pat had started to type something longer but been diverted.

A minute later her phone rang.

'Pat?'

'Yeah.' The clatter and chaos had gone. Pat sounded weary, her voice scratchy. 'I've a three o'clock. Can you take it?'

'Yes, don't worry, I'm on it. What's happened? Where were you?'

'There's been a fire at Babs' house. We thought she was in there. She wasn't.'

'Oh my god! How? When? Was anyone hurt? She had her son and family staying, didn't she?'

'They were out, thankfully, taken the kiddies to Big Fun. They're all fine.'

'But what happened?'

Pat blew out a sigh. 'When she didn't turn up for me and wasn't answering the phone, I went round. Thought she might have gone in without me. We had a bit of a barney yesterday. When no one answered, I opened the letter box to shout. Smelled the smoke at once and called the fire services. I thought she was upstairs. They came real quick but it had taken hold. The back kitchen's gutted but the smoke got everywhere.'

There was a name missing. 'Is Barbara OK?'

'No one knows. That's why I rang you. We don't know where she is. Are you certain you've not heard from her?'

'Not a peep, and we've been in from early. How did the fire start? D'you know?' Aggrieved punters were an occupational hazard, but it was a long time since they'd run afoul of anyone malicious enough to do something like this.

'The fire guy said she'd left the iron on and it had toppled over, likely into the laundry basket. They contained it in the kitchen but it's not nice. It's had all her Christmas shopping too by the looks of it.'

'Let me know what's happening. I'm going to have to go now to get back for your three o'clock.'

As they returned to the office, Annie filled Mike in on the detail he hadn't been able to glean from leaning in to listen. Even he would have to allow them to be late for a house fire.

'Accident?' he asked. 'Or don't they know?'

'Oh, accident for sure. I can't think that we've peeved anyone that badly,' she said.

'Except Lois,' he pointed out. 'If you'd listened to me–'

'If it'd been Lois,' she snapped. 'It'd be our flat gone up in flames. Lois liked Barb. And anyway, a red hot iron on a pile of clothes would do it. She's lost all her Christmas stuff too.'

'Stuff that she's bought on our time, no doubt,' he said sourly.

Annie pushed through the outer door and made for the stairs, then stopped on a gasp. Sounds from above, someone moving about.

'Barbara!' she shouted, taking the stairs two at a time and crashing through the door. 'Where have you–? Oh!'

'Hi Annie, what's up?' said Jennifer.

'Jen, what are you doing back?'

'I had a call as I was on my way. Postponed again. Unbelievable! So I came back.'

'How did you get in?'

Jennifer looked surprised. 'It was open.'

Annie swung round to Mike.

'I locked up,' he said. 'I remember turning the key.'

'But … but why?' Jennifer sounded bewildered. 'You were just downstairs, weren't you?'

'What do you mean? How long have you been back?'

'Not long … couple of minutes … The office was empty but I thought you were in the kitchen. I came in here to take off my coat. Then I heard … well, I thought I heard …'

'What? What did you hear?'

'Someone going downstairs.'

Annie exchanged a glance with Mike. 'A couple of minutes, you said?'

'Uh … well, let's see, I came upstairs. In fact I kind of had two goes at it. I dropped one of my gloves over the bannister and had to go back down for it, but I'd seen that the office door was ajar.'

'Even if we'd forgotten to lock it,' Mike growled. 'We sure as hell didn't leave it open. What happened when you came up?'

'There was no one here, but I thought you were in the kitchen, so I took off my coat, hung it up, sat at the desk and got the file out. I was leafing through it when I heard footsteps going down.' She paused for a moment, narrowing her eyes. 'No, it's been longer than a couple of minutes. I've been flicking through this lot, making notes. Four or five minutes maybe.'

'We've barely been gone ten,' Mike said. 'Didn't you think it was odd that we'd just go out and leave you on your own without saying anything?'

'I didn't think you had. I thought you'd gone down for the post or something.'

Annie put her hand on Mike's arm to stop him moving

158

further into the room. 'Wait,' she said, as she cast her eye all around the space, the desks, the filing drawers, the PCs, the keyboards, the doorway to the back office. She could see where Jennifer had opened one of the drawers to retrieve the file Mike had asked her to read, and the way Jennifer's coat rippled Pat and Barb's spare scarves out of line, but there was more. The light trace of someone's movements shimmered through the space. She felt she could track a methodical fingertip search, starting to the right of the doorway and working round, just the way she'd have done it. Interrupted, thankfully, by Jennifer's return.

'I don't suppose you put the cameras on?' Mike asked.

Annie shook her head. 'We were only going to be ten minutes. We don't turn on the cameras in working hours,' she explained to Jennifer.

Jennifer nodded. 'Same at my old job. Can't spy on your own employees. Cameras are only in the public areas.'

'From now on,' Mike said. 'Those cameras go on anytime we're out of the office.'

That had originally been the procedure, but just as with the clone-phones, they'd grown lax.

'Wait a minute!' Jennifer jumped up from her chair, a triumphant grin on her face. 'Downstairs, the reception area's got a camera. It'll have everyone going in and out. You … you are allowed to access it, aren't you?'

'It's their space, not ours,' said Mike, 'but we look out for each other after a fashion. They'll let us see it. If they don't, you can whip out your warrant card.'

Jennifer gave him a hard stare. 'Don't even joke about it. I'm in enough trouble as it is. Uh … anyway, let's go and see if they'll let us look right now.'

Annie exchanged the ghost of a glance with Mike. Jennifer hadn't meant to say that. She'd almost swallowed her tongue in diving off the topic. *So, you're in enough trouble as it is, are you? I'll find out.*

'You two go,' she said, as the click of the outer door sounded from downstairs. 'That'll be Pat's three o'clock. I'll use my office. Jen, when you heard footsteps going down the stairs, did you think it was me or Mike?'

'I wasn't really paying attention … I suppose I thought it was you. I mean, I didn't think it was Mike.'

Annie nodded. Jennifer had heard a light tread that she'd instinctively classed as a woman's.

* * *

Tommy Marchant kept a close eye on the clock. He had just to finish his report on the missing girl then he was done.

'It had a bad feel to it at the start,' he said. 'It looked out of character, but I don't think it is. It's the parents. Very jumpy and protective. She's left home, goes back reasonably regularly but she's not as reliable as they think. Not according to the group of friends I got to talk to. If she met a guy and decided he was a better bet than an early night at her parents' house, she'd have stayed out and made her excuses later.'

'But she's not turned up?'

'No, not yet. Her friends reckon she's gone off with someone and got wasted. They're confident she'll turn up this evening with a story of having been taken ill.'

'Wasted on what?'

'Just alcohol, they said.' He rolled his eyes. 'A cocktail of whatever's going, I'd guess. My main worry is that she's taken a bad batch of something. They've called up anywhere that any of them could think of calling up; it's all logged. And I've checked the hospitals, she's not landed there.'

'You're saying you think she'll turn up tonight?'

He nodded. 'She needs to, or the stats'll turn against her.'

'You've dinned into them to let us know the second she walks back through the door?'

'Oh yeah, don't worry about that. You'll get calls from the parents whether or not she turns up tonight. Like I say, they're jumpy, see it as out of character, but I think it's more that their little girl has grown up and they hadn't noticed before.' Just like it was for me and Dugs, he thought, when our Jessica grew up.

'What's her name, Elizabeth Suffling?'

'Not Elizabeth, Eloise. Her parents call her Ellie.' As he spoke Tommy pulled himself to his feet, adding, 'Her friends call her Lois.'

CHAPTER 27

'I'll have that data sent on before the end of the day.' Annie ushered Pat's client back downstairs. They exchanged a handshake and he disappeared into the street.

Annie turned and pounded back up the stairs to Mike and Jennifer. 'Well? Did you see who it was?'

Jennifer shook her head. 'Hopeless, Annie. They'd not looked at it in months.'

'It was running,' Mike said. 'But it just showed grey fog.'

'I mean why bother at all?' Jennifer snapped.

Mike caught Annie's eye with the glimmer of a smile. 'I had to drag Jennifer off. She was launching into a full-blown crime-prevention lecture.'

'They need one.' Jennifer looked round. 'With them being so useless, we need to be on the ball up here. I can help you out, placement of cameras, all that sort of thing.'

'Thanks, we're fine for now. We were the ones being lax, not turning our cameras on.'

When Jennifer was a proper member of the team, Annie thought she might issue a challenge. *You've got five minutes, how many cameras can you find?* She wouldn't get them all, and neither would the next intruder. There was nothing Jennifer could tell her about surveillance.

When the locksmith arrived, Annie told Mike and

Jennifer to go. 'I've some data to chase up for Pat's client. No point in all of us waiting around.'

Once he'd done, Annie tossed the new keys in her hand, and wondered whether or not to phone Pat, but there was little chance of either sister coming in over the weekend, especially not now. She had just decided that she would drop a key in over the weekend when an email from Pat popped up.

Babs back. Pissed off. House stinks of smoke. Water everywhere. Fire's had all her Christmas shopping. She hadn't unpacked it. See you Monday.

Annie typed out a quick reply to say she was glad Barbara was safe and sound. 'I *am* glad,' she murmured, just as if Mike was at her side, giving her his raised-eyebrows look.

The last vestige of daylight was long gone; the uncurtained windows showed no definition to the buildings they backed on to, which were largely abandoned and awaiting demolition. She could hear people moving about downstairs but the outer door would be locked by now. As she set the cameras, she checked each of them on her phone, making sure they showed a clear picture.

Should she take Rob Small's papers, because what else could the intruder have been after?

They hadn't left the office unlocked; Mike might be unsure, but she could see the trail in the tiniest of tell-tale signs, drawers that had been opened then closed again, not quite lining up, dust unsettled. She would guess they'd been through one filing cabinet before Jennifer's arrival had cut them off.

She couldn't take the papers. They were a hell of a weight and she didn't have the car.

Satisfied she'd left things as secure as she could, she locked up and headed out.

By the time she reached home, she was damp and cold, but a welcoming smell of frying onions greeted her.

'Get out of your wet things,' Mike called through. 'Food's ready.'

As they sat down to eat, Annie said, 'Could Lois have got her hands on an office key?'

'I wouldn't put it past Barb to have given her one, not that she'd ever admit it. Did you tell her she had to return the agency's property?'

'Uh … not as such. I didn't think she had anything.' Nearer to the truth was that she hadn't given it a thought.

He let out a sigh of exasperation. 'You didn't give her any paperwork, did you? For God's sake, Annie, I told you exactly what process to follow.'

'I didn't have the chance. She stormed out. OK, OK …' She held up her hands in surrender. 'I got things wrong, I admit it.'

'Got things wrong? You totally fucked it up. We might still legally be employing her. Shit, you need to contact her. Text her. Ask if she left any personal stuff in the office and if she took a key away with her.'

'You want *me* to text Lois?'

'Yes. Do it now. Let's get some kind of paper trail in place. No accusations, just a friendly text. OK?'

'But … oh, OK.' She clicked out a succinct message, held it pointedly up to Mike to approve, and then pressed send. 'She won't reply.'

'Never mind, we have an address. We'll get the paperwork in the post to her. Why do you think she had a key?'

'It could have been her today, coming after Rob Small's paperwork. Her way of getting back at me. She was going to take it to Rob Small to show I was lying.'

He looked at her with a mixture of exasperation and concern. 'Lois doesn't know about the paperwork. I'd no idea she'd got to you this badly, Annie.' He reached across the table to take her hand but it felt like he was comforting a recalcitrant child and she pulled her arm away.

'Miriam told Richard Redman that she'd let Lois look through her husband's stuff, implying Lois had taken the paperwork behind her back. Redman must have told Small. He said, "Your junior lifted some paperwork." He knows about Lois.'

'OK, but how would Lois know him?'

'Small could have traced her easily enough. Miriam has her number. She'd have denied having anything but what if she said she'd get it back for him? He might have offered her money. You said you'd seen her watching the office.'

He frowned. 'I saw her over the road; I didn't say she was watching the office. Her friend works across there, doesn't she? But why didn't Miriam just give the papers back to Small?'

'I think she's scared to admit she's seen them. Look how she's been, accusing him of murder one minute, then hanging on his arm at the funeral.'

'And from what I could see, she practically cut Richard Redman.'

'Yeah, I remember. I don't think she likes either of them, but it's Rob Small she's scared of.' Annie thought back over the things she'd seen and heard. 'I hope for her sake she's not fixed on the wrong one.'

CHAPTER 28

Annie woke earlier than usual and slipped out of bed, leaving Mike dead to the world. He'd been up into the small hours planning his and Jennifer's strategy for their big meeting; he'd earned his lie-in. She'd thought she'd earned hers too, but her mind wouldn't rest about the events of the previous day.

It was early enough that she might be back before he woke up, so she plucked the car keys from his jacket pocket, let herself out and headed to the office.

The street was deserted. Blank-faced buildings showed dark windows or closed blinds. In a couple of hours, life would return. A good many of the businesses opened Saturday morning, a handful staying open all day. As she unlocked the outer door, she became aware of someone moving about behind the shuttered reception desk. The camera lens twinkled at her, its pinpoint light showing that it was watching, even if it wasn't recording anything useful.

The stairs creaked as she climbed them. They always creaked. They'd given away Jennifer's approach yesterday, allowing whoever-it-was to go swiftly to the tiny kitchen and await their chance to slip out. She tried the office door to confirm it was locked, then went along the landing, checking behind doors, in cupboards, in every corner that might conceal a person.

Once sure she was alone upstairs, she let herself into the main office and stood just inside the door, letting her gaze take in every millimetre, checking against her mental image of yesterday evening when she'd left. A flashing light signalled voicemail but nothing else had changed. Whoever had tried yesterday had not been back in the night. Maybe they'd given up.

Reaching out, she clicked the button to play the voicemail.

Message for Annie Raymond …

Rob Small's voice.

Annie, I owe you an apology. I've had my paperwork returned. In my defence, I could only think of your people who might have got their hands on it, so I assumed you were holding out on me. If our paths cross again, I owe you a drink.

His words sent her diving for the small office where she flipped the lid on the recycling container. The papers were there in a solid mass at the bottom. 'You haven't,' she murmured. 'It's all still here.'

What was she to make of that? His tone had been relaxed and friendly, as different from his last call as the change she'd seen in him at Havenmere Docks when she'd morphed from an anonymous visitor to a supposed friend of his old mate, Jobsie.

The staircase creaked. She spun round to face the door.

'Miss Raymond,' a voice called. 'Is that you up there?'

She stepped out on to the landing and looked down into the face of the manager from the downstairs consultancy.

'Hi. What can I do for you?'

'My colleague spoke to Mr Connaughty yesterday, and that new woman you have with you, the one with the severe expression. They told me about your intruder. There's something I think you should see.'

Downstairs, behind the still-shuttered reception counter Annie sat at a console where the manager indicated a screen that showed a smudged grey vista.

'That's what we saw when we checked.'

She nodded. 'Camera seized up?'

'Absolutely not!' He gave her a glare. 'After we'd inspected it, I checked some earlier footage. This …' He reached across to click the time back by several hours, 'is yesterday morning.'

This time the picture was clear, showing the reception area, shutter closed, the outer door and the corner of the stairs. The door opened and the man sitting next to her appeared on the screen, stepping over the threshold and pausing to look around, unsmiling, before turning to the door and clicking the catch to leave it unlocked. It had been unlocked when she and Mike arrived. Mike had commented on it. They were used to being first here.

'Well, there's nothing wrong with that shot,' Annie murmured, adding, 'What were you looking for?' His gaze at one point had met her eye through the camera lens.

'I always take a good look at the face we present to the world,' he told her grandly. 'It's too easy to become complacent.'

The seconds ticked by on the monitor; the empty space stared back at them. Annie looked at the timestamp.

'Forgive me, but you're not usually in at that time.'

'Early meeting,' he rapped out. 'Important. Couldn't

schedule at any other time. My girls get time off in lieu.' He indicated the screen that showed the door opening again and a group of five or six people crowding in. Annie cringed a little at 'my girls' and peered closer, not sure there wasn't a man at the back of the group. He/she moved towards the stairs, then stopped, grabbing clumsily at a small case that seemed in danger of bursting open, possibly just using the stair rail to lean on.

The rest bustled across the floor and disappeared under the camera.

At once the figure by the stairs dropped all semblance of clumsiness and darted forward, closing on the camera. A hand holding something reached up. Annie was at the edge of her seat. Whoever it was, kept their head down, showing only a woollen hat to the lens, but they would surely have to look up, if only fleetingly, to see what they were doing.

The head tipped back. Annie gaped at a brief glimpse of a Halloween mask, then the close-up of an aerosol nozzle, and grey fog smothered the view.

She reached out to stop the film and wound it back to when the group came in. Now she knew what was to come, she kept a close eye on the figure at the back. That moment of bending over the small case; that had to be when the mask went on.

This time as the image flooded with grey, the man beside her put out his hand, signalling her to keep it rolling.

'Listen.' He pointed towards the now obscured screen.

Annie heard a click and then a low rumble.

'Click of the door,' he said, with an air of grim triumph. 'That ruffian got out just before we opened the reception shutter.'

Annie looked at the timestamp. Whoever it was had been on the cusp of cannoning into her and Mike on their way in.

'All set for later,' she murmured. No key to the outer door, so the only way to nobble the camera had been to follow someone in and do it before the shutter was opened. It had taken some nerve.

'Clearly, he was preparing the way for later,' the man said. 'If you let it run, you'll hear yourself and Mr Connaughty arrive in a couple of minutes and go up the stairs.'

'The women he came in with. Have you shown them this?'

'I've not told anyone what was done. And I don't want to. It spreads unrest. But I showed the girls those few seconds where the intruder comes through the door behind them. One said they thought it was a woman for upstairs, one said a man, and the rest didn't notice anyone at all.'

'I'd like a copy of the footage, if I may.'

He shook his head. 'I've shown you because I thought you needed to know, but I don't want to invite trouble in.'

'OK, then let me run it through again.'

'Don't be all day. I need to get on.'

He stood up and moved to the photocopier where a stack of papers were balanced. Annie took the footage back to the locked door, slipping out her phone and setting it to video the screen as the early morning scenario played out. Behind her, she could hear the smooth hum of the copier and grinding noise of a shredder in a monotonous rhythm. He was scanning and shredding. Exactly what she would love to do with Rob Small's papers were it feasible.

She let the recording run on beyond the aerosol attack until she heard the outer door open again followed by the unmistakable creaking of the stairs as she and Mike arrived.

Whoever it was could have had almost five minutes uninterrupted if they'd gone straight up.

'No harm done, as luck would have it,' she said as she stopped the recording.

'Hmm, well … Whoever he was, he was after your agency, not mine. But that was my camera he damaged.'

'Did the stuff clean off?'

'Yes, it was paint. Messy.'

She got up to go. If a bill for cleaning the camera arrived, Mike could deal with it.

This had shattered any last sliver of doubt about whether it had been an opportunist, or a planned raid to retrieve those papers. But it didn't explain why Rob Small was claiming to have had them back.

CHAPTER 29

Pacing the office floor, Annie tossed the car keys in her hand, regretting her earlier laziness. A few years ago she wouldn't have thought twice about an early morning run to get here, and after what she'd heard, a jog back across the city was just what she needed to clear her head. But Mike might have plans to go somewhere and she couldn't face his exasperation if he found she'd abandoned the car miles away – again.

From downstairs she could hear the manager walking about, cupboard doors squeaking open and closed. They too were on to some new business angle – or that was the impression she'd got: the big important meeting, his reluctance to rock the boat over what the camera had shown.

Check the cameras, lock the door, and leave the building. A simple enough plan but she found her gaze drawn again to the closed door of the back office.

Rob Small thought he'd had his paperwork returned. His message had been friendly. She could return his call … ask a few questions. It would be natural for her to be curious. Miriam felt like an easier target but was likely to blab to Small anyway. The loose end flapped. Maybe it was time to come in from another angle. Richard Redman was the mystery man who sat somewhere between Small and Miriam; it was his son who had found the body.

'Taking out the trash,' she murmured.

She crossed the room to the cramped inner sanctum, pulled the recycling container out from its corner, dragged it to the top of the stairs and manhandled it down. From behind the shuttered reception counter, she heard the hum of the photocopier and rumble of the shredder. That was good. It placed him at the front of the building and not in the back room that overlooked the yard.

The eagle-eye of the camera twinkled at her.

A blast of cold air pushed the door wide as she unlocked it to let herself out and manoeuvred the load down the narrow passage that led to the back yard, glancing back before turning the dog-leg that would hide her from the street – no one went by, no cars, no sign of life from the building opposite. Round the corner, she faced the gate; solid, sturdy and high with a razor-wire topping that was probably illegal. She unlocked it and pushed through with her cargo, shoving it closed behind her.

The few windows that overlooked the yard were either shuttered or opaque with dirt like the small sixteen-pane aperture to their own back office. No one brought window cleaners round here. She thrust her arms into the recycling container, grabbing the solid mass that was the concertinaed block of paper.

Across the ancient asphalt, a long-obsolete coal bunker sat against the back wall. She balanced the armful of paper as she scrambled up on to it.

Speed was of the essence now. The longer she took, the more likely someone would see her or wonder about how long this routine task was taking her. She tipped the paperwork over in a block, hearing the folds cascade into the brambles. Jumping back down she grabbed the few sheets of legitimate waste and stuffed them into the bin, letting the lid clatter shut.

Returning to the road, dusting her hands down her jeans, she carried the empty container upstairs, checked the cameras and locks and headed out again.

There's no one watching, she told herself, as she climbed into the car and started the engine. This early on a Saturday, where would they watch from?

In an hour or so, she would return by a circuitous route to the backstreet. If nothing seemed out of place, and if it was as deserted as it would usually be, she would fight through the brambles of the waste ground behind an empty terrace and retrieve the papers she'd dumped. If anything didn't feel right, she would leave them there to rot.

Either way, if anyone was watching, and she was sure now that someone had been, they would have seen her clear out the trash, like she'd done numerous times, and then leave empty handed.

CHAPTER 30

Annie and Mike arrived early Monday morning, expecting to be first in the building, but although the street door was locked, they heard voices from behind the closed reception shutter as soon as they stepped inside. They exchanged a glance.

'Business on the up for all of us,' Mike murmured.

Annie made a point of looking directly at the camera which sparkled back at her. If she'd thought to look at it on Friday morning, there would have been no tell-tale glittering star, just a smudge of grey paint.

She and Mike had talked things through but his focus had been on his big meeting. Jennifer was pretty much up to speed, but what if she got called away at the last minute? 'You'll have to make sure it's all at your fingertips too, Annie. In case you need to step in.'

Rob Small's paperwork was now stashed in the flat, tucked inside a double bin-bag. It had emerged from the brambles ripped and jumbled, covered in mud that didn't smell good. Neither of them had felt like looking through it again.

The Thompsons wouldn't be in. Pat had called on Sunday afternoon. 'I'll try and come round Monday evening,' she'd said. 'You won't be out, will you? Babs is fine but we've some stuff to get straight. And there's something I need to run past you.'

Rob Small's message played on Annie's mind. He'd sounded so convincing. Had someone got their hands on a few pages and given them back? But he knew that more than a few pages were involved.

Leaving Mike to prepare the morning coffee, Annie stood in the doorway to the main office and let her gaze scan every inch, although she knew no one had been in, because if they had, the cameras would have told her.

The street door banged and she heard Jennifer's tread on the stairs. Annie intercepted her. 'Mike's making coffee,' she said, and led the way to the kitchen.

He handed over the steaming mugs. 'What are the chances of you being called away on Wednesday?' he asked Jennifer.

'There's nothing scheduled, but I can't promise. Things seem to be ramping up a bit.'

Annie glanced at her. The worry in her voice was palpable. Was this the moment she came clean with them? 'Anything we can do to help?' she asked.

'Uh … thanks … No, no, it'll be fine.'

Fleetingly, Annie met Mike's eye. Jennifer had been close to cracking, but had pulled back.

'Annie's going to get up to speed, too,' said Mike. 'Just to cover the bases.' He turned to Annie. 'It'd be good if you two could go through the stuff me and Jennifer talked about on Friday. I'm going to have to get in touch with a few people now we've lost the Thompsons for who-knows-how-long.'

'Oh? What's happened?'

Between them, they told Jennifer about Barbara's house fire.

'Glad no one was hurt,' Jennifer said. 'Was it an accident, do you think?'

'Barb's careless enough to have done it,' Mike said. 'But there's always a question mark. Cases turn nasty. Revenge attacks can pop up after years.'

The discussion meandered into who would check up on the Thompson sisters' cases to make sure no balls were dropped. Jennifer volunteered to help but Mike vetoed that. 'It'll be easier for me to untangle their records and I'd rather you helped Annie get up to speed on what we went through on Friday.'

An hour later, Annie found herself laughing with Jennifer as they thumbed through files and talked about the people who would be at Mike's big meeting on Wednesday. Mike was at the far desk, head in one hand, phone in the other fire-fighting his way through Pat and Barbara's live cases. Annie flashed him a sympathetic smile. Pat and Barb had their own way of doing things.

It was good to work with Jennifer. Memories resurfaced of her early years in Hull. They'd been thrown into some unexpected tight spots and hadn't done a bad job of looking out for each other, but it had been different then. They'd been on the same side only nominally. If Mike's new initiatives paid off, this agency was really going places, and Jennifer would be a real asset. Annie could only pray that whatever her old job had done to her, it would spit her out intact and ready to join them.

When she heard the street door open, she glanced at the diary to confirm they weren't expecting anyone, but a voice floated up the stairs. 'You want the Thompsons' Agency, Officer. Top of the stairs.'

Officer?

Jennifer's head shot up. Annie met Mike's eye before staring at Jennifer, who had half risen from her chair.

'Thank you,' said a man's voice, and heavy footsteps sounded followed by the creak of the bottom step.

Jennifer was on her feet, her voice a panicked whisper. 'I know him! He'll recognise me. You have to stop him!'

Too late for Jennifer to scuttle through to the kitchen. The stairs choreographed a heavy tread making its way upward.

'My office,' Annie hissed, pushing open the door as Jennifer rushed in. 'Keep quiet,' she mouthed as she pulled it shut, then leapt across to the main door to greet their visitor.

She found herself faced with a middle-aged man, packing a bit too much weight for his height, his expression serious but not unpleasant.

'Ms Annie Raymond?' he greeted her. 'And is that Mr Michael Connaughty?' He nodded towards the desk where Mike was sitting.

'That's right,' said Annie. 'What can we do for you, Mr … uh …?'

'Detective Constable Tommy Marchant.' He held out a warrant card that Annie leant forward to study. 'I wanted to have a word about one of your employees. May I come in?'

'Sure.' Annie grabbed a chair and placed it so that DC Marchant would have his back to the door that hid Jennifer. This had to be about Barb. Pat had said she had something to run past them. There must have been more to her house fire than carelessness.

Once seated, Marchant pulled out a notebook and pen. 'I understand you employ a young woman called Eloise Suffling.'

'Lois?' said Annie, surprised. 'Uh … well … we did, but not any more.'

'She's no longer with you?'

'She was with us for a probationary period,' Mike said. 'It recently ended and we decided not to keep her on.'

'Ah, I see.' Marchant wrote something in his book. 'And when was this?'

Annie thought back. 'The week before last, the Thursday.' She leant to check the dates on the nearest monitor.

'And was she expecting it? Did she seem upset at all?'

'Well … um … yes, I suppose … I mean she must have known things hadn't gone brilliantly, but she wasn't ecstatic when I told her. Why do you ask? Has she made some sort of complaint?'

'What sort of complaint might she have made, Ms Raymond?'

'I don't know … unfair dismissal or something.'

'That wouldn't be a police matter, but she was upset, was she?'

Mike stood up and moved his chair out from the desk, wheeling it closer to where Annie sat facing Marchant. There was tension in the room. Annie knew it was all to do with Jennifer tucked away in the room behind them but what would Marchant make of it?

'What's the problem?' said Mike as he sat down again, leaning towards Marchant, putting on his concerned face. 'Lois is OK, isn't she?'

'I hope so, Mr Connaughty, I–'

'Mike, please. Let's not stand on ceremony. We were saying only the other day we hoped she'd landed on her feet. She wasn't a bad employee, but she just didn't have what we needed. And yes, as Annie said, she was upset that we let her go, but it wasn't anything much. She *is* OK, isn't she?'

Annie thought about Lois ambushing her in the pub four days after she'd been sent packing; the drunken tirade had been witnessed by everyone in the bar.

'As I say, Mr Conn– Mike, I hope she's fine and dandy, but the fact is she was reported missing several days ago and we'd like to find her to make sure. When did you last see her?'

Annie wondered if Jennifer could hear. Not much sound leaked through, but Jennifer would surely have her ear to the keyhole.

Mike looked troubled. 'Not to speak to, but I thought I saw her last Thursday morning. Was it Thursday, Annie? D'you remember, I said I'd seen her across the road?'

'Yes, it was just a week after we'd … uh … parted company.' Annie turned to Tommy Marchant. 'Lois had a friend who worked in the building over the road. It's how she heard that we were looking for someone in the first place.'

He wrote some more in his notebook. 'This friend, d'you have a name?'

'Sorry, no, but I'm sure they'll know if you call in and ask. It's not a big outfit.'

'What time Thursday?'

Annie let Mike take the reins of the conversation. They seemed to have bypassed the altercation in the pub, though

180

it wouldn't be the end of the world to mention it. She listened as DC Marchant and Mike teased bits of information out of each other. Mike occasionally appealed to her to confirm what he was saying. 'That's right, isn't it, Annie?'

The story unfolded. Lois had missed a visit to her parents on Friday night. They were worried. Though she'd not known Lois well, Annie wanted to say, *It's only Monday morning; she'll have been on a bender over the weekend. She'll turn up this evening right as rain.* Then she thought of Miriam telling Richard Redman that Lois had rifled through her husband's possessions ... Rob Small saying he'd had his paperwork back, and said instead, 'Have you tracked down any of Lois's friends?'

'Why? Was there someone in particular?'

She shook her head. 'I just thought her friends might have a better idea where she's likely to be than her parents. She's young, no ties. Maybe she got another job, something casual ...'

His expression was neutral as he acknowledged her point.

After they'd ushered him out, Mike stayed by the top of the stairs watching as he left, then murmured, 'I'll see if he's going across the road,' as he turned towards the kitchen.

Annie followed and they watched Tommy Marchant pause at the kerbside until a car had gone by, then head across to disappear into the building opposite.

'I hope she's OK,' Mike murmured.

'Disproportionate effort,' Annie murmured. 'Lois is not Miss Reliable. She didn't show up at her parents' Friday night. It's only Monday morning. It's a bit early to panic.'

'Just because you didn't like her–'

181

'No, I didn't mean that. I meant if they're making serious enquiries at this stage, there's more to it.'

'Go on.'

'Rob Small thought Lois had taken his paperwork. Now he says he's got it back. But he hasn't. I don't want to tangle us up in anything. It's just that I don't like the feel of it. We need to chase up that voicemail from Rob Small, but not while Jennifer's here.' She glanced round. 'Has Jennifer come out? She might not realise he's gone.'

'He might come back after he's done with them over the road.'

She put out her hand to stop him on the landing. 'It must have been Lois,' she said, keeping her voice low. 'And … Barb?'

He looked at her, puzzled.

She shushed him as he began to speak. 'Let me work it through … fit it together. We'll talk when we're on our own.'

She strode through the main office and pulled open the door at the back. 'Coast clear. You can come out.'

Jennifer was sitting at the desk; Annie's appearance made her jump. She seemed on the point of collapse.

'That was close.' Jennifer tried for a light-hearted tone, but she looked desperate … almost scared. Annie watched her loosen her grip on the edge of the desk and run her hands through her hair, before blowing out a breath and giving a half laugh as she reached down to massage her calf. 'Cramp. I've hardly dared move in case he heard me.'

There'd been no ear to the keyhole. Jennifer had heard nothing; she'd been frozen to the chair.

'I wouldn't have let him through, not without a warrant. Don't worry. He didn't suspect a thing.'

'Annie, there's something … uh … are you sure he's gone … driven off?'

At last, thought Annie, we're going to get the story. 'He's gone to call across the road. We watched him go.'

'I'm going to check from the kitchen window. I want to see him drive off.' Jennifer stood up, grimacing, stretched out her leg, and moved past Mike towards the landing.

Annie let her gaze sweep round the small room. 'Jennifer,' she called sharply. 'Did you shift that?'

Jennifer hurried back. Annie pointed to the recycling container that had been pushed against the wall.

'No, I didn't go over there. I've not moved anything.' She cast a worried look towards the landing, then turned to Mike. 'Mike, could you check that he leaves … drives away?'

Mike, on the point of taking his seat again, gave her a look of surprise. 'I'm listening out in case he calls back. He won't catch us on the hop again.'

'Please … I really need to know he's properly gone.'

'OK.' Mike shrugged and got to his feet.

Annie found herself unsure whether it was a genuine need to know that Marchant had gone, or a ploy to get Mike out of earshot. She said nothing as Jennifer joined her again at the threshold of her office.

'Imagine if he'd caught me here,' Jennifer said. 'I've been sitting on the edge of that chair barely daring to breathe, looking for a hiding place or another way out.'

'There isn't one,' Annie said.

'I know. I doubt I could even have got under the desk. The thing is …' She paused and tipped her head towards the container. 'I didn't touch that. I didn't even notice it.'

183

She met Annie's eye. 'And I didn't do that.' She pointed at the small window that overlooked the yard.

Annie was there in a single stride, gaping at the frame. 'It doesn't open,' she said. 'It's never opened.'

'Well, someone's had a good go at it.'

CHAPTER 31

Mike returned to tell them Marchant was gone. 'He didn't stay long across there.'

Jennifer sagged with relief, then seemed to make an effort to pull herself together. 'I'm sorry. D'you mind? I need to get some fresh air. Five minutes, no more.' With that, she plucked her jacket from the coat rack and clattered down the stairs.

Annie glanced behind her at the now-closed door to her office.

'Could she hear us? She didn't ask why he was–'

Mike's upraised hand stopped her. 'Just a sec.' He grabbed his phone, gave her a wink and said, 'Wait here.'

She watched him tread lightly down the stairs. He'd had a decided cat-who-got-the-cream expression on his face. After a moment's indecision, she straightened the chairs then went to the kitchen where she leant over the counter to see around the intrusive corners of the sign.

No Mike. No Jennifer. They'd had time to nip across the road to where Marchant had been pursuing his enquiries. Whatever was going on, Mike would tell her later. She returned to her office and looked again at the window. It might be opaque with dirt but its frame was sturdy and its sixteen glass panels were thick. Suppose it could be opened, she doubted she'd fit through. Down below, the yard lay in shadow. With the high walls all around, it wouldn't see sunlight until next spring. She braced her hands under the lip of the frame and pushed hard. Not a chance.

But as Jennifer said, someone had had a good go at it; had tried to open it from the inside.

Layers of paint had been scraped away across the joins; bits of wood had been scratched, tiny cuts as though some small creature with sharp teeth had been nibbling along the edge. She could see scraps of curling paint and dust on the narrow sill, a white powdery residue on the skirting board. It was recent damage.

This window as a security issue hadn't been a live topic since … She had to stop to think back, right back, to the Thompsons first taking on the lease. From her point of view, a lifetime ago.

Suppose it could be forced open, no one could get through the gap, except a child or very small adult. She thought of Lois's slight build. But when would anyone be desperate enough to try? It was a long drop to the dank area around the bins, a blank brick wall with no handholds down to solid concrete.

She wiped all around the frame and cleaned the fallen debris from the skirting board. If anyone had a second try, she wanted to spot it right away.

The click of the door from downstairs; a background sound against the everyday business of the agency, but a noise she was especially attuned to just now. It was Mike's tread heavy on the stairs and he wasn't hanging about, taking them in twos. He catapulted into the office and flung himself into his chair to catch his breath.

'Tell you later,' he panted, finger to his lips, then as the click of the door sounded again, he turned his whole attention to the screen in front of him, pen in one hand, mouse in the other.

When Jennifer re-entered, he didn't look up.

'OK Jen,' said Annie. 'We'd better pick up where we left off.'

A glance at Mike who was picking up the phone. He still had that cat-with-the-cream air about him.

She slid her chair closer to Jennifer's and kept her voice low, ostensibly to avoid interrupting Mike's call. 'Before, you started to say there was something you wanted to tell me.'

'Uh … oh, yeah … that was about the window. I've seen enough of it in my time. Usually it's worse damage, with a stack of broken glass and … uh … it's usually been done from the outside. It's recent. Presumably, the intruder I managed to miss the other day.' She gave an embarrassed laugh.

'Well, no harm done,' Annie murmured. Jennifer *had* been going to say something else, but she'd changed her mind.

They returned to the mass of notes and information for Mike's Wednesday meeting. Annie wondered which of them would end up going with him.

It was important she had all this stuff at her fingertips; this wasn't a task to skim; but it was hard to concentrate. She wanted to be alone with Mike to talk through her still half-formed theory about Lois and Barbara. If she was honest, she wanted Pat in the discussion too. She also wanted to quiz him about the way he'd followed Jennifer.

CHAPTER 32

The light was all but gone by the time they finished. Sending Mike and Jennifer on ahead, Annie set the cameras and had a last look round before she locked up. It was as secure as she could make it, but somehow didn't feel that way. She caught them up a short way down the road, and pulled her jacket tight around her against a biting wind. Streetlights picked out gleaming snakes of water; cars swished by, spraying mud. It had rained heavily during the afternoon, and felt like it would pour down again any moment.

Unable to quiz Mike, she turned to Jennifer. 'When that detective was here, could you hear what he was saying?'

'Indistinct voices, nothing clear. There's quite a bit of background noise in that small room.'

'Heating system,' said Mike. 'The pipes run up the back wall.'

As the rain began to pepper them with ice-cold darts, Annie laughed at Jennifer's look of surprise. 'That's right, we have a heating system. I wondered if you'd heard him say what he'd come for, only you didn't ask. In your shoes, it'd have been my first question.'

'I assumed it was something private to do with a case.'

'In this business we don't have hierarchies.' Annie had to raise her voice as they turned the corner and met the wind head on. 'You should ask questions. It was about Lois. Her parents reported her missing on Friday.'

Jennifer half turned to her. 'It's only Monday. She's a grown woman. What's the angle?'

'Yeah, we were wondering. Thinking back, I suppose he was trying to make something of us sacking her.'

'She wasn't sacked,' Mike put in testily. 'She was at the end of her probation and we didn't keep her on. D'you want a lift, Jen?'

Jennifer glanced skywards then down at her watch. 'Thanks, can you drop me at the bus station?'

Annie narrowed her eyes. If she'd known Mike was going to offer and Jennifer to accept, she'd have saved the conversation for the car. It wasn't quite comfortable to be discussing it at volume in the street, not that there was anyone in earshot through the whistling of the wind. The three of them increased their pace as the car park entrance came into view.

Lightning burst across the sky and thunder cracked as Annie sprinted the last few metres to the concrete arch, ducking under cover as a deluge poured down. They shared a look of relief to have missed a thorough soaking, as they turned to plod up the dank cave of the stairway.

'Could you find out about Lois?' Mike said to Jennifer. 'There's more to it if people are out making enquiries. You could ask someone, couldn't you?'

'Like who?' Jennifer sounded as surprised as Annie felt.

'You must still be in touch with people. Or are you *persona non grata* across the board?'

He spoke lightly as though to make a joke of it, but Jennifer's tone was frosty as she snapped, 'Pretty much.'

Conversation was desultory as Annie drove them across town, though she couldn't help noticing the look that was back on Mike's face; cat with the cream.

After they dropped Jennifer at the bus station, Annie drove round to park the car. 'Let's get a drink and some sarnis here,' she said. 'I can't be bothered cooking tonight.'

'You never do,' said Mike, but still with a smile on his face.

She pulled out her phone. 'I'm going to see if Pat can join us. There's something I want to run past you both.'

They found a quiet corner of the large hotel lobby and settled with their drinks, food ordered and on its way.

'What is it you want to talk about?' said Mike.

'You first.' She checked her phone. 'In case Pat joins us. My message is showing read but she's not responded yet. I don't want to have to say it all twice.'

'OK.' He sat forward, the self-satisfied smile became a grin. 'You'll like this … Oh!'

His tone faded to disappointment as he looked over her shoulder. Annie turned.

'Hiya, Kid.' Pat stood there with an enormous umbrella which she shook vigorously. 'I was in St Stephens when I got your message so I thought I'd nip across.'

Annie moved up to give Pat room to sit. A waitress arrived with two plates of sandwiches which she set down in front of Annie and Mike.

Pat tapped her arm and proffered a note. 'Can you get me a coffee?'

'Anything to eat, madam?'

'Uh … nah, I'll be fine. Not stopping long.' The waitress turned away. Pat reached forward, saying, 'Thanks, don't mind if I do,' and plucked a sandwich from each of their plates.

Annie hastily grabbed a handful of her own sandwiches and Mike slid his plate out of range.

'OK.' Annie took in a breath. 'I've not thought this through fully … well I couldn't without you, Pat, because it hinges on something you said.'

'Uh-oh, wild goose chase coming up,' Pat murmured glancing at Mike.

'Just listen. You started this with what you said about Barbara. Or rather what you haven't said yet.' Pat looked blank. 'The fire at Barbara's,' Annie prompted. 'You said there was something you needed to say, but we've not seen you since. For starters, you've been talking with your mate at the fire station.'

'How did you know? I never said …'

'Come on, it's a conversation that was always going to happen with something like this, with our track record.' The worry on Pat's face confirmed to Annie she'd made the right link. 'They've found something dodgy. Traces of an accelerant, I'm guessing.'

Pat nodded.

Mike sat forward. 'So she didn't set fire to her own laundry?'

'Not only that,' said Annie, focusing on Pat as she spoke. 'It wasn't the laundry where they found the accelerant, was it? Whoever started that fire, started it in the Christmas presents. Someone doused her shopping trolley. The so-called collateral damage was the target.'

'Yeah, but …' Pat squirmed and avoided Annie's eye. 'It might have been Babs. She'd bought a table lighter, a real fancy thing, for her godmother. It wasn't new. It could have been full of fuel. Only …'

'Barbara's godmother?' Annie snorted with incredulity. 'The rabidly anti-smoking one. Why would Barbara buy her a lighter?'

'They don't like each other. It's a long-standing thing. They–'

Mike rapped the table with a teaspoon. 'Focus, please. Family politics can wait.'

Annie paused. If the fire had been Barbara's carelessness, it ran a coach and horses through her theory, and maybe she didn't need to confess … except that she did. She couldn't keep this from Pat any longer. 'There's something you need to know. William Marshall stole a stack of paperwork from Havenmere Docks two years ago, and last Thursday Miriam Marshall gave it all to me.'

As Pat gaped, Annie went through what had happened, how she'd been on Miriam's doorstep before dawn and seen Rob Small leave. 'No, he'd not been there overnight, but his visit spooked her, and she basically rammed the bag of papers into my arms and kicked me out. We think Rob Small was pressuring her about them. But she confided in Richard Redman and told him Lois might have taken them. It got back to Rob Small, and he got in touch demanding them back. We think he's tracked Lois down.'

'Are you saying it's tied in with why she's missing?' Mike put in.

Annie didn't reply. It was an uncomfortable idea.

'Lois is missing?' Pat looked from one to the other of them.

'She's not been seen since Thursday night. Her parents

are panicking. There might be more to it. The police seem to be taking it seriously.'

'How do we know about it?' Pat asked.

'A detective called in to the office, Tommy Marchant.'

Pat blew out a sigh and said, 'Hmm, Marchant.'

'What if Small challenged Lois about the paperwork, she denied it, but said she'd track it down for him?' Annie said.

'Why would she?' from Mike.

'Maybe he offered to pay her. You saw her watching the building. She's been stalking us.'

'Stalking you, not us,' Mike murmured. 'Are you saying she was the intruder Jennifer interrupted?'

Annie closed her eyes to bring back the image of the huddled form she'd seen on the camera. 'I'd have said it was someone bigger than Lois.'

'That could be down to clothes,' Pat said.

Annie nodded agreement. 'She was hanging around on Thursday. Mike saw her. The intruder came Friday. It could have been someone checking up on what Lois had told them. Lois was slapdash. She didn't do a thorough job of anything, including watching us. What sort of patchy surveillance do you think she carried out? She wasn't there when I arrived first thing, but she saw you two and Barbara arrive. Then I'll bet she went off for the day; for all we know she has another job, but I think she was back later and saw you and Barbara leave. And I think she thought she'd seen all she needed to see.'

She looked triumphantly at them, but they hadn't got it.

'Think about it, Pat. She didn't see me arrive, I was too early, but she saw you and Barbara. She didn't see any of the comings and goings during the day, but she saw you and Barbara leave for home.'

'Shit!' said Pat, sitting forward. 'Babs arrived that morning with that huge shopping trolley.'

'Yeah,' said Annie. 'And it was very obviously empty.'

'But full to bursting when she went home,' Mike murmured.

'Just like it would have been if she'd stuffed it with Rob Small's paperwork.' Annie gave them a moment to take this in, then said, 'I've known Barbara be careless, but I'm struggling to see her forgetting to turn off an iron unless there's something you're not telling us, like she's really losing the plot.'

Pat stared into the middle distance. For long moments Annie watched her. Eventually she shifted on the seat and met Annie's eye. 'You're right,' she said quietly. 'I was mad at her. I didn't see it for what it was. But *she* knew.'

'What do you mean?'

'From the off, she knew she'd been targeted, just didn't know why.' Pat pulled herself to her feet and reached for her umbrella. 'I need to talk to her. I'll get back to you.' With that, she headed for the far door.

Annie watched Pat clump out into the downpour, then reached for the last sandwich. 'Right then, your turn.' Mike looked deflated as though her theory had stolen his thunder. 'Come on,' she urged. 'You said I'd like it. I'm all ears if it's good news.'

He gave her a wintry smile. 'The good bit was me learning more of those dodgy tricks you're so fond of.'

She laughed. He had started out too trusting, assuming their clients much the same as clients to his merchant bank, that their stories were down the line, straightforward; though he had once confided with some dismay, 'Doing

194

this work with you makes me realise what a bunch of crooks I used to mix with.'

'You know how Jennifer got all prickly when I asked if she could make some discreet enquiries about Lois?'

'I wasn't surprised, Mike. Did you expect her to be on pally terms with any of her colleagues?'

That smile was on his face again. 'I don't know about pally, but yes she's still in touch – very close touch – with at least one person from her old job. She didn't ask why Marchant came round because she had a confidant who was going to tell her.'

Annie stared. Had he really got a step ahead of her? 'When you say confidant …?' she began uncertainly.

'I mean someone she's told everything to; about working with us … everything.'

The waitress hurried up, putting a coffee down on the table. 'Sorry for the delay.'

'Thanks.' Absently, Annie pocketed Pat's change. She watched the waitress walk away, heading for a bar that was beginning to get busy.

Mike pushed the table aside so that he could lean in closer. 'You saw me follow her after Marchant had gone.'

'She said she wanted fresh air,' Annie murmured. 'She looked really rattled.'

'Believe me, she was. She'd gone to make a call.'

'But where? I looked out of the window. I didn't see either of you.'

'Down the side towards the back yard. She went round the dog-leg, so I got as close as I could and listened.'

That explained it. Jennifer had gone out of the door and dived round the corner into that narrow alley with its locked-gate dead-end. Mike too had had time to get out of sight before she had leant over the kitchen counter to check.

'I clicked my phone to record as I left the office. I've got everything I heard. It's not much, but it's enough. If it'd been a still day, I'd have got the lot.'

He looked round. The space was filling up, but there was no one encroaching on their corner. They huddled close to listen as he held the phone.

The recording started on the clatter of his footsteps down the stairs. Then the door clicked open and a surge of noise from the street drowned everything else. Annie couldn't be sure if it was the storm or passing traffic, but she heard him mutter, 'Where the–?' before a car horn cut across him.

'Didn't realise where she was at first, but it was the only place she could have gone. I had some corny line planned about checking she was OK if she'd stayed at this end, but she was out of sight up near the gate.'

The phone gave traffic noise against a stiff breeze, then changed abruptly. The growl of engines faded as the whistle of the wind became shrill. He was now between the high walls of the alleyway.

'I was aware she was talking, but I couldn't make anything out until she raised her voice. Keep listening.'

Annie strained to hear but couldn't distinguish anything from the background noise, until the words cut through, sharp enough to startle her.

'Tommy fucking Marchant!'

Then there was nothing but the undecipherable rumble.

'Could you hear what she was saying, better than this?'

He shook his head. 'Phone's got it all.'

An unintelligible mix of sound followed, with a couple of brief angry bursts from Jennifer.

'… almost walked in on me … why didn't you warn me …?'

Annie felt more than heard a subtle change in the backdrop of sound. 'You're moving away.'

Mike nodded. 'She started pacing about. She was inches from seeing me. But listen, there's more.'

Once again, words emerged from the overlying wind-tunnel effect of the narrow pathway.

'… ridiculous! How could you not know …?'

Mike murmured, 'I'll swear I could hear the voice at the other end of the call when she said that. Having a go back at her. Couldn't make out any words.'

Then Jennifer's voice came through again. 'Well, OK.' Her tone was one of ungracious apology. 'Just make it your business, will you? It won't go well for either of us if …'

A scuffle of movement and the recording cut off.

'That's it,' said Mike. 'She moved. She was coming back towards the road, so I legged it. It has to have been someone back at the station where she worked. She was giving them a rocket for not warning her that Marchant was on his way round, which means that whoever they are she's confided about working for us.'

'Clearly they didn't know about Marchant.'

'No, but they've had their orders now. You heard her: *Make it your business*. So she does have a contact she could pump for information.'

Maybe she will, thought Annie. She would like to know why Lois was considered priority enough for a visit. 'Could be one of those crime initiatives Jennifer complains about,' she said. 'Caring about about missing persons in the run up to Christmas.'

'Or, given your theory about those papers, there could be more to it.'

He was right, and it would settle her unease to know for sure. 'We can't push her, but maybe she'll make enquiries. I just hope she'll drop a hint if she turns up a link to the agency.'

In her head, Annie replayed that final exchange.

It won't go well for either of us …

She'd sensed no trust behind the fragmented exchange. It had been an accomplice rather than a friend; someone who was also caught up in the issue that was dragging Jennifer through disciplinary proceedings, with the difference that this third party did not seem to have been caught. Yet.

This then was someone that Jennifer could drop in the shit any time she liked.

Annie knew it was insensitive, but her first thought was what a useful contact for Jennifer to have once the dust had settled.

CHAPTER 33

Annie watched dawn creep up the Humber. She'd only been out of bed a few minutes. Unusually, she had out-slept Mike who was lounging in an armchair, fully dressed, feet crossed on the coffee table. She was wearing nothing but a shirt of his that she'd plucked from the laundry basket. They'd talked into the small hours about the implications of Barbara's house fire and Jennifer's overheard call without coming to any firm conclusions.

'Did you say Jennifer won't be in this morning?' Annie turned away from the window to face him.

'Uh-huh.' He tipped his thumb towards his phone where it lay on the table. 'Message confirming it this morning. She's been summoned, but she says that's good. It puts her in the clear for tomorrow.'

'Let's not rush in then. I'm feeling quite tired. I hope I'm not coming down with anything.'

He laughed. 'All you're coming down with is a late night and too much to drink, but I suppose if Jennifer's a definite for tomorrow then there's no need for you to cram the rest of that stuff.'

'I want to be up to speed, but I'm not coming in till I've had a coffee and something to eat. Jennifer might get bounced last minute. It's happened before.' She yawned, feeling the icy breeze against her skin as the shirt billowed. She should get dressed, but felt lethargic, unable to get going properly.

Mike glanced at his watch. 'If they cancel on Jennifer last minute like they did before, she'll probably go to the office.'

'So?'

'There'll be no one there. She won't be able to get in.'

'I thought you were on your way now.'

He shook his head. 'I'll wait for you.'

She heard the chair creak as he stood up. His footsteps padded across the floor and she felt his arms slide around her from behind, pushing aside the flimsy material of the shirt. 'Let's go in late for once,' he said. 'We can see what it's like to be Thompson sisters.'

She smiled as she leant back into his embrace. Her phone would tell her if anyone got as far as the top landing.

Later, she surfaced from a doze, to see Mike lying back against the cushions scrolling through his phone. 'What time is it?'

'Just gone ten. Probably time to make a move.'

'Let's have breakfast before we go. We may as well be really late for once. I could just fancy a full English. How about you?'

'You mean you want me to cook you a full English.'

She laughed. 'You know me so well.'

'Fine, but we've no bacon. Or eggs come to that.'

'Toast?'

It was as they were leaving twenty minutes later that her phone pinged a text.

She stared for a moment, not quite believing it. 'There's a turn up. Lois has replied to my text.' She skimmed the words as they headed downstairs, summarising for Mike. 'She says she has some stuff of ours, including …' She paused to shoot him a scandalised glance. 'Including a spare key. Bloody Barb!'

'She *was* the intruder then. Does she admit it?'

They were out in the street now, battered by a stiff breeze off the estuary.

'Hang on.' Annie ran her eye down the rest of the message, updating Mike as soon as they were sheltered inside the car. 'She's sorry for what she said … uh … bangs on about the job being valuable experience. She can't come to the office, she's keeping her head down … I wonder what that's about … but she asks if I'll meet her at the Oddbottle. She'll buy me a drink and return the key, but she only gets a ten-minute break so can we make it at eleven this morning when they open?'

'The Oddbottle?'

'It's a pub out Hessle way, I think. I've heard Pat mention it. I've never been there. Good beer, she said.'

'Annie!'

'Yeah, all right, I'll be having coffee. I'm just saying.'

'You're going to go then?'

She glanced at the time. 'I may as well. I can drop you and head straight there. I'll be back by lunchtime.'

'Should we let that detective know that she's made contact?'

Annie paused. 'We didn't say we would. I think … no, let's not. At least not till I've seen her. If she wants to duck off the radar, that's her business.'

* * *

It was three minutes after eleven when Annie pushed through the door of the Oddbottle into a large well-lit space. High tables with extra tall chairs stood on an expanse of laminate flooring. Lower tables and chairs sat on a wide border of carpet by the windows. She expected it to be empty and on first glance it was, everything neat and gleaming, newly polished for a new day, but as her gaze scanned the room, she realised she wasn't their first customer. Three men huddled at one end of the bar, a couple sat by a window, and a lone woman at the far end of the room leant over her phone. None of them was Lois.

The lone barmaid had her back turned as she polished the glass front of a fridge packed with brightly coloured bottles. Annie took a step towards the bar before something clicked and she spun round for a second look at the lone woman.

Not Lois, but a familiar face.

Perhaps feeling Annie's scrutiny, the woman looked up. Annie saw her eyes open wide in surprise. This sort of coincidence didn't happen. She walked across.

'Hello Miriam. I wasn't expecting to see you here.'

'Likewise.' Miriam Marshall's expression was tight with suspicion. 'Is this … uh … one of your haunts?'

Annie shook her head. 'Never been before in my life.'

'So what brings you here today?'

'I'm supposed to be meeting someone. You?'

Miriam glanced towards the door. In her peripheral vision, Annie could see the reflection of the entranceway in the big window beside Miriam. No one had come in.

'I'm meeting someone too, but you already know that, don't you?'

'Lois?' Annie guessed.

'And you've come instead. Why? If you wanted to meet me, you could just have said so. Why the lies?'

'No, no.' Annie raised her hand to deny the charge. 'I'm supposed to be meeting Lois too. She texted me.' Miriam's air of suspicion seemed to deepen so Annie pulled out her phone. 'I can show you the text.'

Miriam peered at the phone that Annie held out, then heaved a sigh and lifted her own handset.

Annie leant in to see. 'That says it's from the Thompsons' Agency.'

Miriam clicked through the phone impatiently and showed Annie the number. 'Lois was the airhead you sent me, if you remember.'

'Of course, yeah.'

She read the texts that Lois and Miriam had exchanged that morning.

Hi Mrs Marshall. Can you meet me 11 am. The Oddbottle. I've something of yours that I need to give back.

> Not today. I'm in town without the car. I have to be home by 11.30.

Please come, it's important. I'll run you home.

> Can't you come to my house?

Sorry, can't. I'll explain, but I'll get you back in plenty of time, honest. It's really important. I have to give you this stuff back.

Following this quick-fire exchange, there was a five-minute gap, then Lois again:

Please Mrs Marshall

Followed three minutes later by:

It's really important.

A couple of minutes after that, Miriam had replied:

203

> *Alright but don't be late. I have to be home for half past.*

Miriam looked up at Annie. 'She texted you just after that last one from me.'

Annie nodded. The timing hadn't escaped her. Lois had made sure of Miriam, and then texted Annie.

They both turned to look towards the door. No one came in. The three men by the bar were now laughing with the barmaid. The couple by the window remained engrossed in each other.

Annie felt as uneasy as Miriam looked.

'Do you know what stuff she's talking about?' Miriam asked.

'No. You didn't give her anything, did you? Or … uh … could she have taken anything?'

Miriam shrugged, then looked at her watch. 'It's almost ten past. She's not going to show, is she? Sod it!'

'I'll drive you home,' said Annie.

Miriam looked surprised, but her expression softened. It was the first time Annie had seen her smile. 'Thank you, I appreciate that.'

'You'll not get back for half past if you wait for a cab. It's a good twenty minutes from here, isn't it?'

'It's not the first time she's been late, you know. Inconsiderate cow!'

Annie murmured agreement as she stood up. She kept her phone in her hand and tapped out a quick text to Mike as they crossed the car park.

Going to Miriam Marshall's

Explanations would have to wait. She was anxious now to get away from this place. Just because Lois had set up this meeting, it didn't mean it would be her who turned up.

CHAPTER 34

They had barely set off, when Miriam, sounding a little shamefaced, said, 'You don't need to drive me the whole way. That about me having to be home for half past was just for Lois, I was trying to put her off. Take the next right. My car's up at the end. I didn't want to leave it in the pub car park.'

Annie flicked on her indicator and gave Miriam a look.

'You know how it is. You start off on a lie and you keep building on it. I should just have said no. Uh … you know that stuff you took from my house …'

'You mean that paperwork you gave me,' Annie responded firmly.

'Did you …? I mean … what did you do with it? Did you look at it? Did you work it out?'

'Dumped it,' Annie lied. If Miriam turned out to want it back, its mud-coated state would support her story. 'Yes, I looked at it and no, I couldn't work it out. I don't think it was work-out-able to be honest, or only by someone already familiar with whatever system it was describing.'

'Where did you dump it?'

Annie tried to gauge the undertone to Miriam's voice, wanting to keep a step ahead. Miriam had secrets to spill and for once Annie was in the right place. Her offer of a lift seemed to have softened the woman. 'Shredded and gone,' she said, hoping she'd read things right. 'It'll be on its way to being turned into loo paper by now. Sorry, I hope you weren't wanting it back.'

'No, no, that's fine.' The relief was palpable. 'I'm glad it's gone. Uh … I–' Miriam stopped abruptly, then said, 'That's my car.' Annie pulled up. Miriam was slow to unclick her seatbelt. As she fiddled with it, she said, 'I'm glad it's gone, but I'd have liked you to find out what it was about.'

'I would too, but I had no chance on my own. It would have needed a specialist.'

Miriam nodded. 'Or if not a specialist,' she murmured, 'someone who'd seen it happen?'

'What do you mean?'

Miriam was looking ahead, not at Annie. There was no hostility in her expression, just indecision. 'I … uh … Like I said, that 11.30 thing was meant for Lois. I couldn't be bothered with her. Are you tight for time?'

'No, not especially. Why?'

There was a moment's pause. 'I'm going over to my brother's to stay for a few days. I'll have to show my face but I wondered if you might pick me up from there. It's the right direction. Then I can show you.'

Annie's answer was an indeterminate tip of her head.

Miriam gave an uncomfortable laugh. 'It's a good day,' she said at last.

Annie's gaze flicked towards the damp vista showing through the windscreen. It was a dismal day. 'A good day for what?'

'There's a conference in Amsterdam.'

Annie laughed. 'I might not be tight for time, but Amsterdam would be a stretch.'

Miriam looked her in the eye. 'They're all there today. They're all in Amsterdam.'

And although she thought she knew the answer, Annie asked. 'Who?'

'I … uh … I'd like to talk this over somewhere we can get a really good coffee.'

Now she knew for sure who Miriam was talking about. She was still holding on to a secret, but Annie was beginning to see the shape of it, and somewhere at its heart sat William Marshall.

'Just idle curiosity,' she said, 'but did you find out after your husband died or did you know before?'

Miriam curled her lip. 'Oh, I've known about this one for years.'

* * *

Mike sauntered up the road towards the office. He'd had Annie drop him by the store so he could buy milk. He held the carton in his hand. There had been no conscious plan to divert to the coffee bar, but that's where he'd gone, sitting in the window cradling his cup long after he'd drained it, watching the world go by.

He knew everything he needed to know for the meeting tomorrow, now was the time to relax, to prepare himself mentally. This would be the start of their new life, or rather the start of their new work life. On the personal side, he admitted to himself – and might even tell Annie – he couldn't be happier. She'd always been his soulmate. He'd known it from the off, but had muddied the waters with his hankering for conventional goals; marriage, children, money to support the very best of everything for them all. He'd lived the dream. It hadn't turned into a nightmare, just something of a damp squib. He loved his children, and would always be a friend to Amélie, though that had been in the balance once she'd met someone new. He'd fought for reasonable access. Custody was never in question. Annie and children didn't mix. She rubbed along with them when they visited but in the distant way she might treat any acquaintance who didn't speak her language.

He had yet to find out if he'd have Jennifer or Annie with him tomorrow, but it would be fine either way. Jennifer had had time to prepare more thoroughly than Annie, but he could rely on Annie as a safe pair of hands.

As he pushed through the door from the street, raising his hand in greeting to the people behind the reception counter, he thought of Annie's reaction to his overheard call. She'd been oddly delighted with it, whether his part in recording it or something Jennifer had said, he couldn't be sure. It didn't matter. She would work it through and then tell him. It was what she did.

He wondered how she was getting on with Lois. Until they could afford professional staff, he must coach her in some business basics or do certain things himself – if he could keep Barb away from the hiring and Annie away from the firing, they would muddle through.

His step was heading automatically towards the post tray when he heard sounds from upstairs.

Someone moving about in the main office.

His heart thudded in his chest. He twisted to stare at the eye of the camera, expecting the dull blur of a paint-covered lens, but it sparkled back at him.

Whoever it is, I've got them, it told him.

'Who's gone upstairs this morning?' he called across, but softly, not to alert anyone.

'Not seen anyone but we've been busy.' He got a smile but no real interest. He wasn't clear that anyone other than their manager knew about the intruder.

Watching up the stairs, he listened again. One person or two? Hard to say.

At the reception desk, they were in a huddled group laughing. He thought about all the times he'd said to Annie, 'Don't go anywhere at all iffy without letting someone know.'

He almost reached for his phone but he'd taken his time over that coffee. It could conceivably be Annie herself up there.

Now he could hear the pad of footsteps … the click of a door …

Not the main door, that was in his line of sight now. It could only be the small back office, the place Annie had stashed those papers … the damaged window …

Anger blazed inside him. This would not happen again. He was pounding upwards, taking the stairs in twos. No weapon but his own fists, but he didn't care. No one's tampering was going to pull the rug from under his and Annie's new life.

CHAPTER 35

As Mike leapt from the top stair into the main office, his gaze took in the whole picture, the way Annie had taught him. *Be alert, don't miss someone behind you with a baseball bat.* The room was empty, but from the open door to the back office came the unmistakable squeak of the recycling container's wheels and the scrunch of paper.

He crashed through the open doorway shouting, 'What the hell do you–?'

He was met by a shriek as the figure by the container leapt round.

'Jeez, Mike! You nearly gave me a heart attack. What are you playing at?' Pat radiated indignation as she glared at him.

'Pat, I'd forgotten … I thought … What are you doing?'

'Clearing out some old paperwork. What the hell are *you* doing? Where's Annie?'

'I mean what are you doing here at all?'

Pat's glare intensified. 'I work here. Remember?'

'Yes, sorry, I … uh … I'd forgotten you'd got one of the new keys. I thought it was another intruder.'

How was it that he so often felt wrong-footed by Pat? This one was all on him, though he could be forgiven for being surprised to find her in.

'Where did you say Annie is?' Pat asked, turning back to her paper sorting.

'I didn't, but she's gone to meet Lois.'

'Lois? Turned up then has she?'

Mike told her about the text, adding, 'She wants to return our key.'

Pat's gaze shot up to meet his. 'She has a key? It must have been her in the office that time then.'

'I'm hoping Annie'll get the story out of her.'

'Yeah, but wait a minute! How did she get a key in the first place?'

'She says Barbara gave it her.' He was stretching the truth, as Lois hadn't specified, but watched Pat closely as he spoke.

'Babs? Why the–?' Pat stopped abruptly and carried on stuffing paper into the container. His own theory was that Barb had wanted Lois in the office at some point when it hadn't been convenient to be there herself, so she'd handed over a key and never bothered to get it back. That was a huge no-no in their game and he could see that Pat had arrived at the same place, but he wasn't going to push her to talk about it.

'I'm going to make coffee,' he said. 'D'you want one?'

Pat gave him a nod and said, 'Thanks,' which Mike took less for the coffee and more as an acknowledgement that he hadn't pursued the issue of Barbara and the key.

He was satisfied he'd sown the seed. He'd always hesitated to admit it to Annie, but he could work with Pat. Barb was the problem. According to Annie it was Barbara who'd kept the business afloat after Vince Sleeman died. He and Annie had seen little of each other in that period. All he knew was

211

that Sleeman had been a nasty piece of work, and that they'd baled from frying pan to furnace by putting their future in the hands of Dyson and fforbes.

Don't write Barb off, Mike. She lost her mojo when they lost control. They come as a set. Lose Barb and we lose Pat too. His official position was that they were better off without either sister if that was the choice, but he kept seeing glimpses in Pat that chimed with the things Annie kept telling him.

She would be back any minute. He made enough coffee for three

* * *

Ten minutes after crossing the Humber Bridge, Annie pulled the car off the road. It wasn't an official turning, but the start of a rutted track. Miriam was sitting on a fallen log. Annie assumed the track led to a house but the curve of the land took it off behind a screen of bushes and trees. The agreement was that Miriam would leave her car at her brother's place and that they would complete the journey in Annie's.

'Where's your car?' she asked.

'Down at the farm.' Miriam indicated the track. 'You can drop me there after. They'll all be out by then.'

Annie hadn't asked why she wasn't allowed to meet Miriam's family. There had been a time when she'd been phobic about taking anyone to meet what was left of hers. Mike had broken that taboo by appearing at her bedside the time she'd been laid up in hospital in Glasgow. When she'd finally come round, he and her aunt had bonded. She was prepared to allow Miriam her privacy. More concerning were the huge holes and boulders that made up what bit of the track was visible from here.

Seeing the direction of her gaze, Miriam said, 'Don't worry, there's a way round by road. My nephew ran me up here in the quad.' She groaned. 'It's done nothing for my back.'

'OK, let's get going. You can tell me what it's about on the way.'

'I'll do better than that; I'll show you.'

'I want some detail before we get there.'

Miriam fastened her seatbelt and fiddled with the seat controls, tipping the seat right back as Annie set off. 'You don't mind, do you? My back's killing me. If I can lie back I'll be OK by the time we get there.' She squirmed as she wrestled her arms out of her coat sleeves and pulled the coat round so that it lay across her. 'I've caught a bit of a chill out there in the wind.'

No, thought Annie, we're not playing that game. I'm having the information from you before we arrive or we don't go. 'Is that the time?' she said. 'Maybe it would be better to do this another day.'

'But we'll not find the place empty another—' Miriam stopped herself, clearly reading the subtext.

Annie said nothing. Either Miriam started talking or she would turn back and claim lack of time, a forgotten appointment … the excuse didn't matter. What mattered was that she maintained control.

Miriam grunted as she pulled her coat up like a blanket as though to shut Annie out. 'OK, I don't know for sure about the papers, I only have what Will told me, and even if they showed what he said they did, I've no idea how you'd ever untangle it.'

'You'd need a specialist, I suppose,' murmured Annie. 'And it would cost a fortune. Way more than you or I could spare, I'm sure.'

'The police could have done it if they knew it was evidence.'

'I suppose they could, but I doubt they would. Like I say it'd cost a fortune.'

'Yeah, but say it was something like a murder.'

'Maybe.' Annie thought it could cost more than even a murder enquiry could raise. It certainly wouldn't be top of the queue of evidence to be analysed.

She slowed the car for the next exit from the dual carriageway.

Miriam, still lying back on the seat, said. 'Not this turn. Take the next. We're going in the back way.'

Annie speeded up again.

She glanced again at the woman by her side, knowing that all the mud William Marshall had thrown at his old boss at Havenmere Docks had already had a spotlight shone on it.

A sign for the next turn loomed up ahead. 'How's your back?'

Miriam opened her eyes and as they left the main road, eased herself more upright, playing with the seat controls until she was sitting normally again. 'That's better.'

'Did your husband say that paperwork was evidence of a murder?'

'Not directly, but with hindsight, I think that's what he meant.'

The air crackled with Miriam's multiple agendas, but for reasons of her own she was going to tell Annie something that she'd been holding back all this time. Annie looked ahead as a skyline of industrial buildings spread out before them. On their way, they would pass through residential streets, parks, green spaces, but nothing could disguise that this was an unapologetic industrial landscape, alive with the global movement of megatons of goods fed by the wide estuary to the north. 'Whose murder?' she asked.

'His own,' Miriam replied.

CHAPTER 36

Mike went through to the kitchen with his and Pat's empty mugs. He leaned forward to look through the window, round the corner of the sign. The reflection of the low sun made fires rage in the windows opposite, as silhouetted pedestrians strolled up the far pavement. He watched half a dozen cars go by. No sign of Annie. He cupped his hands round the cafetière, now too cold to be retrievable. Where was she? He'd had no word since the text saying she was going to Miriam Marshall's.

As he returned to the office, Pat looked up from her desk. 'What's up?'

'Just a bit concerned about Annie.' He was surprised she'd noticed and unexpectedly relieved to share the worry.

'When was she meeting Lois?'

'Three hours ago and it wasn't meant to last more than ten minutes. She texted me to say they were calling in on Miriam Marshall.'

'What did the text say, exactly?'

He pulled out his phone. 'She just said, *Going to Miriam Marshall's*.'

'I wonder why. Something Lois gave her? Didn't that first text say she had stuff to give back?'

Mike pulled out his chair, grateful she was taking him

seriously. 'We focussed on the key, but yes, she did say more. I don't know how specific she was. Annie didn't read me the full text.'

'Have you tried to ring her?'

He shook his head. 'I didn't want to butt in if she's got Miriam Marshall talking.'

'Why not? It's been three hours and it's not even a live case. If she doesn't want interruptions, her phone'll be off.'

His phone was ringing in his ear before Pat had finished speaking. Why on earth had he hesitated? Annie could get prickly if she deemed him over-zealous in keeping an eye on her, but he'd somehow lost his sense of perspective. This situation had crept up out of nowhere.

The ringtone sounded for a few seconds and then cut off. 'She's red-buttoned me.'

Pat said nothing for a moment, then, 'Give it a couple of minutes. See if she texts.' She turned back to her PC and pulled the keyboard towards her.

Mike stared at the papers on his desk without seeing them. Why hadn't Pat said, 'That's Annie all over, it's what she does, nothing to worry about.' It was what she'd usually say.

'What d'you mean?' he snapped. 'You sound worried. Why are you worried?'

She looked up at him, eyes narrowed, admonishing him for his bad-temper. 'Annie told me you were developing the right instincts. It was a while before I believed her; thought you were a waste of space when you first joined us. You're worried that something's not right. Doesn't mean anything's wrong, but you learn not to ignore these things. I'm worried because you're worried.'

He looked down, not wanting to meet her eye. She was a step ahead of him and must know what he thought of her and her sister. 'What are we going to do?'

'Wait,' she said firmly. 'Give her a few minutes. If she doesn't text, ring back. She knows the score.'

* * *

Miriam directed her through a maze of streets, until the landscape ahead was a deserted wasteland. Whatever Miriam was doing, Annie had the impression it was on impulse. She needed someone to confide in; and circumstances had delivered Annie.

Taking the route that Miriam indicated led them further from any signs of life. The low sun glared through the corner of the windscreen.

'Where's Rob Small in all this?' Annie tried.

'Will might have been wrong about Robbie but that doesn't mean he was wrong about all of it. Will pulled the wool over Robbie's eyes for years, so anyone else could have too.'

It wasn't a direct answer but clearly Miriam thought Annie knew more than she did. For the time being that was fine. What Miriam said fitted what she'd seen of Rob Small; quick to put up the defences but basically lonely. His tones had been warm when he'd talked about his old friend Jobsie and how close they'd been. He'd revelled in showing her what his machines could do. He'd built an impressive enterprise, but it had left him alone and lonely.

'This back way in you say we're going to use, what's that about?'

'It was a legit entrance back in the day when Robbie's father was in charge. Will and some of the others used to use it to skive off without the cameras seeing them. I don't know if Robbie didn't know or if he's forgotten. It's outside what he thinks is a secure inner perimeter. And it needs a key.'

'Shouldn't your husband have given back all his keys?' Annie asked, feeling uncomfortable echoes of her own situation with Lois.

'Will had his father's key. Robbie's father must have had one too, but whether he passed it on, who knows? I doubt Robbie's given that gate a thought in years.'

'But your husband went back in after he lost his job. Why wasn't the gate sorted out then?'

'Robbie never knew how he'd got in. Will told him he'd used his pass to get in through the front.'

It fitted with what Annie knew. Small's agitation at the break in, his over-the-top security push afterwards. 'He broke in a second time, didn't he? Did Rob Small report him to the police?'

'Not that I'm aware.'

'But your husband seriously compromised the security of the dockyard. Why would he let that pass?'

'He didn't. He showed Will what he'd do to him if it happened again.' Annie sensed Miriam's shudder. 'Not that I knew at the time. We … we weren't really talking. See, Robbie had come to tell me before he sacked Will, said he didn't want it to come as a shock. He made it a redundancy so it wouldn't wreck Will's CV, said he'd do a reference and everything … I couldn't argue, the way Will was drinking back then, but Will got to know I'd talked to Robbie and

219

… well, let's just say things got strained. Pull up just here, by the bankside.'

Annie stopped the car and looked at her passenger. 'How's this going to work?' she said. 'Because before I set foot in the place, I want every last detail.'

CHAPTER 37

The road was deserted, its surface cracked and damaged from disuse and lack of maintenance, derelict sites lay to one side, the water's edge not far off the other way. The tallest structure was a hoarding; faded and ripped by wind and rain, its grand advertisement still legible proclaiming the beauties of this stretch of wasteland giving its acreage and an artist's utopian impression of what it might become. Though looking pathetically out of place, it had done its job. A new strip of garish colour bearing the word 'SOLD' slewed across it at an angle.

Miriam nodded towards it. 'Once they rebuild, there'll be no access and Robbie'll be safe in his castle, not that he'll ever know. You leave me here. I'll drop down into the cutting and go along the edge of the bank. It'll take me twenty minutes to get back and get in. Don't be early. You don't want to have to hang about outside the gates. I'll sort it so it lets your car straight in.'

'You can work that stuff, can you?'

'Security gates, yeah, no bother.'

'Wait.' Annie laid her hand on Miriam's arm to stop her getting out of the car. 'You've not told me near enough. I meant what I said. I want to know what you're going to show me before we go in there.'

Miriam gave a huff of exasperation. 'We shouldn't wait around. Someone'll spot us. I can tell you once we're inside. It's warmer in there. We can get some good coffee.' She reached for the door handle.

Annie glanced at the bleak landscape. Any watcher would have to be a long way off. 'I'll ring for a cab for you,' and as Miriam looked momentarily confused, added, 'If you don't want to tell me, that's your choice, but I'm heading back to Hull.'

Miriam sat back and grumbled, 'It might be derelict but it's close to some sensitive outfits. There are regular patrols. If there weren't, you could leave the car and come with me, but there'll be all hell on if they find it abandoned.'

Before Annie could respond, her phone sang out.

She pulled it from her pocket and looked at the screen. Mike. She'd told him she'd be back by lunchtime. She needed to give him an update, but that could wait until she'd got rid of Miriam. She red-buttoned the call and said, 'If any other vehicles show up, we'll drive off or pretend we've broken down or whatever. If you're quick, we won't need to. When you came to our office you implied that Rob Small had killed your husband. Do you still think that?'

'I half believed it because of the way he threatened Will but no, it wasn't him. He could only have done it if the container had gone through his dockyard and it didn't. I had Rich check it out for me. The way it was done, it was as though it was Robbie, but it couldn't have been him. It's like someone knew what Robbie had said to Will and they'd copied it.'

'Someone was trying to frame Rob Small?'

Miriam looked shocked. 'I hadn't thought of that. I

thought if it wasn't an accident then it was to get rid of Will, but if it was to frame Robbie ...'

'I'm not saying it was, I just thought that was what you meant. If it wasn't an accident, it was well dressed up as one. How exactly did Rob Small threaten your husband?'

'Will said to me, "If I turn up dead in a shipping container, it's Robbie Small that's done it." Then of course he went missing and he turned up ... like he did. What was I to think?'

'You didn't mention this to the police at the time, did you?'

'It's going back almost two years when they had that barney, but then when more came out about where he was, I got to thinking back. They saw it as an accident. He had a stack of booze with him. I didn't want to stir up a hornets' nest. They weren't going to take me seriously without any evidence, and I didn't have any.'

'That paperwork?' Annie prompted, checking her mirrors. The industrial wasteland stared back at her. They were still alone.

'I'd thought he'd got rid. Then I dug through his stuff and it was all there.'

'Maybe it really was an accident?'

'So how did he get in there? He might have been able to break into Havenmere Docks but that's only because of this.' Miriam pulled a large old-fashioned key from her pocket and held it out to Annie. 'How's he supposed to have broken into Red Boy's yard or into the container come to that?'

Annie took the key and turned it in her hand. It was old. The bit had been recently oiled but the bow had rust in its curves. She passed it back to Miriam.

'If it was Robbie, then it happened at Havenmere Docks. If he hadn't had the container on site, then he wasn't involved. And it wasn't there, ever. I asked the police, but they couldn't tell me. Confidentiality or something.'

Annie murmured assent. Resources and lack of detailed checking rather than confidentiality might have been at the root of their non-disclosure. 'Who did you speak to, which police officer, can you remember?'

'A woman called Flanagan who brought Will's stuff back. She was OK, a bit wishy-washy.'

Annie felt her eyebrows rise; she'd never heard anyone call Jennifer wishy-washy. 'So you went back to Richard Redman. How did he check it?'

'He looked on one of the online systems. They're all tagged these days, the big containers.'

'Where did he get the info from to check it?'

'From his son. It was his son who found Will. He had the ID number from the side of the thing. That's how he knew it was a rogue crate in the first place. It wasn't on his inventory. So Rich checked and it didn't go through Robbie's yard.'

'So where had it come from?'

'Bristol.' Miriam snapped out the word and turned to look at the road behind them. 'It was lost in a yard in Bristol for the best part of twenty years, then it ended up on the road, but there's another gap before it got to Redman's. Will must have got into it somewhere on the road journey.'

'Or it could have gone to Rob Small's yard,' Annie said.

'No, that's the point, it couldn't. The records of what goes through a dockyard like Havenmere are bang on. They have to be because of smuggling and all that. The road haulage records aren't the same. Yeah for the big companies, but this was classed as a used container, it had been sold on. It left Bristol on the twenty-first of September, heading for Middlesborough, but it was dropped off near Birmingham. Rich talked to people, he got the details. There was a problem with the lorry. But then there's no record of it being picked up again. Next place it turns up is Rich's son's place ... with Will inside it.'

'Could Rob Small have faked the records?'

'No.'

'How can you be so sure?'

'His own local records maybe, but he couldn't mess about with the central ones. They're the ones that Rich checked. Look, I know how this stuff works. I spent the best part of two decades working in shipping.'

Again, Miriam looked round. Annie scanned the mirrors.

'We've got to make a move,' Miriam said. 'Once we're in, we're safe as houses. I'll lock everything up behind me and we can leave through the front. Rob'll never know.'

'Unless he checks his cameras when he gets back.'

'Why would he? I think ...' Miriam's voice wavered for a moment. 'I think I know how to work the simulator. Will told me it took less than three minutes. I couldn't make head nor tail of the printout and neither could anyone else.' She shot Annie a glare.

Those reams and reams of paperwork had been the technical spec for three minutes of ... something. From the scrap that she'd unravelled, Annie knew it was feasible.

'Do you know what–?' she began.

'No!' Miriam snapped. 'Of course I don't fucking know. I haven't a bloody clue, but I've kept the dateline ID. I'll bet you didn't think of that, did you? You just dumped the lot. And I can get into that system, and when I do, I want a fucking witness. I wouldn't have chosen you, but you're all I've got, and I reckon you owe me. OK?'

The outburst took Annie aback, but at last she'd got to the real reason for this jaunt. And was it more planned than she'd thought? Perhaps it was Miriam who'd been back in touch with Lois, persuaded her to reply to Annie's text; the exchange between Miriam and Lois just a smoke screen to explain Miriam's presence in the pub. She could just have asked to meet, but maybe she was scared that Rob Small would find out.

'I've got to go or some bastard'll come along and start shoving their nose in. We're likely being watched now. You get out of the car, come round to my side and open the door, then leave it open while you go round the back and kick the tyres or whatever, just mess about for a minute, give me long enough to slip out and get over the edge of the bank with the car hiding me. Then if anyone's got binoculars on us, they'll not see where I go. Then get the hell away from here and go and kick your heels for twenty minutes. Havenmere's front gates will open for you. In fact, I'll ring when I've sorted them, that'll be safer.'

Miriam had played the ice-woman as the details of her husband's death had come to light, but underneath she was seething with anger, some of which was directed at Annie for the here and now. To avoid observation, she would have to crawl out of the car and across an unedifying stretch of muddy grass, but then if she'd given Annie the full story earlier, they could have stopped the car fleetingly before anyone had the time to take notice.

Annie got out of the car, walked round to open the passenger door, then flipped up the boot and made play of rummaging about inside before bending down as though to check the wheels. After a few moments, she slammed shut the doors. Miriam was nowhere to be seen.

Too quick, too slick. She'd lay money Miriam had been with her husband on at least one of his return visits to the place he used to work.

As she drove off, she propped her mobile on the dashboard and dictated a text to Mike:

Going to Havenmere Docks. Will ring in an hour.

She hesitated, then discarded it unsent. Whatever Miriam's underlying agenda, she wanted Mike to keep quiet about it for now.

Going to Havenmere Docks to find out what really happened. Don't broadcast that. To anyone. Will ring in an hour.

Again, she left it unsent. Her sudden indecisiveness made her uneasy, as though her subconscious was clamouring about something she'd missed. She altered the text's recipient to bypass his clone phone. He would take notice of that. It had been a day shaped by odd texts, starting with Lois's … and she'd bet that had been written at Miriam's dictation. She mustn't leave Mike with any such uncertainty.

Going to Havenmere Docks to find out what really happened. Don't broadcast that. To anyone. Will ring in an hour. Full English without eggs or bacon.

No one else could guess at their unconventional breakfast; it had been a first even for them.

It wasn't until she was on a better-made road and picked up speed round a corner that something clattered in the foot-well on the passenger side. She glanced down to see that the momentum had spread out a mound of crumpled tissues and bits of paper. Clearly Miriam had lost the contents of one of her pockets as she'd slid out of the car. But tissues and paper didn't clatter. When she slowed to peer more closely, she could see Miriam's phone, its black casing almost invisible against the dark floor.

CHAPTER 38

Pat had left the room and lumbered along to the bathroom. Mike stared through the window at the constant drizzle. His files for tomorrow's meeting were open on the screen in front of him but he couldn't focus. Was it time to phone Annie again? He didn't want to wait for Pat to return to give him permission to call, but somehow that was what he was doing.

His phone lay stubbornly comatose on the desk. He couldn't stop himself from clicking it on every few seconds, picking it up to check that he hadn't accidentally switched it to silent mode, agonising over whether he should call her.

When a text popped up on the screen in front of him, he almost dropped the phone in his haste to open it.

Going to Havenmere Docks to find out what really happened. Don't broadcast that. To anyone. Will ring in an hour. Full English without eggs or bacon.

As he smiled at the *full English*, he realised with a jolt, the message had arrived with no sound. If he hadn't been watching the screen, he wouldn't have known it had arrived. Unease shivered down his spine.

Don't broadcast that. To anyone.

They could all send messages that wouldn't land on the clone phones, but he'd never known Annie do it before. She was underlining that not telling anyone included Jennifer, Barbara … and Pat. He shot a guilty look towards the empty landing. The flush sounded and the ancient plumbing clanked its pipes.

He had to tell her Annie had been in touch, but divert her from the contents of the text.

Pat's footsteps padded down the landing.

'Annie's been in touch,' he greeted her, smiling. 'All OK. She's going to ring in an hour.'

'Oh, right.' Pat was clearly taken aback. 'Are you sure everything's OK?'

'Yup, all fine. Um … have you got five minutes? Only there's something I wanted to run past you while Annie's not here.'

That not only got her attention, it put a shifty veil across her face. 'What?' she said guardedly.

'You've a local detective in your pocket. Set us in the right direction on that case the other month.'

Now the shiftiness was pronounced. 'What of it?'

'Who is it?'

She gave him an outraged look. 'You know we don't share that stuff. Why? What's the matter?'

'If … uh … if he's showing too keen an interest in our affairs then we need to share.' He was winging it now. He'd started with no aim other than to divert her from Annie's whereabouts, but an idea was beginning to form. He hadn't entirely believed in Pat's clandestine source. He'd said to Annie once that if they were official investigators who had to register their intelligence sources, Pat's list would shrink to nothing. Suddenly he wasn't so sure.

Taking a shot in the dark, he said, 'It's Marchant, isn't it?'

Pat looked dumbfounded. 'How did you know?'

He gave an indeterminate gesture.

'No, seriously,' she pressed him. 'How did you know? No one knows. Even he doesn't know.'

'What do you mean?'

'Have you met Ryan? One of Babs' sprogs, he's big like you, works in Bridlington.'

Mike sat down and listened in amazement as Pat told him about Barbara's son, Ryan, the keen fisherman, and how he was 'part of the furniture' in one of the seafront clubs where the fishermen often gathered. Tommy Marchant was a regular. 'Him and two mates,' Pat said. 'Been going out for years. They're not coppers, the guys he goes with. It was a long while before we cottoned on that Tommy was.'

It was Ryan, at Pat's urging, who had made a point of getting in with Tommy's group, helping them out with bookings, being on hand to see what might slip out when they celebrated after a good day at sea. It hadn't been much, but with carefully angled comments and questions, they'd had a few nuggets over the years.

'You reckon he doesn't know?'

'No, we've been careful. He's a good lad is Ryan; canny. The times he's got lucky have been when Tommy's been in his cups, accepted that extra pint.'

'He's not bent then?'

'Nah, don't think so. He's just sitting it out to retirement. He'd go early if he could but he can't.'

'You don't sound sure.'

'What, if he's bent or not?' Pat tipped her head. 'Not out-and-out bent for sure. I think there's something dodgy in his past. On the boat, no land in sight, that's the only place he really relaxes, that's what they say. He's desperate to see out his time without damage to his pension. How did you find out?'

'I suppose I clocked something somewhere along the way, but genuinely, it was just a guess.'

'And what's Tommy been doing that's rattled your cage?'

'Presumably, he's the one–' Mike stopped abruptly, then blurted out, 'But he can't be the one who told you about Jennifer.' He stared at Pat who looked puzzled.

'What do you mean?'

Wrapped up in his lucky guess about Marchant, Mike hadn't thought it through. Marchant was the single one of Jennifer's ex-colleagues he knew for sure wasn't her confidant back at the station. 'Who told you about Jennifer?' he demanded of Pat. 'No way did you work it out for yourself. And what exactly do you know?'

Pat sat back, an immovable presence, and looked him solidly in the eye until he felt compelled to break the stare. He grumbled and pulled his chair round.

'Yeah, it was a copper,' said Pat. 'Someone I've spoken to on and off over the years. More off than on if I'm honest. Someone with something to gain from me knowing what you knew about Jennifer, that's my guess.'

So Pat had known all along. 'And I suppose you've been feeding stuff back.'

'Hell, no. You can fuck off with that sort of accusation. There's been nothing like that at all.'

'Yeah, yeah, sorry, I shouldn't have said that. But who was it then?' Could Jennifer's confidant and Pat's contact be one and the same. They must be. Who else would have known enough to have alerted Pat? And why?

'You guessed Marchant, fair enough,' said Pat. 'But that

doesn't mean all the rules we work by go out of the window. We. Don't. Share. That. Stuff. OK?'

As Mike opened his mouth to speak, Pat heaved herself to her feet and headed for the door. He swallowed the words he'd been about to say. She was right. Of course she was right. And this wasn't the way to get information out of her. He'd better rebuild some bridges. That accusation he'd thrown at her was unforgiveable. If Pat was heading for the kitchen to make coffee for herself and not for him, then he had serious bridges to build.

But she wasn't. She was clumping down the stairs.

'Where are you going?' he called, glancing at the window, still streaked with rain. Pat's coat hung behind the door.

'Post,' she called back and there was no mistaking the frost in her voice.

'But we've already–' He stopped. She wasn't going down for the post. She was putting a break in the argument. He leapt to his feet and leant over the bannister. 'I'll make some coffee.'

He saw her pause on the penultimate step, before tossing her shoulders and responding with an irritable grunt. He blew out a sigh of relief. She'd accepted the peace offering.

As he carried two steaming mugs back through, she was just ahead of him, and had a package in her hand.

Putting the mug down in front of her earned him another grunt as she ripped open the package. Something fell from it and clinked on to the desk.

A key.

He looked at it, then at Pat who had pulled out a typewritten note.

'Bloody hell, Mike. Look at this.'

CHAPTER 39

Mike jumped round to Pat's side of the desk and snatched up the note. It was typed.

Here's your key. Lois.

They stared at each other.

'But isn't this what Annie went to collect? Why …?'

Mike floundered. Had Annie sent someone back to the office with the key when she went to Miriam Marshall's? But why? They didn't need it. The locks had been changed.

Pat's eyes narrowed as she looked from the key to the note. 'Maybe Lois didn't have it with her … hmmm.' Mike watched her take a mouthful of coffee before she spoke again. 'She met Annie, but wouldn't hand over the key … then … I don't know … tried a spot of blackmail, bribery.'

'She's handed it over now,' Mike put in.

'Yeah well, Annie wouldn't have stood for any nonsense. She'll have threatened her. That'll be it. She didn't have it with her in case Annie got heavy and tried to take it off her, but something happened and Annie told her she had to drop it in, so she did. Maybe Lois was bluffing, or maybe Annie paid up. God knows what Lois might have found in the files if she's had a key to go rummaging.'

'She didn't get what she was looking for, remember? That's if the intruder was her and if she was after that paperwork. But hang on, we picked up the post earlier.' He tipped his thumb towards a heap of unopened letters. 'That must have come by hand. Come on.'

He leapt up and headed for the stairs. By the time Pat caught him up at the reception counter, he'd already been stonewalled. They were busy. No one could remember who'd brought it.

'It's not our job to track your post, you know.'

'Then I need to see the CCTV,' Mike was saying as Pat arrived beside him.

'I'll ask the manager and let you know.' The supercilious smile that accompanied the words made Mike ball his hands into fists to hold back from slapping the woman.

'Get him now,' snapped Pat, her voice loud enough to raise heads from the back of the office.

The woman turned as though to recruit allies from her colleagues, but the manager rushed out from a side office and strode to the counter.

'You can't keep using our resources like this. It'll have to wait to the end of the day.'

Mike kept his voice level as he repeated his request for sight of the CCTV to know who had delivered the package.

Pat pulled out her phone. 'We're talking about a missing person here, a vulnerable young woman. If you won't cooperate with us, you'll cooperate with the police. Mike, give me the number of that detective who called here the other day … no, no need, I've found it.'

'Alright, alright, just wait a moment,' the manager said testily. 'If it's a police matter, that's different. You should have said.' He glared at Mike who recognised a feeble attempt to save face and remained impassive.

A few minutes later, he and Pat were behind the counter playing back the footage.

They fast-forwarded through the morning until they saw Pat arrive, and then jumped it forward, stopping every time someone came in.

'Busy down here, aren't they?' Pat murmured.

Then, as the timestamp flicked to 11.14, he saw it. The woman's demeanour was surreptitious even as she emerged through the doorway. 'Is that Lois?'

Pat leaned in to stare at the figure who made a beeline across the lobby to the post trays, head down, dropped the package and went back out.

Mike set the sequence to play again. 'Is it Lois?' he asked again.

'Could be anyone all bundled up like that. Can't see her face. Small enough build to be Lois, but it wouldn't stand up in court.'

Mike rolled his eyes. 'We're not taking her to court for returning our key. Just take that sequence back again … There, look at that timestamp. Eleven-fourteen. Could she have met Annie at the Oddbottle and got back here for eleven-fourteen?'

Pat blew out a breath. 'I'd have said ten to fifteen minutes with clear roads. Nearer fifteen, ten'd be pushing it.'

'Annie was probably there a few minutes early. They wouldn't have stayed around to socialise.'

Pat lifted her phone to video the few seconds' footage. 'Do we know for sure that they met? I'm wondering if she sent Annie on a wild goose chase to be sure she wasn't here when she returned the key.'

Mike pulled out his phone. The hour wasn't up, but he clicked out a text to Annie.

Lois was here just before 11.15 to return the key. Did you see her?

He scrolled back through the texts. 'She didn't actually say she met Lois, just that she was going to Miriam Marshall's.'

Pat murmured, 'Yeah, and we don't know for sure it was Lois who was here.'

* * *

The wide approach roads were largely empty, yet had an air of bustle and busyness about them. Annie imagined an invisible army marching towards her from every direction. Close to Havenmere Docks, the background beat of heavy industry leaked in, a rhythmic thump and behind it, a muted roar as though an unstoppable wall of water would burst through at any moment.

She tried to see beyond the high security fences, steel mesh and wires, to spot at least one real person amongst the landscape of metallic shapes, square brick-built structures and glistening towers. The giant cranes were further from the road, down by the estuary, the real highway into these places. The gloom of rising fog melted them into the sky so Annie wasn't sure what she could see and what her mind was making up.

The first sign of life came as the big gates to Havenmere Docks came into view; a car crossed her path up ahead. Even glimpsed through the mist, its security livery was unmistakable.

She kept a wary eye on her mirrors as she swung in to face the blank wall of the gates. If he'd spotted her, he'd be on his way round to challenge her.

A clanking screech set her teeth on edge. The gates slid open to let her in.

The main yard was unrecognisable. The topography had changed with stacks of giant containers dwarfing the office block and leaving no wide space for her to mistakenly pull her car into, but she knew where to go, and familiarity had taken the forbidding gloss off the giant boxes.

You won't get me this time!

She pulled round to the back of the office building and into one of the visitors' parking spaces. She had three phones in the car now; Miriam's, her own and her clone. After a moment's hesitation, she slipped the clone phone into her jacket and put her own phone into the glove box where a small cavity would hide it from a cursory search. Miriam might be wrong about Rob Small's whereabouts. If he found her on his premises unauthorised, she could find herself in customs or police custody and compelled to hand over her mobile. The clone phone had enough on it that it would be a wrench to see it pulled apart and analysed by someone who knew what they were doing, but better that than they got their hands on the real thing with its extra layers of data.

This was exactly the situation she tried to impress on Mike, to get across the importance of the double-phones but he'd only say they should avoid these situations in the first place. She sighed. Maybe he had a point.

Picking up Miriam's phone, she climbed out of the car to squeals and clanking from beyond the building, which surprised her. Was the yard still at work? Miriam had implied that no one would be here … or had she? She'd said Rob Small would be out of the way, but surely the place wasn't automated to the point where it could be left to ply its trade unsupervised. Maybe some minion had been left in charge, someone Miriam knew and could coerce into letting her have range free. But Annie's was the only car in the car park.

She mounted the stairs towards the control room, the route she'd taken when Rob Small had shown her in, and was just at the first landing when she felt the clone phone vibrate. She paused to check. It was a text from Mike.

Lois was here just before 11.15 to return the key. Did you see her?

She thought back. Shit, she'd never told him Lois hadn't shown.

If Lois was at the office at 11.15 then she'd made damn sure Annie was out of the way. Was that the payback for helping Miriam, that she could nip into the agency with no risk of running into Annie? She paused and leant back on the metal handrail. Something screeched and clattered from the far side of the site. The mist in the air was beginning to settle damply on her skin. Or was she wrong about Miriam using Lois, because those texts got both of them out of the way. Had Lois obtained a key to the Marshalls'? And if so, was she still looking for that paperwork? Too much guesswork. She needed to talk this through with Mike and Pat.

She looked down at the car park, at its only occupant, her car. She was tempted to give up on Miriam, to go back down, get in and drive away. This was Miriam's battle with Rob Small, not hers. She clicked out a text to Mike.

No, didn't see Lois. She's up to something. Don't know what but glad she's turned up.

Then she continued up the stairs. The outer door swung open to her touch and she stepped inside.

'Miriam?'

No reply.

The noise from the clanking machinery had quietened as the door closed behind her, just the way she remembered from last time.

A wall of heat hit her as she entered the control room. It might be mid-December but inside here it was tropical. She tried to recall if she'd noticed the heat last time.

She slipped off her jacket and hung it on a hook by the door, pulling Miriam's phone from the pocket and lying it on the side of the console.

Rob Small's wheeled chair sat askew at one end of the console, facing a screen showing the Automatic Number Plate Recognition system. Those were the only obvious signs of Miriam's presence, but Annie knew why she wasn't here waiting. She looked at the screen and used the mouse to click through the controls; Miriam was right, it was a simple system. After putting in Annie's registration, Miriam's plan had been to phone. That would have been the point she realised she'd lost her mobile. Annie imagined her in a panic scurrying to retrace her steps, but she was bound to realise that her best bet was to come back to the Havenmere control room.

Just to be sure, Annie strode the length of the control room and lobby, peering into corners and cupboards. There was a small kitchen at one end but she was alone.

She sat at the console. Miriam wanted to try to find the electronic version of the paperwork her husband had stolen. *I think I know how to work the simulator*, she'd said.

I've kept the dateline ID. Annie remembered the contempt with which she'd assumed that Annie hadn't. But she had. If she could get into this system, she'd like to bet she could find it for herself and run it, maybe before Miriam was back.

CHAPTER 40

Again, Mike felt relief lift the worry from his shoulders, but this time it was tinged with both irritation and puzzlement. It was all very well her saying that Lois was playing games, but what the hell were either of them up to?

Pat rolled her eyes when he told her. 'It's not a paying case, Mike. She's off on one of her side tracks again. Who cares what the real story is?'

He agreed but loyalty to Annie made him point out that a lot of her diversions had enhanced their reputation for doing a thorough job.

The office phone rang. Pat leaned in to look at the number and then plucked the handset from its rest. 'Thompsons' Agency … Yes, that's right, I was going to call you. The documents are all shipshape but I have a couple of queries.'

Pat rummaged through the papers on her desk and settled back for a catch-up session with her client. Mike slid quietly from the room, heading along the landing for the kitchen, his fingers at his phone calling Annie.

She answered at once. 'Mike … Hi …' but sounded distracted.

'What are you doing? Can you talk?'

'You on your own?'

'For the moment, yeah. Pat's in the office. I'm in the kitchen. We've been worried.'

'She doesn't know where I am, does she?'

'Miriam Marshall's is all she knows.'

'Good. Keep it that way if possible.'

'OK, but what–?' He stopped. Footsteps on the landing. 'Pat's coming.'

'OK, I can't give you chapter and verse yet. And I want to get something done before Miriam gets back, but put me on speaker and I'll tell you both what I have so far.'

Mike did as she asked, nodding towards the handset and saying, 'Annie,' to Pat as she came in.

'Hi Pat,' said Annie's voice. 'Listen up, I don't have long. I'm going to get to the bottom of what happened to William Marshall, that is, to the bottom of Miriam's paranoia about it. What actually happened was an accident, I'm pretty sure, but there's something tied in with that paperwork. I've told Miriam we've junked it. I'll get back to you. Miriam lost her phone. It's given me an opportunity I don't want to miss. Speak later, OK?'

The call went dead. Pat looked at Mike. 'Any the wiser?' She gave him a hard stare before turning on her heel and heading to the office.

He followed and found she'd turned her chair to sit at Barb's desk so she faced away from him. For a moment he wondered whether to speak, but even her back looked glacial, so he sat at his own desk and tried to concentrate.

After twenty minutes, he gave up any pretence of being able to focus and stood up.

'Coffee?'

Pat grunted assent so he headed for the kitchen. Too

much coffee by far today. Annie would call anytime now and then they could set aside her diversion and give their attention to what was important.

Pat joined him, going to lean on the counter to watch the grey day outside. After a moment, she said, 'I'd be happier if I knew what was going on.'

'Annie'll tell us when she gets back.'

'I didn't mean that. Where does Jennifer keep ducking out to? Tell me what you're keeping from me and I'll tell you who told me about her.'

So Pat didn't know as much as he'd assumed. Something in her tone made him put aside thoughts of what Annie would say. He needed Pat on side. 'She's suspended,' he told her. 'She's in the middle of a disciplinary. She gets called in for meetings, that's where she's ducking out to. We don't know the detail. We think it's to do with her last posting. If she's not kicked out, she'll resign.'

'Straight-laced Flanagan! Who'd have thought it?'

'So she'll be properly on board with us in a few weeks, unless–' He stopped. He'd said more than enough.

'Unless she gets sent down,' Pat completed for him.

'Yeah, well, we don't know how serious it is.'

'OK, that's the long and short of it, is it? That's what you and Annie have been keeping from us?'

'Yes, that's it. So who told you about her?'

Pat's unfocused gaze was on the world outside. 'What I was told was that she wanted a career change, personal reasons, and that Annie had agreed to give her a trial but was worried about how I'd take it … thought I'd create a fuss, not want her on the team. Of course, I saw what she could be worth straight off. I wasn't about to make any objections. I believed the personal reasons … to start with … more fool me.'

'You said you'd tell me who; a copper you've spoken to on and off over the years.'

She gave a short laugh. 'Yeah, I did say that. But it isn't someone I've had in my pocket. In fact, I'm beginning to think that I'm the one who's been in the pocket – maybe we all have.'

'Yeah, but who?'

She held out her hand. 'Give me your phone. It was Jennifer. It was PC Flanagan herself who told me.'

'Jennifer? But …?'

Pat's hand was still outstretched. Unthinking, he passed his phone across to her. He and Annie had always assumed Pat had been tipped off, but never thought of Jennifer. She must have been desperate to get on board to have risked canvassing Pat.

'But why did you pretend you'd worked it out yourself?'

'More fun that way …' A cold laugh … 'No, it was Jennifer's idea. She didn't want to set off on the wrong foot – going behind Annie's back. Annie's the boss now, after all.'

His phone now sitting in Pat's hand flashed. He saw Pat's eyebrows rise as she looked at the screen.

'Well well, just look who's calling you.' She held the handset up.

'Cut her off,' he snapped. 'She can get in the bloody queue. So listen, do you have any idea what Jennifer's done, how much trouble she's in?'

Pat shook her head as she red-buttoned the call. 'Nope. I told you, I fell for the personal reasons guff.'

His phone screen lit up again and he held out his hand. 'And what do you want with my phone?'

Instead of handing it back, Pat looked at the screen and gave a brief laugh. 'She's pretending to be Annie now. She wants you to ring her.'

He took the phone from her, read the unconvincing message and clicked out a brief response.

Pat leant in to look. 'Full English?'

'Well, just in case it *is* Annie. Pat, you just said you'd be happier if you knew what was going on. Well, so would I. What's the deal with the phone? What's the matter with you?'

She looked up to meet his eye. He saw perplexity in her face. 'I'm not sure …' She turned towards the window and leant across the counter. He looked over her shoulder but could see nothing untoward. 'Come on, we need to be in the office.'

'But what–?'

His phone lit up again. He gasped, suddenly not needing the message to know it was Annie. He could see from the shocked look on Pat's face that she'd realised. 'Is that on silent?'

He shook his head. They'd been too wrapped up in things to realise the caller was bypassing the clone.

As she took the phone from him again, he heard the outside door open downstairs.

'Shit!' she said, furiously clicking out a response to the text, then rushing towards the office, signalling him to follow.

He saw her slip his phone into her pocket as she sat at her desk.

CHAPTER 41

'Speed not haste,' Annie murmured as she played about with the console and its many input devices. She wanted a feel for the system before she tried to dig too deep. There was scope here to get things catastrophically wrong.

Tentatively, she pushed buttons, and slid the various cursors into place on their different screens. The interfaces seemed separate from each other but she guessed they would be integrated behind the scenes, and might even be streaming a record of her meddling direct to Rob Small in Amsterdam.

She turned her head at a loud clanking from outside. She watched one of the giant cranes elevate, then hover over the rows of stacked containers as though wondering which one to move next. The giant boxes were neatly assembled across what had been a wide empty expanse when she'd first visited. Way down towards the far end the pattern broke with a blue container at an angle, mismatched in both height and alignment. She imagined the giant crane spotting it, and tutting as it slid down its tramlines to go and set it straight. Her fingers itched to get at the console, to start to look for the simulator Miriam had mentioned, but she daren't risk causing anything outside to move.

Rob Small was a fool. He'd bypassed his own systems'

security. Everything was password protected, but as soon as she clicked into the relevant boxes, they auto-filled and let her in. And yet it was the electronics he relied on to keep intruders out of the site.

It must have hit him hard to find Miriam's husband had been in.

Annie recalled the ornate old-fashioned key Miriam had shown her. It might have got Miriam on to the site but it hadn't given her access to the control room. William Marshall must have passed on more keys and codes than one for a forgotten back gate. She hadn't thought to ask – careless.

As she watched the scene outside, the big crane lowered on to a container and grabbed its sides with a series of clangs. Then it sat still as another crane slid along its runners. She thought back to the things Small had told her. Data being fed in continuously from external sources, saying where the next shipment was coming from, where its component parts needed to go. The machinery was moving itself into place, the optimum configuration for efficiency as soon as it needed to start hauling things about. That was all that she was seeing; nothing was being lifted or moved. The automatic systems were analysing for future movement and setting themselves in place.

She turned back to the console, glancing at the time.

One screen showed the big gates. She played about with it, cycling it through a series of camera shots showing different parts of the yard; her car alone in the car park, the big gates, large spaces made into geometric mazes by stacked metal boxes, stretches of security fence that she didn't recognise. She cycled through to see if she could spot the forgotten back entrance but there was nothing. It must anyway be in a camera blind spot for it to have remained undetected, and there were plenty of blind spots, even in the small areas she knew. If a vehicle came in through the gates, she couldn't track it round the side of the building; it would reappear in the car park where she would see the driver get out of the car, but couldn't watch them climb the stairs to the control room. Without a map, it was hard to place all the camera shots. She could orientate things with the control tower. The misaligned blue container proved a useful landmark for the far reaches of the yard, but otherwise it was just a maze of machinery and metal boxes.

She watched for any sign of Miriam dodging through the maze. She must have been gone for close on ten minutes now. Annie imagined her retracing her steps the whole way to that deserted road – that would be twenty minutes minimum. Back at the road, she might find some debris from her pocket if it hadn't all fallen inside the car, and surely then she would realise what had happened and make her way back – another twenty minutes.

She split the surveillance screen into several windows, and with the jigsaw in her peripheral vision, she let the wheeled chair glide sideways to the middle of the console.

The simulator subsystem wasn't hard to find. It sprang to life, auto-filled its security boxes and presented her with a screen that included a search facility into which she typed the Dateline ID from the paperwork.

It gave her a single result.

She hadn't expected it to be so simple and glanced uneasily at the CCTV screens.

After a moment's hesitation, she loaded the file and with

249

a brief prayer – *this is just a simulation, it won't do anything for real* – clicked Run.

A schematic built itself on the screen. She scrutinised the graphic, trying to work out what it represented. The rectangular boxes were surely the containers, the lines might be the tracks for the cranes; shaded areas could correspond to buildings and other immovable objects. Several flashing points appeared, some clustered together, some in small groups. Highlights ran down the lines, the boxes twisted and turned and shifted position. Smaller squares zipped back and forth eating up the flashing points like the chaser in a simple game. They would be the autonomous vehicles, one of which Small had told her could have been summoned to push her car out of the way. After the flurry of movement everything stopped except for a single rectangular box that moved forward, then back, then forward again. The screen blanked.

Was that it?

She played it through again, watching the lines and rectangles build and move, the flashing points scurry ahead of the tiny squares, the single box at the end, like a finale – forward, back, forward again.

That was it. That huge heap of paper was the technical spec for those few minutes of action. She'd found what they were looking for but was none the wiser.

Where was Miriam?

A sudden insistent beeping startled her to her feet.

'Miriam?'

She spun round. It was the inbuilt coffee machine. A red alarm flashed in time with the beeps. She walked towards it to see the window playing a looped message: *water tank low … water tank low …*

'It's the bloody heat in here,' she snapped, reaching forward to turn off the alarm, knowing it would probably come on again on some kind of timer. A typed note was fixed to the side of the machine:

Do not fill from outside tap, use drinking water from kitchen.

She'd forgotten the kitchen. The promise of cool drinking water had her striding to the door at the far side of the control room. A galley kitchen with a fridge, a microwave and a chest freezer huddled in a row; a narrow metal door to one side marked Fire Escape, and opposite a deep sink that had several taps, one labelled 'Drinking water'. Helping herself to a glass from the draining board she took a long cool drink, refilled the glass and turned to take it back towards the console.

A movement caught her eye.

'Miriam, is that you?'

The control room was empty but one of the cranes was sliding silently across. She watched it go, left to right. Had she caught its reflection in one of the metallic surfaces? Miriam should still be ten minutes away by her estimate.

Perturbed, she looked around; something was different.

A vehicle began to move on the car park surveillance screen. She hadn't heard the gates. Could Rob Small be back?

The thought sent a shiver through her as her eye turned instinctively towards the door.

The hook was empty. Her jacket had gone.

And with it her car keys and phone.

For a moment she stared at her own car reversing out from its parking place.

'Miriam!' she yelled as she leapt for the door to the external staircase, and grabbed the handle. It wouldn't move. She pulled frantically at it, but it had been locked.

A clanking screech jarred through the air. A familiar sound. The gates were opening.

'Oh no, you don't!' She sprinted back to the console to bring up the security system. One simple command took control of the gates, and with satisfaction, she saw them slide closed as her car nosed round the corner. She watched it creep towards the exit and with a few keystrokes, removed her registration from the ANPR.

The camera angle didn't allow her to see who was driving, but she had no doubts.

'You're not going anywhere, Miriam,' she told the screen. 'Not until I know what the hell you're playing at.'

The car backed off from the gates and stopped. Annie had a feeling Miriam wasn't yet out of options. Sure enough, she was startled by the familiar screech of metal on metal. The big gates started to slide open.

Miriam had remote access. Her car's registration was back on the ANPR authorised list.

Annie overrode it again from the console. 'Think you've got control of the system, do you?' she said as her fingers flew across the keyboard. 'Shouldn't have given me a head start with it. She dug deeper and saw how to blacklist her number. This time as Miriam added in the registration, it appeared only fleetingly on the authorised list before vanishing.

Presumably Miriam would be able to whitelist it, if she realised what was happening, but she couldn't outpace Annie as long as Annie had access to the console.

That metal door in the corner of the kitchen had looked unused but must be a secondary fire-escape. Could she get down there and get Miriam out of the car before she figured out how to get those gates working again?

While she stayed at the console, it was stalemate.

She needed to call back to base, but Miriam had her phone … both her phones; one in her jacket pocket and one in the glove box.

Keeping an eye on the camera, she slid the chair back to the main console and explored the external portals that she'd seen earlier. There was no standard internet connection, everything was tightly tied into a specific network; shipping container movements, shipping … given time she might hack her way to a useable connection, but it wasn't the type of trail she wanted to leave behind her.

Activity on the security system had her scoot back to the end of the console. Miriam had added in the registration again and this time it stayed put. What the hell …?

Annie stared and then smiled. Miriam had transposed two of the digits. She thought she'd input the wrong number. The car edged close to the gates again. They stayed shut, an impenetrable barrier.

She pushed the chair back to the main console to search for some means to communicate with Mike. It took seconds to reach a dead end. These external systems were tied in tight against ad-hoc access to the outside world, and were too sophisticated for her to break without far more time and resource than she had; and even an attempt would count as criminal damage. One of them had been shielded, invisible to a superficial search, much like the hidden phone in her car. She investigated, but it was as tightly secured as the rest.

Oddly, the hidden portal had a replica, right there in plain sight. As Annie opened it she saw an identical security access screen, and when she clicked in the username box, it gave a list with *HavenmereDocksRSmall* at the top. The password field gave her the option to *Use password for HavenmereDocksRSmall*. The clone portal was there for a reason but it didn't have any connection anywhere, and wasn't going to help her contact the outside world, or stop Miriam from trying to get those gates open.

Movement again from the surveillance camera had her back to the end of the console. Miriam was backing the car, turning it towards the side of the building that led to the car park. Was she admitting defeat and coming back?

Annie watched as the car's nose disappeared off the edge of the frame, and waited for it to appear on the car park camera.

Nothing. One screen showed an empty car park, the other an empty stretch of tarmac inside the gates. Miriam had backed the car into the camera blind spot and stopped.

If Miriam got out and hugged the wall, she could make her way back to the external staircase out of view of the cameras. And what about that door in the kitchen? If there was access to the outside, it would be from that side of the building.

Bouncing her attention between the ANPR database to watch for further meddling, the galley kitchen with its narrow fire exit, and the lobby to the main door, Annie's gaze lit on something she'd forgotten.

Miriam's phone.

With a crow of triumph she grabbed it from the side of the console. She could easily hack her way into this at least as far as being able to make a call. When she clicked it on, she saw the battery was low but not yet in the red. Better still it opened up with no security at all.

At once, she put in Mike's number. He would be surprised to see Miriam Marshall on his handset.

The call was cut off, red-buttoned, and she let out an exasperated huff. She'd expected him to answer because he knew Miriam was with her, but he must be busy with something else. Well too bad, she needed to speak to him.

Miriam was fiddling with the security system again, Annie could see signs of activity, but the number remained blacklisted which would keep the gates shut. Annie kept a close eye on both the system and the gates as she clicked out a text to Mike.

This is Annie. I need you to ring me on this number.

Thirty seconds dragged by before a reply popped up: *Full English?*

She rolled her eyes. OK, he needed to know it was her.

Without eggs or bacon. Miriam has my phone, I have hers. Ring me on this number asap.

A movement jerked her attention back to the surveillance screen.

The car had reappeared and was edging towards the gates. Annie leaned in to watch as it turned the corner. For a second, she had an oblique view of Miriam behind the wheel wearing her jacket.

Again the clanking screech of the opening gates. What the hell? The number was still there on the blacklist.

She tried to override it but this time it wasn't listening.

Then as the car swung round, she saw the front registration plate, a dull black smudge. Miriam had stopped out of sight of the camera to smear it with mud or tar, then she'd used some other method to get the gates to open. They wouldn't let through a blacklisted number but the ANPR couldn't recognise it.

There had to be a way to stop it, somewhere beneath the ANPR layer.

As she scrabbled to find it, the gates screeched wider, the car inched closer, and Miriam's phone beeped an incoming text.

It was too late. She couldn't find the right command to stop the gates. Miriam accelerated hard. Annie flinched to see the wing-mirror scrape against the barely adequate gap. And her car was gone.

She looked down at Mike's reply.

You're not on Miriam's phone. It's Lois's.

CHAPTER 42

The rain had let up briefly as Jennifer Flanagan strode towards the ramshackle building that housed the Thompsons' office. She glanced up at the ludicrous sign, feeling the cold air prickle her skin. They could have moved into bigger, more comfortable, more prestigious offices, but Annie had only shrugged when she'd touched on it. At first, she'd assumed lack of money, that they were just bumping along the bottom barely scraping a living just like eight years ago, but she'd been wrong. Surprisingly wrong. In fact, she'd been in for a whole raft of surprises during the time she'd been with them.

Not only had they money behind them, they were good at what they did, though there remained a gaping chasm between the money they brought in by their own efforts and the vast sum that sat in the background.

Did they know what they were doing? It was hardly credible that they didn't.

She'd talked it through with Caitlin. Shouldn't have, but she'd had to after Tommy-stupid-Marchant had hot-footed it round the station raking up dregs of gossip and rung Caitlin with that half-baked tale. Caitlin, typically, had been forgiving of Tommy once she knew the story.

'He rang me as your friend, because he cares what

happens to you,' she'd said, but Jennifer shuddered even now to think what he'd put Caitlin through with his stupid suppositions.

Caitlin's desperation played in her head as she paused in front of the door that led to the reception area of the tinpot little outfit that tried to punch above its weight from the ground floor.

'Our plans,' Caitlin had sobbed. 'What if you lose your job? The baby …? What if you … what if it's worse …?'

She'd had to tell her everything. And of course that caused even more worry. She'd never burdened Caitlin with the worst excesses of the job, the corners that she found herself backed into, that was the way they worked. Their relationship flourished on keeping their lives strictly compartmentalised and now on the brink of such a huge change as this, bloody Marchant had to step in with his size nines.

The road was busy. She could see two police officers sauntering through the crowds, chatting to each other, looking into the windows of the various businesses as they went by. Or were they PCSOs? The sun was low, she couldn't make out the detail of their uniforms. Resources were tight but she hoped one of the two was a fully-fledged officer. She didn't like to see rookies out and about in areas where things could get sticky.

She stepped inside the building. One of the painted mannequins from behind the desk looked up with a welcoming smile that disappeared into a haughty sniff as she recognised Jennifer.

Jennifer threw a scornful glance at the cheap camera lens. 'Less use than a chocolate teapot,' she'd told Caitlin.

If she wanted to go to the dark side, she could turn this place over in minutes and they'd not know what had hit them, though if she went to the dark side, she wouldn't go after small fry like this. Annie's agency upstairs was another matter. Nothing ostentatious but their security was tight – when they remembered to use it.

She'd looked on Annie as a friend, albeit not a close one, indeed a friend who knew more about her than she was comfortable with. It was Pat Thompson who'd given her the 'in' but Annie and Mike had embraced her contribution and she'd found a lot more to the whole operation than she'd imagined.

Even so …

She blew out a breath as she looked up the staircase. 'OK,' she murmured to herself. 'Let's do this.'

* * *

Mike sat at his desk watching Pat who was ignoring him, but puffing slightly, after her quick sprint from the kitchen. The dying vestiges of sunlight speared thin shafts through the window that accentuated the dirt on the glass and the dust in the air. He needed to call Annie, she might be in trouble, and couldn't quite work out why he wasn't demanding his mobile back off Pat.

Not that he needed it, he had Lois's number, and a working phone on his desk. He kept Pat in his peripheral vision as he lifted the receiver. She remained engrossed in her paperwork.

'Hi, it's Mike from the agency.' He kept his voice low and neutral as though talking to a stranger.

Annie picked up his impersonal tone, and sounded worried. 'Mike, what's happening?'

'I'm not sure.' He kept his tone light. 'And how are things with you?'

Her reply came out in a rush. 'Miriam Marshall's stolen my car and she's locked me in at Havenmere Docks.'

'But why …? What …?' It was a struggle to keep his tone even.

'I don't know what she's playing at, but I think she's going to report me and get me found on the premises. She's been outside in the yard. I've no idea what damage she's done.'

'I'll come and get you.' As he spoke the words, he was aware of Pat's head shooting up from the paperwork, but her attention wasn't on him, it was on the main door. He heard familiar footsteps coming up the stairs.

He turned his back to both Pat and the door as he murmured, 'Jennifer's just arrived,' into the phone.

'For god's sake don't let her know where I am. Listen Mike, you can't get here in time. Whatever Miriam's got planned, it's going to happen fast. I'm keeping this phone with me but the battery's low. Head for the bridge, soon as you can. I'll need you to pick me up, but I don't know where from. I'll ring when I'm out of the dockyard. I might have to go the way Miriam got in. If this is Lois's phone then Miriam must have sent the text this morning, but didn't you say that Lois–? No, this has to keep, I need to clear my tracks and get out of here.'

The door swung open and Jennifer stepped in. She began to speak but stopped when she saw Mike was on the phone. He smiled at her and gave her a 'just a moment' gesture.

'So … um … you're absolutely sure about that,' he intoned into the phone.

'Yup,' said Annie's voice. He could tell she was moving about as she spoke. 'I found the simulation that all that paperwork is about. More interesting, there's a clone database that I need to get a better look at if I can before I get out. The simulation's just a few minutes, but I couldn't make out what was happening. Miriam could have shown me. But the bitch took my car.'

'Was that her intention all along or …?' His even tone appeared to have convinced Pat and Jennifer that this was a routine call with a client. They weren't paying him any attention, in fact they seemed to be squaring up to each other.

'I don't know,' Annie answered him. 'That's a good question … oh! I've just put that dateline ID into the hidden database and it's found a match. This is no simulation, this is genuine. I've got to hurry but just let me try it on the replica … There!' He heard satisfaction in her voice. 'Listen Mike, he's hiding stuff he can't erase, masking it behind cloned systems. I don't have time to dig but that's the key.'

'I can get details later,' he broke in, not liking the urgency in her voice, as though she was telling him things because she might not get another chance.

'I'll be OK. I'll clean everything I've touched and I'll leave the system console as I found it. There's a fire-escape. It'll get me outside. I won't have to break any locks or anything. The security in this place is unreal, a mix of over-the-top and wide open. But there won't be cameras in here. Small's got things to hide. He won't want to be watched. That's why you need to know this stuff.'

Behind her words he heard Jennifer ask Pat, 'Where's Annie?'

'Out on a job,' was Pat's unsmiling reply.

'Out where? What job?'

'I don't know.' Pat yawned as she spoke.

The hostility in the exchange startled him.

'Mike,' said Annie's voice. 'What's going on? Who's there? What's wrong?'

'Not sure,' he murmured. 'I'll head out soon as I can. Just … um … listen, OK?'

'I'll keep quiet,' Annie said.

With a glance to check that he wasn't being observed, he slid his hand to the speakerphone button and clicked it on. He wasn't sure what it was he wanted Annie to hear, but that snippy exchange between Jennifer and Pat was somehow tied in with her odd behaviour in the kitchen.

Before anyone could speak again, the click of the door downstairs was followed by the tramp of footsteps coming up.

Still keeping his head half turned away, Mike kept up an intermittent commentary into the silent phone. 'Uh-huh … yes … OK, yes, that's fine …' and watched from the corner of his eye as a man and a woman stepped through the door. He took in the bulky high-viz tabards of their PCSO uniforms. They looked very young and very nervous.

He saw Jennifer look them up and down and give a huff of exasperation. It was as though she'd expected them, but the scorn in her expression was unmistakable.

Were they here to arrest her? Was this the end of the line for Jennifer?

Automatically, he kept up the inane commentary into

the phone, unable to find the words to tell Annie who'd arrived.

Jennifer swung round to face him. 'I'm sorry to interrupt, Mike, but I need you to end that call.'

'OK … I'll have to leave it there,' he said into the receiver. 'Catch up later.' He replaced the handset but left the line open and found he had to swallow against a dry mouth. 'Jennifer, what's up?'

She shot another annoyed glance at the two uniforms, then said, 'Where's Annie?'

'She's out on a job.'

A heavy sigh and she fixed him with a hard stare. 'Mike, tell me where Annie is.'

'For one, what makes you think I know, and for two, it's not actually your business.'

'Oh hell!' She closed her eyes for a second, then looked from him to the two uniforms as though they were the ones being unreasonable.

He noted that she hadn't spared a glance for Pat, who sat glowering at her. Fleetingly he caught Pat's eye and saw a warning look come his way with the ghost of movement, a brief shake of her head, telling him to keep quiet.

'I'm sorry Mike,' Jennifer rapped out in a tone that couldn't have sounded less contrite. 'I genuinely didn't want it to come to this.'

'To what?'

'Michael Connaughty …' He listened aghast as her words washed over him. 'You do not have to say anything, but it may harm your defence if you do not mention when questioned something which you later rely on in court. Anything you do say may be given in evidence.'

263

'But Jennifer, you can't …' What was she playing at? Was this some charade to explain her presence here to the two PCSOs?

'Patricia Thompson …' Now she was cautioning Pat. When she'd done, she turned back to him.

'Where's Annie?'

It was Pat who replied. 'She went to meet Lois.'

'Lois Suffling?' Jennifer sounded surprised. 'Why? Where?'

'Lois sent her a text this morning,' Mike said. 'Asked to meet her at the Oddbottle at 11am. It's a pub–'

'I know where it is. Where is she now?'

'We don't know,' said Mike. 'Lois didn't show. We think Annie went on to see Miriam Marshall. It's out that way.'

'That case isn't even live any more … why would–? Uh … never mind that. All in good time. I need you both to accompany us to the police station and I need your mobile phones. Now please.'

He stared at the outstretched hand. What was it with everyone wanting his phone today? 'And if I say No?'

'Then I'll have to arrest you. I don't want to see you marched out of here in cuffs, but that's up to you.'

He saw one of the still silent PCSOs reach for a set of handcuffs. On autopilot, his hand went to his pocket but it was empty.

'It's on the desk.' Pat's voice from behind him. She was pointing to a handset that looked like his, but he knew it wasn't. 'Here.' Pat reached into her own pocket and tossed a phone across to Jennifer. That wouldn't be Pat's phone either. How much trouble could they be in for the subterfuge?

'But she can't …' He appealed to Pat, who responded with a cold laugh.

'You expected proper coppers, didn't you?' Pat said to Jennifer. 'So you didn't have to do your own dirty work. But you got a couple of kids. Oh and unless you can show me a warrant, you're leaving this place with us and we're locking up.' She turned to Mike. 'Yes, she can. She's no more suspended than the Tacoma Narrows Bridge. She's been under-fucking-cover. Are you going to contradict me, PC Flanagan? No, thought not. You bitch!'

Pat got to her feet. Mike pushed together some papers on his desk using the movement to hit the speakerphone and cut off Annie's call. He felt unable to process what he'd just heard and had no idea if he felt relieved or sorry that he'd made Annie listen. As they left the office, he irritably shrugged off the hand of one of the PCSOs who tried to take his arm.

CHAPTER 43

Annie stared at the now-silent handset.

Jennifer!

All a sham. No suspension, no disciplinary. She'd been sent to spy on them. But why?

'We're not the big fish,' Annie said aloud to the empty room. 'We're not even the tiddlers. You stupid cow! Whatever you're after, we're not it. You could just have asked.'

Odd snatches from the past week played in Annie's head. A blur of Jennifer rushing them from pillar to post, always popping up at just the moment they might have sat back and taken stock. If she took five minutes now, it would all unravel and make perfect sense; the real reason they'd been targeted not just by some police enquiry but by the intruder who'd come for Rob Small's paperwork. But she didn't have five minutes.

The only bright spot was Mike's earlier text that Lois had shown up.

Mike and Pat were being hauled off to a police interview. She'd been robust in telling Mike not to say where she was, and hoped he would stick to it. She'd cleaned the control room of her presence, not from a full forensic search but to the sort of search that Rob Small might make, and now she had to find her way out before someone came to find her. This wasn't a situation in which to concentrate on anything but the here and now.

Except ...

There would be nothing to gain by escaping from here just to walk into a more permanent prison. This was a dockyard, serious stuff, Customs and Excise. This could mean decades behind bars.

For a moment she imagined herself back on that wind-blown stretch near the estuary; the wasteland with its garish for sale sign. The breeze had been sharp in her face as she closed the boot after that charade to cover Miriam's departure; she'd had to fight to open the driver's door.

She might have seen Miriam's phone right away, before she'd even turned on the engine. For instance, if Miriam had left it on the seat. If she had, she'd have leapt out of the car at once to call Miriam back. And if Miriam hadn't answered? Then she'd have just nipped across and over that bank.

Miriam could have hidden herself ... and taken her chance to steal the car from there. It would have been careless of Annie to leave the keys in the ignition ... odd not to have grabbed her jacket given how cold it was. It would all have happened quickly. Her subconscious would need to fill in the second-by-second sequence but it could have happened.

Briefly she put her head in her hands. It was so much more than that. She had to get back to Hull, get back home.

And none of it mattered unless she could get out of here right now.

Through in the galley kitchen the metal door scraped on

the concrete as she pulled it open and slipped through. She could make out a downward staircase, narrow and steep but when she pulled the door shut behind her, she was in darkness. What the hell? This was a fire escape. There should be emergency lighting. She daren't use the torch on Lois's phone, not with its battery so low. Pushing the door open again, she took the stairs quickly, wanting to secure her escape route before returning to close it.

The darkness thickened as she descended. What had looked like the end of the flight was a dog leg to another set of stairs. By the time she reached the bottom, the glimmer of light from above barely showed outlines.

It smelt like a cellar, cold and damp, but was nothing more than a concrete-encased staircase. No side entrances, no access other than top and bottom. The door at ground level was an old-fashioned fire-escape with a bar to be pushed from inside. She leant her weight on the bar and it sprang open a few centimetres then jammed.

Applying her eye to the crack she could see that it emerged just where she'd thought it would, round the side of the building, out of sight of both gates and car park. This was the camera blind spot where Miriam had stopped. Annie could even see the tyre tracks through a slick of black oily detritus, the stuff that Miriam had plastered over the registration plates. If she knelt down, she could reach through the gap and grab a handful of tar.

Putting her back to the door, she heaved at it and felt it give, but then it jammed again. She could see the heavy metal chain securing it from the outside. It looked new and clearly post-dated Small's recent Health & Safety inspection. She stretched her arm through the gap trying to reach the padlock. If she could pull it closer, she might get at the lock.

Frustratingly, the gap was almost wide enough for her to force herself through, but neither the metal door nor its frame had any give in it. She would have to break or unlock the chain.

As she pulled at the heavy links, a high-pitched screech sang out across the site.

The entrance gates!

Within seconds a vehicle was going to drive past. A minute or two later whoever had arrived would be inside the building with her.

She remembered the tell-tale open door at the top that she had to shut if she didn't want anyone on her heels, looked longingly again at the almost wide enough gap, pulled it shut, then turned to sprint up the stairs.

* * *

Mike sat alone in a bare interview room, an untouched glass of water on the table in front of him. They'd offered tea or coffee. He'd said, no, just water. There had been no chance to speak to Pat; Jennifer and her young colleagues had seen to that.

Indignation rose in him at her betrayal. We took you in, we helped you, he wanted to snarl at her, and this is how you repay us. He wanted to get angry because her story, whatever it was, was totally screwed up. We're not involved in anything that could possibly justify this, he wanted to shout in her face.

You could just have asked.

But he'd seen nothing of Jennifer since they'd arrived.

The agency had always cooperated with the police when they'd needed to. He'd been back over the detail of all the big cases when he'd been reading himself into the job. OK, he knew from what Annie had told him that the definition of 'need' might have been elastic at times, but nothing that could warrant this.

His anger evaporated. Annie was expecting him to be on his way to the bridge, except that she'd heard what happened in the office. She might be ringing him now. If so, his clone phone would pick it up, but would anyone answer? He had to assume Pat had turned off both their phones before tucking them away in some corner of the office.

The bigger worry was one that had been nagging at him for a long time, and could be the one reason to justify a police operation against them. Had their owners called in their investment? Were the shadowy Dyson and fforbes behind this? Had the agency been set up to take the rap for something big?

He drew in a breath and tried to relax. It was his first time at the wrong end of a police interview and all that carping on from Annie was beginning to make sense.

'Don't just think about it as some theoretical something that'll never happen, Mike. You need to role play it. I'll help you.'

He'd laughed when she'd tried to play interrogator with him, telling her, 'OK, I can do this myself,' just to get her off his back. He'd been irritated when she'd persisted but he saw the sense of it now.

The sitting still, the relaxed stance, the slight irritation but only at the inconvenience – to be convincing it had to come as second nature.

Annie's voice in his head: *Assume they're watching you all the time.*

His mouth felt dry. He reached for the glass of water and sipped it. They'd be along soon to question him and he had to get straight what he was going to say.

Jennifer had pushed to know where Annie was. He and Pat had confirmed a meeting with Lois at the Oddbottle to which Lois hadn't shown up; then a non-specific intent to go to see Miriam Marshall. Pat had no idea Annie had gone on to Havenmere Docks. It was important that his and Pat's stories tallied. But at the same time, Annie was in trouble. If she was caught in the dockyard, surely it would help to have her version out on the table in advance.

She'd been crystal clear; don't tell Pat, don't tell Jennifer. He had to stick with that. If things dragged on, he'd insist on a lawyer. No, he'd simply get up and leave. He wasn't under arrest, yet. If they went as far as to arrest him, then he'd insist on a lawyer.

CHAPTER 44

Richard Redman drives his car through the tall gates as they ease open. The place seems quiet. Maybe business is bad. He won't shed any tears to see Rob Small struggling; it'll be payback for the workforce he's shafted over the years. He sees dark tyre tracks through a slick of tar dropped by some hapless delivery driver (bet you got an earful, mate). Small likes everything like a new pin. Not just tyre tracks, boot prints. Hilarious if they're the prints from Small's poncy boots.

There's only one other car in the car-park, the one he expects – Rob Small's.

He stops next to it, and glances to the top of the metal staircase. Truth be told, he's not so keen on being here, just him and Small, all this heavy equipment. Accidents happen. Accidents can be made to happen. It might be that Small has figured out what he did for Miriam, and he has no clue whether Small will laugh it off or fly into a rage. But he gets out of the car, because there's a consignment due in through Red Boy's yard and he can't be rocking the boat.

As he sets off up the stairs he feels the weight of an old-fashioned knuckleduster in his pocket; outdated insurance for this day and age but he's old-school.

The door's locked so he knocks. Small's there with a smile opening it and ushering him in, then locking it behind him. That's not usual. His hand creeps to the weapon in his pocket and he decides to take the bull by the horns. 'About tonight ...' he begins.

But Small cuts him off with a raised hand. 'Let's not go into that right now. Later when we're somewhere quieter.'

Who's listening, he wonders, but when they get into the control room there's no one else there.

He sits down, cautious now about what he says. Small makes a few remarks, his tone cautious, so Redman responds in kind, replying to questions but not volunteering anything.

Then Small says, 'Listen Rich, I know you looked up the crate for Miriam, the one Jobsie died in. It seemed to reassure her but tell me straight, did you really look it up? I mean how would you get access?'

Redman pulls in a breath. If Small's asking, then he already knows. 'Right here, Rob. Where else would I get into the systems these days?' He indicates the console, surprises himself with an edge of pride to his voice.

'Oh, is that what you were after? I thought it was the simulation.'

'What simulation?' snaps Redman. He's annoyed at the implication Small knew what he was doing all along. Clearly Miriam's shot her mouth off.

Small looks at him, the stare seems to last a long time but he's not going to be the one to look away, or to break the silence. 'The simulation Jobsie was so scared of. Miriam must have told you about it.'

Redman is about to toss out a scornful, 'Course she did,'

but he hesitates. Small's demeanour is oddly stilted, as though he's acting for an audience. Maybe he's recording this and might play it back to Miriam. So Redman shrugs, like it's no big deal. 'No, what's that then?'

'I showed Jobsie a simulation of what my boys can do, and he broke in and stole the spec for it. I think he had in mind to blackmail me.'

Redman feels uncomfortable when Small talks about his machines as his 'boys', makes him sound mad as a box of frogs, but surprise is foremost and he lets it show, because he thought Jobsie knew just how far he could go rattling this tiger's cage. 'I heard you'd been robbed, but no idea it was Jobsie.'

Small nods. 'Stuff's been destroyed now.'

'I heard someone had had an arsonist on the job,' he says, doing his own bit of cage rattling.

Small gives him a sharp look. 'Don't worry, there'll be no comeback. That threat's neutralised. And no, what Jobsie stole went for recycling. I checked the collection dates; couldn't get it back if I wanted it.'

Everyone knows Jobsie broke back in after Small fired him. He kept his pass and let himself in, but he was just making a point. And after that, Small would have had the place tied down tighter than tight. He's heard rumours that Jobsie got in again, but he's never believed it, no one has.

'How did he get in second time?'

'His pass,' Small says, but avoids his eye. 'I forgot to void it.'

Redman doesn't believe it. Small might have forgotten once but not a second time. So Jobsie had found himself a backdoor, had he? He'd be the one to know about anything like that, length of time he'd worked here. He doesn't pursue the issue, just asks again, 'What simulation?'

Small turns to the console and sets the simulator running. 'That's freight being sorted,' he says, nodding towards the big screen which shows points of light in scattered groups.

Redman watches undersized squares gather the points of light and move them towards larger rectangular areas. 'You don't sort much freight here,' he observes, knowing that Havenmere Docks takes in sealed containers and moves them on whole, rarely if ever splitting cargo.

'No,' says Small. 'But we can.' He points at a cluster of lights. 'One of those is Jobsie. To my boys he's just part of the consignment.'

Richard Redman watches as Small shows how his trucks veer here and there, shepherding the freight inside the big rectangle, explaining how he played it for Jobsie, showing him how the trucks knew which one was him, how they could trap him, shove him along with the rest.

Redman has seen these things before. He recognises the glimmer of light that shimmers across one of the shorter ends of the rectangle. It signifies the door shutting on the recently-loaded freight.

'What's it doing now?' he asks as the big rectangle moves forward, back and forward again.

Small gives a cold laugh. 'I told Jobsie, you're inside there, the load's not tied down. If that crane tipping it up and down doesn't do for you, it won't make no odds. There'll not be much left of you when they bust it open again in Perth or Shanghai.'

Redman begins to understand Small's discomfort. He's

shown Jobsie a blueprint for the way he ended up dying for real. Is he worried someone will finger him for it?

As if reading his thoughts, Small suddenly leans forward. 'I didn't do it, Rich. It was nothing to do with me.'

Redman laughs uncomfortably. 'I know you didn't. I looked it up remember. That crate didn't come your way.'

'Thing is, Rich, what if my boys did it? What if Jobsie broke in again when I wasn't here? They'd have known what to do. I ran that simulation through the system just to see what they'd make of it. I programmed Jobsie in and everything so they'd recognise him.'

'Programmed him in? How? Oh, d'you mean by his–?'

'It wasn't his pass,' Small cut across him, looking desperate now. 'It wasn't his pass even the first time, Rich. I voided it soon as I let him go, 'course I did. I don't know how he was getting in. But what if he did? They'd have recognised him. The only thing my boys are worried about is efficiency. I told them he was bad news on that score. They knew just how to sweep him up; they had that simulation to learn from.'

Richard Redman sits back and surrenders to laughter. He even has to wipe his eyes before he can get out any words. Then he leans forward and pats Rob Small on the knee. 'Rob, mate, your machines couldn't do that. Not in a month of Sundays. You're going bonkers if you think they're that clever. That crate didn't come through here. Your machines didn't kill Jobsie. He climbed into a crate to sleep off a bender and he chose the wrong one. Nowt to do with you. Now for god's sake, get me something to drink before I die of thirst and you have another body on your conscience. Why is it so bloody hot in here?'

'Uh … yeah sure.' Small looks abashed as he gets to his feet.

Redman watches him disappear round the corner towards the kitchen, hears water running, a grunt, the squeak of a door, then Small is back with two cans of orange.

'Listen Rob, are you worried there's someone listening? You're acting like we're not alone, and why did you lock us in?' As soon as he asks, Redman realises that Small has relaxed.

'As a matter of fact, Rich, there is someone else in here. They're hiding, assuming we don't know. I thought they'd be in a cupboard but I've just spotted the fire door in the kitchen, so they're holed up on the stairs. They won't have been able to hear us. But better safe than sorry.'

'Who?' Redman's first thought is indignation that Small didn't come clean about this from the off; his second is to replay Small describing the detail of how 'his boys' might have killed Jobsie. Then a memory comes back to him. 'Fire door?' he says, and stares at Small's feet.

Small looks blank and looks down at his own feet, puzzled, following the line of Redman's gaze.

'When I came in just now, I saw footprints round the side. Boot prints. You're not wearing boots.'

Small's eyes narrow. 'Where exactly?'

'Round the side. Weather we've been having, I thought, they're fresh. Thought it was you, if I'm honest, wondered if you'd wrecked one of those poncy pairs of boots you wear. Just by the fire door.'

Small lets out an expletive and is on his feet diving across the room towards the kitchen. Richard Redman hears a door slam open, then pounding footsteps. He heaves himself to his feet to go and look.

The metal door at the back of the kitchen has been wrenched open. Clanking and swearing comes from beyond it, then Small emerges, pushes past him and strides to the console, tapping in instructions and staring at the screen.

'That's OK,' he says, sitting back with a clear sigh of relief. 'The bitch is still on the site.'

'How do you know?'

Rob Small laughs. Redman can see Small's amused that he's asked how and not who, but he knows Small and he no longer wants to know who.

'Leave her be for now,' says Small. 'I'll get one of the boys to home in on her in a mo. I didn't expect her to get out through the fire door. I couldn't have. Still, she's a lot smaller than me. She can't get off site. And now we know she's not listening, we can settle about tonight.'

CHAPTER 45

Mike felt slightly lightheaded. He set aside the thought that they'd doctored the drinking water. It was the stress. The small bare room was oppressive. He was being as cooperative as he could with the two men who sat the other side of the table with their unnervingly calm manner, but somehow wasn't convincing them. Not that they were unpleasant about it, just relentless. At first he thought every question was going to be a variation on 'Where's Annie?' but they seemed to have moved on now.

'We've spoken to Mrs Marshall. She says she's not seen Annie since the Saturday in November when she called into your agency for a meeting.'

'Well that's not true. We were both at her husband's funeral.' Even as the words came out, he knew they sounded defensive. Why would it be relevant that they'd been at the funeral? Annie had been one in a large crowd, and they hadn't gone to the wake. In truth, he was irritated that they referred to Miriam as Mrs Marshall and Annie just as Annie, as though conferring lesser status.

The man questioning him gave a kindly smile and continued as though he hadn't spoken. 'As it happens, Mrs Marshall *was* at the Oddbottle this morning. Can you tell me how Annie would have known about that?'

'I told you, she went to meet Lois. She didn't know anything about anyone else being there. I don't even think she said she'd met Miriam there. She went on to Miriam's house.'

The man nodded, looking down at the file on the table in front of him. 'Mrs Marshall says she didn't meet anyone at the Oddbottle, she went there to collect her phone. She'd left it the night before. She was very clear that she didn't meet Annie there. Can you explain that?'

Mike thought, haven't I already answered that? He fought back an urge to get snappy and impatient. He hoped Pat was doing OK. 'I don't know exactly where Annie met Miriam,' he repeated. 'I just know that she did.' He was confused now over what Annie's texts had said and what he'd assumed. Maybe he only knew Annie had met Miriam because of the later call about what Miriam had done at Havenmere Docks, but he couldn't mention that. 'You've got my phone,' he said. 'Look at the texts.'

The man sat forward a little. 'We've tracked their phone signals and they were both at the Oddbottle. Mrs Marshall first, then Annie, then a couple of minutes later, they both left. I think that Annie waited in the car park then followed Mrs Marshall. Why would she do that?'

'I don't know. Maybe she got there and found that Lois wasn't there and maybe Miriam Marshall turned up as she was leaving, so she saw her and waited. I don't know. I've not seen Annie since this morning.' He shouldn't have said any of that. They were getting him flustered. They were asking about stuff he couldn't possibly know. *Don't speculate*, said Annie's voice in his head.

'The barmaid remembers Mrs Marshall coming in for her phone, but she doesn't remember Annie.'

'I doubt Annie went to the bar; she wasn't there to drink. She was meeting Lois.'

'Both their phones headed in the same direction away from the pub.'

'Then they were together. They must have met outside.' The man gave him a look. Of course he'd only just said that Miriam claimed not to have met Annie at all, let alone at the pub. 'I think Miriam Marshall's lying.' He knew he shouldn't say it, but couldn't stop himself. 'And no, before you ask, I don't know why.'

More pieces of paper came out. Miriam Marshall's story, apparently backed up by her phone records, was that she went home, then headed for her brother's the other side of the Humber, near Barton. 'The records show Annie's phone and Mrs Marshall's heading from the pub towards where Mrs Marshall lives.'

'Together or apart?' Mike challenged.

'Hard to say.'

'Then who's to say they weren't in the same car?' His belligerence was rising, he couldn't keep a lid on it.

As they kept charting the journeys, it occurred to Mike to wonder at the trouble they'd gone to. He knew Miriam was lying. He knew she'd double-crossed Annie in some way. But he'd promised Annie he wouldn't say where she was.

He struggled to keep track. 'I'm sorry, are you saying Annie followed Miriam across the Humber Bridge?'

'We know they both went across the bridge. Do you think Annie would have been following Mrs Marshall?'

Can't answer a question without asking one, Mike thought crossly. 'You have their phone records,' he snapped. 'You tell me.'

The man smiled almost as though conceding a point. 'Ah well, Mrs Marshall's signal disappeared soon after she left the Oddbottle. The battery gave out apparently. After all, it had been down the side of a chair in the pub all night.'

'So they could have been together when they left.' Mike felt a nub of triumph. 'Who's to say they weren't together when they went wherever they were going?'

'Where was Annie going again, Mike? When she crossed the bridge, I mean.'

Mike sighed. Back here again. Where's Annie? 'I don't know. All I know is that she went to meet Lois and she texted me to say she was going to see Miriam.'

'No, they weren't together.' A piece of paper was spun round on the table and pushed towards him. He saw their car, clear as crystal, Annie at the wheel, the typical road-side camera shot. He peered closely. The passenger seat was empty.

'That one,' a finger tapped on an adjacent photograph, 'is Mrs Marshall.'

It was the approach to the toll booths. He could see it now. He could see it was Miriam. The date and time was printed on the top of each. Miriam had been there just over eight minutes before Annie.

'Then they must have met up on the other side of the bridge, at Miriam's brother's maybe?'

'Not as far as we can see. Mrs Marshall arrived there, put her phone on charge and she's been there ever since.'

'Well, her phone might have been but I don't think she has. Annie told me she met her, and I believe her.' Had Annie told him where she'd met Miriam? Had she said they'd actually met? In his head, he could hear her voice telling him to stop babbling.

The man opposite was leaning in again, his expression troubled. 'The thing is, Mike, Lois Suffling's phone came live about ten minutes after Annie crossed the bridge. Both phones together. We can't track exactly where she went. There are traffic cameras along the main roads but not on the back routes. You've seen where the ANPR got her crossing the bridge. She was on her own.'

He tapped the picture that still lay in front of Mike. Mike looked at it again. He couldn't deny that she was on her own. It was on the tip of his tongue to say, unless there's anyone in the boot, but Annie's voice in his head thundered, *Shut the fuck up!*

A map was laid on the desk. A finger pointed to a minor road somewhere south of the Humber Bridge. It meant nothing to Mike. He'd got to know Hull but work had never taken him into North Lincolnshire.

'Interestingly there was a sighting of her car just there,' the man said. 'Parked up in a disused back entrance to a farm.'

'Sighting by whom?' said Mike. OK, they'd tracked her phone, and they'd got her on traffic cameras, but random sightings felt like a stretch too far.

'Just a passer-by. Farm Watch is active round there. They've had problems with hare coursing, theft of farm machinery, that sort of thing. They think she was there for five minutes, reported that she was rummaging about in the boot. Can you tell me what she might have been doing?'

'I've no idea. Maybe that's where she met Miriam.'

'It's nowhere near Mrs Marshall's brother's house. So it would be an odd place to meet, wouldn't you say?'

'Then I don't know. Maybe she had a problem with the car.'

'A problem with the car? OK.' The map was moved aside and a new traffic camera image put in its place. 'Now here's Annie on the main road near Immingham. Still on her own, would you say?'

He nodded. It was clearly their car and Annie behind the wheel, no one beside her. He checked the date stamp to be sure they weren't pulling a fast one. He looked again at the image of Annie in the driving seat.

'Look closely, Mike. Where's the passenger seat headrest? It was clear enough in this one at the bridge.' The two images were placed side by side. 'Would you say the passenger seat's tipped right back?'

Mike stared, saying nothing, forcing his head to stay still and not to nod agreement until he could process what he was seeing.

'Would you say there's something … or someone … stretched out on that front seat, covered with a coat? The material's quite distinct. Is that a coat you recognise? Is it one of Annie's?'

'No, no it's not. I don't recognise it.' He grasped at the one certainty as he swallowed against a dry throat.

'You see, we've had that image analysed, Mike. It certainly looks like someone's lying back on that seat. And the coat fits the description of the one Lois Suffling was wearing the last time she was seen. Can you tell me anything about that?'

Lois? He could only shake his head as he stared at the image and felt the prickle of shock drain the blood from his skin.

CHAPTER 46

Annie froze as she heard footsteps. Just footsteps. No audible breathing, no muttered words.

As she'd begun her sprint up the stairs, she'd heard something unexpected underlying the sound of the car driving past; the screech of the closing gates had jarred and reversed, they were opening again.

Someone else had arrived.

She'd stopped. That gap in the outside door was so close to wide enough …

It had been a split second decision; one she wasn't sure she'd had the time for.

Now she listened to the footsteps of someone coming into the control room.

Rob Small? Richard Redman? Miriam? Two cars had arrived, but who was here right now, whose footsteps were they? Her mind's eye saw a figure that morphed from the lithe form of Rob Small to the bulk of Richard Redman, stepping silently across the floor towards where she was hidden.

The worst of it was that she had her back to them. The space was too cramped to turn. She'd barely had time to cram herself in.

A sharp knocking sound startled her. The footsteps moved away.

At last, voices. She recognised both and let out a breath. Though neither should instil confidence, it was better to know. She'd debated with herself whether it would be worse if it was Rob Small or Richard Redman. Now it was both.

She listened, fascinated despite herself and breathed a little easier, as Rob Small spelt out the details of the simulation she'd already watched. He wouldn't talk about this if he knew she was listening. And at last it made sense. The detailed specification of his threat to lock William Marshall in a container and leave him to die. She heard him tell Redman that the paperwork had been destroyed, recycled. He could only have had that from Miriam.

Then she heard Richard Redman's burst of hilarity as he pooh-poohed Small's idea of his precious 'boys' working such a stunt, and braced herself to hear Small fly into a rage, but he didn't. He must know it was an absurd idea, however much he would like to believe it. It was as though he was testing it on Redman, seeing if it might be believable. Redman was wrong, though, in his certainty that the container hadn't gone through Rob Small's hands. She thought about that hidden database.

The simulation was just an algorithm for moving freight. It wasn't any sort of conclusive evidence in itself. The smoking gun was the dateline ID. She'd matched it on the hidden database. It showed genuine freight movement, something that Small hadn't been able to erase. Marshall knew how it all worked. He'd been in on it.

If she only had her phone, she would be recording everything, streaming it back to leave a record for someone to find, maybe in time to come and get her, but Lois's phone was low on battery and she wasn't sure it had the capability.

It was uncomfortable in the confined space, but all she had to do was wait them out.

Then she'd heard Small walk to the kitchen, telling Redman as he returned that he'd known she was here all along. Her knees almost buckled as her fleeting security was whipped away. As he told Redman that she was hiding on the kitchen stairs, he sounded almost irritated that she'd been out of earshot. So he'd meant her to hear all this, but why?

She felt sweat at the back of her neck.

Mike was out of reach, trapped by Jennifer's treachery. No one was going to perform a miracle for her now.

The staircase was a bare concrete flight with no doors bar the ones at top and bottom and nowhere to hide, but if he would only go and check it out properly he might fall for the prints she'd made by reaching her boots through the gap and slapping them down in the messy tar.

The boots were on a shelf inches from her face. She could smell the tar on them. She'd had to be so quick it couldn't be a convincing job, but if only he would go down to check and take Richard Redman with him, she would get out of this cupboard, find his key, let herself out ...

Then she listened in disbelief as Redman performed the miracle on her behalf.

Fresh bootprints ...

Small crashed through to the kitchen and on to the staircase, enraged enough that Annie knew he was going to fall for the gap that was almost wide enough.

Redman's footsteps followed as far as the kitchen, but he didn't go down the stairs so she daren't move, not even to ease the stiffness in her limbs.

Then Small was back, his breathing heavy from his

sprint up the stairs. She heard him stride to the console, heard the clicking of a keyboard under his fingers.

He let out a sigh. 'That's OK,' he said. 'The bitch is still on the site.'

With a feeling of being hollowed out, she replayed Redman's words from earlier. *Programmed him in? How? Oh, d'you mean by his–?*

Small had cut him off before he'd said, 'Phone.'

He'd tracked Marshall by his phone and he would track her by Lois's phone, sitting in her pocket, comatose but still on. Could she reach it to turn it off, properly off, without making a noise in the confined space? Her hand began to move, but she stopped.

Despite her so-called escape, Small was more relaxed, confident she couldn't breach his fortress perimeter. He and Redman began to talk about other stuff, about other people.

She needed to get the phone out of the cupboard and into a corner somewhere, preferably on the stairs down from the kitchen, so it looked like she'd dropped it, so they didn't start sniffing about the corner where she was starting to get uncomfortably hot and cramped.

He knew Lois's phone was still on site somewhere and she had no doubt he had the technology to pinpoint it to the nearest millimetre. If he used it right now, it was game over, but if she turned it off so that the signal vanished in front of him … surely he'd immediately pinpoint its last location, and that was game over too.

She had three things to do, but at least she was in a job that had her well prepared for all three: keep still, stay calm … and wait. And while she was waiting, she listened.

288

CHAPTER 47

Mike stood on the street outside the police station. A high fence stood behind him, silver filaments shining out of the dusk. The building stood back from the road, its boundary marked out by a patchy line of dense hard-wearing plants that coiled their woody stalks close to the ground. Discreet concrete bollards reinforced the shrubbery. He felt shell-shocked, not sure where to go or what to do, still unclear why they'd brought him here, or why they'd spat him out again. He sat on one of the bollards, and put his head in his hands.

Footsteps approached. 'What're you thinking?' said a familiar voice.

'That I could murder a cigarette,' he said without looking up.

'Yeah, me too. That's how it gets you. Got any smokes on you?'

He shook his head as he looked up at Pat. 'I've not smoked for ten years.'

'Probably for the best. The urge'll be gone by the time we could get any. Come on, Kid. We can't hang about here. I've called a cab. They're picking us up at the car dealer's.'

You're used to this, he thought, as he stood up and followed Pat across the road.

In his head Annie's voice was telling him to remember everything, to get it written down before he forgot. Had they recorded the interview? He assumed they had. Didn't he have the right to a copy? Nothing made sense to him.

Pat was striding ahead down a side street, heading for the entrance to a car dealership. As he hurried to catch her up, a taxi turned in behind them.

'Pat,' he said, anxious to talk before they had an audience. 'What did–?'

Her sharp look and quickly raised hand silenced him. She murmured, 'Not here.'

They drove across town in silence. After confirming the address of the office, Pat responded only with grunts to the driver's overtures. Mike remained silent as he ran a litany in his head; *they asked where you were … they tracked your phone … they said that Miriam said …*

In his head he was addressing Annie directly, but he needed to get on the road, get over the Humber Bridge, to go to where she'd asked him to go. He almost broke silence to say something to Pat, to divert the driver to the bridge, but he pulled himself up, that was absurd. He needed his own car but Miriam Marshall had taken it.

They arrived at the office to find the outer door locked, though lights still blazed from behind the shuttered reception counter downstairs. Pat continued to flap him to silence as they climbed the stairs, and as they entered the office, she used outstretched finger and thumb to mime *phone* as she held out her hand.

He pulled the clone phone from his pocket, still inside the polythene bag it had been returned in.

Pat had her own phone out and laid them side by side

on the desk. He watched as she pulled a screwdriver from her desk drawer and attacked the casing of his handset. Other than a series of annoyed grunts as the screwdriver slipped, she worked in silence checking both phones, putting them back together.

'Unlikely, I know,' she said at last, 'but they might have put something in one of them.'

'What do we do now? I need to find Annie. Can I have my proper phone back?'

Pat looked troubled. 'Let's stick with the clones for the time being. I doubt they're done with us. We're going to have to split up from here and hope that only one of us is followed. What did they tell you? What did you tell them?'

Mike sat down at his desk and looked at the paperwork he'd left out for the big meeting tomorrow. It seemed like a few minutes ago he was wondering whether it would be Jennifer or Annie who went with him, never suspecting it might be neither. It was way too late to reschedule. You didn't miss a meeting like this and expect to find a way back in anytime soon. He told Pat everything he could remember about the interview, about how they'd tracked Annie's phone and shown him the traffic camera shot of her heading over the Humber Bridge.

'Was it definitely Annie?' she asked.

He nodded. 'The one on the bridge was clear.' He went on to tell her about the report of Annie at the side of the road, rummaging in the boot, and how Lois's phone had come live and tracked the course of hers. 'The next traffic camera that picked her up showed the front seat leant right back. It wasn't as clear but there was someone beside her, covered in a coat. They said it was Lois's coat.'

Pat gave a disdainful sniff as she sat back and crossed her arms. 'They're saying she had Lois stashed in the boot of her car, stopped to drag her out, turn on her phone and lie her on the front seat covered in a coat?'

It sounded absurd when Pat said it like that, but it had been the implication.

'It was our car on the cameras,' he said, 'but that Farm Watch sighting felt like a stretch.'

'Bollocks,' said Pat. 'Either there was no report and it's our local boys in blue who are setting us up … though that's not really their style … or there was a report engineered by whoever actually is setting us up.'

'Not us,' he said. 'Annie.' He glanced up at the window. The roofscape melted into amorphous shapes in the darkness.

'I'm worried something's going to stick,' Pat went on. 'Phone tracing, under-bloody-cover ops. They think we're involved in something big. I could kick myself. I knew Jennifer had been involved in undercover work. I followed her career a bit, after Annie left, all those years ago. She should have been climbing the ladder, you know. She was ambitious when she started. Something happened.' She paused as she stared at him through narrowed eyes. 'Do you know what happened to derail strait-laced Flanagan's career back in the day? Has Annie told you?'

He shook his head. 'I never knew Jennifer till she popped up … Is it only a week ago? It feels like months.'

'It must have been one of the very first cases. You read them all up. Can you remember anything at all about Jennifer?'

'I've only seen your agency's casefiles, and if you mean

292

when she first came to Hull, it wasn't your firm, was it? She was working for someone else.'

Pat looked deflated. 'I'd forgotten that. She worked three cases for Vince. He offered her a job. You know they never really bothered about us before Annie took over. It's since then they've had their eye on us. You know that, don't you?'

He nodded. He'd known. It was one of the things that Annie wouldn't talk about.

'And you know why, don't you?'

He nodded again. 'Penn and Teller.'

Pat gave a half laugh. 'You shouldn't call them that. It annoys Annie.'

'Yeah, well, they annoy me. We're sleepers, aren't we, we're just the collateral damage should they choose to call us in.'

'But is this payback time or have we just stumbled into something with this Marshall case? What do you know about Havenmere Docks? Did Annie go there?'

'Yes! Yes she did. How did you know? She told me not to say.'

'Come on, Mike. We've gone beyond that. The coppers tracked her phone there. They told me … showed me.' He stared at her. This was news to him. 'Not a mention of Lois, interestingly. I said she'd gone to meet Lois. They wanted to know had I seen her texts. I said I couldn't remember, it'd been a busy day, told them to check them out on your phone. That's when they said they'd tracked her and she'd visited the dockyard. So where *is* Annie now?'

Mike went back over everything he'd had from Annie, texts and calls. 'Last she told me, Miriam Marshall had locked her in at Havenmere Docks and taken the car, and her phone. Annie thought she was being set up for something there, that Miriam had done something and was going to leave her to carry the can. She'll have been after the car keys when she took Annie's jacket. Taking her phone might have been a mistake.'

'Ha! Too right it was, and it might be a mistake we can get her on. They really grilled me on where she'd gone after she'd left there.'

'Left there?'

'Looks like I got the other side of the phone tracking. I got the traffic camera stills, all that … only the one they showed me that was supposed to be Annie leaving Havenmere Docks was her driving down some industrial type road. It was your car and her jacket but now I think back her face was half hidden. She was reaching up to do something to the sun visor. Jeez! Imagine falling for that; sodding sun visor, that time of night!'

'It must have been Miriam. Should we tell them?'

'We don't have enough, and it's dodgy to change a story mid-stream. We're out because they think we don't know any more than we told them … well, that and they had nothing to hold us on, thankfully.'

'But what Miriam did. It's not …' Mike stared up out of the window as he searched for the word to describe what he was trying to get across. 'It's not sensible … it's reckless … what's she playing at?'

Pat gave him a speculative glance. 'You're right, Kid. Someone's getting a bit het up about something. I don't mean the coppers, but they were desperate to know where Annie was going.'

'You said they tracked her, thought they were tracking

her anyway, so where did Miriam go in our car? Did they tell you?'

'Yeah, I got all cooperative and put on an act of worrying about Annie. I mean I am worried but I wanted to know what they'd got. They couldn't make out what was going on, and to be honest neither could I, but now I know it wasn't Annie, that puts a different light on it.'

'What did you get?'

'Is your PC on? Get a map up.' He did as he was told and she bustled round to hang over his shoulder. 'OK, they tracked her back across the bridge. I had to push but I got them to show me what they'd got. She stopped somewhere about half a mile from the bridge, not for long, then she headed out of Hull and went to Miriam's place. I said, "There you are; she's going to see Miriam Marshall, that's what she said in the text to Mike," but to be honest I was as puzzled as they were.'

'According to what they told me,' Mike put in. 'Miriam was in Barton somewhere at her brother's.'

'They didn't tell me that, they just said Annie had only stayed a minute and set off again. Back this way.' Pat pointed at the map. 'Almost all the way back to the bridge, and she stopped again same place she'd stopped before, well as far as they could tell. They kept asking why would she stop there … why did she take that route to Miriam's … why did she take a different route back towards the bridge … why was she avoiding the A63 both ways? Where she stopped, it was just a road, no houses, no nothing. But wait a minute, that was when the tech guy said something. I don't think he was supposed to be joining in really, but it was all quite relaxed by then.'

Mike shot her a glance. There had been nothing relaxed about his experience. 'What did he say?'

'Something like, "She's had her phone charging." See, I didn't think about it at the time. I thought they were tracking Annie.'

'Sorry,' Mike muttered. 'I should have told you.'

'No, no, don't worry about it, Kid. I'm glad I didn't know. It made me all the more convincing. He said something earlier, something like he'd thought they were going to lose the phone. Anyway, after that they tracked the car back to your flat near as damn it.'

'Miriam went to our flat?'

Pat shrugged. 'At the time I assumed it was Annie. I said to them, "She's gone back home. What's the fuss for?" and they said they'd been round and there was no one in. Now, I didn't say anything at the time, and I don't want you rushing off to check, we've other stuff to do, but the only way you know the difference between nobody in and no one answering the door is if you break in. What could they have found?'

Mike ran a quick inventory through his head. 'Rob Small's paperwork.'

'Hmm, OK, we'll just have to ride that one as best we can. Let me think a minute.'

Pat leant across him and drew along the route she'd shown him, leaving an uneven red mark behind the mouse pointer; Humber Bridge … half a mile … pause … all the way to Miriam Marshall's …

'Back roads,' Mike put in.

Pat nodded. 'Hard to be a hundred percent about the exact route but that's pretty damned close. She's avoiding

CCTV as best she can, but something'll have caught her.'

The mouse pointer made its return journey, Pat swapped the trail to blue, back roads again, more of a detour, until at that same point half a mile from the bridge. She stopped tracing the route. 'From there she headed back into Hull along the A63 and all the way to your flat.' She stood up straight and turned to him. 'When she stopped that first time, that's where the guy said he'd thought they might be losing the signal, battery going to give up the ghost or whatever.'

Suddenly it clicked in Mike's head. 'Miriam stopped to turn off Annie's phone,' he said. 'But the clone must have been …?'

'Yup, that's it,' said Pat. 'The clone will have been tucked in the side of the glove box, if I know Annie. That would explain a glitch in the signal as one of the phones was turned off. Then when she got back to that spot she turned it on again, which is when the guy said it looked like she'd had it charging. From there, she went to your flat or thereabouts.'

Mike traced the line Pat had drawn on the map – red from the bridge to Miriam's house, blue on the way back. 'So they've made sure, or think they have, that nothing can have tracked them on that detour to Miriam's. We need to tell those detectives. This shows that it wasn't Annie.'

'It doesn't,' said Pat. 'It just shows that the driver didn't want to be tracked on that bit of the journey.'

'OK, but those detectives, they're throwing a load of resources at this. They might be our best chance of finding her.'

'Not while they still think she's involved,' said Pat. 'The

trail they think they left shows Annie coming across the bridge and going straight home, with a long layover at the side of the road. But why different routes to and from Marshall's?'

'What if …?' Mike picked the words carefully out of the calculation he was doing in his head. 'What if it wasn't Miriam driving on the way back?' Pat gave him a tell-me-more look. 'Suppose someone else took over at her house,' he said. 'They drove our car, and Miriam went across to Barton in some other vehicle. She must have done, because that's where she was when they caught up with her.'

'Why not have someone waiting for Miriam nearer the bridge?'

He shrugged. 'Something she needed to get from home?'

'OK, then why the different route?'

'The second driver didn't know the roads as well as Miriam. I mean if you're not a local you'd just pile on to the A63 and go straight for the bridge, but those back roads go all over the show.'

'I can buy that. They wanted to leave a trail showing Annie went straight home. But if they wanted anyone thinking that that's where she's been holed up, they didn't get away with it.'

'How d'you mean?'

'What the coppers saw, but they weren't close enough on her tail, was Annie going to Havenmere Docks … uh … maybe stopping to haul Lois's body out of the boot on the way, from what they said to you. They had her there about half an hour before driving back to Hull, doing that weird detour, then dropping her car at home. When they told me she hadn't been in, I said she might be out getting a takeaway or whatnot. They said her car was there and she'd left her phone in it.'

'They broke into the car too?'

'I don't think so. No, I think they just meant they were getting a static phone signal from the car. I mean, what they implied was that she'd left it behind so she couldn't be traced. I said, "You've just tracked her from Havenmere Docks and you're saying she's gone all secretive to call in the local chippie. Who d'you think she's hiding from, the calorie police?" and that's when the guy said something sarky about her coming back to a flat battery. I wondered if she'd left the lights on, but I think now that he meant the phone. What's the betting the signal had faded again?'

'You mean whoever drove that car took Annie's phone with them.'

'Yes …' Pat nodded slowly. 'Yes, and they must have turned it off or the signal would have split. What use is Annie's phone to Miriam Marshall or anyone in her circle?'

'What do we do? We need to tell them this, don't we?'

Pat looked troubled. 'They won't believe us and we don't need to be hauled back in for further questioning. We need to find Annie. She sure as hell didn't come back over the bridge in your car. Could she still be at Havenmere Docks?'

'She reckoned she could get out. She was going to ring me once she did so that I could go and fetch her.'

'When did you last speak to her?'

'I was on with her when Jennifer arrived with those two goons.'

Pat narrowed her eyes. 'Wait a minute, does Annie know about Jennifer?'

'I put her on speaker when Jennifer came in.'

'What! So she heard it all? Then for god's sake ring her back! Right now! She won't ring you if she thinks you've been arrested.'

CHAPTER 48

Annie listened from within the confined space, the phone sitting heavy in her pocket like a ticking bomb. She was already guilty of breaking and entering, probably criminal damage too, in a highly sensitive area; if Miriam and Small's subterfuge worked, she could be looking at a lengthy prison sentence.

As the talk continued, she realised jail wasn't the threat. It was clear not all containers through this yard were logged, not if they arrived and left by road. Marshall's paperwork was pointing the finger at someone's carelessness. The simulator was the red-herring, it was the entry on the hidden database that held the key to the operation Marshall was trying to highlight. The elaborate story of a threat and a simulated death by robot was insurance in case she escaped the net. She was being fed a ludicrous story to pedal, something easily disproved. Nonetheless, there were nuggets of truth. Small had no clue of the extent to which Miriam was boiling with anger, yet she was still beholden to them. Whatever they were doing, they were in it together and had been for a long time. Miriam had been sincere when she'd pushed that paperwork into her hands. She wanted Small or Redman or maybe both to get their comeuppance, but needed her own hands to remain clean.

Annie thought of the misaligned blue container she'd used as a landmark when cycling through the cameras. It didn't show properly from any angle; its misalignment hiding its ID numbers. Anything could be driven in, kept at the periphery and driven out again.

It might be his insurance, but Small didn't want her in court telling the story of his homicidal robots. His plan A didn't involve her leaving the site at all.

She was a step ahead of Richard Redman, but he would be no ally to her. If she didn't get herself out, she wouldn't be found until someone opened a shipping container in the corner of a dockyard on the other side of the world.

She listened because there was no option. Rob Small was worried, not about her, his captive to be dealt with later, but about their plans for 'this evening'. Their talk was frustratingly full of shorthand and half references to things they knew and she couldn't guess at. Whatever was going to happen, it wouldn't be here, it would be at Redman's Yard the other side of the Humber. She gleaned the interesting snippet that Redman's son knew nothing about it. She might have made an ally of him, but he wasn't here.

'Ah shit!'

The sudden expletive from Small had her heart jumping. The wheeled chair rattled as it was pushed aside.

'What now?' from Richard Redman.

'I was in the substation earlier,' Small muttered. 'Not a hundred percent sure I locked up. If that bitch gets in there … Come and keep an eye out. I don't want to light the yard up like a Christmas tree.'

A heavy sigh from Redman, but Annie heard him get to his feet.

Barely daring to breathe, she opened the cupboard as their footsteps headed for the outer lobby. She heard the key in the door.

'Don't want the bitch pulling the plug. Just keep an eye out. Watch my back.'

Annie stepped out of the confines of the cupboard and eased the door shut. She crept forwards. A substation with access from the car park. If she'd known, she could have cut the power to the entire place, no lights, no electric fencing … would that stop all the machines or did they have their own power supplies? Too late now, Rob Small was securing it.

Keeping low, she peered round the corner of the big console. She could see Richard Redman. He had his back to her, standing half in the doorway, smoking a cigarette.

She watched as he drew in the smoke, leaning his head back, eyes closing momentarily as he savoured the hit, then blowing out a cloud of smoke and peering down over the rail to where Rob Small was presumably checking doors.

She might get close to him if she was careful, but there was no way to slip past without him seeing her. If she could be sure Rob Small wouldn't lock up again, she might try to crawl into the shadows where they would probably walk past without seeing her when they came back in, but then what? Even if he left the door unlocked, she couldn't open it without them noticing, the breeze would rush in, the sound would change. There was no surreptitious exit this way. They'd be on her heels before she was at the halfway landing.

She felt at Lois's phone. She should hide it at the back of the small kitchen, but that would be difficult too. She would have to cross the line of sight from the far door. Redman might see the movement in his peripheral vision. And she risked being trapped on that back staircase with no way out.

Keeping low, practically on the floor, she watched Redman. He'd stepped outside the door now and was leaning on the rail looking over. 'What're you pissing about at, Rob?' he called out.

His attention was all outside. It was the best chance she was going to get.

* * *

Richard Redman strolls back inside as Rob Small climbs the last half dozen stairs. He's uneasy now about tonight. He thought it was all sewn up tighter than a drum, but Small has left loose ends flapping.

He hears Small lock the door behind him as he comes in, but hears the reassuring jangle of keys hanging in the lock. He supposes it makes sense to lock up if Small has an intruder. If it was his yard, he'd be out there right now sorting them out, but he's glad Small's not asked for his help.

There's sailing close to the wind and there's downright recklessness. Time to wrap it up. He's made the decision before but never quite gone as far as to pull the plug. He sits down in a chair and blows out a breath. He wants another fag, though it's seconds since he pinched out the last one and he's supposed to be cutting back.

Small, too, takes his seat and begins to play about with his cameras, letting the lenses roam the site. 'I'll see you over there,' he says.

Redman grunts. He's not so sure, not this time. There's something different. He doesn't like it. He tests the waters with, 'Go over together if you want, time's getting on.'

'Unfinished business here. I'll not be long.' Small means his intruder.

Redman nods. If there's one thing he wants more than to have Small under his eye until tonight's done with, it's that he wants to be well away before Small clears up his unfinished business.

'Yeah, sure.' He has to raise his voice a little. The wind's really howling off the estuary now. There's a sharp chill in the air. He huddles into his jacket, seeing Small shiver at the sudden cold.

A rapid clatter, realisation dawns, running footsteps on a metal staircase. Small's a fraction ahead of him, already on his feet, face puce with rage, chair spinning across the floor. 'What the fuck!'

Redman leaps up and heads for the lobby in time to see Small kick out at a loose panel. So that's where his intruder's been all along. The exit door is swinging wide, gaping on to the darkness below.

He can hear Small racing downward.

When he steps outside on to the top landing, his eyes show spinning patterns in the darkness. The cold wind cuts right through him. He pulls out the half-smoked cigarette and relights it. The flare of his lighter makes no impression on the darkness, just intensifies the swirling patterns.

'Want me to turn the yard lights on?' he shouts down.

'Not yet,' Small's voice responds.

Redman starts to walk down the staircase to get out of the glare of the light from the control room.

Somewhere below, Small is crashing about, putting the fear of god into anyone in earshot. He's systematically searching the car park. Redman can see a bit of movement now, can see Small's track along the perimeter of the space. He's not looking to catch anyone, he's flushing them out of the comparative safety of this side of the building and into the heart of the yard.

He's been kidding himself thinking Small had nothing to do with Jobsie. He's known it all along, deep down, despite the record, despite the crate.

There's a sudden buzz and a flare of light at his feet. He jumps back, as his heart thuds.

It's a phone. He stares at it as it buzzes angrily on the metal surface, showing an incoming call.

He thinks about that clatter of footsteps that had Small hurtling down into the yard. It had gone so far and then stopped now he thinks about it. That intruder was mighty quiet down the second flight.

He picks up the phone, and answers it.

CHAPTER 49

Mike held his breath as he listened to the ringtone, and could see Pat was doing the same. There was a click and a man's voice said, 'Hello.'

For a second Mike froze. Pat was waving at him frantically, mouthing 'Lois. Lois.'

'Uh … I'm trying to contact Lois.'

'Who?'

'Lois Suffling. Isn't this her phone?'

'It might well be, mate, but there ain't no one hereabouts by that name. I've just picked it up off the floor. Wouldn't have seen hide nor hair of it in the dark, if it hadn't rung.'

'Where did you find it?'

There was a pause. 'Tell you what, mate. I'll hand it in, OK?'

The line went dead.

Mike stared hard at the silent handset, then, 'I know that voice. I've heard it before.'

'Rob Small?' guessed Pat.

He shook his head. 'Never spoken to him, never heard him speak.' He closed his eyes.

… wouldn't have seen hide nor hair of it … it's many a year since I saw hide nor hair of Jobsie …

He slapped the desk. 'He spoke at the funeral. His son found the body. That was Richard Redman.'

307

'Redman?' murmured Pat.

They both turned to look at the map on the screen, then looked at each other. Mike could almost hear the jigsaw clicking into place and saw the same dawning realisation on Pat's face.

'Quick,' he said. 'The Marshall file.'

Pat retrieved it and thumbed through for an address, reading out the postcode.

Mike keyed it in and saw the virtual pin drop right at the apex of that detour his car had taken on its way back from Miriam's.

'Pat, we've got to tell those detectives about this. That can't be a coincidence. They'll have to take us seriously.'

'They might take us seriously,' Pat said. 'But that's not to say they'll go in there trying to get Annie out. They think she's in on it.'

'Yes, but …'

'Listen, Kid, this is down to us.'

They both stared at the pin. It sat bang on the location of Redman's Yard, where William Marshall's body had been found.

'Pat, we can't deal with this on our own.'

'You're right but we're not going to offer ourselves up on a plate. If we're banged up in some cop shop somewhere, we're no good to Annie. You get a summary written down. They probably know most of it anyway; they're not doing what they're doing on a whim. Try not to land us in it if you can. Tell them … I don't know … uh … Annie's phone has a gizmo in it or something, that it doesn't turn off fully, and that's why the signal was different. Tell them it wasn't Annie driving. Say we've heard from her but don't be specific as to when. Email it to Babs to send on.'

'Barbara? Are you sure that's–?'

'Yeah, best way. Who knows if either of us'll be in a position to be doing any emailing to anyone. Oh and include the email address of the copper who interviewed me.' She skimmed a card across the desk towards him. 'And yours if you got the details, so Babs knows where to send it. Don't bother with Jennifer, she's just a grunt in all this. And decide which one you want to head for; Havenmere Docks or Redman's Yard.'

Her tone was too authoritative to argue with, but he had serious reservations about bringing Barb into the mix. There was no time to argue. Pat was already on the phone. He typed furiously to the backdrop of Pat scolding her sister.

'Yeah, well you can bloody well get over it and get yourself shifted … the boss has got herself into a tight corner and … I know, I know, but … just don't waste bloody time …'

Mike shook the bizarre image out of his head; Pat calling Annie 'the boss' and over the most unleaderlike stunt she'd ever pulled. He tried not to listen as he concentrated on a concise but compelling summary of what he and Pat had worked out.

He finished, typed in Barb's email and clicked send as Pat ended her call.

'I want to go to Havenmere Docks,' he told her. 'I know she could be miles away but that's where she rang me from.'

Pat heaved herself to her feet and went to rummage through the coats hanging behind the door, pulling out a long raincoat and wide-brimmed hat, which she held out to him. 'You're going to need something more than that flimsy thing you wear. Have you seen what it's like out there? It's pissing down.'

'Yes, but …'

'Believe me, Kid, you're going to get wet, and you don't need to start out soaked to the skin. It'll be a long night. You'll need your wits about you. Where are your car keys?'

'Annie's got them, or rather Miriam. Spares are back at home.'

'According to what the coppers said, the car's back at the flat. The keys might have been left in it, but anyway, come on. We need to get on the road.'

CHAPTER 50

Annie saw Richard Redman move away from the doorway, heard his footsteps descending. She pulled back to where she could see the console to look at the cameras. Rob Small was round by the big cranes where that misaligned container was sitting, well out of the way. There wasn't time to work out what he was doing. She focused again on the car park. Redman had gone down the stairs, but must have stopped halfway. He hadn't emerged into camera view at the bottom yet.

Get a move on, she urged him, and made her way towards the exit, staying low. Rob Small wouldn't be gone for long. She needed to get down those stairs unseen.

Lying close to the floor, she slid herself nearer to the open doorway. The tang of tobacco smoke tickled her nose. Her form would be backlit if she stood up. As she neared the entrance, the silhouette of her head grew on the safety panel of the top landing, barely half a metre high, that was all that prevented a giant shadow show on the car park below.

She edged her head round the corner of the door.

He was right there, four steps down, leaning on the rail, looking out over the car park.

She pulled back, heart thumping.

He'd descended further. She knew he had, she'd heard him. Was this a trap?

And had he seen her shadow on the safety panel? How could he have missed it?

Over the background hum and whirr of machinery, of engines firing, of whatever it was that Rob Small was doing at the heart of the yard, she became aware of a *tap – tap – tap* from just outside the door.

Keeping low, but bracing herself to fight or flee, she sneaked a quick glance.

Tap – tap – tap

He hadn't moved. Cigarette smoke curled around him. His hand held a phone that he was drumming against the metal rail. *Tap – tap – tap*

Her throat was suddenly dry. That was Lois's phone he was holding.

She'd skimmed it out into the darkness to clatter down the first flight; the decoy to make them think she'd got away. She'd assumed it would drop through the open treads and be lost in the darkness below.

Rob Small racing after her must have missed it, but Redman following more slowly had found it. So he knew she was still up here. Yet he hadn't given her away.

'Best place for this …'

Annie froze as she heard his voice. He spoke as though to himself, clearing his throat as the handset drummed a beat against the metal railing.

'… is inside the big blue crate … right at the back … out of sight.'

She heard him blow out a breath. Smoke swirled into the light spilling through the entrance. His footsteps clanged on the metal steps as he began to descend.

Annie slid herself round the corner of the door, flat to

the freezing metal of the top landing, and crept out of range of the spotlight. Redman was stomping his way down, still on the first flight, his back to her. She kept close to the wall and made her way step by step, her hands feeling out in the darkness exploring each tread.

She found the phone on the fourth step, pocketed it and pressed herself into the wall. He was close to ground level before she made her move, grasping the rail, forcing her arms to take the weight as her feet skimmed the steps, so that her rapid descent was silent enough to be drowned out by the ambient noise.

By the time Redman reached the car park she was almost within touching distance of him. He might yet give her a way out of the yard if he gave her the opportunity to slip into the back of his car. But the hope died as she heard the clunk of the central locking before he'd started the engine.

Best place for this … inside the big blue crate …

They were all big crates and there might be hundreds of blue ones, not that she could distinguish colour in this light, but she knew he meant that misaligned one.

Treading carefully, regretting the boots she'd left upstairs in the cupboard, Annie followed the path of Redman's car round the side of the building towards the entrance.

A cold breeze eddied around the tall structure, becoming a fierce wind as she reached the main yard. A single tall light threw eerie shapes and shadows over what had been an empty vista the first time she'd visited, and was now a maze of giant metal boxes. She pressed herself to the darkness of the wall. The cold closed in on her from every angle.

Redman's car was up ahead, driver's window down. He sounded his horn, calling out, 'You there, Rob?'

Footsteps echoed. She saw Small's form jogging towards the big gates.

'Found your intruder?' Redman called.

'No sweat,' Small responded. 'I'll be five minutes behind you.'

'Open up, then.'

'Just a mo.' There was a crackle of static. Small was talking into a hand-held radio.

A car approached along the outer road. A security-liveried vehicle drove up along the other side of the fence and slowed as it approached the gates.

'What're you playing at, Rob?' from Richard Redman. Was there a note of anxiety in his voice?

'I told you, Rich, I've an intruder. Don't want her slipping out in your wake. Give me a sec, I need someone to do a message for me.'

A sharp wind whistled between the giant containers, machinery whirred as though in response. Annie stepped back from the tableau by the gate – no escape route there – and pressed herself into the pitch-black of the corners as she moved towards the heart of the yard, aware of the phone in her pocket, that might give her away at any moment. She was out of sight of the gates now, but an angry exchange floated over to her, followed by the slamming of doors. She had an idea that Rob Small was searching Redman's car.

Slipping round the side of one of the giant boxes, she found herself face to face with a square squat vehicle. Its lights flickered on, and seemed to brighten as she stared at them. Before it could project her shadow across on to the high walls of the control tower, she scurried past it, feeling that it was watching her every move.

Rob Small wanted her in the misaligned blue container, Richard Redman had more or less said so. He'd been telling her to put the phone inside, to fool the tracker.

… right at the back … out of sight …

Was he saying conceal the phone well, or go right in so he can trap you? She had no way of knowing except that he could have given her away to Rob Small before he left and he hadn't.

The screech of the gates echoed off the sides of the containers and merged with the whistling of the wind until it seemed to surround her. While the gates were opening and closing, Rob Small would be there watching that she didn't slip through, so she took the chance to sprint from one metal-walled passageway to the next, trying to get as far as possible while she knew where he was.

Then she was at yet another crossroads, with huge metal walls reaching up into the darkness and she had no clue which way to go. The gates that had been quiet, suddenly screamed loud again. Richard Redman was gone and the only exit was closing, but what direction was the sound coming from? It squealed at her from all around. She was at the heart of the maze, the stacked containers affording no upward view of anything but a swirling inky darkness.

The phone in her pocket buzzed a text. She snatched it out.
Nowhere to hide
Sender: Annie Raymond.

Close by, an engine sprang to life. A bright beam lit up one of the passageways between the containers. Tyres crunched over gravel. It couldn't be Small, not this quickly. These were his 'boys', his autonomous vehicles, the ones that could track Lois's phone.

The revving of the engine bounced off the surfaces, but the light shone from one direction only. Fighting a desperate urge to throw the phone away, Annie raced in the opposite direction.

At almost every turn, a new set of lights snapped on, blinding her.

She dodged and twisted away from them, then found herself in a wider alley, where she ran the length of a huge container.

Grabbing the cold metal corner to dive round the back, she realised she couldn't. This giant crate was pushed up close to its neighbour, no way to squeeze through. From behind, she heard the growing rumble of vehicles.

She tore down the alley, her feet stinging, her socks in tatters, desperate for a side exit.

There wasn't one. She was trapped in the long alley, flashes of light bursting from behind her.

She put everything into sprinting the way they wanted her to go. They wanted her at the misaligned crate, and she had to get there first with enough time to hurl Lois's phone into the heart of it, then dodge away.

She became aware of gaps between the stacks, but didn't deviate until she glimpsed a vista she recognised from the cameras. Light shimmering along a high fence in the distance, familiar shapes rearing up in silhouette. She dived in this new direction, feeling the ground under her feet change in texture. It was no longer the pristine tarmac of the main yard. Gravel tore at her feet like a thousand tiny knives, the uneven surface threatened to turn her ankles. But she didn't slow. This would take her to the back of the misaligned crate. Rob Small's 'boys' had been herding her to the front.

Round another corner and she was out of the metal maze. Lights from the estuary threw the shapes around her into sharp relief, everything a uniform silvery black. The container that loomed in front of her looked out of place, even in the darkness. What the cameras had failed to show was how much smaller it was than everything else. It was neither as long nor as tall despite sitting on a flatbed trailer with a tractor unit attached.

She arrived head on to the cab and skidded to a halt, expecting the lights to flare as they registered the phone. But this vehicle sat comatose and empty.

The front of the box, behind the tractor unit, looked odd. A panel was angled outwards. The whole container was loaded backwards, its doors right behind the lorry cab, one of them swinging temptingly ajar.

The machines that were rumbling after her were coming the long way down the wide tarmacked alley. She had twenty seconds, maybe half a minute.

She pulled herself up on the coupling between cab and trailer, slipping on a length of tarpaulin. Pain jarred through her as her knee banged into something sharp and metallic. She started to shove the tarpaulin down into the darkness beneath the wheels, then stopped. She might need cover. A ripped and oily tarpaulin sheet was usefully anonymous on the back of a truck.

Heart pounding, the rumbling engines creeping closer, she slipped through the container's open door into the darkness inside.

The air stilled, the whistle of the wind fell to a muted backdrop. Her own breathing was suddenly loud.

Using the phone's torch, she flashed the beam all around, allowing herself a single second to take in her surroundings before she snapped it off again. The space was crammed with old furniture and battered appliances. A tall sideboard stood upright beside her. There was a narrow corridor leading through the chaos. She must hide the phone well enough that Small couldn't retrieve it, because he mustn't guess that she was no longer with it. And she must be quick.

His 'boys' wouldn't catch her without a phone signal to guide them, however much he would like to believe it.

In the darkness, she put her hand on the sideboard to steady herself, then started back with an involuntary gasp. It had tipped. It wasn't tied down.

She scrabbled at the phone to allow herself another brief burst with the torch.

Something soft flopped on to her foot. Forget trying to get to the heart of it. Time was running out.

Judging her aim, she cradled the phone prior to tossing it over to the far corner, at the same time shaking her foot to free it.

The soft something snaked round and grasped her ankle.

A voice croaked, 'Help me!'

Shock coursed through her as she yanked back with her foot and fumbled for the torch beam. It lit up a pallid-skinned hand and thin arm. She wrenched aside a cardboard box, coughing involuntarily at the dust that billowed out.

'Oh my god! Lois!'

Lois lay on her side, crushed between the old boxes, a

desperate plea in her eyes that stared at Annie. If she hadn't spoken, Annie would not have been sure she was alive.

Grabbing the hand that had snagged her ankle, she urged her, 'Come on, Lois, move. We have to get out.'

A brief moan was the only response.

The seconds leaked away.

Drawing in a breath, Annie hurled the phone to the back of the container, hearing it crash and skitter down into the jumbled mess. She dropped to her knees, grabbed hold of Lois under the arms and pulled. Lois's slack body slid out from where it had been lying, but it was clear she couldn't move on her own.

Panting hard, Annie hauled the inert form towards the sliver of light that was the door. She peered through the gap, and round the side of the container. As the wind hit her face, she saw lights bouncing from between the stacked containers. Rob Small's 'boys' were here.

She dragged Lois on to the surface of the flatbed. Their cover was scant and temporary. The vehicles were approaching from the back. If she tried to get down either side, she'd be lit up like a stage act in a spotlight. She might lower Lois to the ground between tractor and trailer, but as she looked down, even that space became more defined as the light crept in. And it was a mass of wires and bars. There was no easy way through.

The tarpaulin was where she'd left it, caught on the kingpin of the coupling. If she could get them both off the flatbed and on to the back of the tractor, it might be possible to wedge Lois low down in the tangle of wires, maybe cover them over with the tarpaulin. Just long enough for Rob Small to believe that she was trapped inside.

If he could pinpoint the phone, and clearly he could, he would know she was in there. He would reach up and slam shut the door. Then they just had to keep quiet and wait.

She envisaged it as she hauled Lois upright, leaning in until her lips were almost touching the side of Lois's head. 'Come on, Lois, try to help me, and keep quiet. This is what we're going to do.'

It was all wishful thinking.

Rob Small would go inside with a flashlight. Even if he believed the fiction that Annie was hidden and decided it wasn't worth his while to push through the unstable mountains of furniture, he would check on his original captive and find her gone.

'Well done, boys.'

His voice was so close, it speared a shard of ice through her. The engine noises subsided to a gentle hum. They might be purring at his praise as the wind sang a chorus through rows of containers.

The tramp of footsteps, the crunch of gravel. Pulling the tarpaulin over their heads, Annie pressed herself close to Lois and held the girl in a firm grasp.

'What's this, boys? Wrong way about. Dear me, how could that have happened?'

Annie held her breath. Small's tone was playful, but she hadn't heard him climb on to the flatbed yet. She cringed at the thought of his hand grasping the tarpaulin and whipping it away.

A sudden metallic clang made her ears ring. She felt Lois start in fright and gripped her tighter. *Hold it together, Lois.*

She wasn't sure, but a spark of hope ignited. Had Rob Small believed his phone tracker without question? Had he just slammed shut the door? She could hear bolts and the click of locks. *A mix of over-the-top and wide open*, she'd said about Small's security. He'd done it again. Believed implicitly in his own systems, his own plan. Not that they were anywhere near out of the woods yet.

A new sound began to swell. Annie recognised it. One of the big cranes. The low hum grew in intensity until it pulsed from all around them. She clutched tight to the tarpaulin, afraid the vibrations would make it fall.

The clang of the grabs clutching the sides of the box, hit like a physical blow. Annie's head swam as the whole edifice shook. She could only cling to the tangled wires, with Lois wedged against the back of the cab, and hope they wouldn't be shaken loose.

The shaking stopped abruptly. A dark shadow engulfed them. She risked turning her head slightly to look through a tear in the oily fabric.

The container was hanging in the air, a solid black oblong against wisps of light. It began to sway as it turned. *Wrong way about*, he'd said. It was, too. The wrong way round on the flatbed. The big crane was turning it in the air so that the doors would face the back.

As she watched, one end suddenly dropped with a terrible squeal. She couldn't stop herself from clutching Lois and heard the girl whimper in fright. 'It's OK, it's OK,' she whispered urgently.

The big crane didn't let go, it tipped one side sharply and then the other. She could hear the crash and clang as the heavy contents hurtled from side to side. Forward, back, forward again – the finale for anyone still inside.

CHAPTER 51

Jennifer Flanagan accepted a Werther's Original from the packet her colleague held out. The paper rustled as she unwrapped it.

'Not the ideal snack for covert surveillance,' she said, popping it into her mouth.

He stuffed the sachet back into the door pocket beside him. 'Chewing gum in the glove box if you prefer. Anyway, no need to be covert at this distance.'

She'd meant the hardness of the sweet, not the noise of the packet, the sort of thing you might choke on if you had to move quickly. Chewing gum was as bad, but she didn't pursue the point. It had been at least ten minutes since they'd had word Pat Thompson and Michael Connaughty had set off in Pat's car.

She glanced at the clock; another late one. 'I stayed in uniform to avoid this stuff, you know.'

'You're good at it. Ayaan Ahmed told me about the undercover you'd done down south. You should step up. You could.'

'I know I could,' she snapped, annoyed. 'Where I have trouble is getting across to people like Sergeant Ahmed that I don't want to.'

'Come on, I'll bet you've enjoyed this last week.

Makes a change from pulling drunks apart on Saturday nights.'

'I'd sooner pull drunks apart than deceive people, to be honest.'

'They're villains, Jennifer. They'd deceive you, soon as look at you.'

'Oh come on, you said Connaughty looked shell-shocked, like he hadn't a clue what had been going on, and Pat Thompson's never been a big player.'

'Yeah, he'll have some sleepless nights, for sure. If he's any sense he'll go back to banking, and back to his wife.'

Mike had a wife? That was news to her, but she just said, 'I've known Annie Raymond for over ten years. Not that I've seen anything of her for the past eight, but I knew her when she was just starting out. She runs close to the line, but I'm not convinced she'd step this far over.'

'You think she's just naïve?'

'I guess.'

'Does that really wash for someone of her experience?'

She knew he was right. 'Oh, I don't know. I just didn't feel she'd changed that much.'

'What about the woman she used to work with in London?'

'Hell, no doubts there. Bent as a butcher's hook. What happened to her?'

He shrugged. 'With luck, wilds of South America planning a coup that's never going to become our business. Or maybe an assassin caught up with her. She just vanished off the radar.'

'Mike Connaughty could be good for that agency, you know. He has big plans, totally legit. It could all fall through because of me. I don't feel good about that.'

'You didn't know he was married, did you?' Surprised he'd cottoned on, given that his listening skills weren't great, she shook her head. 'Wife lives in Switzerland. They have two kids. He left her to take up with Annie Raymond again.'

The radio crackled to life. Pat and Mike had arrived at his and Annie's waterfront flat.

'He's heading into the flat,' the voice said. 'She's waiting outside … OK, he's back, got his keys. They're checking all round the car. Not sure if they're looking for booby traps or trackers but unless they get right underneath with a torch they won't spot what we've put on there. He and Thompson are talking. Right then. He's locked the car. She's gone back to hers … He's heading back to the flat, going up the staircase. She's setting off now.'

'Have they seen you?'

'They're pretending not. You've got Connaughty's car?'

Jennifer's companion checked his screen. 'Loud and clear.'

'Right, we're going with Thompson. Keep me posted.'

For a couple of minutes they sat in silence. The road where they were parked was a residential street a mile or so from the flat Mike shared with Annie. Lights were on behind drawn curtains. The few people who had arrived or left had paid them no attention, being intent on getting out of the cold drizzle that was thickening into a downpour.

'Here we go.'

Jennifer looked back at the screen. Mike's car was on the move. He must have turned round almost before he'd made it into the flat.

Jennifer's companion fired up the engine.

'Wouldn't it be ironic if some opportunist has just nicked his car?' she said.

'Yeah, hilarious.' He gave her a look. 'He's on the ball, his phone's disappeared.'

As they'd predicted, Mike had made a play of going home, waited until Pat and the car following her had disappeared then gone back out. It surprised her that he'd thought to turn off his phone. She'd like to bet Pat had put that idea in his head.

'OK,' she murmured. 'Lead us to Annie. What do you reckon east or west?'

'West for sure,' he said. 'She dropped the car off to make it look like she went home, then she went back over the bridge to join the action.'

'You mean Havenmere Docks?' She glanced sideways at him as she asked the question.

He shook his head. 'No one can figure that link. It's more like the shiny object to keep us all from looking in the right direction.' He began to inch the car forward as he spoke. 'It's only a small outfit in the grand scheme of things, not enough clout to be the main player, and squeaky clean as far as anyone can tell. But maybe she's the missing link. He's going to take us west and then south over the Humber, I'll put my shirt on it.'

That was the most anyone had told her about the innards of this operation. She thought back to the day she'd gone to Ayaan Ahmed with her intel about Annie, what she'd seen at the funeral; that Annie knew Rob Small, and she'd watched the introduction between Annie and Richard Redman. Ahmed's words: *I know a good deal more about you than I did last time we spoke.* That sinking feeling that the job was about to ask for more of her than she wanted to give. He'd looked up her record, checked out the undercover work she'd done. 'You're perfectly placed,' he'd said, 'to renew your friendship with Annie Raymond. He'd given her scraps and no more. The theft from Havenmere Docks. She was to find out if the Thompson agency had the paperwork and get it back. Look for this … look for that … Annie could be loose-tongued, get her confidence. Ask about who was backing the agency … where all that money was coming from … what they were doing in return.

Jennifer felt a little warmer towards her companion for not treating her as a grunt to be worked to death and otherwise ignored.

They watched the tracker on Mike's car approach the big roundabout. Her colleague's fingers tapped the steering wheel as he waited for Mike to commit to a route. The tracker failed to turn left. 'Missed your turning, buddy,' he muttered.

'Maybe he's coming through town?' Jennifer said. 'Going back to the office for something? Oh …'

They looked at each other in surprise as Mike swung round the roundabout, on to the A63 in the other direction and headed off at speed.

'Where's he going?'

Jennifer wanted to say east, and that she'd won the shirt from his back, but she settled for, 'God knows! But he wants to slow down or traffic'll pull him.'

They followed from a long way back, too far for him to see them or for them to see him.

'What's out this way, Jennifer? Where would he be going?'

She let out a tut of frustration. She was supposed to know these people. 'He might be going to do that about-turn thing, round the next roundabout and back again, checking for anyone following. Either that or I was right about the sneak thief and we're following a joy rider.'

'Don't even joke about it. We get enough earache about costs as it is.'

She thought through the agency's ongoing cases. Nothing out this way. Mike carried on east over the first roundabout, no U-turn. She watched his approach to the next.

'He's certainly in a hurry,' she commented. The tracker carried on east.

'Here we go,' said her companion. 'He's turning left at Marfleet.'

'Got it,' said Jennifer. It wasn't a case at all. 'Barbara Caldwell, Pat Thompson's sister, lives out this way. She's been largely absent. They had a house fire. That must be where he's going, but I can't think why.'

'Then quick, get me an address. Get us there first.'

She scrolled through her phone and clicked the postcode into the SatNav. 'Hell,' she muttered. 'We can't get there ahead of him. There's no viable way round that won't take twice as long.'

'Then we're going past him. He's only just turned off. I want to know what's so important that he's making the detour.' The car surged forward, blue light strobing around them. There weren't many cars ahead and they all obediently slewed to the inside lane to let the blue flashing vehicle pass. A single wail of the siren got them through Marfleet roundabout.

'Duck down. He's just ahead.'

Jennifer slipped low in the seat as they careered on up Marfleet Avenue with bursts of siren to get them through knots of traffic.

'Coupla minutes,' he said. 'I want to be well out of his way.' After the promised two minutes, Jennifer felt the car slow and swing round to the right. 'OK, get up. We're plain clothes again. Talk me in from here.'

Barbara's road was empty of parked cars. The rain began to drum down, bouncing off the lids of the brown wheelie bins sitting along the wide pavement. The Caldwell house showed lights upstairs and down. As they drove past, Jennifer could see the bulk of Barbara's form, her back to the uncurtained window, facing what looked like an enormous TV screen. She peered for any sign of the recent fire but it had been round the back and nothing showed.

Her colleague pulled up half a dozen houses past Barbara's on the other side of the road. Killing the lights, he reversed into a lane that led to a row of garages. In the downpour and with some cover from a line of bare trees, it was camouflage enough.

They'd outpaced Mike by several minutes. If it hadn't been for the tracker creeping closer, Jennifer would have lost confidence in her guess. They watched his car appear round the corner at the far end of the road and surge towards them.

'Go easy, Mike,' Jennifer murmured. 'You'll aquaplane.'

He swung the car on to the hard-standing outside Barbara's house, jumped out and dashed for the front porch, whose outer door swung open. Through the frosted glass she could make out his hand raised to knock.

Barbara's rotund form appeared briefly in the doorway and Mike disappeared inside.

'He didn't lock up.'

'We don't know where Annie went after she left the car,' Jennifer began. 'Could–?'

Barbara's door re-opened. Mike rushed back out into the downpour, clutching a fat carrier bag. He dived into the shelter of the car. Its lights blazed as he reversed on to the road with a sideways swerve. As he set off in a fountain of spray, the rear end fishtailed, then straightened and he headed off the way he'd come in.

'Someone's in a hurry,' her colleague said. 'What's he's got in the bag?'

'Shit,' Jennifer let out her annoyance. 'The paperwork that was stolen from Havenmere Docks. I've been moving heaven and earth to get my hands on that.'

After radioing in to update on this development, her colleague started the car. 'We'll go out the other way. Don't want Mrs Caldwell clocking us and letting him know.'

Jennifer glanced across towards Barbara's house. 'She's back in front of the TV. And anyway, his phone's off.'

They cruised steadily retracing their route. Mike was going at a more sedate pace now, heading back towards the main route.

'When did they take it to Barbara's!' Jennifer burst out. 'I was certain it was at the office.'

'It's only two rooms, isn't it? How long does it take to search two rooms?'

'It might look ramshackle, but their security's shit hot. I had to figure out when the cameras weren't on, then I'd to get my hands on a duplicate key, then I had to pull a stunt with a clown mask and can of spray paint to get in there on my own.'

He guffawed. 'I'd like to have seen that.'

She laughed too. It had been quite a trick. 'All that and it got me about three bloody minutes on my own,' she told him. 'Next thing they're back, poring over camera footage, changing the locks. Sergeant Ahmed said he'd find an excuse to send someone in on the fly, take everyone by surprise, so I could act all shocked and hide in the back office, which was the one place I hadn't looked.'

'Oh right, that's where the missing woman came into it then?'

'Yeah, she'd worked there. Did she turn up?'

'Not yet.' His tone was clipped in a way that made Jennifer think there was more to this than she was being told.

'She's not involved too, is she? It was just meant to be a handy excuse to send someone round.'

'Let's just say Miss Suffling's whereabouts are a cause for concern, and we might find her when we find Annie Raymond.'

'Yes, but is–?'

'Did it work?' he cut across her, making clear she would get no more on that topic. 'Getting you time to search?'

'He sent Tommy-fucking-Marchant of all people, or anyway, he didn't hand pick who went and that's who turned up. Half an hour before I was expecting him. Have you ever known Tommy arrive early for anything? Can you imagine if he'd caught a glimpse of me? I tell you, there was nothing put on about my panic to get in that back office.'

She laughed again, imagining Tommy diving in all guns

blazing to 'rescue' her. She'd ransacked that small area, barely got it back together and herself behind the desk before Annie was opening the door to tell her it was safe.

'I went through everything,' she told him, laughing. 'I must have looked like I'd run a marathon after Tommy left. They took it for shock.' Her laughter ebbed. She remembered her verbal assault on Ahmed, the call she'd made from the alleyway beside the building. She might have been a bit over-the-top with that.

The tracker showed Mike leading them to the route they'd expected him to take in the first place. They settled in for at least half an hour's journey, keeping a minimum of half a mile between them.

'If they're so shit hot on security,' he said, 'they must have seen that you'd searched.'

'Oh, I arranged a diversion, made it look like someone had had a go at the window. Exactly where's he going?' She nodded towards where the tracker showed Mike's steady progress along the A63.

'I'd say he's off to find Annie Raymond wherever she's gone, but if you're right about what he picked up from Caldwell, then maybe he thinks he's going to take a detour to Havenmere Docks to put it back.'

'How would he do that?'

'Who knows? Maybe he's hiding the evidence to keep her out of trouble.'

'Poor Mike. He hasn't a clue. Wait a minute, what's he doing?' She watched the tracker move into a slip road as though to leave the main carriageway.

They watched the tracker duck under the flyover and on to Hessle Road.

'Now what? What contacts have they round here? Come on, Jennifer, where's he going?'

'I'm good but I'm not psychic. It's kind of the direction of the Marshalls' house, but it's not an obvious route.'

On the smaller roads, in the rain, with parked cars and darkness to conceal them, they came close enough to catch an occasional glimpse of his car on the longer stretches.

'Annie Raymond went close to the Marshalls' on her way home,' he told her. 'There'd have been no one in. Marshall's widow was in Barton with her brother. Maybe he's completing whatever her errand was.'

'Like dumping the paperwork there? I suppose it would make more sense than trying to get in the dockyard.'

'Maybe this is his job before he goes to find her. Pick up the papers from Caldwell, dump them at the Marshall house. We should get there ahead of him again, watch what he does.'

Jennifer peered through the gloom and the driving rain, then down at the screen. 'I'm not sure. This route doesn't make any sense. Why didn't he stay on the A63?'

'Avoiding cameras?'

Jennifer huffed unconvinced. 'I suppose he might have been rattled by seeing the way you tracked Annie's phone, but …' Her voice tailed off.

'OK, we'll leave it a while.'

They drove on in silence. Mike, half a mile ahead of them, had slowed considerably. They crawled along in his wake until the tracker took an unexpected right turn.

They both stared at the screen. Right turn, immediately left, then it stopped.

'Where the hell's he stopped? What's there?'

'It's … I don't believe it! It's the Oddbottle pub.'

'That's where she followed Mrs Marshall from. What the fuck's he doing there?'

Jennifer was pressed back in her seat as the car accelerated. She saw his hand hover over the lights, but he held off. The road was quiet enough that they didn't need to shout out their arrival.

In less than half a minute, the pub was in sight. She just caught Mike disappearing through the double doors as the car swerved across the road, bumped up the kerb and slewed to a halt within inches of Mike's back bumper.

'Straighten it. Stay out of sight,' her colleague rapped out as he leapt from the car and sprinted through the rain towards the doors.

Jennifer glared after him, pulling in an exasperated breath as she felt the car begin to slide. She yanked the handbrake full on and clambered into the driver's seat to back it into a discreet corner.

After a few minutes, she pulled up the hood of her jacket and climbed out of the car, locking it and running to the inadequate shelter of the building's wall. There were no windows this side. It wasn't great cover because of the external lights, but she hugged the wall as she made her way towards the door.

It made sense for him to go inside. Mike didn't know him. She kept half an eye on the double doors and half on the path from the other side of the pub, convinced Mike's ploy in stopping here was less straightforward than a quick pint on his way to meet Annie. Could Annie be here?

She approached the doors at an angle, peering through to be sure Mike wasn't in range. She didn't see him until she was almost close enough to see her own breath condense on the glass, then she had to fight an urge to wipe the pane clean to get a better view. Whatever she'd expected, it wasn't this. Her colleague was leaning back on the bar, his face creased to a grin, and would be looking right at her if he wasn't focussed on the closer target of Mike, who had his back to her but she could tell he was enjoying the joke. Nodding, smiles, more laughter … for all the world like two guys enjoying an evening pint.

She recalled his, *Who the fuck's he meeting?* and thought, from here, it's looks like it's you.

The tempo of the exchange changed. They were saying their goodbyes. Some comradely slapping of arms. It was clear her colleague would head for the door and Mike would turn to watch him go.

Jennifer leapt back round the corner of the wall. She'd aimed to be back in the car before he came out, but the door banged open before she had covered half the distance.

He strode past her with a growled, 'Get in the car,' from the side of his mouth. His expression couldn't have been more different from the smiling bonhomie she'd just witnessed. He was furious with her.

'I made sure he didn't see me.' But between keeping her voice discreetly low and the drumming of the rain, she doubted he'd heard her.

In the car, he put his hands on the steering wheel and laid his head on his arms.

After a moment, he looked across at her. Then with a speed and force that made her jump, he slammed his fist on to the dashboard.

'Bollocks!' His fist crashed down again. 'Bollocks! Bollocks! Bollocks!'

CHAPTER 52

On Pat's instructions, Mike put his foot down on his way from the flat to Barbara's. The road was reasonably quiet at this hour, though there was one heart-stopping moment when a siren wailed behind him and a pulsing blue light loomed in his mirror. He pulled in fully expecting to be stopped, but it shot past on some mission of its own and snaked off into the night. He slowed after that, concentrating on the road. The weather was foul, visibility getting worse by the second.

Barbara's street was quiet. He flew along towards her house, too fast for the conditions. Annie was in trouble. He didn't know where she was. And from out of nowhere, he was wholly reliant on the Thompson sisters.

He swung into Barbara's drive, killed the lights, jumped out, hat on, collar turned up and rushed for the door leaving his keys in the ignition.

Barbara had the door open almost as he knocked. He took one stride across the carpet of the small hallway as she pushed the door shut, smothering the beat of the rain, then he fell to his knees and stretched flat out over the threshold to the living room. He smelt the dust from the multi-coloured weave of her carpet. Boots stepped over him. A rush of cold air as the door swung open and banged shut. His engine revved, tyres squealed.

Barbara's feet clambered over him and she walked to a red two-seater settee set in front of the living room window and sat down. He turned his head sideways to watch as she picked up what looked like a TV remote on a stick.

'I wasn't followed,' he said.

'Stay low,' she replied, 'There's a car across the road, arrived a couple of minutes before you did. Could be a courting couple.'

'Can you see who's in it?'

She tutted. 'It's a mirror on a stick, Mike, and it's pissing down out there. If I hadn't been watching and seen it arrive, I wouldn't know there was car there at all, but I'm pretty sure they didn't back all the way in ... ah, hang on, here we go. Yup, they're on their way.'

She got to her feet, pulled shut the curtains. 'Right, through here.'

He scrambled to his feet and followed her to a small kitchen, taking in the still blackened walls.

She pushed a set of car keys into his hand. 'Down the garden.' She pointed through the kitchen window. 'Gate at the end. Leads to a ten-foot. Blue Renault parked up on the bottom road. It's Julie's, our Ryan's missus. Company car so it'll not flag up any of our names. The Humber Bridge is your bottleneck. That's where they'll stop you, or catch up with you. You need to get there fast. Wear this.'

He looked with some dismay at the chequered flat cap, long wisps of grey hair hanging down from inside. 'I'll look like a clown.'

'In this weather it'll make you look old. More to the point, you won't look like you on any cameras. Now listen.' She grasped his arm and looked up into his eyes, face stern.

It's like she's lecturing one of her sons, he thought. 'Whose numbers are in your head? Mine? Pat's? Annie's?'

'Uh … yeah. Yes, I can do those from memory.'

'Keep your phone and Annie's off. And don't use this … ' She pressed a handset into his hand. 'Unless you really have to.'

'Whose is it?'

'Burner phone, it isn't anyone's. Turn it on but not until you're across the river. If anything happens you need to know about, I'll use it to call you. There's nothing on it. Pay-as-you-go sim. Disposable if need be. If not, I'll have it back when you're done. Now listen to me; this is what you're to do when you come back.'

He took in what she was saying, dumbfounded at the way the sisters had sprung into action like a well-oiled machine. So many times Annie had told him they had contingency plans, how things could go pear-shaped all too quickly, that sometimes official routes weren't the best solution. And so many times she'd told him the sisters were more capable than he gave them credit for.

'Thanks,' he said, briefly putting his hand on her arm.

She gave him a quick unsmiling nod. 'Now get going, and get that lass out of trouble.'

CHAPTER 53

Jennifer looked at her colleague to be sure the outburst had subsided. 'I made sure he didn't see me,' she repeated.

'Wouldn't have mattered if he had,' he replied with a wintry smile. 'It's not Connaughty.'

'What! Then who … how …?' Shock robbed her of a coherent question.

'I can tell you who.' The words were ground out. 'Because it's someone I've met. Tommy Marchant introduced me in Bridlington, must be two years ago. One of his fishing friends. Ryan Caldwell.'

'But that's Barbara's son.'

'Yeah, I'd figured that. Have you met him?' Was there a note of suspicion in his voice?

'No, never, but she's talked about him. We need to call this in, don't we?'

'They're going to love us for this. Just let's think a minute. His version is that he borrowed Connaughty's car and Connaughty is back at his mother's, but is that where they swapped?'

'They could have swapped at the flat in town.'

After a moment, he said, 'No, I think it's more likely Caldwell's. Otherwise, why the detour?'

'But he went in, grabbed that bag and came straight out. We barely lost sight of him.'

'He has the carrier with him, by the way. It's full of fishing magazines.'

'What were you talking about with him?'

'When I saw who it was, I didn't know if I wanted to nick him or punch him, but I did the whole Hi-how-are-you thing, any good fishing trips and so on, then I asked if he knew Mike Connaughty. He says yes, his mum works with him, so I ask is he here, because his car's outside and I need a word. And he tells me he's borrowed Connaughty's car and Connaughty's back at his mum's. Load of shite, of course, but I pretended to buy it. Decided I didn't want to haul him in just yet. There'll be conspiracy in there somewhere but no obvious crime in borrowing a car. If they swapped in town, what was the point of that detour?'

'It gives Mike longer to get away,' she suggested.

'OK, and how? Whose car's he in?'

'Presumably Ryan's or is that too obvious?'

'No, you're right. They didn't have long to plan this, it was done on the fly. Whichever way they did the swap, he'll be in Caldwell's car. Radio in and get them to check the bridge.'

She gave him a hard look. If he thought she was carrying the can for this debacle, he was mistaken. 'Do we even have an address? I don't think he lives with Barbara.'

'What?' He was still glowering at Mike's car.

'Registration, make, model … are we relying on him being the only Ryan Caldwell in the area?'

He started the engine and pulled the car in front of the double doors. 'Give me a minute,' he said. 'I'll get all the detail you need.'

As the doors swung shut behind him, the radio buzzed. Still watching the doors, Jennifer answered the call.

'You still with Connaughty?'

She didn't want to be the one to break the bad news, but reasoned that the call could easily have come in on her colleague's first foray into the pub.

'He's stopped at the Oddbottle pub. We're checking it out now.'

'The Oddbottle?' She heard the surprise. 'OK, well listen, Annie Raymond's phone's live. It came on briefly a while ago and she texted "Nowhere to hide" to Lois Suffling, but turned it straight off again. It's come on again now and stayed on. She called Connaughty. No reply, his phone's off. She let it go to voicemail but didn't leave a message. She texted "Call me". It came from …' There was a pause as coordinates were checked and read out.

Jennifer input the data into the map as the blurry view through the panes in the door showed her colleague on his way out. 'We'll get back to you in a moment, but we might be able to divert.'

As he climbed behind the wheel, she told him what had happened and saw hope dawn in his eyes. If they could collar both Annie and Mike, they could be forgiven for losing him in the first place.

'He'll be heading there too. Let's get after them.'

She looked again at the coordinates. 'Hang on, I was near there just over a month ago.' She remembered the feeling that something wasn't right; her uneasiness replayed itself in a sudden shiver. 'I answered the triple nine,' she said. 'Marshall's body in a shipping container.'

CHAPTER 54

In her head, Annie replayed Rob Small's words to Richard Redman. *I don't want to light the yard up like a Christmas tree.* No one must remember unusual activity here tonight. It was all she had. If the big lights went on, then the anomalous bundle balanced above the trailer hitch would stand out a mile.

She concentrated on absolute stillness, but as soon as a chance came, she must lower Lois to the ground and drag her to a dark corner until Small had gone. But she must act soon because Lois's comatose form was gradually slipping from her grasp and would become irretrievably tangled in the spiral of wires and network of pipes and struts.

Through the tear in the cloth, she could see one edge of the container and a small gravelled patch.

Small's footsteps crunched back and forth as he spoke into his phone. 'I know what I said, but I don't like it. Get the coat back, burn it, and turn the bloody phone off. Now! Just do it!'

The yard was noisy enough to provide some cover, but Small was too close. She needed him at the far end of the flatbed or better still back in the control room. There were camera blind spots within reach if she could just get off this lorry. On her own, she could be down and away in a moment, but she needed whole seconds to get Lois clear too. Her option to abandon Lois had been back inside the container. Too late now. Unsupported, Lois's unconscious form would fall heavily on to the ratchet between tractor and trailer, then slump to the ground.

If Lois had only come back and told them when Rob Small had approached her, but Annie knew she was partly to blame for that. From what she'd overheard, she knew Lois had been the arsonist at Barb's; careless, slapdash Lois, not even checking the contents of the shopping trolley before she tipped petrol all over it. They were desperate to get rid of it, Small had gone as far as to check out their recycling collection times. She supposed Lois had been well paid, but had always been too loose a cannon to let go.

The echo from Rob Small's voice changed. He'd moved to the far end of the flatbed. On her own, she would take the chance to jump down and slip away. A spark of resentment at Lois died as it was born. A new voice called out from in front of the lorry. If it wasn't for Lois, she'd have jumped down into his arms.

She froze and tightened her grip. How and when had this second man come on the scene?

Now Small was striding up from behind the trailer.

He crossed her line of sight.

She held her breath and fought against an urge to close her eyes.

The new voice said, 'I could just go–'

'*That's* your route,' Small cut across him. 'Unless I say otherwise, you stick to it like glue and you follow every detour.'

'Sure, sure. Just thought it'd be quicker.'

'I'm not paying for quick. I'm paying for that exact route and for you to drop off that crate at exactly that time tomorrow. No detours, no funny business. Understood?'

'Yeah, yeah.'

'Because if you think you're not being paid enough for a bit of a zigzag route to Portsmouth, there are other ways we can … acknowledge your contribution.'

'No worries, boss. I'll go that exact route.'

'I'll know if you deviate. I'll know the second you deviate. OK?'

The panel behind Annie shook. The man was climbing up into the cab.

She willed Rob Small to get on one of his small vehicles and go ahead to the gates, because she wasn't confident she could hold Lois steady if they began to move.

The vibration from the engine coming to life almost pitched her backwards. The tarpaulin slipped and Rob Small's form loomed over her.

Her hands began to let go, her feet began to brace for a leap into the darkness.

It wasn't him. It was his shadow.

With gritted teeth, she braced her one-handed grip on Lois, and hauled the tarpaulin back over them. She clutched at a pipe as the truck bumped forward.

Then they were moving at speed. Lois slipped. As Annie grabbed out, she felt Lois's body jar to a stop and slump forward into her legs. Somehow, she was stable, but her feet must be dangling down. It was a miracle they hadn't already pulled out any wires. The ride was smoother, but the oily cloth now pressed into her face. She had no hand free to move it, and no idea if Lois was still concealed.

This must be the wide alley between the giant containers. The truck slowed, she heard the screech of the gates. The lorry was sure to stop before it drove through. With Lois's body more stable, she risked reaching downward to be sure the tarpaulin covered them both.

It would be a split-second decision on fragmentary data.

Small had searched Redman's car … they were close to the glare of the solitary light … another few metres and they'd be outside the perimeter … was it worth the risk? Was there another option? The wide alleyway had felt fast, but would be nothing compared to the open road. Could she keep herself secure, let alone Lois, who would gradually be shaken through the tangle of wires and pipes until some part of her hit the road?

If she could just hang on until there were people about. They'd argued about the route. She thought Small wanted him to go over the Humber Bridge, an unnecessary detour on the way to Portsmouth. The Humber Bridge was perfect. It had cameras and people. Even if he had a Humbertag and didn't need to stop for the toll, she could attract attention.

The lorry juddered to a stop over the familiar squeal of the gates. She tried to gauge if Small was nearby. She could only pray that he didn't decide on a final search and that the driver stuck to the route he'd been given.

The gates fell silent. They bumped forward.

'Hey!' Rob Small's voice called out.

Under the cloying darkness of the oily cloth, Annie froze.

CHAPTER 55

Mike slowed as he neared the approach to Havenmere Docks. Annie had told him private security prowled these streets. He could expect them to appear any time now.

The burner phone lay on the seat beside him, on since the Bridge but silent.

The rain had let up as he'd crossed the estuary. He'd driven through a sea of dark fields with the angular gleam of heavy industry along the seaward horizon. Annie had hinted at a back route but, without detailed directions, he had no chance of finding it. His intention was to loop round and come past the entrance to Havenmere Docks without appearing to make a beeline for the place, but that was as far as his plan went.

Up ahead he saw the left turn that would take him along past his target.

A sudden buzz startled him. The burner phone's screen lit up. He grabbed it.

'Yes.'

'Pat's been in touch,' said Barbara's voice. 'Annie's phone came on.'

'Where?'

'Our side of the Humber, pretty much where Pat's headed. Redman's Yard.'

He squashed an impulse to swing the car round and head back. It wasn't Annie. She didn't have her phone. 'Do we know who she called … who the phone called?'

'You, but don't turn your phone on to check, it could be a ploy to pinpoint you. Where are you?'

'Almost there. It's quiet.'

'Well it's not quiet where Pat's heading, not if all the radio traffic's to be believed. Something big's going down.'

'No point me turning round. Not yet.'

'No, but watch your back.'

Havenmere Docks was both darker and quieter than other places he'd passed, yet the big gates were open, a lorry stood in the entrance and he could see two people, which was two more than he'd seen anywhere else. With a jolt he recognised the man on the ground as Rob Small. He was talking to the driver. They turned to look his way. He realised he'd slowed right down and was staring. He snatched his gaze back to the road ahead, feeling a flush creep up his neck.

In his mirror a liveried vehicle appeared at the end of the road, but he only had a glance as he passed the big entrance, because the lorry pulled out behind him, filling his rearward view.

He didn't know what he'd seen, didn't know if he'd seen anything at all, didn't want to tangle with private security this close to the docks, but Rob Small had stayed behind, and that looked like it had been the last vehicle out. He wanted to talk to the driver, but how could he stop him and what could he say? The bedraggled hat and wig forced him into the role of dozy old duffer; *I've lost my way*.

He wasn't sure he had the nerve. With a security car hot on their heels, he didn't want to challenge anyone about anything. He had a feeling they would pull guns.

* * *

Rob Small was running. Annie heard his footsteps pounding closer. He must have seen something. She should jump now and run, not wait for the tarpaulin to be whipped away, but where to? If she made it through the gates, there was nowhere to hide. He would outpace her in seconds. Could she dive back into the heart of the yard, trust to luck to find Jobsie's backdoor, if it even existed. And what about Lois?

'Change of plan,' Small's voice called out. 'Something kicking off. Go this way …' The words faded as Small reached the cab and lowered his voice.

The driver's response wasn't audible, but the truck began to roll forward again. Annie tightened her grasp on Lois, hardly daring to breathe as she felt the mechanism below her feet twist for the sharp turn on to the road.

We're out, she thought.

The truck straightened and surged forward, knocking Annie off balance. She felt Lois's body shift and start to slide. The tarpaulin slipped off her head and she breathed clear air, but the relief was momentary.

The feeling of speed inside the yard had been a relative crawl. Everything vibrated. The glow of the streetlights flashed over them, bright-dark, bright-dark. Her one secure handhold was heating rapidly; she would soon be reliant on the spiralling wires that gave no stability at all.

The thought they might hold on as far as the Humber Bridge was absurd. She doubted they could go half a mile before she slipped or Lois fell.

Their speed decreased. They must be approaching the junction. At this time of night, there would be no other vehicles. He wouldn't stop. He would simply swing out and take the right hand turn. The mechanism would twist; Lois would slide out of her grasp.

A ditch might make a temporary hideout, but only if she could jump and pull Lois with her. Rob Small told Richard Redman he'd be five minutes behind him. He would be on their tail any time now.

The truck jerked to a sudden halt. A horn blared. The driver yelled out. 'What're you playing at!'

Annie had Lois under the arms and was heaving her up out of the tangle of wires, gasping with the effort as she hauled her across the coupling. A wire had wrapped itself round Lois's foot.

She fought rising panic as she tried to unravel it, untwisting loop after loop.

Another car approached. Annie crouched on the road between truck and trailer, barely breathing. If the lorry moved now she'd be under its wheels.

She saw the security livery as the vehicle glided past.

Voices reached her as she wrestled with the wire.

Words heavy with worry, the raised volume of someone slightly deaf. 'Can you help …? Lost my way …'

Shock bolted through her, bringing sudden hope.

Leaning in close, she unwound the final loop from Lois's ankle and dragged her down off the coupling. Lois slumped to the tarmac. Grabbing her under the arms, Annie hauled the girl's dead weight across the mud and into the darkness of a shallow ditch.

A scornful laugh from the driver. '... way out of your way, Pal ...'

A car door slammed. 'What's the trouble?' The voice of officialdom butted in, laden with suspicion.

'Geezer here ... a right tangle ... sort him, will you ... I need to get on ...'

Sudden loud regular beeps of a truck reversing, then the engine revved, the load rattled and moved off. Appalled, Annie realised how much of the darkness had come from the shadow of the container. A streetlight threw out a treacherous beam. Through the wet foliage she could see two figures in the road as the lorry roared off.

She pressed herself into the damp earth. Without the bulk of the lorry blocking them the voices were clear, and far too close.

'Let me look.' Officialdom stamped his authority on the incident. 'You can't hang around here. Follow the lorry to the junction, then follow your SatNav. In future, use it or you'll be in bother.'

The figure looked nothing like Mike. It wasn't the right car. And yet ...

She watched the stony-faced uniform stand rock solid in the road as the car drove away. Tears of frustration pricked the back of her eyes. It was only the thought of Rob Small's plan B that stopped her showing herself. She didn't want to spend the next decade behind bars. Mike was right about Penn and bloody Teller, that was the route they were going if they didn't break free. If she could just get out of this ...

The uniform was at his car. It wasn't too late to call out. She listened to the rev of the engine, watched through the grass as he swung the car into a U-turn and headed back towards the docks.

As soon as he'd gone she was on her feet sprinting across the road, staring desperately into the darkness for any sign of the car but it had gone.

The sudden swell of sound of a vehicle approaching fast from the wrong direction had her dashing back to the muddy ditch beside Lois, feet ripped and on fire. She recognised Rob Small's car as it raced up to the junction. He took the corner without stopping.

Her options had spiralled to a stark choice. Wait for the security car to come round again and flag it down. How else would she get Lois the help she needed? The wind whistled across the open countryside, chilling her to immobility. It wouldn't just be Lois who would die out here if she didn't act.

The next vehicle came slowly, a low purr that drew nearer. Frozen now into indecision, she watched the shape glide past the junction and stop. She heard the whine of its reverse gear as it backed round the corner.

Then she was scrambling to get to her feet, stumbling, unable to stay upright.

'Mike.' Her voice came out as a croak. 'Mike! Over here.'

From under the weirdest straggly hair, she saw the shock on his face, saw his hand reach out towards her. 'No,' she said. 'Help me with Lois.'

She tried to pull Lois out of the mud, but her strength had gone.

'Get the car door,' Mike rapped out. 'Quick before the security guy does another circuit.'

He hoisted Lois in his arms as Annie stumbled ahead, climbing in to help pull Lois across the seat. Then he was behind the wheel driving them away.

CHAPTER 56

'We need you straightened out,' Barbara greeted Annie, hauling her inside the dark kitchen by her upper arm. 'Get upstairs in the bath. I've put some of Julie's togs in there. And don't hang about.'

'Yes, hurry,' Mike urged. 'We don't know how long we've got.' He turned to Barbara as he offloaded the fat carrier bag of fish and chips on to the kitchen side. 'Yes, you heard right,' he said. 'It was Lois. We dumped her at A&E in Scunthorpe. They'll be a while putting the pieces together, but–' He stopped and turned to Annie. 'Do you need a hand up the stairs?'

'I'm fine,' she snapped, throwing off Mike's arm. He wasn't exactly siding with Barb, but he wasn't exactly not. It unsettled her. Hobbling towards the staircase, she tried to tread lightly. The warmth of the house had begun to thaw her feet and she felt the sting of a thousand tiny knives.

Back downstairs, wearing one of Barb's daughter-in-law's outfits, she rubbed at her head with a towel while Mike blasted her hair with a hairdryer.

'It's dry.' She pushed his hand away. 'Can we eat now? I'm famished.'

Barbara looked at her through narrowed eyes, then

marched out to the kitchen. Annie lay back in the chair and closed her eyes, waiting for the aroma of fish and chips to draw near.

A pair of hands were in her hair, rubbing roughly. She sat up with a start and jerked away from Barbara.

'What the hell?'

'Just a bit of cooking oil,' said Barbara with a triumphant smile. 'Don't want you looking like you've only just washed your hair.'

Mike nodded approval. 'Good idea, that looks better.'

Annie glared at him.

Barbara's phone pinged a text. 'Ryan's on his way back,' she said.

Everything in the room stilled. She, Mike and Barbara looked at each other.

Ryan might bring company with him or it might arrive in advance … if it wasn't already parked outside. No one was going to disturb the curtains to be caught checking.

Their cover story was reliant on the flimsy foundation that Rob Small would not yet have discovered their deception and would be working to his plan A; wafer-thin but all they had.

'He didn't want me caught there,' Annie had told Mike on the journey back to Hull. 'But he'd factored it in. Plan B, the intruder doing damage. He really wanted me inside that container with Lois.'

If he'd managed to lock her in, could she have survived? She'd have realised when it began to lift; she'd seen the simulation. Those containers had grips and handles all over the place for stuff to be tied to. Could she have thought quickly enough and got high enough to cling on above the mayhem? He'd tipped it back and forth, but not upside down. She couldn't have saved Lois.

'Let's eat,' said Barbara.

Annie's hunger was gone, but she didn't object as a crackly package was dumped in her lap.

No one had called at Barbara's since Ryan had left in Mike's car, but that didn't mean no one was watching.

Mike's voice, snapping, 'Eat!' woke her from a doze. He'd reached across to pull open the paper. The smell of chips with a hint of vinegar rose around her and she was ravenous again.

She took a huge bite of fish in batter, crunching it as she watched Barbara opening the door to the wood burner and pushing something inside. Then she recognised the cloth of her good jeans and managed an indignant grumble through a mouthful of haddock, meant to convey that the trousers would wash, that they were a favourite pair.

'Better safe than sorry,' Barbara rapped out. 'I've already burned your shoes.'

Mike sat bolt upright. 'Shit! Those weren't Annie's shoes. They were Lois's. Annie took them off her in the car. I didn't think at the time, there was too much to do. Annie, where are your boots?'

Her heart sank. Potential time bomb. 'Sorry,' she mumbled through a mouthful of fish. 'I had to leave them in a cupboard in Small's control room.'

'How the fuck do we explain that?'

'Same way we explain any trace of me that's in that place. I visited once before, all legit, Rob Small let me in. There's bound to be traces.'

'Yeah, fingerprints and such, but boots! Could you say they must have fallen out of your car?'

'Don't speculate!' She gave him a hard stare. 'If they're found … If he makes anything of it … We don't know. We have no idea whatsoever. That's it.'

'Let's hope it's too late for him to try that line,' Mike said. 'There'll be evidence in that container when they find it.'

'*If* they find it,' corrected Barbara. 'They won't even be looking unless they get something from Lois. She's the real time bomb.'

'As far as we know, there's been no whisper of her having anything to do with Havenmere Docks, has there?'

'There's no way of knowing if the coppers' operation had linked her in, other than to you via her phone.'

'But why else did Marchant come round to ask about her? I said there had to be more to it than a simple disappearance. She'd only been gone over a weekend.'

'We think it was something Jennifer set up, not that she was pleased at the way it went.'

Annie's mind was too tired to do the heavy lifting but pieces began to fall into place. 'Bitch!' She let out some of her anger at the betrayal. 'If she …'

'No time for that now.' Barbara took charge. 'We don't know anything about Lois, OK?'

'Small's going to deny all knowledge,' Mike pointed out.

Annie yawned. As soon as the edge was off her hunger, tiredness descended like a heavy blanket. 'It had to be tonight,' she said. 'Because of what they were having delivered into Redman's Yard. All their focus was over there. Havenmere was where it was controlled from but Redman's did the dirty work. Do we know what exactly?'

'The coppers are all over it,' said Barbara. 'Partly because Pat led them there.'

Annie remembered the snatches of conversation between Small and the driver. 'He was sending that container over that way to start with. Would he have risked dropping it in Redman's Yard again, after William Marshall? Redman's son knows nothing about it. He's the one who's in Amsterdam. Small and Redman have had this side-line going for years.'

'I assume drugs,' Barbara said. 'Except that Big Daddy Redman didn't want his boy mixed up in it. He thinks he's running a legit business. The Marshalls must have been in it up to their necks, until he became a liability with the drinking.'

Annie tried to get her thoughts in line, to superimpose what she now knew on to what she'd heard. 'He wants to cut Redman out of it,' she said. 'He wants to play in a bigger league. He was trying to upend Redman's side of things at the same time as get rid of Marshall. Another body in that yard would do it. But could he have kept his own fingers clean?' She thought about the cloned databases. Small wasn't as clever as he liked to think but his trap had worked on Richard Redman. 'As long as he thinks I'm with Lois in that container, he's going to clear all trace of me out of his dockyard.'

'Play in a bigger league?'

She looked up sharply at the apprehension in Mike's tone. He and Barb exchanged a glance.

Barb murmured, 'Penn and Teller?'

Annie started to say, 'No,' then subsided. It would take too much energy to tell them she'd changed her mind. She wanted out as much as they did. Dyson and fforbes weren't behind this. If they were, none of them would have known anything about it until the prison door slammed shut behind them.

She'd had the details from Mike and knew where they'd caught her on camera, knew that some of it had been Miriam. There was one other stretch where a stray camera could have caught her, but it had been dark, and her jacket was the distinctive marker. *Hard luck, Miriam; that's going to be you, too.*

'We're as ready as we can be,' Barbara said, making her way to the settee, her fish and chips on a plate.

'Why didn't they come back sooner?' Mike asked.

'They had no reason before they got my email.'

'But I thought you'd sent that hours ago.'

'Hell no, these things need timing. And this might be it …' Lights across the curtains showed the slew of a vehicle pulling up outside. 'Bit too soon for our Ryan.'

Mike ran his hands through his hair. 'It'll all fall apart. Lois is bound to say who got her out.'

'Keep your cool,' ordered Barbara, and to Annie's surprise, Mike made a visible effort to relax.

A hand had reached out of the darkness and closed round her ankle. *Help me!* They were the only words Lois had spoken. Mike wanted to convince himself they'd done the best they could for Lois, and she thought they probably had, but it was far from clear that Lois would emerge from this unscathed, if at all. 'I doubt Lois'll remember anything from tonight,' she told him.

They fell silent. The fish and chip papers crackled, Barbara's knife and fork clattered against her plate. Over the whistle of the storm, came the tramp of footsteps towards the front door.

'If they don't get Small,' Barbara said to Annie as she put aside her plate and heaved herself to her feet. 'He'll come after you. You know too much.'

A strident knocking echoed through the house. If Small dodged this bullet, he surely wouldn't risk doing to her what he'd done to Marshall. But she'd left him plenty of pieces – fingerprints, boots, the forensic traces – to put together a set up that could have her locked away for years. Was she Small's ticking time bomb? Once he discovered Lois had survived, they both were.

CHAPTER 57

Annie woke with a start. A face swam into view, a man with a kind face watching her quizzically. He was a stranger and not quite smiling but she could see how concerned he was and felt instinctively safe. He wasn't here to harm her.

She snapped properly awake and sat up. Barbara's living room. Fish and chip papers in her lap. There had been footsteps … a knock at the door. It felt like hours ago, but must only be minutes. They'd been talking while she slept.

The man with the concerned face perched at the edge of the armchair opposite. He was watching her but speaking to someone else. His voice was soft.

Barbara cut across the peaceful tableau. 'She's going nowhere. After the day she's had, she needs a good night's sleep.'

Barbara wasn't deceived by a kind face. Mike looked frozen to his chair. If this was the detective who'd questioned him, no wonder he looked worried. Those velvet tones could draw blood from a stone.

It was time she was back in the game.

She took in a deep breath. 'I'll tell you everything you want to know, as long as you don't want me to move. If you want to take me to a formal interview, then you'll have to arrest me.'

He gave her that quizzical look again and an almost-smile. 'I'm not here to arrest you, Annie, but I need to know where you've been, what you've been doing and who you've seen. Can you tell me that? And you won't mind if my colleague records us.'

She glanced round to see a second man standing near the door behind Mike. More surprisingly, Jennifer was there too, not meeting her eye.

After a sharp glare at Jennifer, she turned back to the chief interrogator.

'It started with a text from Lois Suffling,' she began, and sketched in some background. 'When I arrived, Lois wasn't there, but Miriam Marshall was.'

'Was it crowded?'

'No, practically empty.'

'The landlady doesn't remember you being there. That seems odd when there were practically no other customers. Can you tell me why that might be?'

'I didn't go to the bar. I saw Miriam straight off and went over. I knew it was no coincidence.'

She related their conversation more or less word for word.

'What made you follow her when she left?'

'I didn't. I offered her a lift.' Miriam's fabricated bus journey from town, her car on a nearby road to deceive Lois, sounded far-fetched as Annie told it, which was annoying because it was the exact truth. It felt now like the implausible story it had actually been. She shouldn't have fallen for it.

She drew in a breath, feeling Jennifer as a looming presence behind her. It seemed reckless to have her here, but if it was a ploy to wrong foot her, it was close to working.

She related the story Miriam had given her. This, after all, was the easy bit.

His prompts allowed no ambiguities to slip through, and though his questions several times had her at the verge of railing against Miriam in a way that would have helped no one, she focussed on relating the facts.

He told her Miriam's brother lived nowhere near the place Annie had picked her up. He lived in a semi on an estate, not a farm. She parried his prompts; no, she knew nothing about Miriam's family; and no, she hadn't checked. 'When was I supposed to check? I accepted what she told me.'

His tone never wavered from calm and reasonable, yet he conveyed an air of finding it harder and harder to believe her.

'You were reported via Farm Watch. Someone saw you parked up, looking in the boot of your car. Can you tell me what you were doing?'

'I never went near the boot of the car. They were mistaken.'

'And yet they gave a good description and your registration, and you've just told me that you stopped in exactly that spot. Are you sure you've remembered everything?'

'I stopped to pick up Miriam. She was there waiting for me. I didn't get out of the car. She got in. Neither of us went near the boot. I hope you're checking your source.'

'We check everything.'

Sometimes he glanced at Barbara who sat on the settee

glowering at him, and sometimes he glanced up over Annie's head, maybe at Jennifer. Annie watched him, transfixed at the way he spoke, as though he had her best interests at heart; an effective technique, one she wished she could emulate. But despite everything, she was convinced of a hint of steel behind those concerned eyes.

Her story neared that derelict stretch of coastline. 'I could show you exactly where she took me, but I'd need a map.'

He got to his feet, pulling a tablet from his pocket, and came to sit on the chair arm beside her.

It felt uncomfortable to have him so close, but she squinted at the map and started from the point Miriam had joined her, tracing the route with her finger. She told him about Miriam lying back on the seat, leaving him to join the dots as to what the cameras would and wouldn't have seen.

'We stopped here, waste ground, it's derelict. She said she knew a back way into Havenmere Docks and she could access it from there.'

As she spoke, she saw the absurdity of the claim. The aerial view made a nonsense of it. Miriam must have had someone waiting. While Annie was giving her the twenty minutes leeway she'd said she needed, someone had driven her straight to the front entrance.

'She had a key, a big ornate thing. It was old and heavy.'
'Heavy?'

'She gave it me to hold.' *And yes, my fingerprints will be all over it. Rob Small's plan B. What was that key really for?*

He probed about the route, pushed her to speculate about the things Miriam had said. She parried his invitations to tell him more than she could have known about.

'I'm puzzled, Annie. Why would you go along with a plan to break into somewhere as sensitive as a dockyard?'

'I didn't.' She picked her words with care. 'I pushed her to tell me what it was about, and it was the paperwork her husband stole.'

She looked up at him as she spoke, and wanted to add, Move back over there now, we've done with the map. Only they hadn't, and she must keep a clear head because the difficult bit would arrive hot on the heels of the paperwork.

'Tell me about the paperwork.'

She gave him an account that was largely factual, including their suspicions about the fire here in Barbara's kitchen. 'We couldn't make head nor tail of it, but Miriam told me it was the spec for a simulation that her husband's ex-boss had threatened him with; a way for him to die inside a shipping container.' She outlined roughly what Rob Small had explained to Richard Redman, putting the words into Miriam's mouth.

'And where is this paperwork now?'

'It's in our flat.'

'Unless you lot have already broken in and taken it,' grumbled Mike.

She couldn't shoot Mike a warning glance because she couldn't see him through the bulk of the man on the arm of her chair, but she saw Barbara look across.

Her interrogator half turned. 'We're the other side, Mr Connaughty,' he said drily. 'We don't do the breaking and entering.' He turned back to Annie. 'So you dropped Mrs Marshall off. Then where did you go?'

This was the difficult bit, and Mike had unsettled her with his sniping. 'No, I didn't. That's what she said she wanted, but she lied. She got me to open the car boot to give her cover to slip over the bankside.'

'Didn't you just tell me you never went near the boot?'

He was right, she had. 'I meant earlier.'

It would be easy to succumb to the trials of the day, the agony in her feet, just to slump in the chair and beg for something to ease the pain. But that would give Rob Small his plan B on a plate.

She couldn't see Mike to signal for help, but Barbara was there, a solid disapproving presence on the settee. A brief glance was all it took and Barbara was on her feet, reaching for the chip papers from Annie's lap.

'All done with these? How about a nice cup of tea? You haven't had enough to drink.'

'Coffee?' murmured Annie.

'And give Annie some space,' Barbara barked at the detective on the chair arm. 'Can't you see she's all in?'

'Of course,' he said, and moved an inch or so.

'Mike!' Barbara snapped her fingers. 'Coffee for Annie.'

The chair creaked as Mike stood up. 'Yes, sure,' he said. 'How about …?'

'I'm OK for now,' Barbara rapped out. 'And these guys …' She took in the two detectives and Jennifer with a disdainful nod of her head, 'don't drink on duty.'

'Can I help?' Jennifer said from somewhere by the door.

Barbara swung round with a glare. 'You want to rummage about in my kitchen, Constable Flanagan, you show me a search warrant, and otherwise you stay put.'

Jennifer started to say something, but the man on

Annie's chair arm glanced round and Jennifer shut up. There, thought Annie, there's the steel showing. She relaxed and almost smiled. Barbara had given her the space to get her head back in the game. Without waiting for the prompt, she related how she'd given Miriam the cover to slip away unnoticed.

'So you opened the boot while Mrs Marshall got out of the car, and when you looked she'd gone. Is that right?'

She closed her eyes briefly, imagining herself back on that wind-blown stretch, feeling the sharp breeze off the estuary sting her face. 'Her phone was on the seat. I assumed it had slipped out of her pocket. I shouted, but she didn't answer, so I jumped out, and went down the bank the way I thought she'd gone.' She let her mind conjure the feel of slick mud under her feet, imagined herself momentarily phased to be looking out across the foreshore and there being no sign of anyone. 'Then I heard the car start up.'

They sparred for a while. She allowed herself to be annoyed when he highlighted her beginner's error of leaving the keys in the ignition. 'I was only going to be a second.'

'If I had a quid for every time I've been told that.'

Yes, she was cold without her jacket. 'It was a bloody long walk back to the main road. I soon warmed up.'

When it came to the lift she'd hitched back over the Humber, she was openly uncooperative. 'He was a commercial driver. He shouldn't have picked me up at all. I'm not putting his job in jeopardy.' She overrode his next comment with, 'I deliberately didn't look at him, or his vehicle reg or colour or anything. I was knackered. I got in the back and dozed.'

She wondered how far they would dig, because Julie Caldwell's car was waiting to be found not too far below the surface, though it wouldn't show the Caldwell name and Mike had looked like an old man in that wig in the dark.

'And he drove you back here?'

'He dropped me on the main road. It's not that far to walk. And I don't know where he was going, I didn't ask.'

'Straight off the bridge, east through Hull on the main road. No detours. Would that be accurate?'

'Yes, but I can't give you times, not even approximately.'

'So he went pretty much past your own front door. Why did you choose to come here?'

Annie felt more than heard a reaction from Jennifer, a satisfied but smothered murmur of triumph. This was the most far-fetched part of the fiction, and Jennifer knew it better than anyone.

She looked up to meet his eye. 'If I'd known she'd left the car at the flat, I might have, but I'd had a hellish journey back. No phone, no money. Of course I came to Babs. It's what we do when we're in trouble.'

'You could have gone in anywhere and called 999.'

'Why would I? It was a stupid feud with a client. It's happened before. I was mad at Miriam but I was willing to let her simmer down and explain herself.'

An unfamiliar phone shrilled. There was a mumbled, 'Excuse me,' as someone moved out to the porch to take the call. Annie's interrogator stood up and followed. There was a low-voiced exchange.

Annie looked round. The two men were outside the room leaving Jennifer on her own with them. Jennifer didn't attempt to meet anyone's eye.

Her interrogator stepped back into the room. 'Good news, Annie. We've found your phone.'

For form's sake she gave him a smile. 'Where was it and can I have it back?' Until the clone was back in her possession, her own phone was out of bounds.

'When we've checked it out. It was just by a container yard west of Hull.'

Redman's Yard, she thought. That's why Small had wanted the lorry to do the detour so they could get her phone into the container. Miriam hadn't meant to take it.

'Don't suppose you found my jacket, too.' She knew they hadn't. She'd heard Rob Small give the order to burn it. It was a pity because it was the jacket that would bear indisputable forensic traces of Miriam and back up her version of events, both the truth and the lies.

Where would they burn it, she wondered. Late at night, unexpected police activity, the need to stay hidden. As the thought crossed her mind, he said, 'Yes, the jacket was with it.'

Annie slumped back with a huge sigh of relief and gave him a genuine smile. 'Thank God! Now you can prove it was Miriam driving the car, not me.'

If he responded, she didn't hear him.

There were voices, people moving about. At one point, someone's arm was under hers, helping her up the stairs.

CHAPTER 58

Annie surfaced from sleep feeling relaxed and refreshed. Barbara's spare room was a mass of floral prints and frills into which snaked the irresistible aroma of bacon frying. It led her down to Barbara's kitchen where both sisters were tucking into substantial breakfasts. Barbara retrieved a laden plate from under the grill and put it in front of her.

'Were they trying to pin Lois's death on me?' she wondered as she speared a sausage. The full implications of what Miriam and Small had planned were beginning to hit home. They'd finessed her through a traffic camera with an apparently unconscious body hidden under Lois's coat; her phone and Lois's had been tracked together; and she might have been found in a shipping container with Lois's body. 'None of it felt planned, but it was,' she said. 'To the last second. Well except that Miriam wanted revenge on Rob Small at the same time she was doing his dirty work.'

'And Lois did this lot,' Barbara grumbled, looking round at the blackened walls. 'Ungrateful little cow.'

'Wonder how she is,' said Pat.

'We can't go making enquiries,' Annie said. 'Have I got to go and do a formal statement?'

'You might be off the hook, Kid. Seems like they've done

some better digging on Miriam's story after they had Babs' email. They'll have found a few holes.'

'What about Rob Small … Richard Redman?'

Pat shrugged. 'I didn't see much. They got Redman and whatever was being delivered to that yard, but I'm not sure Small was in the thick of it. I'll ask around.'

Annie nodded. They would get to know.

'When you first came to Hull,' Pat said, 'you did a drugs case and a missing girl case, but what was the third one? Mike was asking and I couldn't remember.'

'Accident on a building site.' Annie pushed aside her empty plate and gave Barbara a smile. 'That was spot on, thanks. We *are* going to make formal statements, all of us, whether they want them or not.' She laughed at the looks on their faces. 'We're doing it because it's time we got out from under Penn and Teller.'

She saw the sisters exchange a raised-eyebrows glance at her use of the forbidden nickname. 'Go on,' said Pat.

'Right, as long as– Oh my God!' She leapt to her feet, feeling the blood drain from her.

'What! What is it?' Pat was on her feet too, looking panicked.

'Mike's meeting. It's today. Now. We've got to get going!'

'Shit!' Pat clapped her hand to her mouth. 'Clean went out of my head. It's too late, Annie. It's in Wakefield. If he's going, he'll be there by now.'

'Someone give me a phone.' Annie clicked in Mike's number. After a few moments, his voicemail cut in with his 'in a meeting' message. 'He can't be,' Annie wailed. 'He can't do this on his own. After all that work! Why didn't he ring? Why didn't he take me home with him last night?'

'Don't write him off so fast,' said Barbara. 'He smashed a bloody miracle yesterday; he might do it again today. He's not the dozy lummock he looks.'

Annie glared at her. 'Come on, we need to get to the office, pronto. Let's at least be on the spot in case anything can be salvaged.'

The office was quiet, but the crucial file was gone from Mike's desk.

Pat made coffee. They lingered over it for longer than usual. Occasionally one of them made a comment on a case, and now and then Annie retried Mike's phone only for it to tell her that he was still 'in a meeting'.

Eventually, Pat said, 'What have formal statements to do with Penn and Teller?'

'Probably nothing now. But think about it, what's the one thing they've put their foot down about? Relocating. They don't want us to be high-profile. They set us up to be low key, quietly efficient and fading into the wallpaper.' She let out a huff of exasperation as the weather battered the window behind her. 'Sodding rain! Ms Dyson and Mr fforbes won't like this Marshall business one little bit. That police operation was big and well financed. They've been after Redman, Small and whoever else for a good while. And to go as far as to plant Jennifer on us! That was aimed at them. We were digging into Marshall's death and they must know who we're bankrolled by. You can see where they joined the dots wrong.'

'Who's to say the terrible twosome aren't behind it?' Pat put in.

'Not a chance,' said Annie. Her years working with the London firm had taught her all she needed to know about people like Dyson and fforbes. 'Believe me, this isn't their game, but that doesn't mean they'll like the way it shone a spotlight on us. We could use it.'

Pat leant forward. 'Are you saying you're prepared to walk away?'

'It's not that simple. You can't walk away from people like that, but if we become more trouble than we're worth, they might just decide to drop us, but if they do, we'll plummet to rock bottom. We don't have the cash flow to keep going and we don't have the collateral to finance a loan. We could have had. One signature on a deal like the one Mike's chasing and we'd be laughing, but he won't look credible going into this on his own.'

The hours dragged on. It was after two o'clock before the downstairs door banged open and Annie recognised Mike's tread on the stairs.

She listened intently. The sisters were doing the same. It was a slow heavy tread, presaging bad news.

As he came in, he said, 'I'm sorry about this,' and Annie thought, No, it's us who should be apologising. 'But I had to bring her.'

It took a second to register that he was ushering Jennifer in.

'What the hell?' Annie half rose from her chair, fists balled, but Mike stopped her with a gesture.

'You were out for the count and I thought she owed us this at least.'

Jennifer looked uncomfortable as she met Annie's eye. 'Least I could do,' she murmured.

'Well?' said Pat.

Mike stepped forward so his back was to Jennifer and gave them a discreet thumbs up and a wink. Annie felt an electric current run through her, standing the hairs at the back of her neck on end. He'd done it.

'Why did you bring her back here?' Pat shot at him. Yes, thought Annie, why spoil the moment?

'Paperwork,' said Mike, reaching into a desk drawer. 'Do you have any personal possessions here?'

Jennifer shook her head. 'OK, sign here to say so.' She signed. 'And I want you to read and sign this …' He passed Jennifer a form. 'It's to say you haven't taken anything of ours and you won't use anything you've learnt against us.'

'I was wondering …' Jennifer began tentatively.

'You want information from us,' said Annie. 'What do we get in return?'

'Whatever you want to know.' Annie took that as confirmation Jennifer had been a minor cog and knew very little.

'Where did you go last Wednesday?' Barbara said. 'You were gone hours.'

'I was called to a briefing.'

'You caught the 11.10 York train, I saw you.'

'Uh … yes … the whole operation's being run from York. The debrief was with the detective super over there.'

Annie smiled at Jennifer's surprise. Yup, she thought, you didn't even spot Barbara Caldwell on your tail. 'I'm not sure you could have cut it in our business,' she said, twisting the knife with, 'Who was it you were tearing a strip off for not warning you about Marchant?'

'Sergeant Ahmed. He was supposed to be looking out for me. Do I get to ask my question now?'

'Did you take a key?' Pat said in what Annie thought was a wild shot, but Jennifer nodded.

'I got a colleague to return it. She's Lois's build and I thought she might be taken for Lois on the CCTV. That's the truth. I'm sorry about it all. I was doing my job. For what it's worth, I'm glad you're not involved. I wouldn't have wanted to see you in court.'

Annie exchanged a quick glance with the sisters. This was the first they'd heard they were officially in the clear. 'Go on then, what do you want to know?'

'Where was that container in the gap between leaving Bristol and turning up in Redman's Yard.'

It wasn't what Annie had expected but it was the right question for her to pass on what she needed to. 'This is purely speculation,' she said. 'The driver was bribed or blackmailed to stage a breakdown. The lorry parked up in Birmingham and was gone the next morning, taken on the QT to Havenmere Docks.'

Jennifer stared at her intently.

'If you dig, I think you'll find more stuff going in and out of Havenmere by road than the records suggest. Small has a fake database on his system. It mirrors the real one.' She watched Jennifer swallow involuntarily and knew she'd given her gold dust. It should be the nail they needed to close the coffin around Rob Small. 'Check out the IDs on that paperwork Marshall stole. He was pointing you at clandestine shipments.'

Jennifer seemed to snap to. 'Thank you,' she said, then looked at the form in her hand as though she'd never seen it before. 'I can't sign this.' She slapped it back on to Mike's desk, before turning on her heel and heading down the stairs.

By unspoken agreement, they waited in silence for the

slam of the outer door, then Annie said, 'We've some fizz in a cupboard somewhere.' She looked at Mike, sitting back in his chair, grinning broadly. 'How did you persuade her? And none of that guff about her owing us.'

'Blackmail. Your bad habits are rubbing off on me. I said you'd told me everything about the early case that stopped her career in its tracks and that I'd set it all out for her bosses if she didn't play ball.'

'What early case?'

'Pat could only remember a drugs thing and a missing girl. I took a chance on the missing girl and hit the jackpot.'

'But that was a lifetime ago.' Annie struggled to recall any detail. She was amazed Jennifer could think anything from back then still mattered.

Barbara poured Prosecco into their coffee mugs and lifted hers. 'To Mike's golden goose.'

'Bright futures all round,' added Pat.

Annie caught Mike's eye. 'And to Penn and Teller dropping us like hot cakes.'

Mike gave her an incredulous stare, then raised his mug. 'I'll drink to that.'

The end

AUTHOR'S NOTE

The books in this series are not tied to explicit dates, though I always know what year I'm writing about when I write them. In this way, I keep track of things like how old the characters are, what the weather is like in the area where the story is set, and I sometimes track things like the phases of the moon so that if characters are out and about at night, I know whether or not they have moonlight to guide them.

I once wrote a book set in a future year. That was *Syrup Trap City*. I wanted it both set in Hull City of Culture year and to be published that same year, 2017, which meant writing it the year before. It was a struggle and I had to gamble that a freak of nature would not occur to pull the rug from under the whole plot. I was lucky; it didn't. The notional year for *Boxed In* was 2019, and given how easily I could have pushed it to 2020, it was a stroke of luck that I dodged the upheaval of a global pandemic, the presence of which would have meant fundamental changes to every aspect of the plot.

The brand new area for me in researching this book was the world of container shipments. Before I began the book, containers were giant metal boxes that sat on the backs of lorries, the decks of ships or stacked Lego-like in vast dockside yards, and I'd thought no more about them. But as with anything, once you start to look below the surface, all kinds of things emerge.

The container that was lost through being painted into the middle of an office block comes from a true story; as does the speculation about the container having falling from a ship in a storm. Many do, and they often float just below the surface posing a real hazard to shipping. The ID numbers on containers should make them easy enough to track, but the systems are not fully standardised nor fully automated, and containers go missing from time to time, not always by accident.

Electronic tracking devices exist, but are neither universal nor straightforward. A device, such as used in aviation, that can always signal a container's location might mean it can't get lost, but will significantly add to its costs, because unlike an aeroplane, a container is often buried many layers deep in other containers, has a typical journey time measured in weeks rather than hours, and unlike a plane, tends not to make the return journey. After its maiden 'flight', it is rarely cost effective for it to be repacked and returned, it is more likely to be sold for repurposing. Although some elements of the container shipment world are highly automated and controlled, there is enough of a Wild West fringe to allow for chancers to take advantage, be they insurance fraudsters, opportunist thieves or jobbing crime writers.

ABOUT THE AUTHOR

Penny Grubb is a scientist, a researcher and a teacher as well as a novelist. She wants everyone to know about the power of the written word and how it works in academic, creative, journalistic, reflective and indeed all contexts. She believes that once people understand the power of words, they are protected from exploitation by mendacious purveyors of half-truths and propaganda.

Penny is author of the Annie Raymond mysteries, a crime series published both sides of the Atlantic. She is active on social media when she can find the time and loves to hear from readers. Come and join her over on her website (pennygrubb.co.uk) where she regularly blogs, her Facebook page (pennygrubbauthor) and on Twitter (@pennygrubb).

THE ANNIE RAYMOND MYSTERIES

Annie's career was kick-started in Hull by what she initially saw as a lucky break in *Like False Money*. After that *The Jawbone Gang* saw her settling into her new role but with seriously itchy feet. These took her both south to London and north to Scotland as she faced an appalling dilemma at the start of *The Doll Makers*. An odd set of circumstances landed her once again in Hull in *Where There's Smoke*, facing down an enemy she'd not seen since her early career.

Buried Deep took Annie to York from her London base and was a crossover book that for the first time put a police investigation front and centre alongside her own work. This was the book that introduced DC Ayaan Ahmed and Det Supt Martyn Webber. *Tiger Blood*, the next in line, took a step sideways and majored solely on a network of police investigative work, following the tangled career paths of Ahmed and Webber. Despite it being advertised as the sixth Annie book, she gets no more than a passing mention.

Syrup Trap City returned both to Hull and to Annie although Ahmed, now a sergeant, had a role. It was Webber who had become the unnamed passing mention.

Boxed In follows Annie's fortunes after major changes in both her personal and professional life. It isn't the first time she has become entangled with the shadier side of life, but on this occasion she walked in with her eyes open.

Book 9 will take the concept of 'eyes open' to an unexpected context for Annie, Mike and the Thompson sisters as they struggle with the realities of earning an honest living. Watch this space.

The Annie Raymond Mysteries
Book 1: *Like False Money*
Book 2: *The Jawbone Gang*
Book 3: *The Doll Makers*
Books 1, 2 & 3 are published as a trilogy:
Falling into Crime
Book 4: *Where There's Smoke*
Book 5: *Buried Deep*
Book 6: *Syrup Trap City*
Book 7: *Boxed In*

The Webber/Ahmed series
Book 1: *Buried Deep*
Book 2: *Tiger Blood*
Syrup Trap City & *Boxed In*
also feature Webber and Ahmed

If you have enjoyed this book, please consider leaving a review for Penny to let her know what you thought of her work.

You can read about Penny on her author page on the Fantastic Books Store. While you're there, why not browse our other delightful tales and wonderfully woven prose?

www.fantasticbooksstore.com

www.ingramcontent.com/pod-product-compliance
Lightning Source LLC
Chambersburg PA
CBHW061303170626

46817CB00001B/36